NEVER *dig* BENEATH A GRAVE

NEVER
dig
BENEATH A GRAVE

ISBN-13: 978-1-964967-02-8

Editor: Jennifer Speck

Cover Artist: Dark Hart Designs

First Edition: October 2024

10 9 8 7 6 5 4 3 2 1

Dedicated to the girls who dream of a bad man who's willing to be good, just for them. This is for you.

AUTHOR'S NOTE

Dear Reader,

This book is NOT a clean romance. It is dark. It is sexy. It is in no way, shape or form, a reflection on the government of California. It is purely a work of fiction and is meant to entertain . . . and maybe to make you question your morals.

This book is significantly darker than the first three, so please read through these trigger warnings carefully. I have taken the liberty of listing them, so they are easy to read. Your mental health matters, too.

P.S. I feel it needs to be said: DO NOT MIX DRUGS AND/OR ANY KIND OF ALCOHOL just because you read it in this book. Black Dahlia is not real. It's not meant to be realistic. It's meant to entertain. In fact, it might kill you. Who knows? Don't find out.

- Explicit sexual scenes in great detail
- Graphic violence and gore
- Drug abuse
- Torture
- Psychological abuse
- Physical abuse
- Mental abuse
- Emotional abuse
- PTSD/CPTSD
- Sleep paralysis and vivid nightmares
- Murder
- Human trafficking
- Descriptions of sexual slave trade
- Mentions of a cult

- Breath play
- Degradation/praise kink
- Someone gets shot in the dick
- Kidnapping
- Murder, again
- Stalking
- Organized crime
- Desecration of a corpse
- Mentions or rape
- Descriptions of torture such as ball shocking, stabbing, and body part removal
- Fingers
- Crude and obscene language. Like a lot of it.
- Closets
- Ill-advised method of firearms training
- Slight breeding kink
- Spanking
- A hot man on a motorcycle
- Strangulation

"We're darkness and mine has fucking craved yours since the moment I laid eyes on you."

-Mason Carpenter, *Never Dig Beneath a Grave*

PROLOGUE

This was a stupid plan.

Carpenter's Auto Services may as well be Fort Knox with how daunting it feels. My nerves are all over the place. My stomach feels queasy as I reach for the door, stopping to inspect the logo. *Carpenter's Auto* scribbled in front of a skull with two wrenches for crossbones.

Somehow, I can't think of anything more fitting for a business owned by Mason Carpenter.

I should have gone home and changed. Maybe brushed my hair. It's braided and frizzy from the heat, despite there being low humidity on this hot LA summer day. I've covered it with a Laker's hat, but the wild strawberry blonde hairs surrounding my face still escape.

Not that I'm here to look pretty. Those days of secretly wanting to impress Mason are long over, but . . . it would have been nice to show up wearing something a little nicer than a pair of old jeans and a worn T-shirt—it was moving day, okay?

It's been two years. He doesn't know I'm coming. A fact that I have reminded myself of for the last twenty-four hours since moving to LA. I *also* can't seem to stop thinking about our last conversation. The brush of his tongue against mine. The feel of his fingers gripping my hair while he ground out my name.

Oh, and the way he ghosted me after the fact.

Rejection still burns in my stomach when I think back to that night. How stupid and young and naïve I was to think I could mean anything more to him.

Still . . . I need his help and I'll be damned if I walk out of this place without it.

Tugging on the glass door to the lobby, I step inside . . .

And almost step right back out.

The place is horrifying. From the dirt on every surface, to the papers stacked high on the counter, it's a wonder anything ever gets done around here.

I can hear the sound of an impact running in the garage, but no one is up front.

"Hello?"

No answer.

Grumbling under my breath, I step toward the door that leads to the garage and peek my head out. I can't see him, but I can smell him.

Sweat, grease, and that little bit of essence of *hot* man—in the attractive sense.

"Hello?" I try again.

The impact drowns out the sound of my voice, so I step fully into the garage, looking at the space around me. In contrast to the office, this area is well organized. The tools are all in their places and the floor has been swept. Though I know nothing about garages this one seems . . . comfortable.

I step around the car that's being hammered into oblivion by the old, tired impact, spotting long, strong legs covered in denim leading down to old work boots. The shirt covering his torso rides up just enough to catch a glimpse of hard, trimmed abs underneath and I swear, my heart beats just a little bit faster.

Yep, that's Mason, alright. All six foot, five million inches of him.

Suddenly, the impact stops and he's sliding out from under the car on a creeper, those hurricane-colored eyes I've tried to forget glaring up at me like I'm here to tell him he's been denied from participating in the rapture.

Okay. Maybe this was a bad idea.

"Hannah."

There's no question behind it. Just my name. Like he's acknowledging my presence, but he's pissed about it.

Yep, definitely a bad idea.

My mind struggles with words because all I can think about is the way he touched me. As if I were precious to him. Like I mattered.

And also his muscles.

This must be some sick joke the universe is playing on me. Like *Punk'd: Fuck Hannah* edition.

Two years have been good to him. He's not just the strong guy I once knew, but a whole ass man, now, complete with every ingredient to make the perfect dirty fantasy to come to life.

Heavy, broad shoulders. Tattoos rippling over strong muscles that slip up his arms and into the sleeves of his T-shirt. Harsh jawline.

Stop it, Hannah, I chastise myself. *He's probably married with children now. We've got other priorities that he wouldn't understand . . .*

"Are you going to speak?"

Shit.

"You know, you should really hire a receptionist," I ramble because that's what I do when I'm nervous. "Someone could rob you blind and you'd be none the wiser. Though, I'm not sure there's much of a market for dust bunnies right now."

He's not amused.

"I mean, you know what they say about a clean . . . garage, right?"

I have no idea what they say. Again, I tend to ramble when I'm nervous.

And Mason Carpenter has *always* made me nervous.

"What are you doing here, Hannah?"

The silence hanging in the air between us is palpable. Tense.

Fuck.

"She's missing, Mason."

His jaw ticks, but apart from that, he doesn't react.

He has no reason to help me. After his stepfather was arrested on heinous crimes, I'm sure Missy is the last person anyone in his family is concerned about saving. Hell, it feels like she's the last person *anyone* is thinking about right now.

Except for me.

Stay strong, Hannah. The worst he can do is say no.

"No."

Everything is doomed.

"Mason," I start, but he chooses this time to stand, his big self *towering* over me and every bit as wide as the best linebacker in the NFL.

I'd forgotten how tall he is . . .

His muscles ripple under the thin black T-shirt he's got on. Those aren't gym muscles. They're earned over a lifetime of hard work.

My mouth is suddenly very, very dry.

"You're the only one I can trust. My mother's brushing it under the rug because of who she was involved with and the cops aren't looking. I mean, they say they are, but not really. The FBI is after her and God only knows who else."

"I said no." He stalks toward a tool cart, away from me, but I follow him. He doesn't appear to like it judging by the tension in his shoulders.

"I *know* something bad has happened. Missy's smart, but she's not very good at hiding."

"Your sister is being accused of some very bad shit, Hannah," Mason bites, still not looking at me. "And you want to help her?"

"*No*," I snap. I know what she's been accused of. I just don't believe it. I mean that's my twin. My sister. She wouldn't do those things. "I just want to make sure she's okay and convince her to turn herself in. I just . . . I don't have a good feeling."

"I have enough problems to deal with without having to worry about you, too."

Rude.

"What if I agreed to work for you? For free?" He starts shaking his head before I'm even done speaking. "I could clean up. I could organize. I know all about invoices and billing." I help run the charity my mother founded for children overseas. Coincidentally, that's how no one knows I'm *here* right now.

"Not happening," he grits, voice rough as he slams a drawer on the tool cart shut. Finally, he turns back to me and I realize, with some panic, that he's entirely too close. Like a foot away.

My head spins at the proximity. Strange for me, but then again, everything has *always* been strange where Mason and I are concerned.

"Tell me," he murmurs, voice dark and his eyes like a Category 5 hurricane. "Where is your dear mother? She know you're here?"

He *would* ask about her.

"No," I say, squaring my shoulders. "And she doesn't need to. I'm not a child." He chuckles, shaking his head in disgust. "And I live in LA now. I don't need permission from her to visit an old friend."

Okay, friend may have been a poor choice of words. I don't know what I'd call Mason, but even before, he was the furthest thing from a friend you could get. Sexy acquaintance? Object of every dirty fantasy I've ever had?

Still . . . my mother is *not* a topic we need to discuss right now. Or ever.

"I'm not asking for anything else. I just . . . I can't do it on my own. I've tried. I'm failing miserably. No one will speak to me because of who my mother is."

And because my twin is wanted for murder and human trafficking, but I digress.

"Then give up."

If I were a violent person, which I'm not, I would kick him in the shin.

—Then run away as fast as I can because I've seen Mason's dark side. We'll just say a grizzly looks tame.

"What if it were your sister?"

It grows so silent, you could hear a mouse queef in the back of the garage.

His gaze hardens, his jaw ticking in that way I used to think was endearing. Now that I know it seals my fate, it's more like a stab to the chest.

"No. It's final."

Without even a word, he nods over my head to the door and with bitter embarrassment, I realize I've lost.

Defeat crushes through me, but . . . it's not like I haven't been here before. It was a long shot, anyway.

"Goodbye, Mason."

He doesn't seem to like that response because his eyes narrow dangerously, but he doesn't say a word as he watches me leave. As soon as the door shuts behind me with a metallic finality, I suck in a shaky breath and head toward my old, beat up bumblebee yellow VW Bug—It was cheap, okay?

That was . . .

Rough.

Mason looked at me like I was sin incarnate. As if everything that happened was my fault. God knows, sometimes I feel like it.

I fall into the front seat of my car, forcing the tears burning in my eyes back. I refuse to cry. Not here.

My gaze catches on the picture in the dash. Missy wouldn't cry. She'd take the rejection with class. She'd wait until she was home and completely alone before a single tear fell.

She smiles back at me, as if reminding me of who she was. That was nearly six years ago. What may as well be a lifetime. I was seventeen and everything made sense. I knew my next move. I knew what life would be like when I reached the age I am now. I was going to marry that boy in high school who told me I was pretty, because of course, he didn't just want to get in my pants. He wasn't like other guys.

Boy, was I wrong.

I lean forward, laying my head against the steering wheel and toss my hat on the passenger seat, hair be damned.

"Where in the world are you, Missy?" I whisper to the picture, ashamed when a tear manages to break free and fall to the old polaroid, sun-faded and covered in dust.

A sharp rap at the window causes me to let out a squeak and throw myself back in the seat like I've been shot, but . . . it's Mason, staring down at me like he's studying a map to some forbidden treasure he *really* doesn't want to go out and find, that makes my heart hammer in my chest.

Like he's already regretting what he's about to say.

My heart bottoms out, laying in shambles in the pit of my chest as I prepare myself for more of the mental lashing that comes with Mason Carpenter and roll down the window.

"Be here at nine. Don't be late or you're on your own."

My mouth falls open like a chicken waiting for rain. Unfortunately, he doesn't give me time to ask questions because he turns and stalks off back down the sidewalk. All six foot, five inches of him.

Scrambling, I hurl myself from the car, banging my head painfully on the doorframe, but I don't stop.

"You'll help me? Tomorrow?"

He stops up the sidewalk, turns around, and regards me with a bored expression. One that says he really doesn't care if I show up or not.

"If that's a problem for you, you're welcome to continue searching on your own."

Jesus. He's so harsh now.

"Nope," I say, popping the *P*. I really want to tell him to shove it, but I need his help if I'm ever going to find Missy. "I'll be here, bright and early."

I hate early mornings.

He doesn't say anything else, but his gaze lingers for a second longer than it should. As if he's looking for something. Waiting for some big *gotcha* moment or for Missy to pop out of the trunk like a mentally ill Jack in the box.

Then he shuts the garage door behind him.

What the fuck just happened?

Did I just get rejected and then . . . I don't know . . . *un*rejected all in the course of ten minutes?

By Mason Carpenter, no less? The man who's haunted both my wildest dreams and my darkest nightmares since I met him?

This is either going to go really, really bad. Or . . . really good. I'm hoping for the latter. I'm betting on the first.

With Mason, there is no in between.

"I'm going to find you, Missy," I whisper, pressing a kiss to my fingertips and then pressing those same fingers to her picture. "I promise."

Then

CHAPTER One

MASON

3 YEARS AGO, MAY

I fucking hate Malibu.

The money, oozing out of every mansion. The people with their high society standards and self-entitlement. The fucking secrets.

I can't remember the last time I was here. Probably when Savannah graduated high school two years ago. It's just not the place for me. While I try to be there for my sisters whenever they need me, I also prefer to stay in my half of LA, far away from Parker Estate and my stepfather with a penchant for illegal activities.

I've got enough problems.

But . . . Bailey— the first out of three sisters— is celebrating her graduation from college and not even Marcus Parker could force me to miss it.

So, here I am, cruising down the busy streets toward the shiny mansion Mom and the girls moved into after she married Parker. The one place that makes my fucking skin crawl like I'm covered in a thousand fire ants.

I thought about backing out. I really did. Bailey wouldn't care. She knows I hate it here, but I also don't want to be the shit brother who never shows. I didn't come for Christmas, even though she begged me to. I owe it to her to at least make an appearance tonight.

Pulling up at the gate, there's a line of cars waiting to enter. Mom is throwing the party for Bailey and her best friend Andi, so I knew there would be people, but damn. Even I didn't think they were this popular.

"Jesus Christ," I murmur when I spot a guard waving a metal detector over the gift bags someone a couple cars ahead of me brought. Like they'd bring a bomb to a graduation party.

Then again . . . Parker is into some bad shit, so I guess it's warranted to be a little paranoid.

Too bad he's got his security searching out threats to him like bloodhounds.

I wait in line for twenty minutes before finally, the car in front of me begins their federal prison-style search and seizure. It's a group of kids. I wonder if Bailey and Andi even know them, but knowing Mom, she didn't invite their actual friends. Just the people she could claim she knows.

The problem with my mother, like a lot of people in LA, is they're too worked up over who's doing what, when, and with who. Mom loves anything to do with a high-class party and Bailey's graduation was the perfect opportunity for her to show off the wealth that oozes out of every brick in the Parker Mansion.

I remember when things were different. When us kids came first and she loved Dad. When she would make pancakes every Saturday morning, even though they were awful, and when she and Dad ran Carpenter's Auto together.

Now . . . I don't even recognize her.

The brake lights in front of me flash and I realize it's about to be my turn, the whole time, my stomach filling with dread at the prospect of having to let Mom try to force another one of Bailey and

Savannah's expensive friends at me.

The women Mom tries to throw at me . . . they're beautiful, don't get me wrong, but they aren't for me. I'm too rough for a soft girl. Too big a dick for someone who expects elegance and grace. Who was raised on money and fine dining, instead of hamburgers and Kool-Aid.

I move to pull up, but before I can, a young girl storms through the gates, so close to the front of my truck, I have to slam on the brakes to keep from adding a new addition to the cobblestone drive.

The guard yells something at her, but she just wipes dark black tears from her face and keeps marching down the sidewalk, wrapping her arms around herself.

Don't.

It's a busy road.

It's Malibu. She'll be fine.

I think we all know just because there's money, it doesn't mean there isn't also danger.

I war with myself, toying with the idea of going after her. I shouldn't. I don't know who she is. I'm here to see my sister. Not play Superman for the crying girl shuffling down the street.

A car horn honks loudly behind me and I stick my middle finger up at them out the window.

Dickhead.

"Fuck me," I grumble, whipping the truck into the grass beside the gate while two of the guards yell at me. "Tell Daddy dearest I say hello."

They glare at me, but neither says a word when I pull back out onto the street and make my way off toward the city where the girl went.

She didn't make it far. Probably because she doesn't have shoes on and she's soaking wet, for some reason, but I pull up beside the curb in front of her and roll the window down, anyway.

"You alright? I almost ran you over."

She pauses on the sidewalk, turning toward me with black-tinted tears streaming down her face.

I think she's going to start crying again when her lip wobbles. I've dealt with my fair share of upset women. Three sisters and all. Instead, she sucks it in and lifts her chin, glaring at me.

Yep. That's fucking Malibu for you.

"I'm fine."

I shrug.

"Suit yourself."

I put the truck in drive, debating on whether I want to sit in the line of cars or just go home and see Bailey tomorrow when the girl jumps toward the truck.

"Wait!"

I can't help but chuckle.

Fresh tears brim in her eyes and now that she's closer, I can see she's young. Pretty, but young. Probably no more than eighteen.

"Get in."

She doesn't argue and for a brief moment, I wonder where this girl's sense of self-preservation is. Then, I'm hit with the aroma of her perfume when she climbs in the passenger seat and despite myself, I fucking like it. Like sugar and honey and everything sweet.

"Where to?"

"Um . . ." she stammers. She's obviously been drinking. Doesn't surprise me coming out of Parker's place. "Do you know where the Kappa Nu house is?"

A sorority girl. Makes sense, I guess, hanging with Bailey and Andi.

"UCLA?"

She nods, buckling her seatbelt and hugging her arms around herself.

"I'll find it."

"Why are you helping me?" she asks quietly.

"Why are you soaking wet?"

She blinks at me, finally looking at me head-on with two of the brightest fucking green eyes I've ever seen. Like mint leaves or the trees up north. Fucking breathtaking.

And also highly unobtainable.

When she turns away, I start back down the highway toward the city, deciding I'll take Bailey out for ice cream and whatever else she wants to do in a couple days once things have settled down. She'd like that more than Mom's party, anyway.

"My boyfriend—sorry, *ex*-boyfriend, pushed me in the pool."

I raise a brow, but she doesn't look at me.

"Why did he do that?"

She shrugs. "I don't know. Because he's an idiot. And a child. And a cheating jerk."

Cue another brow raise for her choice of *jerk* as an insult. I can think of plenty of things to call the little bastard, none of which are nearly as kind as jerk.

"So you found out he cheated and he shoved you in the pool?"

"I guess. It sounds silly. Childish."

"You're not wrong there."

She regards me for a moment, probably trying to decipher what to say.

"Now you."

"What about me?"

"Why are you helping me?"

I let out a breath through my teeth as Malibu and that shit party slips away and the few miles of quiet country road takes us back to Los Angeles. Well, as country as it gets around here.

"Because that was my sister's party and she'd be pissed if I didn't help you."

"Bailey? Or the other one?"

"Andi. And yes, Bailey is my sister."

She shivers in the cool air of the AC, so without taking my eyes off the road, I pull an old flannel from the back seat of the truck and hand it to her.

"It's not much, but it's warm."

"Clean?"

"Probably not."

She seems to contemplate it for a moment but ends up slipping it on anyway.

"Thank you. I'm Hannah, by the way."

"Mason."

"Well, thank you for giving me a ride Mason. I'm sure you didn't want to leave the party."

I chuckle and I can feel her watching me.

"How do you know my sister?"

"I don't."

"So, why are you at her party?"

"My boyfriend— God, *ex*-boyfriend— is Drew's cousin."

Fucking Drew Marshall. I can't stand the kid, but Bailey loves him, so I tolerate him, for her sake.

For now.

Lately, he's been a little too controlling, from what Mila reports. Mila's the youngest of us and the most awkward, but she listens and she's good at keeping an eye on things when others think she isn't paying attention.

I had planned to talk to Bailey about Drew's controlling nature tonight, but that was before I realized Mom invited all of Los Angeles.

"The Marshall's are all rich kids who couldn't hold their own in a thumb war."

She laughs, a real laugh, and even in that moment, I don't think I quite understood the role that laugh would play in the rest of my life.

"Isn't he a little old for you, anyway?"

She rolls her eyes like a petulant teen. "I'm twenty. He's only twenty-six."

Shit. My age.

I guess a couple years really does make a difference. Where she's still naïve to the world's dark side, I've lived it. Though, from the looks of the expensive dress covered up in my old flannel, the sorority at the biggest college in LA, and the personal invite to a Monica Parker party, I'd say she hasn't had to live through much.

"A lot can change in a couple years."

"Maybe I just like older guys."

I glance at her and she's watching me. For a moment, I forget she's some random soaking wet twenty-year-old college kid and not a fucking siren here to drag me to the bottom of the ocean.

Then I remember. College. Twenty years old. I'm twenty-eight. I've got a business. A house. All of which I got because Dad died, but still. I've got responsibilities that don't interest someone so young. Or of her class.

"What is your major?"

She rolls her eyes, turning away from me.

Yep, a kid.

"Communication and Economics."

"Fascinating. You'll have to tell me more next time."

She pauses for a moment, but when she catches on that there won't *be* a next time, she gasps, laughing and punching me in the arm.

"Could you have picked a more boring degree?"

"Fine, what did you major in?"

I side-eye her. "College wasn't for me."

"Don't like school?"

"Don't like shelling out unnecessary money."

She shakes her head as we pull onto a busy campus street. For the end of the year, it's packed with people leaving or partying away their last days before summer break. To our right, Greek Row has houses lined down the street that all look like some poor attempt at replicating the Parthenon, each one with the trademark Greek symbols above the door.

"So, what *do* you do Mr . . ."

"Carpenter," I finish for her, spotting Kappa Nu and pulling to a stop between a Beamer and one of those new electric cars that look like a toaster. "I'm a mechanic."

"You don't strike me as the glamorous party-type like the rest of your family."

"And *you* don't strike me as the type to allow a Marshall to push her into a swimming pool." I lean across her, ignoring her gawking face and mouthwatering perfume and push the passenger door open. "Your stop."

She pauses for a moment and I hang there, balancing on the center console and holding the door open for her, our faces inches apart.

"Thank you for the ride, Mason Carpenter." Slowly, she exits the truck. I don't bother to ask for my flannel back. It looks better on her.

I chuckle darkly, for no other reason than dry amusement. If she knew what was going through my head at the sight of those pretty eyes, soft red hair, and a smattering of light freckles across her cheeks and nose, she wouldn't think I was her knight in shining armor, coming to rescue her from walking the twenty miles back to college.

"You're pretty, Hannah," I say quietly and her mouth parts over a soft breath. "But stupid. Don't get in the car with strangers."

And with that, I shut the door on her and she stumbles back a few steps. She stares through the tinted glass for a moment, glaring at me before finally, she turns and marches up the stairs to Kappa Nu.

I watch her go inside before I pull away, all the while my skin crawling and my nose filled with the scent of her perfume. Sweet and honey-like. The soft southern accent that's barely noticeable under that California exterior. Perfect body hidden under a sopping wet dress.

Yeah . . . whoever she is, she's going to be a problem.

And that, my friends, is what I get for trying to play hero.

CHAPTER Two

HANNAH

SEPTEMBER

"I fucking hate the tramps at these parties."

"Missy," I scold, surveying the people around us to make sure none of them heard. "Keep your voice down."

She shrugs. "Look at them." She nods to where the three Carpenter sisters are laughing, completely oblivious to my sister's death glare from across the room.

Must be nice. Laughing with your sisters. Mine always seems to be pissed off or sneaking out.

A waiter passes by with flutes of champagne, so I grab two and hand one to Missy. She's not normally in this bad of a mood, but lately, she's been in a constant state of *I hate everyone and everything* and I have no idea how to help break her out of it.

I've tried the mani-pedi route. The movie night. The twin sister gossip trick.

Nothing works.

"They're so happy to wallow in Daddy's money. Ignore the world's problems, so long as they don't affect them."

"Isn't that what we do?"

She shoots me a dark look, brown eyes like two little laser beams aimed at my head.

"God, how are we so different?"

I shrug, forcing a smile on my face. Mom's watching. "We weren't . . . until you decided the world was out to get you and started keeping secrets."

"Maybe I had to grow up quicker than you."

I resist the urge to roll my eyes and down my flute of champagne, sipping it instead, like I'm supposed to.

I'm going to need a whole keg if she keeps this attitude up.

"You forget we're twins?" I chuckle, though the declaration is clear. She's literally two minutes and fifteen seconds older than me. "We even share the same birthday."

"I'm still older," she murmurs, still deadlocked on Bailey, Savannah, and Mila Carpenter. "More mature. I've done things you wouldn't dream of."

I hate when she says things like that. Like she's going on world tours every night, only to slip quietly back in her bed before anyone notices she's gone. Can't be that exciting because she still lives at the LA mansion, and I can't think of anywhere else I'd rather be less than this city.

"Dramatic much?"

In a lot of ways, Missy and I are almost exactly the same. We're the same height, shoe size, and we used to be the same dress size until I grew hips and boobs and she grew more elegant and thin.

That's where the similarities stop, though. Where my hair is a lighter, cool red, hers is a darker fiery chocolate, appearing brown in regular lighting, but filled with red highlights in the sun. Not that she ever goes out in it from sleeping as late as she can every day.

Her eyes are brown. Mine are green. She has a dimple in her cheek. I don't.

Where I'm constantly trying to see the good in the world—

sometimes to my own downfall—Missy's hate couldn't be more apparent if it danced naked in the center of the room.

I guess, that's why we grew apart over the years. The old stories about twins are true. You can sense each other's presence. Emotions. You share in their pain.

Of course, that's only if the other half is willing to let you in.

"Look at them, Hannah," she says quietly. She steps closer and the scent of her Chanel No. 5 washes over me like a haze. It's Missy's signature scent. I don't know that she even owns anything else. It used to comfort me. Now it just makes me sad. "They're happy to be controlled by men."

She says it so vehemently, for a moment, I can feel her loathing seeping through my veins like poison.

"Don't you want to be in control of your *own* life?"

"I am," I argue, though it sounds meek even to my ears. Missy just chuckles darkly

"No, Mother's in control of your life. Just like she's in control of mine, or so she thinks. Until the day we're married off to the highest bidder to be controlled by another boring, unfaithful man to further her political agenda."

"Mom wouldn't do that."

"Are you sure?"

The way she says it makes my stomach turn.

Of course, I'm sure. I hope. She may be running for governor, but our mother's not the arranged marriage type. Not now, in modern-day America. That's something that happened hundreds of years ago.

Missy's just being cynical, as always.

"Could you at least *try* to be happy for them? It's Bailey's engagement party. She's marrying Drew."

Missy pauses, inspecting me and that fake smile threatens to crack.

And . . . now I've pissed her off.

"Fuck you."

And then she's gone.

I watch her storm through the crowd, toward the back of the venue where the gardens sit beyond the double French doors. All the while, the stepfather of the bride-to-be watches her, quietly sipping his own flute of champagne.

Ew.

I'll admit, I don't know much about the Carpenter sisters, save for what they show the outside world and that Marcus Parker, their stepfather, is one of my mother's biggest supporters.

Oh, and that their brother is the hottest man alive.

I thought he might be here. I mean, it *is* his sister's engagement party, but we've been here an hour and I've yet to see him and let me tell you . . . he sticks out in a crowd.

It's not just the height—he's practically a tree—but the glimmer of darkness that coats him like an invisible second skin. The pinnacle "bad boy" your mother doesn't want you to bring home. The rough, blue-collar man that every woman from eighteen to ninety-nine can't help but notice. It could be the tattoos on his arms and the way he doesn't say anything more than is absolutely necessary. The body built like a machine, trimmed with muscles I didn't even know existed.

It could also be the eyes like a hurricane rolling in off the coast and the growly voice that sends shivers down my spine.

I've yet to meet another man like him.

Unfortunately, I've also yet to meet *him* again.

I don't actually want to *do* anything about my little . . . crush on Mason Carpenter. Mom would lay an egg.

I just want to . . . look at him, I guess. It's been a couple months, so I'm sure he's all but forgotten about me and my pitiful dress soaking his truck's interior, but I haven't.

Too bad he's not here.

With some guilt, I realize, I should go after Missy and see if we can be excused. I've had enough fake smiling for one night.

"Let her go." My best friend, Michael and practically the only person I can talk to about Missy steps up beside me, holding out his hand. "Come on. Dance with me."

Across the room, my mother is watching, smiling while in conversation with another woman. She nods to me, encouraging it.

I don't like her ulterior motives.

In that moment, I feel the piercing gaze of everyone in the room, even the ones not looking at me. Part of me feels guilty for upsetting Missy. The other half feels guilty for refusing Michael's subtle advances . . . again.

All's not well in friendship paradise. Especially since my mother seems hellbent on playing Cupid.

Michael comes from a wealthy family, and I have my suspicions that Mom has had her sights set on him for me for a long time.

Joke's on her. I could never be intimate with Michael. He's too much like the brother I never had.

"Just let me go check on her." I wince at the exasperation he hides well behind a colorful smile. "I'm sorry."

I should change my name to Hannah *Running* Gaines. It seems to be my solution to every awkward situation.

Run from the uncomfortable position my mother is putting me in with Michael. Run from Missy and her bad attitude. Run from Mom and her political BS.

Run from a party hosted by the Carpenters because I caught my boyfriend cheating.

I hurry through the crowd, away from Michael and Mom and everyone's prying eyes.

A few people stop to speak to me—only because of my mother—but I just smile politely and wave before hurrying on toward the terrace and gardens beyond. I don't know that I have it in me to spread Mom's political jargon tonight and God knows I don't want to screw up and say the wrong thing.

Mom's tantrums make a nuclear meltdown seem like a minor

inconvenience.

And then Missy's words ring in my ear.

Don't you want to be in control of your own life?

I grit my teeth, ignoring the prying thoughts at the back of my mind and press through the double doors to the sprawling back gardens of the Pleasant Hills Country Club.

One thing Missy isn't wrong about? The Carpenters have money. Money-money. Like so much money, you could swim in it. Mom's wealthy, but I guess I've never really recognized the wealth that surrounds me until right now when it's staring me in the face.

Sometimes I feel guilty. Other times I don't because I know Mom worked her way up from nothing. When Dad left us, Missy and I were only seven and Mom became a single parent. We moved from Virginia to California, Mom started her political climb at the ripe old age of thirty-three and now, she's become the governor of California.

For a lot of reasons, I admire her perseverance.

For others . . . I hate her.

Stepping through the hedge maze where I'm sure Missy must have gone, I hear the sound of hushed voices. I follow them, but when I round the corner, my heart bottoms out in my chest.

Marcus Parker is standing in front of my sister, his lips locked with hers in a fevered embrace. He's got her dress hiked up, her knee over his arm as he thrusts into her.

I fall back a step and just when I think I can't move, a hand wraps around my mouth and I'm hauled back before I can even get a peep out.

Strong arms envelop me and though I try to fight them off, the person they belong to isn't at all swayed as they drag me back out of the hedge maze.

When I'm finally set to my feet, I spin around to unleash on whoever the hell grabbed me when I'm struck, yet again.

Hurricane eyes. Hard jaw. Broad shoulders.

So, he did come . . .

"What the hell are you doing?" My voice is breathier than usual as my heart feels like it's going to high step out of my chest.

"Saving your ass," Mason Carpenter says, lighting the end of a cigarette. I've always hated the scent of cigarettes and maybe it's just my schoolgirl crush on the titan of a man, but now, I find it . . . attractive.

Cue the internal eyerolls.

And then my cheeks burn when I remember the old flannel he loaned me that I never gave back.

"Again," he adds, drawing on the end of his cigarette.

Because I'm a glutton for punishment, I reach for the cigarette, plucking it out of his fingers and raising it to my lips. I feel like a toddler, mimicking the actions of an adult. Especially when he watches me, gaze as dark and all-consuming as it was four months ago when I put my lips to it and pull. The moment the nicotine-filled smoke hits my lungs, my throat closes and I cough.

Great, Hannah. Really cool.

I don't miss the amusement in his eyes when I hand it back to him and for some reason, I'm surprised when he raises it back to his lips, pink lipstick stain and all.

"What are they doing?" I ask quietly, wrapping my arms around myself. It's chilly in September at night, despite the warmth of the daytime weather in SoCal, but I refuse to ask him for his leather jacket.

I'd probably end up keeping it and sleeping in it every night, anyway.

Mason cocks a brow, taking a long drag and billowing out a puff of smoke. "You really have to ask?"

My stomach twists painfully. My sister, having an illicit affair with a married man.

No wonder she hates the Carpenters so much.

"That's horrible," I murmur bleakly.

"Thought you *only* date older men?" At the time, my little joke seemed funny, especially because I was drunk and he was both older, as well as the most attractive man I'd ever seen. Now, I'm embarrassed. His eyes travel over the blush on my cheeks and neck, his jaw twitching before he looks away.

"I would never date a married man."

Mason shrugs. "Takes two people to commit adultery, little doe."

"Don't call me that," I stammer, my cheeks blazing like the surface of the sun. Little doe. What does that even mean?

He ignores me completely.

"Though, I can't imagine having the infamous Marcus Parker grunting and sweating all over you would be the desire of any woman your age."

I roll my eyes, crossing my arms over my chest. "You act like you're so much older."

His eyes flash with something dark before it's quickly replaced with a look of indifference.

Is everyone going to be cryptic tonight?

"Congratulations, by the way. Bailey and Drew seem really happy together."

He chuckles sardonically.

"Seems that way, huh?"

I don't have either the brain power or the desire to understand what that means, right now.

"I take it you don't like him."

"Dislike isn't strong enough a word."

I shrug. "He seems nice enough."

"You've got a lot to learn about the world, Hannah. And the people in it."

"Please," I shoot him a glare. "I don't live under a rock."

"No, but you do live under Mommy's thumb."

"As if you don't."

"I made my own way. Do I look like a frequenter of country clubs to you?"

Right now, he looks like he could be a model for sexy, blue-collar men.

"Okay, you got me there."

"Look at this place. People surrounded by their wealth. They're so shallow they forget to see each other for who they really are."

"And who do you think I really am?" I ask quietly, regretting it the moment it's out of my mouth.

Mason studies me for a moment, tossing the butt of his cigarette. His eyes flash with something dark and repressed and when he takes a step forward, my heart skips a beat.

Careful not to touch me, he places both hands on either side of the wall behind my head, caging me in. He smells like leather and sin and everything that makes my mouth water that shouldn't.

My mother would kill me if she could see me right now. Practically salivating for this man.

He reaches up and I freeze in place, blinking up at him while he gently brushes a stray lock of hair off my cheek. It's intimate, like a lover's caress and my skin tingles where the backs of his fingers brush against it.

"Men like me break girls like you, little doe." A shiver moves down my spine and my heart stalls in my chest when I force myself to meet his eyes, like a storm at sea. "I would shatter you. Watch you crumble from my fingers, my mouth . . . my cock. Then when I was finished with you, I'd put you back together again, so you'd be mine to do with as I please."

I let out a breath, though it shakes as my chest tightens, my body growing hot with a desire I'm not sure I've ever experienced before.

Mason presses forward until his front is barely brushing mine. He leans in, his stubble on my cheek sending electric shocks through my veins and all the way down to my core.

"What do you think your mother would say if she knew I could make her sweet little daughter's pussy wet with just a few words?"

"I'm not wet," I lie. I definitely am. "I just think you're crude."

He chuckles darkly, lingering against my skin for a moment

longer. His breath is warm and I fight the instinct to tilt my head to grant him better access to the pressure point there.

"Run inside to your mother before they come back," he murmurs, pulling away and leaving my skin cold and tingling at the loss of him. His eyes burn with intensity as he pulls out another cigarette and lights the end. With the flame of the lighter burning in his eyes, he looks like the devil.

If the devil were as hot as Mason Carpenter.

Then again, isn't he meant to be a fallen angel?

Mason leans back against the stone railing of the terrace, facing the building. His eyes sweep over the huge country club, filled with disdain and something black as night.

He hates this place.

"Why do you hate your stepfather?"

His eyes flick back to me and I take a single step backward. I never realized how much bigger than me he was the last time I saw him. Now, I feel like a toddler in comparison.

"Besides the obvious."

"What makes you think you're at liberty to ask?"

I'm so taken aback by his sudden harshness, my mouth actually falls open.

Still, he doesn't look like he regrets it. Not with the harsh set of his jaw and the way his shoulders stiffen.

"Okay . . ." I start, but he cuts me off.

"We aren't girlfriends. We aren't sharing our darkest secrets. I helped you once because my sister would have wanted me to. That's it."

I stare at him for a moment, shell-shocked at his outward rudeness. He seemed like such a nice guy. A *man* among all the boys I've been dating.

Guess I was wrong.

"Have a good night, then."

I turn to march toward the door, cheeks burning hot and hands vibrating with either anger or adrenaline. I don't know which, yet.

"Oh, and by the way." I pause at the door, turning back to him watching me with a darkness in his eyes I'm not accustomed to. "I

---

would have rather walked."

Missy is quiet while our mother berates me on the way home.

"That boy is *trash*," she slurs and some of the ash from the end of her cigarette lands on the leather seat of the limo. It seems someone had a little too much fun at the party. "He's a thief and a drug dealer."

Mason doesn't seem like a thief *or* a drug dealer. In fact . . . he seems to be one of the only sane people I've spoken to in the last six months.

My mother doesn't know about Mason taking me home a couple months ago. Somehow, I convinced Michael to say he left early to drive me back to the university, only because I knew this was how she would react.

Mother doesn't like anyone different than her. Case in point, Missy and me and her affinity for harsh punishments and cruel assessments disguised behind that fake Virginian accent.

Laura Gaines didn't grow up in Virginia. She was born in fucking Wisconsin.

"Why do you dislike him so much?" I actively work to keep the annoyance out of my voice, but Laura is a bloodhound. She can sniff out any sign of disrespect.

Like right now. Her eye twitches when she blows out a cloud of smoke, eyeing me like she's inspecting me before a big benefit or an event where my presence is required.

"You like him, don't you?" I pause, my heart nearly stopping in my chest. Mason Carpenter is handsome, but that's where the attraction stops. He's crude and an asshole. His fingernails are stained with motor grease and he's covered in tattoos.

Tattoos that make him hotter, my brain chimes at the worst moment. *And the callouses on his hands that felt good against your skin. The way he says your name. Almost like he's growling it.*

Okay, shut up.

My cheeks flame and, of course, Laura picks up on that.

She sneers behind her cloud of smoke. "You do."

"I'm indifferent toward him."

"Oh, please." She rolls her eyes, laughing sardonically.

I glance at Missy beside me for a little backup. I mean, she's *sleeping* with Marcus Parker. Mom's business partner. A *married* business partner. Unfortunately, though, she's got her head leaned against the window, her eyes darting back and forth as she watches the buildings pass by on our way back to the Bel Air mansion.

Is she high?

"You were practically fornicating with him in the garden," Mother grits, disgust dripping from her tone. "I didn't raise you that way."

"You didn't raise me to be judgmental and cruel, either," I retort and I know as soon as it's out of my mouth, it was the wrong thing to say. "We were just talking."

"The problem with you, Hannah dear, is you're too naïve. You think he wants to talk to you? He doesn't even *like* you. He just wants what's between your legs."

My mouth fills with saliva at the sick feeling brewing in my stomach. I know it's of my mother's design, but the sad part is, she's probably not wrong. Mason's the same as any other guy that comes to call. They all want the same things. Sex. A good time. Some claim to fucking the governor's daughter because it's a fun little story to tell their friends.

I'm an idiot if I don't accept that he's not just like the others.

Mom points the glowing red end of her cigarette at me.

"I want you to stay away from him."

My stomach clenches, remembering the way he'd looked at me

in the garden. Like I was something special to him, and he hated it.

"And if I say no?"

She narrows her gaze, finishing the last of her cigarette and smashing it out a little too aggressively in the limo's ashtray.

"Try me."

The way she says it, it's more of a threat than an actual warning. Like she's hoping I'll slip up.

A shiver rolls down my spine when I think of that dark, dark place.

"Fine."

She watches me for a beat as if she's trying to read my mind and see if I'm lying or planning to sneak out to meet the bad boy in the middle of the night.

"Good."

We pull through the gates of the Gaines' LA mansion moments later, after the car falls into an awkward silence of Mom replying to emails, Missy on the trip of her life, and me . . . thinking about my conversation with Mason.

Am I really that different from the rest of my family? Is he?

I suppose he is. The pinnacle black sheep.

Mom answers a call as we pull up to the house and Missy and I climb out. She stumbles away from me, but I race to keep up with her.

"What did he give you?" I ask quietly, grabbing her hand to stop her before she climbs the stairs. I can hear Mom on the phone outside, complaining about the Carpenters.

Missy's eyes dart to mine and her brow furrows, but I can see in the way her pupils are nearly completely dilated and the way she licks her lips, she's definitely on something.

"Stop it, Hannah," she snaps, ripping her hand out from mine. She climbs the stairs in a huff, but I follow after her anyway.

"Missy, he's married." She stops at the top of the landing, turning back to me with a smile.

"To a whiny bitch with no ambition," she says sweetly and my stomach turns when the fake smile falls off her face, being replaced with a dark scowl. I take a step back at the look on her face, almost toppling back down the stairs. In the dim lighting of the upper floor, she almost looks demonic. Terrifying. "He's making me a partner at one of his companies."

"It doesn't mean it's right. He has a family."

She regards me with dull indifference as if I'm nothing more than a doorknob in a department store.

"You're so naïve, it's almost pathetic, Hannah."

Okay, ouch.

Unfortunately, Missy takes a step forward and I can't take a step back because the stairs are right behind me. In a rush, she lifts her hand and I actually jump as if she might hit me. Instead, she brushes the red lock of hair off my cheek, the same one Mason had.

"My poor prudish sister, pining after Mason Carpenter. As if he'd want a girl like you," she coos, and acid turns in my stomach. "A word of advice, Hannah. You'll never be more than Mom's little doll because you refuse to fight back. Marry Michael and have boring sex with the lights off every Saturday night and raise two boring children because that's all you'll ever succeed at."

Tears burn in my eyes and just as one is about to fall, Mom walks through the door, still on the phone and completely oblivious to what's happening at the top of the stairs.

"Of course, Hannah would love to come with me."

Missy cocks her head, a sinister smile tugging on her lips.

"*Boo.*" She jumps forward, almost knocking me down the stairs and I clamber for the railing in my heels. Missy just chuckles and goes to her room, shutting the door behind her with a final click.

"I said carnations!" My mother screeches from downstairs and I jump, again nearly toppling down the stairs and ending it all.

I go to my room, taking a shower and thinking about tonight's events. Missy. Mom. Mason. The dark side of my sister I never knew existed. The words Mason murmured in my ear that should have sent me running in the other direction.

Men like me break girls like you, little doe.

Somehow, I know he's right.

Still, as Mom screams from somewhere downstairs, barking orders into her phone like a deranged dictator and Missy cuts on some heavy screamo music like a teenager going through a "phase", curling up in that old flannel, surrounded by the scent of leather, smoke, and something else that must be *him*, I find I feel the safest I've ever felt.

And I sleep through the night.

CHAPTER *Three*

HANNAH

DECEMBER

"I'm not going!"

"Like hell, you're not! I'm giving a speech. You're expected."

Missy growls dramatically, stomping her foot the same way she does every time she and our mother get into a fight. "I'm sick and *tired* of going to these stupid charity benefits. I don't care about these people and neither do you!"

"Your sister's not complaining," Mom fires back and Missy's ire is then turned on me.

Thanks, Mom.

"Because she's too afraid of you. You're both pathetic."

And cue the belligerent disrespect that always goes unchecked.

I'm used to Missy and Mom and their tender way of throwing me under the bus whenever they get into an argument. The only reason I'm complaining now is the blistering migraine throbbing in my temple.

The girls from Kappa NU and I went out to celebrate Christmas before we went our separate ways for the holidays, last night. I guess one drink led to five and now, I'm paying the price.

So, donned in the golden Tom Ford evening gown Mom picked out for me, I sit in the foyer of the LA mansion, practically begging the Advil to take over and hoping to God Missy stops screaming soon.

Of course, in true Missy fashion, though, she doesn't.

"You're going and that's final," Mom snaps, face red under her perfect blonde French twist. "Go change. You're embarrassing me." Mom waves a hand to the people waiting in the foyer. Her staff, right-hand woman, and I suspect, secret lover, June. My best friend Michael. Mom's driver, Donatello.

I roll my eyes. As if none of them haven't seen Missy throw a fit before.

Missy opens her mouth to refuse again, but Mom stops her with a look. I know that look. It's a warning. One more toe out of line and the already dire consequences will turn into dictator-like punishment.

"I hate you!" Missy spits at Mom, storming back up the stairs to her room. Seconds later, her door slams with enough force to rattle my brain.

"Christ," Mom grits in her gentle Virginian accent, patting down her already perfect hair. "You would think I had asked her to chop off a limb."

"It's okay," June soothes, placing a hand on Mom's arm. She's good at diffusion situations, especially with Missy. I suppose that's part of why Mom keeps her around, apart from her . . . *other* talents. "Hannah can go speak with her. We have to go."

"Let's not," I shoot back, and everyone's eyes turn on me. My cheeks burn red under their gaze. I'm not used to being the center of attention. That position is normally filled with either Mom or Missy. Truth be told, I'd rather remain in the background. It's simpler there.

Less yelling.

June shoots me a look, warning me not to upset my mother any more than she already is and I resist the urge to roll my eyes.

Right about now, I'm pretty tired of everyone in my general vicinity. I just want to get this benefit over with, come back home, and climb into a bubble bath. Now that Mom's governor, we've been splitting our time between LA and Sacramento, though I prefer Los Angeles. Mom's agreed to let me stay this time, with the promise that I won't do anything stupid, but I think she just wants me to keep an eye on Missy.

Always babysitting Missy.

"No, that's a good idea," Mom murmurs, completely disregarding I already said no. "She'll talk to you if no one else is around."

"Then it's settled." June smiles at me, not even bothering to hide the triumph in her gaze. "Hannah, you go and get Missy ready and the rest of us will head over. We're going to be late if we don't leave soon."

"Of course."

Mom stares at me for a moment, as if she's testing me to see if I'll argue with her again, but I know better. I'm not an idiot.

She nods once and then she and June head toward the door with the rest of the party while I prepare myself for the mental warfare that comes with calming down my sister.

"You look like shit," Michael chuckles quietly, joining me now that everyone has dissolved into idle chit-chat about tonight's events.

"Thank you," I grimace.

"I didn't mean it like that," he murmurs. "I meant you look like you don't feel well. You actually look beautiful right now."

Actually?

Ass.

"Wait," he calls, following me as I climb to the second floor. "That wasn't right, either."

"Is this about what my mother said?"

If awkward tension was a liquid, we'd be drowning in it right now.

"Well—"

"Michael," I stop on the landing, lowering my voice now that we're out of eyesight of everyone downstairs. "You're making things awkward by worrying about what my mother thinks." His eyes flash with something incredulous before it's quickly replaced. "You and I both know we're just friends. Isn't that enough?"

He lets out a deep sigh, shrugging.

"Of course. But what if there's something there we're not seeing that she is?"

"There's not, though."

I roll my eyes, resuming my trek toward Missy's room. He follows along behind me.

"You don't think so?"

"Michael, I'm *really* not in the mood to have this conversation."

He cocks his head. "When, then?"

I ignore him, stopping in front of Missy's door, agitation winding through me.

"Missy put the damn dress on and let's go."

Michael stares at me like I've lost my mind, but right now, my head is nearly splitting in half.

No answer.

"Missy!" I yell, banging my fist so hard on the wooden door, my hand tingles.

Still no answer.

So, like a thin, invisible string, my temper snaps.

"You're twenty-one years old. Stop acting like a whiny brat and let's go!"

"Hannah," Michael cautions, holding a hand out to stop me.

Coincidentally, his palm brushes my stomach and I shrink back. His eyes darken before he turns away.

"Missy, it's Michael. Can you please come tonight?"

"Doing my sister's bidding won't make her love you, Michael."

I wince at her words muffled through the door.

Damn, Missy. You just had to go *there.*

Michael seems to take it in stride, though, chuckling and shaking his head.

"You Gaines girls should become lawyers," he says to me. "Come on, Missy. It's just for a night and then things will die down for a while."

"No, they won't. You forgot New Year's."

He looks back at me across the hall for help and I shrug.

"You did."

He growls under his breath and shakes his head.

"Missy—"

"Just let me handle it," I say softly. He looks down to where my hand rests on his arm as if I am personally responsible for the death of his grandmother.

"That's the first time you've touched me in months," he says quietly, jaw tightening.

And then, without a word, he retreats down the hallway to go with my mother.

I let out a sigh, staring after him with all manner of conflicting emotions hurtling about my head.

What the hell have I gotten myself into?

One night to destroy a happy, fifteen-year friendship.

To make matters worse—a night I regret more than anything else in my life.

And then, I'm back to thinking about Missy's illicit affair with Marcus Parker.

To my knowledge, she hasn't stopped and in fact, he's been doting on her more in the last couple months. Since she got a job working for him, she's been gone a lot and I haven't spoken to her about it any more than for her to tell me to "mind my own fucking business".

I know it's wrong, but . . . what can I do? Forbid her from seeing him? Like that will do anything. All I can do is try to show her how wrong it is, but she doesn't care.

I thought about mentioning it to Mom, but God knows she can't be trusted. For all I know, she could have put her up to it.

"Missy?" I tap lightly on her door, but she doesn't answer. The silence is nearly deafening. "Missy, please let me in. Are you okay?"

"Fuck off, Hannah."

I bite back the retort on the tip of my tongue. This is just her getting out her anger for our mother. I'm used to it. Fighting with her won't make it better.

"Missy, I know you're angry, but Mom was only trying to—" Before I can finish my sentence she flings the door open. Her hair flies around her face in a wild tangle, her eyes and cheeks red from crying.

"*Don't* finish that sentence," she growls, fresh tears glistening in her hateful gaze.

I falter for a moment, stepping back from the venomous rage that seeps off her in waves.

"I'm sorry. I was only going to say she just wants us there. I don't think she was trying to upset you. It's Christmas. We always spend Christmas together."

"That's the problem," she spits through clenched teeth. "You don't *think*. You just say whatever nonsense comes to mind and expect everyone to listen to it as if it's gospel. Well, I'm not one of your little friends you can order around."

It's at that moment, I realize, I really don't know my sister at all anymore.

All the times I've stayed to coax her out of her room. All the times I've tried to comfort her after a particularly bad fight between her and our mother.

All the punishments I endured to save her . . .

"Go to hell, Missy," I snap, turning to march away from her. "Don't expect me to save you this time."

A hand clasps in the ends of my hair, yanking me back and I let out a startled cry of pain.

Missy pulls me backward until I fall to the ground at her feet, banging my head on the tile floor in the process. She crouches down over me, taking my chin in her hand and gripping my skin painfully until her manicured fingernails dig in.

"In case you forgot, dear, *stupid*, sweet sister, we were born in hell."

And then she's off me and slamming the door in my face while I lay there, sputtering and disoriented.

CHAPTER Four

MASON

The annual Christmas charity benefit has got to be the biggest fucking waste of time.

That money doesn't go to help people. Not most of it, anyway. Of course, they pay for the venue—the most expensive one they can rent—the staff to cater that event, the musicians in the live orchestra, and any high-ranking member they want to attend.

Laura Gaines will be giving a speech tonight. Probably another tale about how she's saving the lives of millions as governor. But if Governor Gaines is. . . that means her daughter will be, too.

Of course, I'm not here to see Hannah Gaines, but if she happens to cross my path, I won't say no.

The little redhead is becoming a problem. One I'm not accustomed to dealing with. It's been three months since I saw her in the back gardens of the country club and each day, I've grown increasingly agitated.

It's why I've always tried to keep my distance where she's

concerned. I knew she would trip me up and after she started asking about Parker, I started picturing all manner of things I'd love to do to her to shut her up.

Her under me, spread against my sheets and begging for my cock. My name a plea on her lips. Her on her knees, pretty green eyes flashing up at me with that fire I've come to seek out.

Heat rushes to my groin and my heartbeat pounds in my ears before I quickly push the fantasy away.

She'll never be mine.

Now, like a cuck, I'm holding my dick for a chance to see her again. Watch those pretty freckles disappear when I make her blush. See her green eyes flash with that fire I can't get enough of.

And her scent . . . Jesus fucking Christ. Like something I want to worship and degrade, all at the same time.

I know as well as any other guy not to fuck around with the governor's daughter. *Especially* the daughter of Laura Gaines. Want to kiss life goodbye in the blink of an eye? Fuck around with the prized princess she parades around like a show poodle.

"You're early."

I blow a cloud of smoke at my reflection in the window in front of me. It's cracked because the hotel doesn't allow cigarettes, but I've never been one to follow the rules.

"You're late."

The FBI agent steps into the room with a dark chuckle, sitting down at one of the chairs. This room is another banquet hall, dark as it's not being used for tonight's benefit in the main room. Vaguely, you can hear the muffled sounds of the party beyond as all manner of LA's wealth convenes for charity's sake.

"Come. Let's have a little chat."

I don't move from my spot by the window. The FBI agent chuckles again.

"You don't trust easily," he points out, lighting up the end of his own cigarette.

"And you do?"

He nods. "No. Though, it is my line of work to seek out liars."

"What about . . . traffickers?"

He pauses for a moment, pulling hard on the end of the cigarette and blowing a cloud of smoke into the air.

"Depends on the kind."

"Both."

His eyes glint black in the darkness.

"I'm told you have some information that might be useful for me."

"My stepfather," I start, turning around and leaning against the wall. "Is trafficking drugs and people in and out of the state."

"And you know this, how?"

"I have my sources. Before I give you the proof, I have some things I'd like in return."

"I could just have you detained and then we'd get the proof, anyway."

I chuckle darkly. "That's where you're wrong, Prince."

"So, what is it you want?"

"I want my sisters and mother granted immunity. They didn't play a part in this."

Logan Prince seems to mull that over for a moment.

"And yourself, of course."

"Yes."

"Is that it?"

It should be. Fuck, it really should be.

"Hannah Gaines."

"The redhead."

So he has noticed her.

"She's not a part of this, either."

Logan sits forward, resting his elbows on his knees. I can see the plan weave its way through his mind as if it's second nature for him. As if we're all just NPC's and he's the controller of the game.

Good. It's what my family needs. Someone who won't get tangled up in emotions and shit that could make this plan go south. They need an out. Logan Prince *is* their out.

"So, you're telling me, not only is your stepfather in on this, but also the governor? What about the other daughter?"

"She's as much a part of it as Parker is. Maybe more."

"How can you be sure?"

"You'll get all that as soon as I get a document stating my family and Hannah will be safe."

"Expect it in your mailbox this week."

"Then you can expect an envelope with all these details after that."

Logan watches me for a moment, studying me. It's a classic FBI move. They try to get in your head. Make you tell them shit because they make you uncomfortable.

"So that's Hannah Gaines, Monica Parker, Bailey Carpenter, Savannah Carpenter, and . . ."

"Mila."

Christian steps out of the shadows, blue eyes grim in the dim lighting provided by the lowered wall sconces.

"Ah, yes, the more the merrier," Logan says bitterly.

"Christian has an in for you, but we can't be sure how soon."

"And does Christian know what we're up against?"

"I've been guarding the Carpenter girls for years. Marcus Parker is a cockroach and the world needs to be rid of him," Christan says, as matter-of-fact as if he were talking about the Sunday paper. "You'll see to it, it's done, correct?"

Logan flashes a cocky grin.

"Oh, it'll get done."

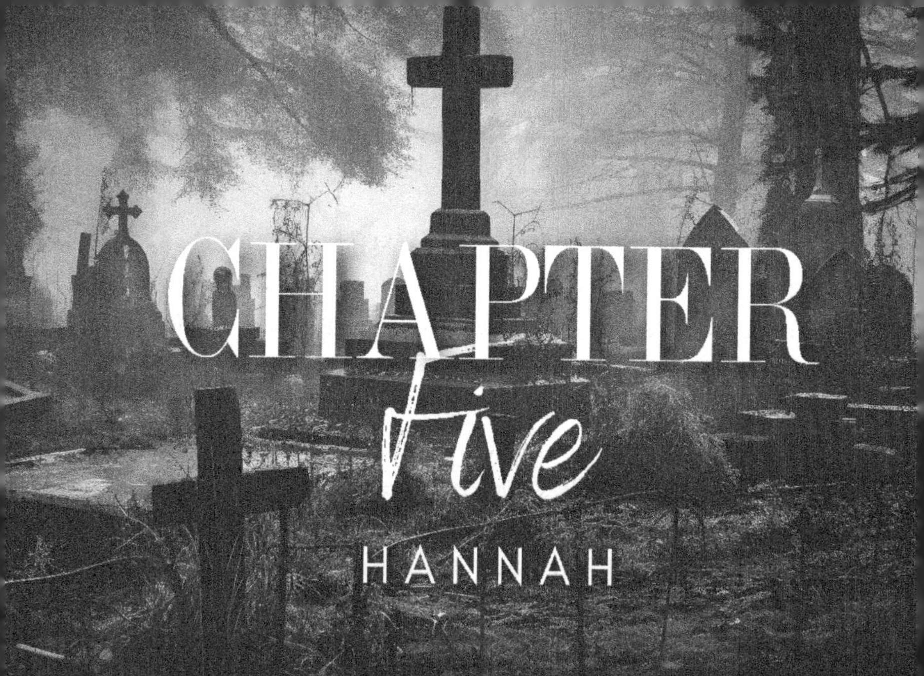

CHAPTER *Five*

HANNAH

The Christmas charity gala is being held at one of the most prestigious hotels in LA and tonight, it seems everyone, including their brother, came out to support the cause.

The cause being . . . I don't know, but it beats sitting around in Missy's angry cloud of hate all night.

My jaw is sore and though I applied concealer like a face mask in the car to cover the red scratches from Missy's nails, the raised skin still shows through if you look close enough. The driver, Paulo, is kind enough not to ask.

He knows my mother.

He knows Missy, too.

He and Missy even had a tryst a few years back and I remember him panicking because he thought he was going to get fired when he cut it off.

Unfortunately, I think losing his job would have been better.

Somehow, Missy snuck into his apartment and added hair removal cream to his new girlfriend's conditioner. It completely ruined her pretty black curls and her head had to be shaved because of all the bald patches.

That was when I realized my sister could be pure evil if she really put her mind to it. Vindictive.

"Need me to escort you in, Ms. Gaines?" Paulo asks from the front seat of the Bentley.

Since I'm arriving late, I didn't have to sit through the insufferable limo drive with my mother and her team. Even if they weren't there, Michael still would have been and I just need space from him right now.

"No, thank you, Paulo. I can walk in by myself." As soon as I say it, my door is opened and one of Mom's security is staring down at me. "Or so I thought."

I let out a deep sigh, forcing my best face and take the hand extended to me.

And so it begins.

"See you later, Paulo."

Four men are waiting to escort me inside. Not unusual in my mother's line of work. Back in Sacramento, we're surrounded by security constantly.

But LA is my "safe spot". I can breathe—which is ironic considering the city I'm speaking about—without having to worry about someone watching me like I'm the Declaration of Independence. Here lately, though, with my mother spending more time here, it's starting to become Sacramento 2.0.

Sometimes I feel like a marionette doll, being controlled from all directions. Which dress to wear, which shoes would look classy and chic instead of trashy. What to say, how to walk. When to smile and when to be completely devoid of expression.

Sometimes, I even dream about going back to college. Back when I had the freedom to breathe and do whatever girls my age do.

I'm twenty-three, but I feel older. Like a forty-two-year-old married and kept woman whose husband runs around behind her back and commands her every waking moment.

Just like Monica Parker.

I've seen her. The wife to the other-woman scenario my sister is playing out. On the outside, you wouldn't notice the cracks in her porcelain exterior. I know, on the inside, it's broken and bloody— a mess from her husband's betrayal.

She hates me by proxy and though I would love to speak to her, just once, to see what she's really like, I know no one's getting through that cool exterior.

It's no wonder Mason hates his stepfather so much.

Somehow, I feel like if I married Michael and accepted this fate, I would end up just like Monica. Internally tattered. Broken.

Of course, there's something darker where Marcus Parker is concerned. I could see it in the caustic glint in Mason's eyes the night I asked him about it. I haven't seen him since, but I reckon he still hates me for prying into his internal struggles, almost as much as I hate myself for bothering to care.

I wish I was like Missy. Cold. Passionately unfeeling, if that's even a thing. But I'm not. I care too much and that will be my downfall. Mark my words.

"Ms. Gaines." The doorman tips his hat at me. For a moment, I wonder how he knows my name and then I remember the four huge men surrounding me like I'm a priceless jewel.

Oh, yeah. My mother's the governor.

God, don't let her find out I forgot. I'll have to hear her speech about paving the way for women in politics and changing this state for the good.

As if she's any different from the last governor.

The hotel lobby is filled with familiar faces. Men and women dressed in their best gowns and tuxes to show off their wealth for the photographers to capture for the less fortunate. Because that's what we are, right? The unobtainable, used to remind the average citizen that while they may succeed, they will never be on our level.

It's disgusting.

"I have to use the restroom," I announce loudly to my four bodyguards and none of them make a move.

I attempt to step away from them, but they only follow, silent and expressionless behind dark glasses as if they're the secret service and I'm the president of the United States.

"I need to change my tampon," I lie and one at least has the good sense to grimace slightly at the connotation. "Do you really need to follow?"

"We go where you go, Miss Gaines."

Of course. Who am I to demand privacy while using the restroom?

"Fine," I grumble under my breath, "but you aren't coming in with me."

Somehow, I manage to break myself free from my throngs of man-muscle and slip quietly into the bathroom. Alone.

I let out a sigh of relief, sinking back against the door and closing my eyes.

"Tough crowd?"

I nearly jump out of my skin at the sound of the voice. I hadn't expected anyone else to be in here. Stupid, I know.

Bailey Carpenter, oldest sister of the Carpenter bunch stands at the sink in front of me, fixing what looks to be black mascara streaks under her eyes. She smiles humorlessly at the grim expression on my face.

"We really are all alike, aren't we?"

I don't know what she means by that, but I did hear about her fiancé and the atrocities he committed against her recently. Of course, some of those had to be rumors, but just how deep was the truth buried under that fake smile?

"Come here," she beckons, pulling concealer out of the small Versace clutch lying on the counter. When I don't move, she cocks a delicate brow. "You missed a spot."

Slowly, I approach her and she pushes me back against the counter and raises my chin to the light. She's taller than I am. Older, by only a couple years. Being in this proximity to her, my sister's vengeful hate for the three sisters comes back to me. I always thought it was because of Marcus, but maybe it's something else.

Bailey carries herself in a way that the outside world wouldn't understand. The constant need to be "on", lest the world catch you having a normal human emotion. It's what's expected of women in our position and something Missy never mastered.

"Sisters can be such bitches, can't they?" Bailey asks softly, carefully applying concealer to the scratches on my face.

At this proximity, I can see the massive resemblance between her and Mason. The light eyes, the high cheekbones. The sort of parental authority both seem to carry in themselves.

"Mine seems to have lost her mind," I whisper. I don't even know why I tell her. Bailey owes me nothing. In fact, our families couldn't be more at odds than the Hatfields and McCoys now that my sister's affair has reached the surface.

"Did you tell your mother?" I can tell by the glimmer of displeasure in her eyes, she knows as well as I do, it would do nothing.

"I can't run off to my mother every time my sister and I get into a fight."

"Perhaps," Bailey says, patting the concealer into my face with a towel from the sink. "Though, do you really think she'll stop here?"

"We have security—"

"Security that will stop her from shoving you down the stairs? Or throwing a toaster in your bubble bath? Perhaps she'll just poison your food."

Fuck. My lip wobbles and I'm disgusted with myself. Mom *hates* it when we cry. You would think raising two daughters, she would be used to it by now, but as a kid, the more tears you shed the worse the punishment was.

"A word of advice," Bailey murmurs, sealing her concealer back up and sliding it back in her clutch. "You sister's a loose cannon. And violent. Get out while you still can. Before Parker sinks his claws into you, too."

"He's a creep," I grumble, shuddering at the thought of a very sweaty Marcus Parker thrusting over me.

Bailey shrugs, heading toward the door. "This is LA. They all are."

"Bailey," I call and she stops, hand on the door handle. "Are you okay?"

She turns back to me, tears glistening in her eyes, but they never fall.

"Of course."

And with that, she's gone.

I suck in a deep breath, willing my hands to stop shaking and wash them in the sink before heading back toward the door.

It's time to face the music. My mother will undoubtedly be pissed I didn't manage to coerce Missy into coming, but there's nothing I can do about that now.

I suck up my pride, force the fake smile to my face, and head toward the door, stopping dead in my tracks when I open it to the dark, heavy gaze of my mother.

Well, shit.

"Come."

"Mom—"

In a flash, she reaches for me, her hand gripping the crook of my neck so hard her fingernails dig into the exposed flesh there.

"Make a scene."

Fuck.

I swallow my fear and let her lead me like I'm marching from the Tower of London to meet the executioner.

I didn't do as she told me.

Now I have to face the consequences.

Mom leads me to a room off the back hallway. A theatre of sorts. The only light illuminates from the dim sconces on the wall, casting everything in shadows.

"Make sure no one comes in here," she murmurs to one of her guards, her face expressionless as she shuts the door behind her with a final click.

Now all the sound that's left is the faint whir of the air conditioner and the dull, muffled sound of the party beyond this room.

We're completely alone. Nothing good ever comes from being completely alone with my mother.

"Hannah," she says, lighting up a cigarette, even though we all know she can't smoke inside. "When I give you instructions, what are you to do?"

I swallow over the lump in my throat, my hands knitting together in front of me.

"Follow them." I'm ashamed of how small my voice sounds.

"Correct." She nods, taking a long drag until the end of her cigarette glows cherry red. "So why didn't you bring your sister, like I told you?"

"Sh—she didn't want to come," I stammer, anxiety bubbling inside me. "I—I tried."

In an instant, she snatches my jaw in her hand almost as forcefully as Missy had.

You know, for as much as they fight, they sure are a lot alike. Both fucking psychotic.

"You know damn good and well when I say bring her, I mean *force* her if that's what it fucking takes. It wasn't a suggestion."

"I'm sorry," I whisper, my voice clouded with the tears brimming in my eyes. "She threw me on the ground. S—scratched me. She wouldn't come."

"I don't give a shit what she did. You are to be presentable. Wherever I want. Whenever I want. That's what comes with this job, Hannah. Or do you not understand?"

I'm the governor of California, my brain mocks.

"I'm the goddamned governor of California," she spits and under different circumstances, I would laugh at the irony. "If I can't control two girls, how will people expect me to control a state?"

"I'm sorry," I repeat, flinching from the pain as she digs her nails down to my jawbone. "I'm sorry."

She stares at me for a moment, and I think, with all manner of sickness bubbling in my stomach, that she's going to hit me.

Instead, she releases me.

And then her hand slaps across my face so hard, I taste blood in my mouth. I stumble, managing to grip the back of a chair, my vision growing spotty for a moment, before the feeling passes, leaving behind the burning sting of a sliced lip.

There's a sickening moment of roaring silence.

Then a throat clears from the shadows.

Mom's eyes go wide, but when Mason Carpenter steps out from a spot by the window, her gaze narrows to small dark slits.

"The funny thing about abusers," Mason says, voice cold as winter and eyes dangerously dark in the dimly lit room. "Is no one ever thinks it's a woman."

Mom doesn't say anything for a moment, instead choosing to smooth down her already-perfect hair, instead.

Something passes between them. A warning. I can't tell from who, but the tension is so thick you could cut it with a butter knife. Mason steps up beside me, towering over both my mother and me in a suit that looks like it was hand-crafted for his body. His scent envelopes me, bringing about an odd sense of safety.

My mother ignores him completely, turning back to me with a simmering rage behind her blue eyes. "Go home. Don't let me see your face before I leave tomorrow."

She turns for the door, only stopping before she opens it, sinister gaze flicking back to Mason.

"Oh, and don't forget to take out the trash."

And with that, she's gone, leaving me still clutching my cheek as the blood oozes from my lip.

Her ring. It cut me.

I hate it here.

I need to go home. I need to hide in my room with the door locked, away from Missy. Away from Mom. Away from Michael and his expectations. I need a bandage and a bottle of wine.

I need to be alone.

Mason doesn't say anything, though he turns to me with that same cold indifference he'd shown my mother. He takes my chin in his hand, softer than I would have ever thought possible out of a man his size, and lifts it to face him. Something dark and caustic passes over his gaze, before he quickly snuffs it out and pulls a handkerchief from his pocket.

"You shouldn't have said that," I say softly while he dabs at the blood on my lip. "My mother . . . she'll make your life hell."

"Seems she's already doing that enough, for you."

I swallow, my throat constricting when he shoves the handkerchief back in his pocket and steps away from me.

I don't miss the way his hand clenches to a fist before he shoves it in his pocket.

"Come. I'll drive you home."

I almost open my mouth to argue, but what's the point? For some reason, I would rather be with Mason than anyone on my mother's team right now.

I follow him out the door and through the back hallway to the alleyway out the back door. He stays close to me as he walks me to the parking garage and toward his truck. The same truck he took me home in months ago.

The ride home is silent, save for the rock music playing quietly in the background. Mason seems to be lost in thought, but so am I.

When he pulls through the gate at home, I realize I haven't said a single word the entire way home.

"Thank you for the ride. Seems you're always saving me," I chuckle, though it lacks any humor.

Unfortunately, Mason doesn't seem to find it funny, either.

"Give me your phone," he murmurs darkly, holding out his hand. I open my mouth to protest and he cocks a brow.

Fine.

I place it in his hand, ashamed at the tremor that moves through mine when I do. He notices, but he doesn't say anything, typing something I can't see.

"My number. In case you find yourself without a ride again." The way he says it, I know he's not just talking about taking me home.

I open my mouth to speak, but I have nothing to say. And then, I realize what Bailey meant.

We really are all alike, aren't we?

Silent. Me, Bailey, Mila, Savannah, every other woman our age in this position. Even Monica Parker. We're silent in the face of the people that control our lives. In my case, my mother. We put on a pretty face, disguise our battle scars, and pretend our lives are as perfect as the media makes them out to be.

It's a disgrace.

"Goodnight, Hannah."

I swallow.

Guess that's my cue to leave.

I climb out of his truck, stumbling on my heels ungracefully before I right myself.

"Goodnight, Mason."

CHAPTER Six

HANNAH

What did you do?" Mom snaps, her teeth barred and her gaze full of disgust.

She looks down at the little cat at our feet, her eyes flashing wickedly between both of us.

Tears well in my eyes.

Missy glowers at her.

"Which one of you did this?" Mom snaps, her face turning tomato red as she hovers over us.

I don't want Mama to think I did that, but I don't want Missy to get in trouble either. Mama is harder on her than me.

Floof was a good cat. My cat *and now, he's gone. All because he scratched Missy's hand.*

He never liked her. She hated him.

"Hannah did it."

I gawk at her, fresh new tears slipping down my face at my sister's betrayal.

"Mama—"

"What did you do, Hannah Marie, and you better not lie to me."

"I didn't do anything, Mama," I whimper, but Missy steps in to handle that, too.

"She was petting it too hard. Broke it's neck," Missy shrugs. "I tried to save it, but . . . I think it's dead."

"Mama, I swear, I didn't do it."

"You've been acting out," Mama says, taking hold of my wrist. "I don't know how else to help you and God knows your father's not here to help. Bastard couldn't take raising two spoiled and evil little girls, such as yourself."

She tugs me toward the house and when I realize where we're going, I fight against her.

My lungs restrict, the air refusing to slip past my throat.

"Missy, tell her I didn't do it," I beg, looking back over my shoulder, but Missy just stands beside poor Floof, her gaze unfeeling.

Cold.

Thud.

"Mama, please?" I beg as she tugs me toward that dark place where my nightmares live. "Please."

Thud.

"It's time you spent a little while in the closet, Hannah." Her piercing brown gaze shoots back at me over her shoulder and she only tightens her grip. "Maybe it will fix you."

Thud.

I blink up at the stars on my ceiling.

Thud.

The knock startles me awake

Something is knocking against a wall.

I scrub a hand over my eyes, sitting up in bed and staring around my room.

Everything's in place. It's just Missy and I in the house and there's a guard outside the gate.

Still, the even thump against the wall continues, like a bass drum from somewhere near.

I suck in a deep breath, slipping from the bed and tugging the flannel tighter around me.

It doesn't even smell like him, anymore, but it's become a source of safety in the darkness and I'll be damned if I play Detective Hannah without it.

I slip into the darkness of the hallway, swallowing the sound of my heartbeat thumping in my ears and listening for the sound.

Missy's room.

I've tried to speak to her this week, but she refuses to come out of her room.

I've seen her once and that was only when I caught her sneaking back with something to eat, long after I was supposed to have gone to bed.

Mom's gone, so she's no help. I don't know where Marcus Parker is, but I haven't seen him since the Christmas gala. Even Michael has been scarce and he's staying with his parents in their LA mansion for the holidays.

"Missy?" I tap on her door, but the only answer is a resounding *thud*. Carefully, I push the door open and stand back as the darkness looms at me like a monster from within is daring me to take another step. "Missy? Are you okay?"

I'm ashamed of the tremor in my voice because it means that my earlier suspicions are correct.

I'm terrified of my sister.

Cautiously, I take a step into the room, searching for the sound of the banging, but she's not in her bed. I cover my nose, the sickly sweet scent of something herbal mixed with unwashed skin filling my nostrils.

"Miss—"

I freeze. Missy is on the floor near the corner of her room, a little bottle sitting beside her while she bangs her head against the wall, muttering something under her breath.

Oh, fuck.

I step over the throw pillows and clothes littering the floor and my hands shake when I reach for her, my skin glowing in the darkness.

"Missy?"

In a flash, her eyes shoot to mine, her sinister smile gleaming wickedly in the darkness.

"Come on, Hannah," she coaxes, lifting the little bottle beside her. "Just a little sip."

I fall back, my heart lurching in my chest at the madness in her eyes.

"Missy, what is that?"

"Just a little sip to make the demons go away," she whispers and my stomach fills with nausea. I stumble, tripping on a pillow and falling flat on my ass.

"Missy, stop!" Panic wells in my voice, fear gripping me by the throat when she climbs over me, little bottle in hand.

"Drink up, sister," she hisses, her fingernails digging into the flesh of my lips until I can feel blood seeping from my once healed-over cut.

The cut from the Christmas party.

I scream, fighting against her hold and she cackles, only tightening her grip.

"Don't you want to do this together?"

I kick, and her hand rears back, connecting with my cheek with blinding, stinging pain. I throw myself and finally, she topples off me, still laughing in that deranged shrill tone as I hurl myself from the room and nearly bash into the wall across from her bedroom door.

What the fuck?

I stay frozen in place, listening for the sounds of her footsteps on the hardwood floor, but they never come.

My skin burns and I have no idea what to do. Carefully, I tiptoe into my room and grab my phone, sneaking past Missy's room on my way out to the sounds of that even, steady thump against the wall.

I dart for the stairs, my hands shaking when I try to make a call.

Michael doesn't answer. Mom doesn't answer.

So, I call the only number I can think of that would at a time like this.

"Hannah?"

"I need you to come over. Something's wrong with Missy."

"I'm on my way."

CHAPTER *Seven*

MASON

Hannah's crying when she opens the door, but it's not the first thing I notice.

It's the busted lip.

"What happened?" I grit, stepping into the foyer of the oversized mansion and taking her chin in my hand to inspect the damage.

"It's Missy," she shivers. "She's lost her mind."

Of course. The evil twin.

"What did she do?"

"She's been banging her head against the wall and she lost it. She attacked me. She was talking about demons," she stammers, voice choked with the tears still streaming down her face. "I'm sorry, I just didn't know what to do. No one would answer me," she rushes.

I step closer to her and she winces when I raise my hand. My blood simmers beneath the surface of the meaning behind that. She expects pain, but when I wipe the tears from under her eyes, she sucks in a shaky breath.

"Take me to her."

Carefully, she nods. Right on cue, something shatters somewhere upstairs, causing her to jump into me.

"She's in her room," Hannah says softly.

I step up the stairs, a sniffling Hannah on my tail, and take a left at her instruction. It's not hard to find the room. I can smell it from here. A sickeningly sweet odor, like burning herbs and unwashed skin.

Makes my fucking skin crawl.

"Please be careful. She's dangerous," Hannah whispers, her little hand holding onto mine when I step into the door.

Funny, but not funny in a laughing way. Funny in a dangerous one because I like the way her fingers feel in mine.

That's new.

"So am I."

Her eyes widen, but she doesn't say anything when I step toward the room, releasing her.

"Missy," I call, cautiously stepping into the doorway. It's dark, save for the moonlight streaming through the window.

"Get out!" Melissa screeches and seconds later, a lamp flies at my head. I step out of the way just in time, spinning to find her huddled in the corner like some kind of forgotten feral beast. She doesn't have a stitch of clothing on and her hair is a wild, matted mess against the moonlight in the window behind her.

Fucking hell.

"Missy, stop acting like an idiot and talk to us."

I'm sure it's not the recommended form of communication for dealing with a murderous psychopath, but it's all I've got.

"I *said,* get out," she hisses, throwing a pillow my direction next. I want to pick it up and throw it back, but I know that's probably not conducive to talking her down from whatever proverbial ledge she's on.

"I can't do that, Missy."

"Mason," Hannah whimpers behind me when Melissa growls like a deranged puppy dog. She tugs on my hand, but I stay put. I'm not leaving her here if her sister's gone off the fucking deep end.

"Hannah . . ." Melissa snickers, getting onto her hands and knees. "Take a sip, Hannah. It'll feel so good."

Hannah steps back into the wall behind me, eyes going wide at the little bottle in Melissa's hand.

"Stay here." I drop Hannah's hand and step into the room, ignoring Melissa's angry fists when she tries to bat me away from her and pluck the bottle out of her hand.

"You bastard!" she screeches, launching herself off the floor. I manage to turn away before she produces a goddamn steak knife, making a poor attempt to lunge at me and throw her onto the bed.

"Hannah, get something to tie her down," I grit, peeling the knife out of Melissa's hand and pinning her down.

"Get off me!" Melissa thrashes underneath me, rearing her head and smashing it back against the mattress.

"*Hannah*." Hannah's eyes wide with fear and locked on Melissa finally snap to mine and she darts into motion, rushing to the dresser and rifling through drawers.

"I'll fucking kill you."

"I'd love to see you try," I murmur, voice strained from holding her down.

Listen, I'm a big guy. I'm six-foot-five, two hundred and fifty pounds and I can deadlift a transmission without any problems.

Tell me why I'm struggling to hold down a little five-foot-five woman who can't weigh any more than a wet dishrag?

"Tie her hands to the bed."

"Isn't that mean?" Hannah breathes, stalling.

"She tried to stab me. I hardly think it's mean."

Hannah nods, sidestepping around Melissa and wrapping a scarf around the hand that I'm holding, then the bedpost. Her hands shake while she ties the other off in a knot, her bottom lip trembling as Melissa spews all manner of disgusting threats at me.

"*Pig. Your mother's a slut. She's going to get what's coming to her. Your sisters, too.*"

"It's done."

I step off the bed, my muscles tight from holding Melissa down and pull Hannah back when Melissa tries to lunge a kick in her direction.

Definitely not the best experience I've had with a girl naked underneath me.

"Come." I pull Hannah from where she's rooted in place and lead her to the bathroom off Melissa's room.

"What is that?" Hannah asks, eyeing the little bottle in my hand.

I hold it up, inspecting it in the light. It looks like a shooter—if standard liquor was the bright green color of acid. I pop the cork, smelling the contents and my stomach churns.

"It looks like poison," Hannah says softly when I screw the lid back on.

"Absinthe," I murmur. I didn't know anyone still drank the shit.

"I thought that was fake." Hannah's brows knit together.

"No. Though what they sell in stores is diluted. This . . . appears to be mixed with something."

"*Heaven* . . ." Melissa chimes from her bed like she's on another fucking astral plane. Hannah's spine stiffens and she turns back to look at her sister.

I step back out of the bathroom, holding up the bottle for Melissa to see.

"I need you to tell me what's in this."

Melissa just cackles.

"What is it?"

"Black Dahlia."

My spine stiffens, the sound of my stepfather's voice like nails on a dusty chalkboard.

Melissa, on the other hand, gasps softly, the evil puppy act dropping almost completely.

"You came for me."

I grimace, putting myself between Parker and Hannah when he

steps in the room, eyes trained on Melissa tied in the bed.

"What did you do to her?"

"What did *you* do to her?" I retort, holding up the bottle. "This has your name written all over it."

He doesn't deny it. Sick fuck.

"The black dahlia is harmless . . . if taken correctly."

"And if taken *in*correctly?" Hannah chimes from behind me. She steps beside me and I have to restrain myself from pulling her back. "Is she in danger?" she asks, voice softer.

Parker regards her for a moment like you might regard a fine art piece.

I fucking hate it.

Probably because I know that if he touched her, killing him would be the only painless thing I do to him.

"No," he says turning back to Melissa who's desperately trying to reach for him despite her hands shackled to the bed by a pair of ugly scarves. "Though she will need rest. A lot of it." He sinks down on the side of the bed, wiping a stray tear from under her eye.

Too bad he's never shown this much kindness to my mother.

"Jesus fucking Christ, Parker."

"We all have our vices, Mason," he murmurs darkly, his eyes flashing to Hannah.

Fucking prick.

"Why do they call it the black dahlia?" Hannah asks quietly, completely oblivious to what Parker just said.

"Because someone drank a whole bottle and tried—and nearly succeeded—in skinning themselves alive."

Hannah falls back a step, her face going white.

"What the fuck is in it?"

Parker shrugs. He couldn't care less.

"A bit of ecstasy. A bit of extra wormwood. Whatever else she decided to add to it. It's highly effective in helping with depression."

"Looks like it," Hannah sneers.

"I'm taking her home."

"You aren't taking her anywhere," Hannah declares, head held high and lips pursed.

"Let him," I murmur quietly. It's better she goes with Parker than stays here with Hannah where she can slit her throat in the middle of the night.

Hannah opens her mouth to argue, but I wrap an arm around her waist and pull her toward the door. It's intimate. It's too close, but I'll be damned if I let go of her until I get her out of harm's way and I know, once Parker unties those scarves, there's no telling what Melissa might do.

"Come on," I tell her, gripping her chin and turning her eyes back to mine when she stops to look back at Parker and Melissa. Her green eyes are filled with worry. Worry I can't stop, but I can understand.

That helpless feeling when your family is in danger and you're fucking powerless to stop it.

I lead her down to the foyer and not even five minutes later, Parker is escorting Melissa downstairs, wrapped in a blanket. His dark gaze pierces into mine as if warning me, but I'm past giving a shit.

He's been trying to get rid of me for years. It's unfortunate for him that he hasn't succeeded.

"I'll be in touch," he murmurs and then the door shuts behind him.

"Thank you . . . for coming. I don't know what I would have done if you hadn't."

Hannah hands me a beer before nestling into the opposite end of the couch and tucking her knees up to her chest.

Those fucking legs. They've been burned into my brain since I got here. Taunting me.

It was a mistake to come here. An even bigger one to stick around after Parker left. Now, with the empty house, I should be leaving, but . . . like a moth to a flame, I can't seem to stay away.

Even if she pisses me off, there's some masochistic, fucked-up part of me that still wants to be here. Like a moment with Hannah is a friendly handout from God.

Right before he kicks me in the dick again, of course.

"Stop thanking me, Hannah."

She opens her mouth to apologize, but stops, popping the top on her own beer instead. "I don't know who these belong to, but they can spare a couple right?"

"Why do you live here?"

She stares at me a beat, swallowing some of the cheap beer and wincing when it hits the back of her tongue.

I almost chuckle. Seems California's princess doesn't like the taste.

"Where else is there to live?" she challenges.

"I'd have to think anywhere would be better than here."

She shrugs. "I wouldn't know. I've thought about moving out a few times, I just . . . my mother's not the easiest person to get along with, but she'd be on her own. With Missy staying here most of the time."

"She's not your responsibility."

"Maybe not," she offers. "But she's still my mother."

"A mother who beats you."

Hannah fixes me with a look.

"She doesn't beat me. She's just . . . I don't know."

"What about your father?"

"Gone," she says. "He left with his mistress back in Virginia when we were kids. Haven't seen him since."

It's dangerous to ask questions like this. Questions I'm not even sure I want the answer to. Still . . . the nagging little voice in the back of my head forces me, because it's fucking Hannah and I've never been good at following the rules. Not where she's concerned.

"Funny," she chuckles humorlessly. "Our families keep intertwining even if they hate each other. We're like the LA version of the Montagues and the Capulets."

"Your sister is the mistress of my stepfather. It seems our families are intertwined already."

Hannah shifts on the couch, taking another drink and otherwise, looks uncomfortable.

"Missy hasn't always been like this, you know? She used to be . . . more normal, I guess."

"Does your mother know?"

"Well . . . we're not really supposed to speak about it. She's always been a little different. A little more headstrong. She and Mom can fight for hours." She shakes her head. "Is your family like that or is mine just crazy?"

"All families are crazy."

"Yeah," she muses, voice low and soft. Finally, she tears her eyes to mine and I can't fucking look away. "Is that what it's like? Being in love?"

She looks like a little deer in this light. Timid and fragile. The freckles on her nose make her look younger than she is. Too soft and sweet for someone like me. Unfortunately for her, my cock doesn't seem to care.

"I couldn't tell you."

She shrugs.

"If it is, I don't want to experience it."

"Hannah . . . This isn't—"

"No. We aren't the modern-day Romeo and Juliet," she says, eyes trained on the expensive rug on the floor. Thing's as cold and uniform as the rest of the house. And then, just to drive the knife a little further, "I don't want to be."

I grit my teeth so hard I fear they may crack. I *want* to tell her I know she's lying. We both know it, but I also know she's right. I don't want something serious, and we're both already in well over our heads by now.

Even if I could look past the shit with Parker and Melissa. Her mother. Her unwillingness to get out from under her mother's thumb, there's still that nagging voice in the back of my head telling me she's too fucking good for me.

She's too sweet. Too innocent. Too fucking perfect. I'd break her. Ruin her until I'm the only one she'd see because that's what guys like me do to girls like her.

We claim them. Keep them addicted to us so they can't see what kind of monsters we really are.

I have to face the fact that I'll lose her because she's got responsibilities I'm not willing to accept as my own.

And that someday, someone else will.

I want to kill him, whoever he is. Beat him to the punch, before he can rip her away from me again.

When I don't say anything, Hannah takes another drink of her beer, wincing when it hits the back of her tongue.

"This tastes awful. I don't know why people drink it."

"I knew you wouldn't like it."

She eyes me pointedly. "And you do?"

I shrug. "It's a means to an end. That's why anyone drinks it."

"Well, you can have it," she murmurs, leaning forward and placing it on the coffee table in front of me.

"I need to leave. Got to get up early. Been here long enough as it is."

She rolls her eyes. "You act like the FBI is going to leap out from behind the bookcase. It's just us."

"Yeah, and your mother doesn't like me."

She snickers, a breathy sound that goes straight to my dick.

"She doesn't like anyone. Especially not attractive men who stick up for her daughters."

"I see. She doesn't like men who her daughters have a little crush on." I chuckle darkly as she leans back against the mass of throw pillows, her foot resting on the cushion between us.

Let me fucking tell you, I've never given a single shit about someone's foot until I saw the red polish on hers.

Her eyes lock with mine, half-lidded and hazy. "Maybe I just wanted to piss her off."

"That it?" Don't ask me why. Maybe she spiked my beer or some shit, but I reach out, my fingers brushing over her calf. Goosebumps rise in their wake and Hannah's eyes widen at my touch. "That why you're still wearing my flannel?"

Her tongue darts out to lick her bottom lip and my cock pulses at the motion.

Fuck me.

What the hell am I doing?

"It's warm. This house gets cold," she lies quietly when my hand travels higher on her skin, almost reaching her knee before I drop it back down to her foot. In a flash, I yank her upright and forward until her ass is resting on the middle cushion and her foot's in my lap.

Fuck, this has already gone too far.

Her breath hitches when we come face to face, my hand on her knee hooked over mine and her fingers dancing across the skin on the back of my arm.

She feels so good. Soft and warm. My cock throbs with the need to bury myself inside her, forget all the shit that's happened and make her mine. Even if only for a night.

"Prove it."

"Prove what?" she asks, voice barely above a whisper.

She must realize what I'm saying because she pauses for a moment, eyes sliding down to my lips. I can feel her heartbeat hammering in the pulse point behind her knee. Funnily enough, it matches my own.

She swallows hard, slipping closer and I can taste the mint mixed with the beer and something so her, my blood simmers in my veins.

"If you didn't care, prove it, little doe."

Her gaze narrows at the challenge. Like she's as determined as I am to prove to herself that there's nothing there, but a deep understanding that we're just two people in a long line of bullshit.

Gently, she places her hand on the back of the couch, rising up and closer to me. I watch her, cock hardening to the point of pain in my jeans.

This is probably the stupidest thing I've ever done.

Still, I don't stop her.

Carefully, she closes the gap between us and neither of us breathes. She brushes her lips over mine, and I realize, I'm fucking done for.

Hannah tastes exactly as I thought she would. Like honey and sweetness and everything I've been fucking dreaming about for a year.

She pulls back just enough to catch her breath in the air between us, eyes closed.

So, I follow her.

That was . . . not what I expected.

And now she's got me by the balls.

I bridge the gap between us, my hand slipping into her hair and tugging her lips back to mine, and she whimpers into my mouth.

Fuck. Me.

I slip my tongue in her mouth when her hands come to rest on my shoulders, flexing over the material of my T-shirt. I circle her back with my arm when those hands slide up to fist the short roots of my hair.

I pull her closer to me until she's straddling me and a breathy moan leaves her lips.

Kissing Hannah is a bad idea. This thing between us will only end one way. I need to stop and I'll be damned if I don't try to talk myself into it, but when her pajama-clad pussy brushes the denim over my cock, that same voice of reason shuts right the fuck up.

I break away from her kiss, nipping a line down to the side of her neck and sucking the flesh below her ear into my mouth. She whimpers, fingers tightening in my shirt as she arches her neck to give me more room.

"*Fuck,* little doe," I grind out between my teeth, hand on her ass while I grind her overtop my cock. She gasps at the friction, lips parted and her eyes screwed shut. "Look at me."

She opens her eyes, her bright green gaze locking with mine, and it's at that moment, I know I've just signed my fucking death warrant.

And then, a throat clears.

In a flash, Hannah pushes me away, scrambling off my lap and falling to her ass on the couch beside me.

"I came because you said it was an emergency," Michael says, eyes twitching back and forth between Hannah and me. "But it seems you've got all the help you need."

Hannah wipes the corner of her lip, face flaming.

"Michael," Hannah grits between her teeth. "Don't."

"I'm afraid she already knows, Hannah," Michael chimes as if he's a disappointed dad.

"She doesn't need your permission," I mutter, stepping in front of Hannah. She may trust this cuck.

I don't.

"It's fine, Michael," Hannah warns, putting a hand on my stomach. "Come on," she says softly. "I'll walk you out."

I step out onto the landing, shooting Michael a wink before I go and Hannah follows, oblivious. She shuts the front door behind her quietly, pausing to wrap her arms around herself a few feet back.

"You going to be okay here by yourself?"

There's a twinkle in her eyes. A flash so quick I almost don't notice it.

Fear. Worry?

"I'll be okay. Michael will probably be here . . . and the guards."

There's a tension in the air that wasn't there before and now, I can't get the taste of her lips off my tongue.

"He your boyfriend?"

She narrows her gaze. "No."

"You sure he knows that?"

"Michael's been my best friend since we were kids. We grew up together. He's just acting like a protective older brother."

Yeah, sure he is.

She chuckles sheepishly. "Guess I better let you go. I know you said you get up early."

I nod, though it was a lie to get her away from me. Back when I could fucking think rationally.

"Yeah."

I shove my hands in my pockets because if I don't, I run the risk of reaching for her.

She looks up at me with those big green eyes and those freckles on her nose under the pale glow of the porch light and all I can think about is how badly I want to taste her again.

"I'll be back tomorrow to check on you."

She smiles softly. I'm digging my own grave.

. . . I can taste her on my tongue. Feel her in my veins like heroin.

It's become a problem I'm not sure I'm man enough to handle.

"Goodnight, little doe."

I turn and leave before she can pull me back in.

Tomorrow. I'll come back tomorrow.

I drive home in silence, the trek from Bel Air to North Inglewood seeming to pass by in a blur because I can't get her out of my head. Not to mention, the shit Melissa is on, Parker, what her mother's going to do when she finds out I had her precious daughter in the palm of my hand.

I scrub a hand through my hair and I'm annoyed to find my hand shaking. Fucking hell.

Tomorrow, I'll put an end to this . . . if I can. I'll check on her and then back off because while it feels like Hannah fucking Gaines was made for me, I know she wasn't.

I resign myself to the fact that shit just fucking sucks when I get home, parking in the drive in front of my house. What used to be Dad's house.

The place is small, especially compared to the Gaines' estate, but it's home. It's where I grew up until Dad passed and it's where I've lived since Gran signed it over to me before *she* passed. It's got everything I need. Three bedrooms. A nice backyard. It's right across the alleyway from the shop, so the commute can't be beat and it even has a garage out back where Dad's old Challenger is stored.

Seeing the cold, harsh interior of Laura Gaines' LA mansion, tonight only solidified for me that I'm not cut out for life behind that kind of wealth. For *that* life.

And her daughter's not cut out for mine.

The streets are quiet tonight. Damn near silent as I unlock the front door to the house.

I pause at the front door. The crickets are quiet.

Someone's watching me.

Carefully, I unlock the door, and step inside, watching my back as I go, but no one's there.

But it's when I turn around and notice the light over the stove is off that I fucking know, someone's here.

A throat clears behind me and I reach for the gun at my back before the deafening sound of a pistol clicks only inches from the back of my head.

And then I notice all the fucking people coming out of the dark shadows of my house.

Well, fuck.

"On the ground." Someone shoves me down, and I go, falling to my knees with a grunt.

"Got to hand it to you, it's not easy to surprise me."

A chuckle sounds from behind me, and the cold steel of a barrel presses to the back of my head.

"Want to tell me what you want?"

The gun is pressed harder to my head as a warning.

"Move an inch, and this bullet goes through your skull."

"Funnily enough, you're the second person who's threatened to kill me tonight. And she was actually dangerous."

A fist connects with my mouth, and I snarl through the blood staining my gums.

"What's the matter?" A man chuckles from the shadows. His heavy boots scuff along my floor, black eyes glinting in the night. He flashes a smile, teeth shining menacingly in the moonlight streaming through the window. He pauses in the center of the room as more men step from the darkness. "You don't look happy to see me?"

"Not ready for guests. Didn't even get the punch bowl out."

The man just snickers, ignoring my taunt as the room chuckles around me.

"*Él es chistoso.*"

More demented laughter sounds through the room.

"I think you and I are going to get along just fine, Mason Carpenter. Don't you?"

"I'm pretty hard to get along with."

The devil in front of me chuckles.

"So it seems." He kneels down in front of me, his voice dropping to a quiet growl. "Pity, you pissed off the wrong person."

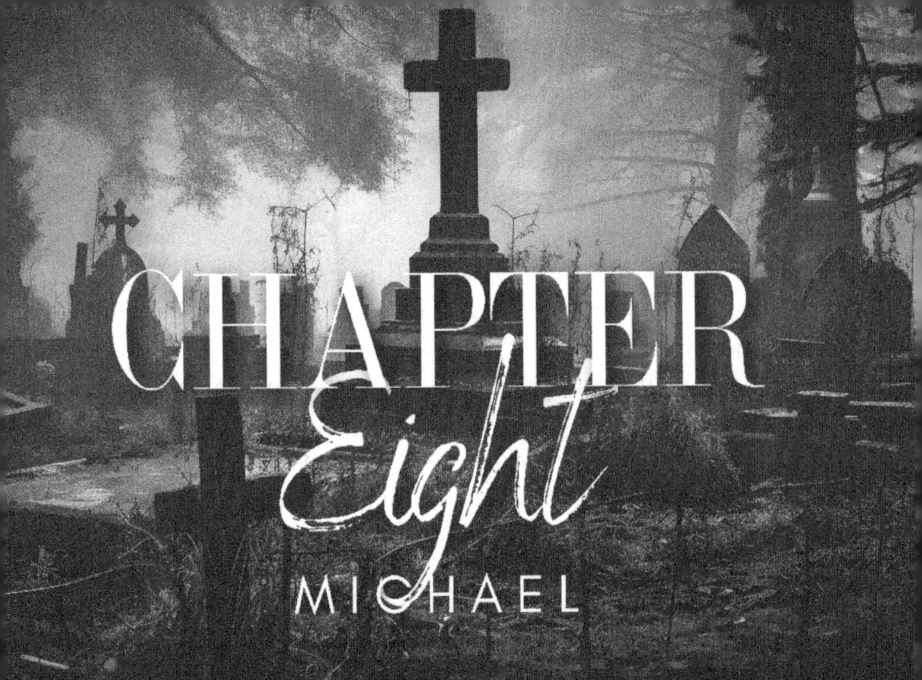

CHAPTER Eight

MICHAEL

"Mom, stop!"

"This is for your own good, Hannah!" Laura drags Hannah by the hair at the crown of her head toward the doorway at the very back of the basement in the Sacramento estate the governor calls home.

Not the home in which she receives the state, of course. This one is more . . . secluded.

"I have *tried* to beat it into your head that you are better than them," Laura growls, shoving her through the small, narrow door that ensures no light will reach the room and Hannah falls to the ground, cowering away from her.

I'll admit, it's not my finest moment, turning her in for what she's done, but . . . my mother always said, *You have to do the hard things for the people you love.* And well, I do love her.

I love her enough to put her in a dark closet and throw away the key. Mason Carpenter is bad for her. She just doesn't see it. Fortunately, I do. So does Laura.

"Mom, please!" Hannah cries, tears streaming down her beet-red face, but Laura can't be swayed.

There aren't many things that scare me in this world. Laura Gaines on a rampage would be one of them.

"I give you a home, designer clothes, fancy gowns and bags, and you open your *filthy* legs for that mongrel—"

"He didn't do anything!" Hannah screeches, though it lacks any real bite from the tears still streaming down her face.

"You and your sister have made a mockery of me for the last time."

Hannah's eyes go wide and she lunges for the door just as Laura slams it shut, muffling her cries in fear. Unfortunately, she can't muffle the banging that ensues seconds later.

"Don't worry," I murmur, placing a hand on Laura's shoulder and stepping from the shadows. Hannah doesn't know I'm here, but I *had* to see that she was taken care of. She *needs to learn.* I can feel the tremors of rage still moving through her. "You're doing the right thing."

Laura's fingers slide up and intertwine with mine. It's not something that we partake in often, but the affection is welcome, given how I found Hannah last night.

Laura lets out a breath, turning back to me and wiping a stray tear off her cheek. I pull a pack of cigarettes out of the front pocket of my suit and hand her one.

"Missy is dead to me," she says quietly, taking my lighter and billowing out a cloud of smoke. "This is Hannah's last chance. I won't have her screwing up everything I've built."

"Thank you," I murmur and she shoots me a warning look.

"Don't thank me, yet, Michael. The Carpenters are a cancer. Impossible to get rid of."

"Let me . . . get rid of him," I volunteer.

"I've dealt with Mason Carpenter. For now. And as far as Parker's concerned, I only have one daughter now." She blows out a cloud, thinking. "That guy of yours. The one who says he can get close with the Carpenters?"

"Johnson."

She nods. "Johnson. Put him to work. I want that family eliminated. Before they can cause any more damage."

"I'll see to it that it gets done."

"Good." She looks back at the door, which is moving with the force of Hannah's fists beating against the other side. "She never did like the dark."

"Could this be . . . damaging? I only ask because if we are to marry . . ."

"She'll be fine. A couple hours in the hole is good for them. You'll see." She shrugs. "Of course, the next step is a gentle lobotomy."

"Help!" Hannah screams and I grimace from the terror in her voice. Laura just chuckles, wrapping her arm around my shoulders.

"Come on," she says, leading me down the hallway and away from the sounds of terror coming from the closet. "You'll get used to it."

Now

CHAPTER Nine

MASON

JUNE, EIGHTEEN MONTHS LATER

"This is the last of it."

Ian nods, the welding helmet covering his face while he torches the VIN numbers off plates we took off what was once a nearly pristine G-Wagon.

I yawn, checking the clock on the wall of the old shack behind the garage. It's late. Past midnight and we both have to be up early, but that doesn't matter.

Not on nights like tonight.

No, tonight, we're stuck in what was once the parts building, cutting up cars. Removing pieces and parts and loading them into the back of a waiting van in the back lot.

Each time, more and more show up and I'm starting to run out of room for this shit and the patience for it.

They always come. They never give a time. I guess their people are probably watching me. They have to be to know my schedule and know who's working. That's what worries me. Them snooping around here while *she's* here is only going to make shit worse.

I mean, they have to know my future brother-in-law is a fed, but I'm guessing they just don't give a fuck.

Or they're just fucking stupid.

I'm going with the latter.

The cars come in off the streets and they're stored at a warehouse in some undisclosed location before they're carted here under the cover of night. We cut them into pieces and load the parts into the van that arrives shortly after the cars do. They leave.

I never see what happens after that. Judging by the blood I've seen in a few of the cars, I don't want to, either.

Chop shops are illegal. What I'm *doing* is illegal, but it's not like they sent a door-to-door salesman around, trying to get people to sign up to do their bidding.

No. The cartel takes. Whatever they want. When they want. It doesn't matter if you say no. You'll do it, or bad shit will happen to the people you care about.

Especially when they've got the government in their pocket.

The last time I refused, I received a picture from an anonymous number of my sister at the bar her husband owns in New Orleans. You could tell it was candid. She didn't even know.

I stopped refusing after that.

"Thank fucking God," Ian grumbles, finishing the last of the VIN plates. He tosses it in the bucket beside him and pulls the welding helmet off his head.

Ian's my right-hand man here at the shop. My best friend, if you want to call him that. He's the motherfucker I call when shit goes down. Does that count? He's been around for years and I've known him since tech school.

We were both rowdy. We hated class and we hated our lives even more. We bonded over our shared *fuck the patriarchy* attitude and now, here we are, in Dad's shop, cutting up stolen cars for the cartel.

"I'm fucking beat," he grumbles, swiping his forearm across his sweaty forehead. It's hot as fuck in the back garage with no ventilation, but we can't risk getting caught.

We get caught doing what we're doing? It doesn't matter if we were forced into it, we're going straight to prison. Right next to my stepfather.

Part of me likes that idea. It would give me the chance to handle our unsolved business, but I also need to be here. Mom needs me. My sisters need me. The shop . . . *her.*

Right now, there are too many priorities standing in the way of me and revenge. Someday, though, I'll find him and one of us will leave in a body bag.

It won't be me.

"Let's get this shit loaded up. I want to go home."

"You got shit else to do?"

"Yeah," Ian quips. "Come to work for you, asshole."

My spine fills with lead and pretty cinnamon-colored hair and soft green eyes flash through my mind. "Got a new person starting tomorrow, by the way."

I haven't had the chance to tell him about Hannah because, well . . . I don't even know what the fuck to do about it.

"What's his name?"

I steel myself.

"Her name."

He pauses, a smirk pulling on his face. "You, uh . . . hit your head or something?"

"Or something."

If only that were the fucking case.

When I saw her standing in my shop, I thought I had.

Hannah fucking Gaines. A girl I never thought I'd see again and consequently, the girl that's been in the back of my mind for years. Festering. Haunting my fucking nightmares.

She looked good. Better than good. She's still got that same innocent look and the prettiest fucking green eyes I've ever seen. Like mint leaves or Washington pine trees dripping in moss. Those eyes that keep me up at night.

Coming to me to ask for help in looking for Melissa Gaines took balls, I'll give her that. It's only because I knew if one of my sisters went missing, no matter what they'd done, I'd want them found, too. Fuck, I'd do everything I could to track them down, even if it meant turning them in.

She acted like I was just some fucking asshole off the street. Like I didn't mean a damn thing to her. I guess I probably don't, after the way things ended.

Good.

"Never seen you go to this length to get pussy," Ian chuckles while we clean up. "You losing your touch?"

I grit my teeth. That's what got me into this fucking mess, but he doesn't know that. No one does. I fell for her sweet charm and soft voice and let myself get carried away in her cinnamon-colored hair and those fucking freckles on her nose.

Now . . . I'm paying the price.

"Just tell the driver to get the hell out of here."

Ian gives me a salute before heading toward the back door. As soon as he's gone, I work on torching the VIN numbers on the plates we pried off the car one last time, my mind stuck on the girl I thought I'd never speak to again.

Now here I am, agreeing to help her find the woman who aided in ripping apart my family. Her evil twin.

She must think I'm a fucking idiot. I know shit about Hannah that even she doesn't know. I know underneath that perfect exterior is a darkness not many people can stomach. She's just better at hiding it.

But, fuck. Something still draws me in. Maybe I'm a masochist.

God knows I feel like it.

Maybe she'll disappear again, and I won't have to worry about it. Maybe she won't even show up.

Somehow, though . . . I know she fucking will.

Like some sick fucking joke, Hannah's right on time the next morning, bright-eyed and cheery, as if she doesn't have a care in the world.

It pisses me off. I'm fucking spiraling trying to figure out how to make this shit work while she's just relieved I agreed to help her find her sister. Part of me wants to punish her for even thinking about going after Melissa fucking Gaines. The other fucked-up part of me wants to punish her for forgetting I existed.

Unfortunately, that's the part that doesn't shut the fuck up.

"Good morning," she beams, rocking back and forth on the balls of her feet as if it isn't too fucking early in the morning. Ian and I didn't leave the warehouse until after two and by the time I fell into bed, it felt like dawn came five minutes later. Especially when the little redhead in front of me was bouncing around my brain like a damned battering ram.

"Yeah," I grumble, unlocking the door to the office and striding inside. It closes on her and for a split second, I feel guilty. I have more manners than that. Then, I remember how she moaned my name and suddenly, shutting the door in her face doesn't seem all that rude anymore. Especially when she pulls it open and steps inside, smiling like it doesn't bother her at all.

And now I'm pissed off all over again.

Why the fuck did I agree to this?

It's not my problem that Melissa Gaines is missing. The world would be a better place if she turned up dead somewhere. Hannah Gaines *also* isn't my problem, but . . . then again, she wasn't two years ago, either.

I made her my problem the day I saw that perfect ass and her pretty smile. Now, I'm wishing I'd never met her in the first place.

"So . . ." she starts, looking around at the clutter in the lobby.

I know where everything is and it doesn't bother anyone. People are only inside to pay their bill before they get in their fixed cars and leave.

Besides, I don't have time.

That or the thought of changing shit with Dad not here feels like spitting in his face.

"What do you want me to do first?"

She follows behind me, way too fucking close, though I'm not even sure forcing her to work out on the street would be enough distance. I can smell her perfume. The same goddamned perfume that used to make me hard— *still* makes me hard.

I fucking hate it.

I step behind the counter and she steps up in front of it. I'm grateful for the barrier between us because I need to keep my distance.

"You haven't told me anything about the job," she explains when I don't answer.

After much debate when I should have been sleeping last night, I came up with a plan. It's a shitty one, one I know I'll feel guilty about later, but if it gets Hannah out of here, I'm willing to follow through with it.

"Your job is to sit here and answer the phone. That's all. All quotes get written up and come through me. You can write up the job, including make and model, and put the notes in that basket. You set up appointments when I tell you to. You can even talk to the dust. Just don't fuck with anything."

She looks around at the abhorrent stack of papers strewn about the desk.

"Can I clean?"

"I said, don't fuck with anything."

Her lips twitch at my words and I almost chuckle when she doesn't say a word.

"Okay."

"I'll pay you weekly. You get here at nine and you leave at five.

Same as the guys. There's no special treatment here."

I know I'm being harsh when she winces, but the sinister motherfucker in the back of my head chuckles. I'm getting under her skin.

Just like she's always gotten under mine.

"What about . . . the other?"

Oh, yes. The *other* part of this arrangement.

"I'll see what I can do, but I'm not making any promises." I don't miss the way her eyes light up, but . . . I can't let it deter me. She can't be here.

"What about the garage? I don't know anything about it, but I can try."

She's grasping for straws. Anything to get me on her side to help her sister. Having Hannah in the garage is the *last* thing I want.

Having her under my roof is bad enough. Having her out there, right under my nose. Watching the guys trip over their dicks all day to talk to her?

Hard no.

I'm not too proud to admit that even if I want her gone, there's still that urge to shield her from this life and the closer she gets to me . . . the more dangerous it is.

I want her as far away from *that* as possible. Not to mention myself.

"No. This is temporary. If you have a problem with it, you're more than welcome to quit now. Save us both the hassle of firing you later."

She cocks her head, those emerald eyes narrowing to slits. She thinks this is a challenge. A game.

If it is, I'll make sure I win this time.

"No problem at all."

The phone starts ringing as if it's mocking her and I hide my amusement, turning away to head out the side door and into the garage. The guys should be here any moment.

"Have a good day," I pause, nodding to the phone that's caked in years of dirt and grease. "And don't forget to answer that."

CHAPTER *Ten*

HANNAH

"Can you repeat that, please?" I swear this phone is affecting my ability to hear clearly. It has enough prehistoric dirt and grease embedded in the receiver that it's hard to tell if it's a phone or an ode to uncleanliness.

This is *not* what I signed up for. Part of me wanted to run for the hills this morning when Mason presented my "job". The other, more stubborn half couldn't let him win.

It's a game to him. I know it. He wants me to quit.

I'm not going to make it easy on him. I'll make him fire me before I ever give up.

I hope.

I mean, why can't I clean? There's so much dust in the office, I haven't stopped sneezing since I sat down. The counter is piled high with what looks like every piece of paper Los Angeles has to offer and the lobby looks like a tomb for old, torn car magazines.

My skin itches to clean, but I also don't want to get fired on my first day. Mason said not to touch anything, so apart from the phone and my one brave trek to the bathroom that ended in me chickening out — it was bad— I've sat right where he told me to, all day.

No one has come to check on me. Make sure I'm still alive and haven't been devoured by a dust bunny yet. Not even Mason. I haven't seen a soul all day and I think I'm starting to go stir crazy. Like the people on the phone aren't real people and just a simulation to drive me to quit.

I wouldn't put it past him.

I don't even know why he hates me. Every time he looks at me, it's like he's thinking about how I personally wronged him. Like my breathing air is sucking the life from his lungs.

Like I'm a cockroach that needs to be exterminated.

Well, screw him. I have been nothing but polite, given the circumstances. He's the one who cut all ties. He couldn't even give me the decency of a polite *fuck you* before he vanished.

Okay, Hannah . . . Let's not rehash *those* old scars.

Believe me, if he wasn't the single person who might be able to help me find Missy, I would have never bothered to come here, but . . . unfortunately, Mason Carpenter knows a little more than he lets on.

My first day ends five minutes after five when Mason stalks into the lobby without even looking at me and orders me to go home. Then, he promptly shuts his office door in my face.

He's got a bad habit of that.

If I didn't need his help so desperately, I wouldn't have come back the next day, but I do, so I make sure to arrive ten minutes early, just like the day before.

Plus, nothing beat the satisfaction of seeing the disgruntled look on Mason's face when he realized he hadn't, in fact, won this little game we're playing.

My second day's a bit slower. A whole lot lonelier. Only so many people call an auto shop. One elderly man called three times to ask if his car was done before lunch, but I think he was just lonely.

Honestly, I didn't mind.

Michael: When are you coming home?

I chuckle at my phone, rolling my eyes. Listen. I know it's bad to text at work, but there are only so many ceiling tiles in the lobby and I've counted them enough times to know there are exactly twenty-two.

Sliding my phone behind a stack of papers that make it impossible to do anything else, I shoot him a quick text back.

Hannah: Mom that bad?

Michael: She hasn't left me alone. I don't think I've had a moment off in the last week.

Hannah: I hate to be that guy, but I told you so.

Hannah: Mom makes a dictator seem tolerable.

Michael: Ha Ha. Very funny.

Michael: But really, when are you coming home?

My stomach drops. Is it wrong of me to enjoy the solitude LA has offered me? The break from my overbearing mother and her team constantly worried about what I say or wear?

I ate ice cream last night. Fucking ice cream for the first time in years because no one was around to stop me. Should I have? I don't know. It came from a less than desirable corner store on the way to my house, so God only knows what someone could have done with it, but dammit, I ate the whole container because no one was around to chastise me with their cruel words disguised as polite reminders for me to watch my weight.

I've been the same size since high school. I've eaten the fish and the bland chicken put on my plate for years, because God forbid Hannah eat something that has a little more flavor than soggy cardboard. I've worn the same, subtle makeup since Mom moved us to this Godforsaken state and I've never even *thought* about wearing anything too revealing.

I've been the poster child for political finishing school and have nothing to show for it but a face that many mistake as the woman involved in a sex trafficking ring and a mother in office who's jammed economics and polls down my throat for four years.

If I was smart, I'd just move. To Greenland, or somewhere the sun doesn't try to cook you alive for walking down the sidewalk. Somewhere no one would know my name or my face and all the atrocities its mirror is rumored to have partaken in.

Michael: I miss you.

Sighing as the guilt washes over me, I type out an apology. Erase it. Type out an *I know*. Erase that, too.

What do I say? I don't miss you as much as you miss me? That's a great thing to say to your childhood best friend.

Hannah: I'll be home soon.

Michael: Good. Save me from your mother.

Hannah: Again, I hate to be that guy, but I told you so.

Michael: Her schedule is stricter than a queen's.

I chuckle. Ever since Mom hired Michael early this year to be her assistant, she's been running him ragged.

Hannah: Hell hath no fury like a woman in an Armani pantsuit.

I'm still laughing at my text when the door to the garage opens and I nearly launch my phone into the abyss in fright.

Mason will totally fire me if he sees me texting.

Only, the face at the door is not the scowling one of my employer.

The man chuckles, a dimple giving way on his cheek. "Don't worry," he says quietly, shutting the door behind him like he's not supposed to be here. "I won't rat you out."

He's young. Probably around my age. He's cute, though he's about a head shorter than Mason and his prickly hair reminds me of Michael and how much I really do miss him. That's what we used to call a buzzcut when we were younger and Michael's mom kept shaving his head.

Glad we're out of that phase.

"Sorry," I blush, sliding my phone back under the top of the counter. I tidy the stack of papers in front of me, realize my mistake and quickly fuck them up again because I remember Mason likes his trash organized *his* way. "Just checking to make sure there were no emergencies back home."

He waves it off and holds out his hand, wincing when he sees his fingers are stained with dirt and grease from working in the shop.

I roll my eyes, taking it anyway and shaking his hand. I mean, has he *seen* the office I'm "working" in?

"Ian," he greets, dropping my hand and using the same one to lift his shirt to wipe the sweat off his forehead.

Gross . . . but expected.

"Hannah."

"Carpenter told me we'd be getting a new employee. Wanted to come say hi. Probably pretty lonely up here."

"Yeah, I thought I would be— nevermind."

"He giving you a hard time?"

"Doesn't he give everyone a hard time?"

The glint of amusement in Ian's eyes tells me that no, he doesn't. And Mason said there would be no special treatment.

"He probably just wants you to prove yourself."

"How do I prove myself answering calls? Go out and dance in front of the shop to get more customers?"

"Depends on what kind of dance," he chuckles. "Just do what he tells you. He'll make it worth your while. Maybe even let you out to work in the garage."

I resist the urge to roll my eyes again. Mason will let me in the garage when hell freezes over.

"I'll make sure to answer the phone really, really well, so maybe he'll let me out to play with the big kids."

Ian grins. "All I'm saying is just take the initiative."

I eye him, and that cheerfulness dissipates. "You're a mole, aren't you?"

He pauses for a moment, studying me. Time passes slowly for that split second, but before I can analyze it, that smile returns.

Weird.

"No, he didn't send me in here to try and get you fired. I'm just saying the place could use some cleaning. Customers can't even sit down up here."

Immediately, I shake my head. "He said not to touch anything."

Ian waves a hand. "He was just pissed off because it was morning and we were up late the night before."

Doing what, I wonder?

"Mason's a good guy. You've just got to win him over."

I'm not winning shit over. He's the one who acts like I'm Typhoid Mary, walking around and handing out death warrants.

Sadly, I think those days have passed. I did win him over, one time. It was the closest I've ever felt to the sun. Electric. Dangerous. Now, it's gone.

"Thanks for the advice," I grumble, memories of the past flashing through my mind like some kind of messed up zoetrope. Mom, Missy, Mason, and I. A little glass bottle. A closet.

A sinister smile.

"Anytime, rookie."

"Don't call me that."

Rookie sounds like an insult.

"Nah, that's your nickname, now. Everyone here has one."

"Okay, what's yours?"

"Pit. The other kid is Puke."

"I don't want to know, do I?"

"Probably not."

"What's Mason?"

"Boss. Bossman. Big Daddy if you really want to get under his skin."

Somehow, I feel like calling Mason *Daddy* is not a good idea for me.

"I better get back out there," Ian announces, heading toward the door when Mason comes into view through the bane of my existence— a window that shows the garage. I can feel him watching me all day, waiting for me to crack.

This time is no different. His eyes bore into mine through the glass and the thick layer of dust does nothing to stop the weight of that stare. Like a hurricane. He pauses for a moment, then his gaze sweeps over to Ian and his jaw ticks.

Then he looks away.

"Yeah, you better go," I roll my eyes. "Wouldn't want you to get whipped for speaking to the lowly office maid."

My mother has been giving me an allowance since I was seven years old.

When I was a child, it was a dollar for every household chore I completed. Two for vacuuming, because she hated it. I hated it, too, but I came to secretly enjoy sweeping up the debris and hearing the decrepit Hoover crackle as it cleaned our old carpets.

After . . . Dad . . . things changed. The allowance was no longer about household chores, but instead, about days that I was the perfect little soldier, fighting in her political warfare as she clawed her way to the top and eventually, governor.

Ten dollars turned into a hundred. A hundred turned into a thousand. Mom became governor and I became her perfect little doll that she could dress up and parade around as if to say, *look, I was a single mother for years and my child is near perfection.*

Any misstep resulted in a punishment, no matter how insignificant. And let me tell you. Mother's punishments are more like nightmares.

Missy never fell into line. Maybe she was a "bad kid" or maybe she was just better at living her own life than me. Either way, after we moved to California, Mom's punishments were no longer about teaching us discipline, but more about silence. The louder you are, the more it hurts.

That sort of thing.

Now that I'm making money of my own again, I won't have to use Mom's allowance she still transfers into my account every week.

Mason pays me, though our agreement said otherwise, but I'm not complaining. When he hands me the envelope, right along with Puke and Ian, he doesn't say a word and I don't bother to argue because I need his help. He's quite literally my last option if I want to help my sister.

By the middle of the second week working for Mason, I decide to take Ian up on his offer. I bring cleaning supplies from home and smuggle them inside. Don't ask me why. Maybe I knew I was doing something I wasn't supposed to.

Maybe this would show Mason I'm genuinely trying to help. Maybe he'll finally grant me an olive branch and give me *something* to go by. Maybe it'll just piss him off, but dammit, I'm bored and with all this time sitting around, the racing thoughts have never once stopped.

The same mantra repeats over and over like a broken record. Missy. Mom. Michael. Africa. Missy.

I can't take it anymore.

I'm going to clean and if Mason Carpenter doesn't like it, then I guess I'll deal with the consequences later.

Call it "taking initiative".

I start off by organizing the desk. I match car keys and invoices for pickup on one end and bills for drop-offs and services on the other. I move everything and scrub away the years of dirty, sticky fingerprints and even deep clean the chair.

Let me tell you . . . that chair has seen some shit.

I take apart the phone enough to scrub the gunk out of the earpiece so you can actually hear people call and then I work on the lobby area.

I mean, yesterday, an elderly woman *stood* and waited in the lobby for Mason to pull her car out. I felt so guilty I offered her my chair which she took one look at and declined. I honestly can't blame her.

People can't sit because the chairs are either filled with magazines or car parts. So, I scrub those, too, stacking the parts on a shelf in the corner and organizing the magazines in the rack in the corner with care. I don't know why, I just feel like they mean something to Mason. Why else would he still have them?

The last area is one I have yet to venture into.

The bathroom.

I've been holding it all week and by the time I get home, I'm surprised I haven't peed myself. I'm going to catch a kidney infection and hot or not, Mason is *not* worth that.

Stepping inside looks like a warzone. Smells like one, too. I'm not sure if the men have ever even hit the bowl or if the floor is just their preferred battleground. I scrub everything, including the walls and then I have my first pee at the office before I decide it's time to get out when my head gets dizzy from the chemical warfare I've taken against myself.

The final step of the day?

Mopping.

That's what I'm doing when Mason decides to step into the office.

Looking like he's ready to either wring my neck or drag me down to the pits of hell.

Uh-oh.

"Goddamnit, Hannah," he grits, searching through the papers on the desk and no doubt, throwing them everywhere and fucking shit up. "Where is the paperwork for Mr. Stevens?"

I drop the mop where I'm standing and hurry to grab a paper that's literally *right* in front of him.

"Jesus fucking Christ," he growls, those hurricane eyes boring into mine. The tone of his voice sends a shot of panic through me, freezing cold like adrenaline, but deadly warm from the shame creeping in. That little girl that used to run and hide peeks her head around the corner. "What did you do?"

"I—I cleaned," I stammer, cheeks so hot you could fry an egg.

"And I told you not to touch anything," he snaps, face equally as flushed. Only he's not embarrassed. He's enraged. "Why can't you just do what you're fucking told?"

He stares at me a beat and my mouth falls open, but nothing comes out. He's right. He told me not to touch anything. This is my punishment for doing just that.

I should have never listened to Ian. Initiative doesn't get you anywhere. Not with Mason.

Shaking his head, Mason storms back out to the garage, leaving me staring after him, my feet rooted in place.

Mason's always been harsh, but he's never yelled at me. Not even . . . before.

No.

The angry, bitter adult version of the little girl inside me bites back. I did something that needed to be done. Nothing was ruined. Everything is almost in the same spot. Just cleaned.

I shake my head. I need to get out of here.

I step out on the back dock, away from Mason and his anger. Away from where he can see me. Away from the chemicals and the magazines and that damned phone.

Fuck that phone.

Everything from the last week comes bubbling to the surface and my eyes burn.

Please, no.

But it's no use. Tears well, blurring my vision and everything I've been trying to push down meets in my chest. I can't handle it anymore.

So, while I'm alone before I get fired, I take my moment. I let a couple tears fall and wrap my arms tightly around my knees.

God, it's pointless.

But hey, at least Mason won't be able to find anything in his precious pile of trash.

I guess it really is the little things in life.

CHAPTER Eleven

MASON

She never did like to fucking listen.

Why is it so hard? Don't touch shit. Don't move shit. Don't fuck with shit.

I know where every part, piece, and sheet of damned paper is in this garage. Or at least, I fucking used to.

One thing I hate more than anything is people touching my shit. Dad's shit. This garage has been the same since he died and it wasn't hurting anyone the way it was.

Now, I have no idea what she's moved. What she's thrown out. Whether customer invoices are still there.

And now . . . *they're* going to know something's different.

"Sorry, Mr. Stevens," I murmur, handing over the keys and the invoice to his BMW. He takes it, looking past me.

"Everything alright?"

"Yeah, just hired some new help."

He gives a disappointed smile, looking past me again. This time, I turn and follow his gaze to the small window in the back to where the little redhead of my fucking nightmares is sitting on the dock. The same one where Ian and I loaded parts into the other night, knees drawn up to her chest.

Jesus fucking Christ.

"Well, son, you know," Mr. Stevens starts, placing his hand on my shoulder. "My wife and I used to fight like cats and dogs, too. Then, I learned how to apologize. Once I figured that out, my marriage was perfect. Smooth sailing."

I have half a mind to tell him marriage is not in the cards and especially not with a woman like Hannah. She's beautiful, yes, but she's also a fucking tornado. One that cleans and moves my shit and gets under my skin like no other.

"She's not my wife," I murmur, tension like steel rigid in my spine.

"Oh," Mr. Stevens says, looking back at Hannah and shaking his head. "My condolences, then."

Fucking prick.

I wait here while he climbs in his car and drives off, debating on what I should do. I knew this shit wouldn't work out.

Then I turn to head back into the office and spot her, a sinking feeling fills my gut. It's hot. Past four, and she's been working hard. It's just the two of us and we're done for the day, despite the brake job I've been working on the last hour after I sent the guys home.

I know I should send her home, too.

I *should* tell her to not come back. God knows it would make my life easier. If I could convince myself Hannah Gaines is not my problem and send her back home to her mother. Let her sister rot for all the shit she's done.

Maybe then, I could accept that Hannah's not mine. She never has been.

But . . . even as I think it, I know it's not fucking true and *that* seems to be the root of all my problems.

She came to me because she was desperate. Because she knew she could count on me. I could see the defeat in her eyes when I told her no the first time. I could feel the worry and regardless of how I feel about Melissa Gaines, I know that if it were my sister, I'd want to find her, too.

Fuck, I wouldn't stop until I did.

"Jesus Christ." I run a hand over my face, scrubbing away the regret from watching her tear up. So she's upset. You know who else is upset? All those families her sister helped ruin.

I step back into the office, looking around. It's nice. Cleaner than I've ever seen it. People can sit down in the lobby now. I inspect the counter and find everything laid out and labeled. It looks a hell of a lot better than anything I could have done. Dad's magazines are neatly arranged in the rack. The old fake plant Mom brought when I was only twelve has been dusted and the bathroom has been cleaned for the first time in years. Maybe ever.

Something about how clean everything looks pisses me off. Who does she think she is? She can't just show up and fuck up the one thing that's kept me going. Maybe I've just gotten used to the dirt or maybe it's because I can't be mad at her, even if I try to be.

I've done everything in my power to get her to quit at this point, but she just rolls with the punches. Her being here is dangerous and if *they* find out about her, that'll be me signing my own death warrant.

I don't need these problems. She doesn't need these problems.

So, why then, do I feel like I got kicked in the dick when I walk out back and see her crying?

Fuck me.

God, if you're trying to punish me, just take me out. I'll deal with whatever the hell you've got down there over this, any day.

My boot scratches along the old concrete on the dock and Hannah jumps, hastily turning the other direction and wiping her eyes. As if I couldn't see her crying.

As if I didn't feel shitty enough.

"Sorry, just needed a minute," she mumbles. "The fumes were too much."

"They're pretty strong," I agree, swallowing over the lump in my chest. "Look, maybe I was a little harsh."

She chuckles dryly, shaking her head and staring out at the backyard. It's full of old tires. Parts. A broken car or two. Nothing that should interest her, but she'd rather look at it than me.

She doesn't meet my eyes. Not anymore. She had trouble with that before and I didn't get it back then. Now, I understand and it pisses me off, even if it shouldn't.

"A little?"

I deserved that.

"Okay," I concede. It occurs to me, then, that I am absolute shit at apologies. Maybe I should have asked Mr. Stevens for some tips. Three little sisters, yet, I can't look at a girl crying without feeling like the world's biggest piece of shit. "You're going to have to show me where everything is. I'm not used to it being organized."

She shakes her head.

"I should go, Mason," she says softly, gaze bright with unshed tears.

She moves to stand, but a strange bolt of panic pinches me in the chest and forces me to drop to my haunches next to her.

This is what I wanted, right? Her to quit?

But, when I think about her disappearing again, something dark inside me growls. Low and menacing.

What the fuck is wrong with me?

I don't know what she's got going on. I've got my own shit to deal with and I don't want her to be a part of it.

She doesn't belong in my world, any more than I ever belonged in hers.

I still don't want her to leave, though . . .

"What about Melissa?"

She finally turns those pretty eyes on me and in the glint of the evening sun . . . fuck.

"Mason, have you even tried to find anything out?" Not exactly.

I've been dealing with the fucking head trip that comes with having her around. "I didn't think so," she says quietly after a moment.

"I need your help."

"It's not working out. I shouldn't have bothered you."

The rational part of me knows her quitting is for the best. The other half—the half that has *never* been rational when it comes to Hannah Gaines—snarls at the thought of her walking out of the garage and out of my life.

Again.

"Bummer," I murmur and she looks away. Suddenly, my mission is to get her to look at me again. "I'm finishing a brake job and can't fit under the car."

"Bull," she mumbles, rolling her eyes.

"I'm serious." I stand, jabbing a thumb back at the garage. "I need someone small enough to fit under there."

"You have other workers."

"Not right now."

She regards me for a moment and I think she's going to say no. Hell, I wouldn't blame her. She knows I have a lift. I don't need someone smaller than me.

"Fine. But I'm not finishing the mopping until tomorrow. It'll probably need it again, anyway."

I hold out my hand to her and she stares at my fingers as if they might bite her.

Finally, her palm slips into mine and I haul her off the dock, forcing myself to take a step back from her when she's on her feet. I force myself to ignore the dull ache in my chest and I *force* my eyes not to follow the sway of her hips when we walk back into the shop.

Fuck, I force myself not to breathe because the scent of her perfume has been burned into my brain for the last week.

Yeah, Hannah Gaines is going to be a real fucking problem.

I'm a fucking idiot.

That much is evident when Hannah's on her hands and knees in front of me, head under the car, and that glorious ass in the air.

"I can't reach," she grumbles under her breath, rolling over so her back is on the creeper.

Thank fuck.

Asking her to stay and help was a mistake. It's hard enough to ignore her presence when she's under my roof. It's a completely different animal when she's right under my goddamned nose.

I don't need the help. She knows it. I could've just as easily put the car up on a lift or dealt with it tomorrow, but something in me didn't like that idea.

Not nearly as much as having her in my fucking space.

"So, what? You just run your mother's charity and that's it?"

Hannah's quiet under the car, taking the wrench when I hand it to her. I *could* raise the car up for her a bit. I mean the jack's right there, but watching her work like this is better. Keeps me from getting too close to her. Keeps *her* and that pretty smile under the car.

That is, if she still smiled at me.

"Hey, it's busier than you think . . . sometimes."

"I'm surprised she let you leave the house."

She shrugs. "She doesn't have much choice now. I'm twenty-three."

Fuck, where has the time gone? I'm going to be thirty this year and yet, I feel like I've barely got shit figured out. I can pay my bills. I can buy groceries. Taxes? Retirement? No fucking idea.

"Can I be honest?"

"Aren't you always?"

She ignores me, letting out a deep breath.

"I lied to her to come here. She thinks I'm in Africa, helping build a school. Does that . . . make me a bad person?"

"A bad person? No."

She rolls out enough to stare at me. "I didn't come back here for *you*, if that's what you're insinuating."

"I wasn't aware I was insinuating anything," I murmur, though there's a bitter edge to my voice I fucking despise.

She's silent for a moment, probably chewing on her words. I can see it by the way she bites her bottom lip; I've gotten under her skin.

Not that I've paid attention enough to notice those quirks.

"What about Michael?"

Even at this angle, I can see her spine stiffen.

"What about him?"

"Seemed like he was cozying up pretty well when I was around."

"I am *not* going there with you." I can see her cheeks flame and while I chuckle under my breath, something dark inside me stirs.

"So, I shouldn't expect a wedding invitation?"

She hands me the wrench back and I hand her the next size down. Not that I already knew what she'd need, or anything. Call it a lucky guess, fueled by me already finishing the other side before I asked for her help.

"Michael and I are friends," she declares to the undercarriage of the car. "Nothing more. If he wants that, then that's his business, but it doesn't mean I have to be accepting."

"Your mother sure liked him."

"Then she can marry him."

"So, it has been a topic of conversation."

"Why are you pushing me?" she snaps.

"I'm not pushing. You volunteered that information yourself. I merely made an observation."

Right now, it's like we're kids, again. She's only twenty-three. So fucking innocent and naïve, she'd blush at anything I'd say to her. Those pretty fucking eyes would still sparkle when she'd look at me—me, of all fucking people—and I actually had the gall to think that maybe I could keep her if I tried hard enough.

She scoffs, sliding out from under the car and standing off the creeper.

"You're still an asshole."

"And you're still a brat."

I grab the wheel, securing it back in place and she watches as I run the lug nuts in with an impact.

"You want to try?"

Hesitantly, she holds out her hands and I give her the impact, resigning myself to the fact that I like seeing her delicate hands covered in grease.

I motion for her to kneel on the ground beside me and take her hands in mine—big mistake—aligning the tool with the lug nut and pressing in.

"Press the button," I murmur, voice gruffer than usual. She notices because her tongue darts out to lick her lips and my cock presses against my jeans.

She does and we drive the lug nut in place together. Except when it's done, neither of us moves.

She's too fucking close. I can smell her. Feel the heat off her skin. I can see the little gold flecks in her eyes, despite how tired she looks.

I don't know this girl. Not who she is now. This Hannah is broken. Scared of something. She's running from a past I was thoroughly removed from.

Fuck . . . it would be so easy to lose myself in her for a couple hours. Remind her why we fit so well back then. Forget about the outside world and the bullshit with the cartel. Reclaim what would have been mine.

But—

"I'm . . . uh . . ." her cheeks flame and that moment passes.

She clears her throat, her gaze going to anything but me.

It pisses me off.

I want her gaze. I want her touch. I want her to leave so we can put this shit behind us. Forget each other again, if that's what it takes.

Even though I've never fucking forgotten her.

I turn back to the wheel, breaking the eye contact that fucking seared something into my chest, like a damned branding iron. "Go home, Hannah."

She doesn't say anything and time seems to stand still for a moment while she processes my request.

Then, finally, she quietly rises to her feet.

There's no use delving into the past. What's done is done and apologizing for it now, a couple years later, doesn't mean a damned thing. I was just an idiot kid pretending to be a man who thought he was falling for a girl when in reality, I didn't know shit.

Love's a made-up construct for two people to justify the worst parts of their relationship. All the reasons why they shouldn't be together look a whole hell of a lot better when you say, *oh, but we're in love.*

Fuck that.

Love . . . the biggest corporate scam there is.

"Goodnight, Mason."

I listen to the quiet sounds of her footsteps echoing on the concrete as she retreats and then moments later, the garage door closes and I'm alone in the aftermath of what happens when I let Hannah Gaines get close again.

"Goodnight, Hannah."

CHAPTER *Twelve*

MASON

Hannah Gaines is without a doubt, the most annoying woman I've ever met.

And I'm fucking obsessed with her.

She's cheerful when I'm not. Sunny when it's pouring down rain and her goddamned smile lights up the fucking room.

She's funny. Smart. Sexy as fuck, especially when she's concentrating on something or trying to hide the blush on her cheeks.

She's wormed her way into every facet of the garage. I give her free rein over the lobby. She keeps up with the invoices and the customer calls. People love her.

She's a fucking godsend, but I'll be damned if I tell her that.

I have resigned myself to the fact that I must be a masochist. Why else would I keep her around? I know the repercussions of having her here, but even those don't seem to matter anymore.

The problem?

I can't stand her.

I also can't convince myself to get rid of her.

I should have said no when I had the chance. Now, it's too late.

She's become an itch I can't scratch . . . a nuisance fucking with my head. Every time she laughs. Every time she smiles. When I catch a hint of that damned perfume.

She's burrowed her way back into my head.

I fucking hate it.

She hasn't spoken to me, save for the few occasions when she needs a quote for a customer or to set up an appointment.

As if she's avoiding me as much as I'm avoiding her.

Part of me is pleased she's not speaking to me. Makes it easier to ignore her long enough to get something done. To not think about the inevitable when this shit comes crashing down on top of me.

The other half is pissed that Puke won't stop staring at her ass and Ian has taken it upon himself to act as her personal bodyguard.

Fucker better watch himself.

There's a whole twisted, fucked-up past between Hannah and me and though only I know the truth about what happened between us, I can't deny there's still that urge to try and keep her for myself. Lock her away and stake my fucking claim.

Fortunately for him, I'm not an idiot. I can't have Hannah and her being here puts us all in danger, no matter how pretty the freckles on her nose are in the evening sun. I've built a life for myself here. One that doesn't have her in it.

But fuck, if the idea isn't entertaining.

But . . . I'm still not above knocking his teeth in.

She's probably noticed I've been avoiding her, but I don't care. I'm in no mood to talk about her sister. I did call a few of my . . . connections. None of them had any idea where Melissa Gaines disappeared to, so it's back to square one.

I keep telling myself I'll give her the bad news any day now, cut her free and tell her to never come back here, but . . . I just don't.

She finds out I can't find Melissa Gaines, she's gone and while life was so much simpler without her in it, there was that voice in the back of my mind.

I try to tell myself Hannah isn't my problem, but we all know it's a damned lie.

I made her my problem the moment I set eyes on her.

Now she's my fucking addiction and it'll take a fucking exorcism to forcibly remove her from me.

Accidentally—or so I tell myself—the monitor on my desk allows me to keep an eye on the shop while I'm in my office *supposed* to be doing other shit. It's become my greatest tool for keeping a bird's eye view on her and I know it's becoming a problem.

Just like she's become my obsession.

Right now, she's at her desk and I need to get out to the garage, but there are also bills that need to be paid. Keyword: Need to. I haven't fucking touched them.

It's easy when I can keep an eye on her from the cameras. She's got her hair piled up on top of her head while she organizes today's invoices. I can see she's quietly singing to herself, even though she can't carry a tune to save her life. From here, she looks innocent.

Fucking perfection.

And *that's* what I'm watching when the high-rolling fed walks in the door.

Fucking Logan Prince.

My sister's fiancé. Also the biggest pain in my ass.

Besides Hannah, of course.

He says something to Hannah, flashing that devil-may-care smirk and my first thought is to kick his ass for daring to go near her. My second thought, though, is that I know this man is damned near obsessed with my sister and for that, I know he'd never hurt her.

Hannah may be the beginning and end of my world, but she's just another girl to him.

Seconds later, my little sister's fiancé waltzes in without knocking, FBI swagger and attitude wrapped into one cocky smile. Sometimes, I think he and Savannah are perfect for each other. Other times, I'd like to wring his neck for touching her.

"Long time, no see," Logan murmurs, shutting the door behind him. Last year, Logan went undercover and brought my stepfather, Marcus Parker, in for crimes against humanity. Trafficking. Sex slavery. Nasty shit you only read in fucked-up books or hear about on the news. I had a part in all that.

Now, he's taken it upon himself to propose to my sister.

"What?"

He smirks, slinking into a chair in the corner. I should throw it out. Gives people the invitation to sit down and stay.

"You're a fucking idiot," he says cheerfully.

I grit my teeth and Logan's eyes flash with humor. Fucking prick.

He jabs a thumb back at the closed door.

"She know your little secret?"

"Why are you here?"

Don't get me wrong. Logan's not a bad guy, but he knows too much, something he likes to remind me of every fucking chance he gets. Unfortunately, Savannah loves him. I know he'd die for her, just like Charlie for Bailey . . . but if either of them hurt my sisters, I'd make sure no one ever heard from them again.

Logan's not the only one good with a bullet.

"I heard you've got family therapy next week."

"That why you came? To remind me for my mother?"

Logan just chuckles, shaking his head.

"Maybe you can all chat about why the sister of your stepfather's mistress is working for you there."

Jesus fucking Christ.

"Keep your mouth shut." I don't need my family breathing down my neck about this.

"You know they'll find out."

"It's none of their concern."

Logan narrows his eyes, inspecting me in that annoying way he does when he's trying to get inside my head. Some FBI shit I don't like.

"Does this have anything to do with the leading lady in Parker's fucked up line of bullshit?"

"And if it does?"

"Just making sure you know where your loyalties lie."

"That's rich," I scoff and Logan cocks a brow.

"She's dangerous, Carpenter."

"So are you."

His lip perks up at the corner, a devilish smile pulling on his face. "I am. So are you. Which is why I'm here. Parker's dying."

The room buzzes with silence.

This has got to be a fucking joke.

I open my mouth to ask, but he cuts me off.

"Brain cancer." He sucks in a deep breath. "They won't let him out, but with his year left to live, they aren't prosecuting him any more than they already have."

"So they're going to drop it . . . just like that?"

"Yeah. Just like that."

I shove out of the chair, nearly toppling it over on the ground. I need to walk. I need to punch something. I need to fuck my pretty little receptionist, but we all know, none of those things are going to happen.

"And everyone's just supposed to forget about everything he did?"

Logan doesn't answer, but I can see in the darkness of his eyes, he agrees.

"Your sister is upset. Which is the other reason I'm here."

It feels like someone stuck a steel rod down my spine.

"They're worried about you."

Cement fills my veins. I've been dodging Mom's calls for two weeks. She wants to forget about the past. Move on with the millions she got in her divorce agreement with Parker and live in her fancy ass house in Santa Monica.

She wants the same relationship we used to have. Before she

fucked Dad over and before he died. Before she abandoned me with my grandmother because her new husband didn't like me around.

"There's more, isn't there?"

The humor in his eyes fades and he gets that serious look. I fucking hate it. Usually, it means bad shit is happening.

"Melissa Gaines' finger appeared in your mother's mailbox last week."

That throws a wrench in shit.

"Fuck," I curse under my breath and Logan chuckles.

I scrub a hand over my face. This is getting too twisted.

"Who mails a fucking finger? That group Parker was in?"

That group being the Brethren— a conglomerate of sick fucks, mostly billionaires who prey on the young and less fortunate with their twisted games. Savannah was one of those victims and I'll hate myself until the day I die for not being able to save her.

For not being around to notice.

"We don't think it's them. They've laid low since Parker was caught. They know we're investigating them."

"Why would they send it to Mom? Isn't that a little fucked?"

My first thought is the cartel. Maybe they're trying to send me a message because they think I'm going to rebel, soon, but . . . it doesn't have their names written on it. They like to make it known who's in charge. They'd never do something like this anonymously.

Logan shrugs. "Pretty fucked to send a finger in the first place."

Touché.

"Who all knows about this?"

"Just me. Your mother. Your sister."

"Half the FBI."

"No, just my team. I'm going to make myself perfectly clear because you seem to have . . . other things on your mind. This stays between us." His eyes harden. "She can't know."

And now that Hannah's involved, it makes shit a whole lot more dangerous.

"I thought you were supposed to be getting out of this shit?"

Logan's eyes flicker with something dark for a moment, before that cold mask of indifference slips back into place. "I will. When she's safe."

Because Savannah knows about the Brethren. Because knowing makes her a target. I can't fault him for making it his dying wish to protect my sister. What more could I fucking ask for? He could hire a dozen men to protect her. At the end of the day, I know she's safest with him.

"Any update on your little . . . situation?"

"Unless you call watching my back an update."

"I told you. I've got men watching. They'll see to it nothing bad happens."

"Forgive me if I don't find that as comforting as you seem to think it is. I didn't ask for this."

"This is what happens when you go fucking around with the forbidden fruit."

I grit my teeth until they threaten to shatter in my gums. "These people aren't ones you fuck with."

He shrugs. "Neither was Parker. Look at the world, Carpenter. You really want to raise kids in this shit show?"

I don't bother telling him I don't plan on raising kids, at all.

"You can't stop them all."

"No, but I can try," he agrees, standing. His gaze hardens. "I asked your sister to marry me, by the way."

"Yeah. You should've fucking said something. Asked, maybe?"

He just shakes his head, a dark look in his eyes. "No. Had to be her choice. No one else's."

He reaches for the door and I get up to follow him, pissed off that I can't argue that and even more pissed off when I see Hannah standing at the desk when we step into the lobby. Her eyes lock with Logan for a second, then with me before she looks away, her cheeks glowing red.

Fuck me.

Logan smirks, heading for the door, but he stops, hand on the handle.

"For the record," he murmurs, keeping his voice low so Hannah can't hear when she takes a call. "I only asked you to stay away while I was trying to save her. Until it was safe."

I grit my teeth. I know it's my fault my family worries about me. Wonders why I don't come around. I just . . . I can't.

"I know."

Logan nods and with that he's gone, leaving me alone with my thoughts and the girl who won't leave them.

She hangs up the phone a second later, her gaze meeting mine and for once, she doesn't have that cheery smile.

"Are you okay?" she asks quietly when I stride past her and back to my office.

"Fine."

Then I shut the door.

CHAPTER Thirteen

HANNAH

Today is a day for awkwardness.

"God fucking dammit."

—That's part of it. Mason's been in his office all morning, door open, with expletives rolling out at every opportunity.

The other half is the argument we had the other night. His apology. The strange . . . tension in the air between us since.

He hasn't told me if he's been looking into Missy's disappearance. I haven't asked. I know if I push him, he'll probably tell me to fuck off back to Sacramento, so I've been giving him some space.

"Of course, it doesn't match. Why would it?" he grumbles and I finally decide I can't take it anymore.

"Are you trying to perform open heart surgery in here or are you just trying out new things to say when you're pissed off?"

He doesn't look up to where I stand at the door to the office, but I can see a spreadsheet on the screen in front of him.

He scrubs a hand over his face, letting out a deep sigh. "I don't have the patience for you right now."

"Rude." I step into the office, looking over his shoulder. I don't miss the way his spine stiffens with my proximity, and to be honest, it's a little humorous.

Mason's not as indifferent as he likes to pretend.

"Your equation's wrong."

"Thanks," he mutters sardonically, erasing the whole thing. "Don't you have some dirt to victimize or something?"

"Nope," I answer, popping the *P*. I step back, giving him a little space. "Everything's spotless. You could eat off the bathroom floor, though I wouldn't advise it." No response other than a shake of his head. "You know, I could probably figure that out."

"No," he answers coldly before I'm even finished. "I'll figure it out."

I shrug. Fine. He wants to be miserable, then he can be miserable. Who am I to stop him?

"Suit yourself . . . though, spreadsheets were kind of my whole degree in college."

His jaw ticks, but he doesn't look at me as he tries, once again, to figure it out.

Five minutes later, the cursing starts again.

"Hannah," he bites and I chuckle under my breath.

I take my time returning back to the door and this time, he's looking at me like he already regrets asking me for my help.

He mulls the words over for a moment.

"Can you show me how to figure this shit out?"

I stare at him for a beat, unable to mask the coy smile from slipping out.

"Am I hearing things or did Mason Carpenter just admit he needs *my* help with something?"

He shakes his head, turning back to the computer.

"I'll figure it out myself."

I sigh, rolling my eyes. So dramatic.

"Move over. Let me see."

I shove his arm and he lurches it back like I just doused him in gasoline and lit a match. He eyes me menacingly before vacating his giant chair and allowing me to take his place.

My feet don't even touch the ground, a fact I'm only slightly embarrassed about. Mason may as well have auditioned to play a tree in the *Wizard of Oz*.

"Okay, obviously we just need to start over," I murmur, trying to make sense of whatever he's done. "Are these the books?"

"Invoices for the month," he grumbles, sitting a battered chair from the lobby behind me.

Right behind me.

The back of my neck burns when he sits down, watching me work.

I never knew simple accounting could be so . . . alluring.

"How do you normally figure this stuff out?" I ask to break up the overwhelming silence.

At this proximity, I can smell the soap on his skin from a shower. He hasn't been in the garage, so he's not been sweaty and greasy today, but even that smells heavenly.

Is it creepy to get turned on by the scent of someone else?

Do I just need to get laid? It's been . . . God, I don't even know how long.

He clears his throat shifting in his chair and I just so happen to peek down at his denim-clad thigh, right next to mine.

Okay, I *definitely* need to get laid. A man's thigh has never turned me on before and right now, there's a steady pulse in my core.

"Figure it out at tax time."

I'm pleased to see his voice is no longer pissed off. It's softer. Nicer.

"It's probably all fucked up."

"Mason," I scold quietly, turning back to him. "People get thrown in jail for that."

His eyes zero in on mine and I almost look away from the

intensity behind them. He shrugs. "No one's said anything yet."

"Trust me," I grimace, turning back to the spreadsheet. "No one ever says anything, they just show up one day and shut you down." I start building a new spreadsheet for last month, completely ignoring what he's already done. It's just easier to start over at this point.

"Then where would you turn?" he murmurs darkly and I swallow past the lump in my throat.

"Mason, I know I haven't said this, yet," I say quietly, afraid to look at him. Fortunately, when I'm stressed, I do a better job. I always hated what I went to college for. It was boring, but Mom insisted, stating it would land me a better job in the long run. "But thank you."

If only she could see me, now. Sat in Mason's little dusty office, typing away on an ancient computer and fixing the books for his mechanic's shop. Something about knowing she would be angrier than a cat in a laser factory makes me almost laugh.

Mason, on the other hand, doesn't reply, but he doesn't need to. I can feel the animosity firing in the air like electrical charges.

"Why are you doing this, Hannah?" he asks after a long time of watching me work.

"You needed help."

"You know what I'm talking about."

I swallow, sucking in a deep breath.

How do I tell him and make him understand when I don't even know myself?

"I just . . . I can't abandon her."

"She abandoned you."

I peek at him over my shoulder and find him watching me. For once, he doesn't look like he hates me. He's inspecting me as if he's trying to find something. Some shred of doubt that maybe I won't follow through with this.

"She did," I admit, finally. I can't tell if it feels good to say that out loud, or not. "But where would we be if we were always keeping a tally on who owes whom?"

He doesn't have an answer for that. His gaze darkens, but he doesn't say anything, so I turn back to the spreadsheet.

"You know what they're accusing her of."

It's not a question.

A pit forms in the bottom of my stomach. The same one that always comes with racing thoughts about Missy.

"I know." I'm ashamed of how small my voice sounds when I say it.

"And if it's true?"

It can't be. Sure, she slept with someone else's husband. That's not a crime, though it is disgusting. Especially with Marcus Parker, but . . . human trafficking? The Missy I knew wouldn't have been able to stomach it.

But . . . the same Missy I knew *also* wasn't deranged and sinister. Or hooked on some illegal concoction that makes people eat each other.

That night flashes back across my mind. The night Mason came and brought Marcus to take Missy away.

The night I kissed him. If I think about it for a moment, I can still feel the way his calloused hands felt against the smooth bare skin of my legs, my back. The way his fingers gripped the roots of my hair, pulling on the strands like he couldn't get me close enough.

A shudder rolls through me, but I readjust in the chair to hide it.

Mason doesn't need to know I still think about that night. Or the way he tasted like nicotine, whiskey and sweet, sweet temptation. Like a bad man who would do all the right things for a good girl.

—Or that I still have that damned flannel.

"*If* it's true," I mumble, "then I can't help her. I'll turn her in because it's the right thing to do."

"And you could do that? To your sister?"

I don't like what he's implying, but I ignore it. As if I'm not strong enough.

"Doesn't sound very loyal of me, does it?"

"Doesn't sound very *Hannah* of you," he corrects.

"Maybe you don't know me as well as you thought," I challenge.

"Oh, little doe, I know you very, *very* well."

Holy shit.

My cheeks flame and that burn in my core amplifies. *Little doe.* It's been years since he's called me that, but even now, it has the same effect it did back then. My stomach tightens and I get all these crazy ideas in my head before I brush them to the side and remind myself that Mason and I are nothing more than unwilling partners in a battle between families.

And then I remember the way he completely cut me off after that night.

"It's done," I say quietly after a long, harrowing silence. "You're in the green for the month by fifteen thousand and some change, though I don't know if that number's really correct because the rest of the months might be wrong."

"Can you . . . " he pauses when I turn around in the chair to face him. It feels like looking into the eye of a hurricane. "Can you look at the rest of them?"

I cock a brow at him.

"Are you giving me free rein to fix stuff?"

His jaw ticks.

"Yes."

Finally. Some common ground.

"I'll move the computer out there and you can go through all of it. I just . . ."

"It's okay. Sometimes math is easier for some, and cars are easier for others."

That actually seems to work because he nods solemnly.

"Hannah . . ." he starts to say something else, but he cuts himself off while I wait on bated breath. Is this where he finally gives me whatever information he was able to find out about Missy? Or is this where he apologizes for being a ghost of a dick for almost two years?

Unfortunately, neither.

"Were you able to find anything out?"

Something flashes across his gaze, but it's gone before I can read it.

"No. I spoke to some contacts, but . . . nothing."

Fuck.

Tears burn in the corners of my eyes, but I shove them away before he can see them and turn back to the computer.

"Well, I guess I'll get started on this. There's no telling how long it'll take."

"Hannah," he murmurs, though there's something conflicting in his voice. A guilt that wasn't there before. "I'll keep looking. I've got a couple other people to talk to."

"Okay," I nod, my voice higher than usual.

He waits for a moment as if he's going to say something else, but eventually, he just gets up and heads toward the door.

"I'll move the computer Monday. We're almost done for the day, so why don't you go home."

"It's only four," I point out and he shrugs, not looking at me.

"And it's hot." He starts to walk away but stops at the door. "Have a good weekend, Hannah."

I almost smile, despite everything.

That's the nicest he's been to me since I started.

"Have a good weekend, Mason."

My house is pink.

Like Barbie went manic and redecorated on a Tuesday pink.

The outside is pink. The linoleum floors in the kitchen and bath? Pink sparkles. The couch that came with the house? You guessed it. Pink. There was even some custom pink toilet paper that I put away when I moved in.

Normally I wouldn't complain. I was fortunate to find a place this cheap in a moderately decent neighborhood in LA and that's saying something. Most of the places I looked at were either overpriced cardboard boxes or felt like at any moment, I was going to find some creep living in the walls.

I just feel anything but cheerful tonight, and the pink makes me feel like I have to be.

Like one of Mom's parties.

I still haven't finished unpacking, but if Mason really is looking into Missy's disappearance, I may not have to. If I can find Missy, I can go home, or . . . something. I still haven't decided.

To be honest, the prospect of coming back to LA freaking petrified me. The people aren't the same here. They're more . . . in your face. Everyone's trying to make something of themselves, as opposed to back in Sacramento that's full of the elderly and politicians.

I'm well and truly on my own for the first time in my entire life.

It's liberating, but . . . it's also fucking terrifying.

Imagine being murdered and the police show up at your house, only for it to be some bubblegum pink nightmare dollhouse?

I don't know. Maybe I'm just being cynical.

This is the part where I always come up short in my irrational plan to take the law into my own hands.

I thought I had it all figured out. My Barbie's dream house Airbnb is rented under a false name—not hard to do. My mother thinks I'm in Africa on a mission trip for her charity—something I've done before. Even Michael, my *best* friend, doesn't know I'm here.

I don't even know where Missy's been living the last two years and LA isn't exactly a small town. I can't just ask the neighbor if they've seen a woman who looks like me at the local 7-Eleven. I have no real concrete evidence to go by and that's not exactly conducive to completing my mission.

Which is . . . I don't really know.

Find Missy? Take her home?

I've heard things about what she's done. Some bad. Some worse. I can't stomach the thought of her doing any of what the rumors say, so I choose not to believe them.

Does that make me the problem? An enabler?

I've gone over the places she could be hiding in my head a billion times. I'll be honest, the odds of finding her are not in my favor.

Especially if I can't find somewhere to start.

And to think . . . I lied. I lied and told my mother I would go help build a school in a little village that really needs it, yet, here I am, sitting in my pink house trying to piece together the clues to my sister's disappearance. Does that make me . . . bad? Mason said no, but there's still that part of me that wonders if all these lies will eventually start to tumble down on one another until I'm left in the rubble.

Fuck.

"What am I going to do?" I groan, laying my head in my hands because that seems like the best course of action when you're all alone on a Friday night.

And then my phone buzzes.

There are only three people that could be.

My mother, who won't call because, again, she thinks I'm off the grid.

Michael, who also won't call because he *too* thinks I'm off the grid.

And . . . them.

Begrudgingly, I check the screen and find a number I don't know, but hey, at least it's not *Unknown,* right?

"Hello?"

No answer, save for the sounds of idle background noise.

"Hello?"

Again, no answer.

"Look asshole. I don't know who you are or why you keep calling me, but if you don't even have the balls to say it—"

"Ha—Hannah?"

I freeze as ice fills my veins. I know that voice.

"Missy?" I jump up from the couch and cut the TV completely. "Missy, is that you?"

"Hannah, I'm in trouble," she whispers, voice barely legible over the racing of my heartbeat in my chest.

"Missy, where are you?"

"I—I don't know," she stammers. "You've got to help me. They're going to kill me."

"Missy—"

"I don't have a lot of time," she whispers, voice cracking. "They're going to come back."

"What's it look like where you are? Are you still in California?" The panic in my chest swells at the sound of her quiet crying on the other end of the phone. "Who is coming for you?"

"I—I'm in some kind of warehouse. I think I'm in LA, but I don't know. Hannah, they've been drugging me. They're going to kill me."

"Who?"

"*Men*," she cries, but she doesn't explain. "These men are after me, because of Marcus. Because he loved me and took care of me. Oh my God, Hannah. I miss him so much. Our home."

"We can get you back home, I just need to find you."

"*No*," she hisses, almost venomously. "My home. With Marcus." She sucks in a deep breath. "With the man I love."

"Missy, where was your house?"

"I've got to go," she says hurriedly. "I can hear them coming. Find me, Hannah."

"Missy—" I growl, but a cold, harsh *click* followed by silence is all that greets me.

I stare at the phone in my hand for a moment, Missy's words repeating over and over again in my mind.

They're going to kill me.

"Fuck!" I curse, throwing my phone across the room and instantly regretting it. I rush to it, letting out a deep sigh of relief when I realize it's not broken.

She may call back.

"What the hell am I supposed to do?" I repeat, looking up at the ceiling. What do you know? It's pink, too.

But of course, it doesn't answer.

My phone does, though, as another buzz against the hardwood floor startles me into scrambling to grab it.

A text.

You'll never guess from who.

Unknown: I wonder why Mason Carpenter hasn't told you about your sister's finger ending up in his mother's mailbox yet.

Unknown: Curious.

Unknown: Curious, indeed.

My heart bottoms out, reading the message, but it's quickly replaced with revulsion when the picture comes through.

Because there it is. The mustache tattoo I always hated.

Only, now, it's detached and lying next to a photograph of Missy, tied up. Gagged. Tears streaming down her face.

Unknown: Seems time's running out.

Unknown: Tick Tock.

CHAPTER *Fourteen*

HANNAH

As it turns out, Marcus Parker owned a *lot* of property.

Mansions in three states, the Parker Estate in Malibu, a penthouse in downtown LA, a *bunch* of warehouses and businesses, and one, smaller water-side home in Venice.

I know that's the place, just from looking at the picture and once I use my mother's system to locate Missy's mailing address, I sigh in relief.

I've found it.

Step two is complete.

It's a short trip from my house, but I'm not going alone because, well, that would be idiotic of me. While I really don't want to ask Mason for help, he owes me after I agreed to completely revamp his books and fix years of accounting errors, which, might I add, date back to the early two-thousands.

Plus . . . if he did know about Missy's finger, why is he keeping it a secret?

So . . . here I am, standing outside Rummie's, along with what appears to be every SoCal motorcycle gang in the surrounding four counties.

This should be fun.

I'll admit, it's a little embarrassing, pulling to a stop in front of the crowded bar in my little bright yellow bug, especially with the laughs it garners from the . . . *cough* . . . locals. It's a *lot* more embarrassing that I have to hunt him out and ask for help.

Again.

Luckily, Ian let it slip that he, Mason, and Puke were coming here tonight to "unwind". As soon as I step out of the car, my flight or flight reflexes kick in and I'm ready to sink right into the pavement with the urine from a man peeing on the side of the building, not too far away.

Anywhere has to be better than here.

"Oh, baby," a woman in tight leather leggings and a tight bustier top coos the moment she sees me. She either looks like she's auditioning for the remake of *Grease* in a few minutes, or like she might put a cigarette out on my face for looking at her the wrong way.

Honestly, both.

"Are you lost?"

I totally should have worn something . . . I don't know, sexy? My "out of style" denim shorts and bright green T-shirt don't fit in here. I'm not showing nearly enough skin. Not to mention, the sneakers I've had for years that I threw on because I was in a rush to get out the door.

I didn't even wear makeup and I'm supposed to coax Mason out to come break into my missing sister's house with me?

Fuck me.

"Need us to call your mama?" another girl, this one snarkier, chimes from her cigarette-smoking perch beside the door.

"No, thank you." I'm ashamed at how timid and . . . *southern* my voice sounds next to their cool California accents. "I'm looking for Mason Carpenter. Have ya'll seen him?"

God, Hannah, get it together.

"Ya'll," snarky girl snickers, mocking me, but the other shoots her a look of reproach.

"Honey, they're going to eat you alive in there," first woman says, eyeing me up and down. "Mason's busy. Why don't you go on home and wait for him there?"

My stomach slips uncomfortably. *Busy with what?* "It's . . . um . . . important."

I can see at this distance, she's not much older than me, though probably a hell of a lot more fun. Bet her mother didn't force her to brush her hair with one hundred strokes every night.

"Fresh *meat*." A man throws his arm around my shoulders and I cringe at the scent of his breath. "Want a beer?" he asks, offering me his.

"No," I wince, unable to force the politeness out of my tone. It refuses to die. "No, thank you."

I duck down and out from under his arm and first woman eyes the man.

"Oh, leave her alone, Bill. Poor thing's shaking. She's scared to death."

I wouldn't say that, but then again, there is a slight tremor in my hands that's not normally there.

Missy, you asshole. You're lucky you're my sister.

"Hey, ain't you the governor's daughter?" a new man asks, sliding up on the other side of me.

I'm effectively cornered.

I open my mouth to speak, but the words get stuck on my tongue.

"I'm—I'm looking for Mason."

"M—M—M—Mason," second guy mocks, and he and a few of the people surrounding us chuckle.

"Aww . . . you got a little crush on Mason?" second girl chimes. Of course, she would. She's been quiet for far too long. "Well, get in line, honey."

"I just need to speak to him."

"He's busy," Bill says and the original woman rolls her eyes.

"He's inside. At the bar." She steps forward, putting a hand on Bill's chest and pushing him back. He's so drunk, he nearly falls on his ass. She turns back to me, giving me a quick nod of her head and a scowl, telling me I better hurry or she's not covering for me any longer.

"Thank you," I breathe, and rush through the door.

—And stumble right into pandemonium.

I've never been in a bar before. It was forbidden like most things that involved fun, but even if I had, I don't think it would have compared to the inside of Rummie's.

The crowd is thick and overconfident; a drunken haze, hanging over the room. A woman's dancing on a tabletop in the back, surrounded by a group of rough, cheering men. The bar is lined with loud people, most not even fully involved in a conversation because there's just so much going on around them. Some people even dry hump against tables and chairs, "dancing" to the rock music blaring over the radio as if no one else is in the room.

First woman was right.

These people are going to eat me alive.

Come on, Hannah. Doesn't mean they're bad people, I chastise myself and even though I agree with the tyrant that is my inner monologue, I still feel like a mouse walking into a viper's den as I slip through the crowd.

Someone tries to pull me into a dance, a drunk man I'm sure won't remember my face after the next five minutes.

"Hey, babygirl. Daddy know where you are right now?" another asks, grinning at me through broken teeth. Looks like he's already been in a bar fight tonight.

I ignore him, only to turn and run into a woman who sloshes her drink on me.

"Fucking cow," she growls, lunging at me as if she might really bite me.

Suddenly, I'm missing the protection of first woman.

"Excuse me," I squeak to a group of men gathered in front of the bar, but none of them move. They don't even look in my direction, save to produce a truly long list of shitty pickup lines.

"Wow, she's warm," one comments, snickering sickeningly when I squeeze through them.

"And short. I like 'em small. Makes 'em tight."

God, I could vomit if I'd actually eaten dinner.

Jesus, Mason. Where the hell are you?

And then, as if on cue, I spot him. He's leaning back against the bar, Puke and Ian beside him and for a brief, shining moment, relief floods through me.

However, it's quickly replaced by something else when I spot the girl beside him, her hand on his stomach. She giggles while she whispers something in his ear.

"Hannah." Ian's as surprised to see me as Mason is when his eyes flash to mine and instantly darken.

"What the hell are you doing?" I growl putting on my best angry wife voice and putting every single one of my shower acting skills to the test.

Mason's jaw ticks.

The sinister voice in the back of my head chuckles.

"Umm . . . Mason," the girl next to him asks, blue eyes flashing me up and down. "Who is this?"

"His *wife*," I snap before Mason can even get a word in. "Who are you?"

She at least looks horrified, looking back and forth between Mason and me like we've lost our minds. Maybe I have, at this point.

"Our baby is sick at home and you come *here*?"

"Okay, I think it's time for me to go," the woman says, wincing as she disentangles herself from Mason.

Unfortunately, for both her and me, Mason's eyes never leave my face, but instead of the burning hatred I expected, there's a flicker of amusement and something else that makes my body tighten as the girl disappears back into the crowd.

Puke and Ian look terrified. Mason looks like he's ready to whip me for his own amusement.

"I'll take a shot of whatever the most expensive vodka you have is, please?" I say to the bartender who nods at my request. "Oh, and you can put it on his tab. Right, honey?"

Now Mason looks like he's ready to kill me. Or fuck me. I'm not sure which would be more terrifying, right now.

"Alright, Hannah," he murmurs when the bartender slides me my drink. I down the shot, letting the silky sweetness slip down my throat. Listen, I'm no drinker, but I was in a sorority. You can only sit out so many frat parties before people start asking questions. "You have my attention. What do you want?"

"That," I say, dabbing at the corner of my mouth and sliding the shot glass back on the bar. "Was for not telling me about the mysterious package that showed up at your mother's house last week."

I can see the darkness coalesce in his eyes the moment he realizes what I'm talking about.

"*This*," I hand him the paper with Missy and Marcus's address on it. "Is where we're going."

He looks down at the address, handing the paper back to me.

"I'm not going anywhere."

"Is that so?" I raise my hand to the bartender, who nods. "Can you make it a double, please? Guess I might as well stick around." I chuckle when he slides me another shot. I sit down at the bar beside Puke, who looks like I'm the Grim Reaper coming to collect his soul. "I'm no expert, but I think this vodka runs about fifteen dollars a shot. What's that? Forty-five dollars for wasting my time? I think it's worth more than that, don't you, Puke?"

"Ye—Yes, ma'am," he replies without looking at Mason.

I down my second shot, this one sliding down a little rougher because it's a double, but I drink it anyway, because I have a point to make. Mason can't avoid me forever.

Speaking of which, he stares down at me, his head cocked and his eyes portraying a bored indifference, even if the tick in his jaw tells me he's anything but.

"Shall I continue?" I ask, sliding the shot glass up the bar again.

He stares at me for a beat, as if he's trying to read my mind.

Still . . . he doesn't reply.

I move to raise my hand again, but before I can, Mason's scooping me out of the barstool and hoisting me over his shoulder, caveman-style.

"You can't ignore me forever," I grit, smacking at his back because that's all I can reach at this angle as he carries me out of the bar. People around us hoot and holler, but he pays them no attention as he carts me through the front door and out into the parking lot beyond.

"Hey, Mason. Some girl was looking for you. She was real pretty," Bill says still drunk as a skunk and in the same place I left him.

"Shut the fuck up, Bill," Mason grumbles, marching me through the crowd.

"Thanks for the help, Bill!" I call and I yelp when Mason's hand smacks my ass. "Asshole," I grumble under my breath.

The group at the door dissolves back into drunken chatter, forgetting all about Mason and me. Don't ask me why, but now that Mason's here, they don't seem all that bad. Drunk, but not scary.

Maybe it's because I know none of them would actually hurt me with Mason around. Maybe it's because facing Mason is far more frightening than anything they could dole out.

"You go, Red," first woman calls, putting a hand on Bill's shoulder to turn him away.

Mason deposits me right in front of my bright yellow bug and all the blood rushes to my head when he leans in so far, I have to slip up the hood to keep from being pressed against him.

"What kind of game are you playing?" he asks, voice barely above a whisper.

I've got to hand it to him, it's no wonder all the women are falling all over themselves when he's around. The man may as well have invented the sexy smolder.

"I'm not playing any game," I say innocently, though we both know, I definitely am. "You and I had a deal. You haven't followed through with your end even though I have *more* than followed through with mine."

His eyes flash menacingly and he leans forward, placing his hands on the hood on either side of me, effectively caging me in. My breath hitches and heat pools in my core at the press of his thighs against my knees, forcefully spreading them apart.

Yeah . . . I definitely need to get laid.

"You know B and E is a crime, little doe?"

I swallow over the lump in my throat, my heart hammering in my chest from the proximity of him. His scent encompasses me and something warm flutters in my core. Fresh soap, smoke, and leather. Him.

"So is hacking into the governor's private databases," I whisper, and his jaw flutters dangerously.

Gently, almost involuntarily, his finger traces the line of bare skin that shows where my T-shirt rests on top of my jeans. I let out a shaky breath, and even though my palms are slipping against the hood of the car, I force myself to stay rooted in place.

He doesn't say anything, but if the heat in his stare was enough, I would have gone up in flames.

"Get in the car."

He steps away from me in a flash and my heart nearly bottoms out from the wash of intensity firing in the air between us.

Good. Distance is good.

Carefully, I slide to my feet, stumbling—unfortunately—into Mason.

Maybe I shouldn't have drank so much to prove my point.

"What's the matter, little doe?" Mason cocks a brow at me. "Too much to drink."

He holds out his hand and begrudgingly, I give him the keys.

He chuckles darkly, moving to the driver's side of my little yellow bug, shaking his head.

"Passenger seat."

CHAPTER *Fifteen*

MASON

Hannah is a shit criminal.

"It's that one," she whispers loudly, pointing at a blue two-story house off a canal in Venice.

I shake my head, grabbing her hand and pushing it down.

"No. It's that one." I point next door to Melissa Gaine's orange adobe "house" that cost Parker a fortune. The two buildings are almost identical. Like most things in LA, everything's a carbon copy of something else and I'm not just talking about houses.

"No, it's not," Hannah argues, stepping up to the back gate of the blue house and peaking her head over the bushes that are almost as tall as she is.

I step up beside her, nodding to an upstairs window.

"There's a TV on in the bedroom. You really want to go breaking into some random stranger's house in the middle of the night, or do you want to get what we came for?"

She narrows her eyes on me. I wait for her to admit she's wrong. She doesn't.

Instead, she steps up to the bushes behind the orange house, sneaking down the line of foliage as if she's auditioning to be the next James Bond. I resist the urge to chuckle. It's evident she's never fucking done this before.

California's princess, breaking the rules.

"Just so we're clear." I feel the need to reiterate this to her because Hannah's never been in a single ounce of fucking trouble. "You know breaking and entering is a crime, right?" I don't really care at this point. I'm as good as dead when they find out where she is, but Hannah wouldn't make it in prison.

"Okay?" she challenges, brows furrowed in concentration as she stares at the wall in front of her. "So is jaywalking."

Like a fucking spider monkey, she attempts—and fails— to jump up and climb the wall. She manages to reach the top, I'll give her that, but halfway over, she gets stuck, perfect ass in the air.

"Can you give me a boost?"

I have half a mind to smack her ass, again.

Stepping up behind her, I put a hand on the back of her thigh and raise her up so she can climb on top of the wall.

"Here," she whispers, holding out a hand.

I eye it for a moment because she's fucking crazy if she thinks her little ass is pulling me up, and stride over to the gate flipping the very noticeable lock on the top and pushing it open, striding into the backyard.

"Asshole," Hannah grumbles, even though she lets me help her down from her perch on the wall. I'm careful not to hold her too long. Shit like that is how I got in this mess, but I can't deny the possessiveness that washes through me with her in my arms.

I set her on her feet and move to the back door. The house is pitch black, obviously, but the curtains are drawn, blocking out any vantage of the inside.

"Are you expecting landmines?"

Hannah glares at me from across the yard. Finally, she swallows nervously, stepping down the path as if Melissa's going to pop out of a bush at any moment with a knife.

At this point, it wouldn't fucking surprise me.

"There's going to be a security system," I tell her quietly. The curtain is drawn over the window of the sliding glass door, but the cobwebs shining against the white fabric means no one's been here for a long time. "Do you have any idea what the code might be?"

She winces. "I didn't think of that."

"Not very criminal of you."

She shoots me a glare.

"Maybe our birthday."

"Okay . . ." I wait. She doesn't answer. "What the fuck is it?"

It's surprising to me that I don't know her birthday. I know everything else about her. At least, the shit I've made up in my head. The girl's a fucking mystery to me.

Melissa Gaines was easy to figure out. Shit parents. Childhood trauma. Some big-time rich guy swoops in and promises her the world and she gets caught up in it. Liked the dark side of the moon a little too much.

Hannah, though?

It would take a thousand years to figure out what's in her pretty little head and I don't have that kind of time before she leaves, again.

"You're awfully rude, tonight." She pauses, cocking her head. "Every night, really."

I let out a deep breath, willing my self-control to keep hanging on by a thread.

"Birthday, Hannah."

"September fifteenth."

"Good girl."

Hannah's eyes widen and her lips clamp shut, cheeks flaming even in the darkness. It has the effect I intended and shuts her up for once, while I try to figure out the back door.

Listen, I'm not a criminal. I do, however, have a lock picker's tool kit. It can be useful if you really can't get a car door open, but mostly, it sits on a shelf in my office.

Now, it's helping me commit a crime for the little brat behind me.

"Can you hurry up?" Hannah whispers after a few minutes of me fucking with the lock. And failing. "I feel like someone's going to catch us."

We're standing in nearly complete darkness, save for the small penlight in my mouth to light up the lock. I shoot her a look and she concedes, standing quietly beside me, once more.

Finally, after a lot of bullshit, there's a click and the lock inside disengages.

"September fifteenth."

Hannah nods, opening her mouth to speak, but I don't give her time before I'm sliding the door open and stepping into the darkness inside. I locate the control panel on the wall beside the door and type in the code, but it flashes red.

"Hannah, plan B."

"Shit."

"*Hannah*."

"Umm . . . Oh, August fifth! I remember her saying that was her anniversary with Marcus."

I type it in and miraculously, the control panel beeps once, signaling the house is unarmed.

I hope.

"You've really got to get better at this if we're going to be breaking into people's houses," I murmur as she steps through the curtain, hastily brushing off old spider webs.

"Oh, pardon me," she sneers. "Let me see if they have a B and E class down at the local tech school."

I swear to fucking God.

This little brat is going to be the fucking death of me.

"It smells really bad in here," Hannah winces, looking around and covering her nose.

"Rotten food. No one's been here for a while." I keep the penlight low, looking at the stack of mail on the table. Bills Melissa didn't pay, junk, more bills.

"What was she going to do with all this space?" Hannah looks around, waving her flashlight around the room and, consequently, the walls and windows.

Jesus Christ.

I push it down towards the floor and she opens her mouth to argue, but for once, she doesn't.

"Parker bought her this place," I murmur, stepping out of the kitchen and into the living room. "Way too fucking big for one person."

"No kidding," Hannah says, from where she stands at the mantel. There's a picture there and upon closer inspection, I realize it's Melissa and Parker, dressed up. Probably for a "party".

Black venom slips through my veins seeing his face. He should be dead. Not cozy in his little private prison cell, being waited on hand and foot. Safe and fucking sound.

Hannah looks at me for a moment, then carefully, she reaches up, takes the picture, and lays it face down.

I move away from her, scanning the rest of the room and Hannah seems to abandon her search for evidence in favor of prying.

"I know you don't like him, but . . . was he really into everything they're saying he was?"

I can hear in her voice she's not accusing me. She's merely curious. As if she accepts my judgment, but like a child, wants to know the reason.

Unfortunately, for her, that's the last fucking thing I want to talk about. She's so fucking innocent, I'm not sure she'd even believe me if I tried.

"I thought we were here to look for clues?"

She takes a step back at the bite in my voice.

"Right. Sorry."

You know those moments where you feel like a grumpy asshole, even if it's completely warranted?

Yeah, they fucking suck.

"Hey, look," she says suddenly, stalking across the room. I follow her to where an entryway table is crushed to pieces on the floor.

"Someone was here."

Hannah falls silent, shining her flashlight on a trail of blood leading towards the stairs.

"Mason," she says softly and I can hear the slight tremor in her voice.

"Don't tell me you're chickening out, now."

She shoots me a look.

"Sometimes, I can't stand you," she grumbles as she marches past, towards the staircase.

"Right back at you, little doe."

She rolls her eyes, carefully climbing the stairs and avoiding any of the dried blood on the floor.

I follow behind her, careful to keep my distance because, well, the view is something to be admired, even if she pisses me off.

Hannah goes in one direction and I go the other at the top. The house has four bedrooms and two of the four are filled with racks of designer clothing. Melissa has enough Gucci to feed every homeless person in the city twice-over. The third bedroom, *actually* a bedroom, must be the guest room because there's nothing in any of the drawers but blankets and sheets.

"Mason," Hannah calls out from across the house after I've just stepped out of the nearly empty bathroom connected to the guest room.

Tension coils through me at the sound of her voice. I step through the house, to the open door of the master—

—And stop short.

"Jesus," I mutter, looking at the pictures above the California king bed in the center of the room.

Three pictures, all of a naked Melissa Gaines sit above the wall, all smiling coyly at us as if she knows what we're up to.

The only problem is the eyes are cut out over every single one.

"There's this, too," Hannah grumbles, handing me a pamphlet. I check it over in the dimming flashlight in my hand and it feels like someone injected cement into my spine.

You've got to be fucking kidding me.

"What is that place? The Inner Sanctum."

I almost chuckle. Almost.

I hand it back to her. "A sex club. Invitation only."

Hannah grimaces, her spine stiffening. She peeks back at her sister on the wall, then at me, and I'm reminded of her little jealous streak at the bar. Truth be told, Melissa Gaines could give the best head in this state and I wouldn't find her attractive.

No, unfortunately, that spot's reserved for her fucking sister.

And only her fucking sister.

"Did you find anything else?"

"That."

She nods to a glass decanter on the dresser. It glows green like the color of Hannah's eyes in my flashlight.

Neither of us needs to ask what that is.

"Do you . . . do you think something bad happened?"

"Hannah—" I grit and I almost feel guilty when she winces at my tone.

"No, Mason. I know you don't care," she snaps, actually stomping her foot. "But if someone *took* her, don't you think it's a good idea to find out who? I mean, what if they're coming after everyone attached to your stepfather."

"Parker," I correct and she growls under her breath, shaking her head.

"Okay, fine. Call him whatever you want, but this concerns more than just me. Your mother got a finger in her mailbox." She squares her shoulders. "I'm going to that club."

Immediately, I shake my head. "No."

"I didn't ask you to come with me."

"And you aren't going alone, either."

"You aren't my father," she bites, eyes flaring in the pale glow of her dying flashlight.

"No, but I'm all you've got. We aren't going."

She opens her mouth to say something, but a creak downstairs causes her to shut her mouth tight, eyes going wide.

"Security! Anyone inside?"

Oh, fuck.

Hannah jerks at the sound of the voice downstairs, but I seal a hand over her mouth to silence her and push her back against the wall. It's not the best position. My front pressed completely against hers, her wide eyes staring up at me in fear. I know she can feel my cock and the evidently permanent hard-on pressed into her stomach, but there aren't a lot of choices in a situation like this.

We listen to the sounds of two pairs of feet moving about the house downstairs, and I wrack my brain for a way out of this situation.

Fuck. Fuck. Fuck.

"Take off your shirt."

Hannah's eyes turn to sharp points. She mumbles something against my hand and I remove my fingers with a sigh.

"No," she whispers.

"*Take off your shirt,*" I growl, stepping back from her. "And get on the bed."

She starts to argue, again, but I don't let her. I crush my lips to hers, lifting her quickly and spinning her back toward the bed before depositing her on top of the covers. I rip my shirt over my head, then hers, and pull her back to me in a rush.

She tries to push at my shoulders, but I only tug her closer until her body lines up with mine. Only then, does she seem to understand the plan.

I try not to think of the way she fucking feels in my hands. How much I've craved the taste of her. How little convincing it would take to get me to abandon my morals completely and fuck her right here, in her missing sister's bed. Despite everything, a groan rumbles from deep in my chest. Tasting her feels like coming home.

Somewhere along the line, the kiss becomes blurred, but not enough that I don't hear the footsteps of the men on the stairs. Just when they breach the bedroom door, I'm rolling my hips into Hannah's and a soft moan slips free from her lips.

"Hey! You two didn't hear us calling?"

Fucking hell. It's about fucking time they showed up.

They flick on the light overhead and Hannah breaks away from me with a gasp, working to cover herself up with the comforter below her.

I hate to fucking think about what's on it, but there aren't many choices when you're caught breaking into the house of your newfound obsession's twin sister.

"What are you doing here?" I snap, stepping off the bed. Both men reach back like they're going for their guns, but I'm not an idiot. I can see they're both poor excuses for Tasers from here. Nothing like the nine in my back.

"You the homeowner?" one snaps. I can tell he's new. Probably no older than Hannah from the looks of it. He keeps his gaze pinned on me—smart—while the other guy just looks around like a dumbass.

"I am," Hannah says breathlessly, slipping her shirt over her head as discreetly as possible.

"You have your ID on you?"

She nods quickly and I steel myself for the handcuffs that are likely about to come. Imagine my surprise when Hannah reaches into Melissa's purse sitting beside the bed and pulls out her wallet.

How the fuck didn't I notice that?

She hands over Melissa's ID and the younger guy inspects it, then Hannah.

"You set off the alarm," he says, almost pissed off that Melissa's

ID checked out. Idiot didn't look close enough. Hannah and Melissa look nothing alike. "Said you entered the wrong code."

Hannah waves a hand, climbing off the bed to stand next to me.

"Sorry," she laughs sweetly. "Must have made a mistake when we got here. We just got in from a long stay in Aruba. Have you ever been?" She makes a show of placing her hand on my stomach and nestling into my side. My cock pulses in response, particularly when her nails dig into my skin.

Little shit.

"Can't say I have. What happened to your table downstairs?"

"Yeah, and why does it smell so bad in the kitchen?" the other guy chimes. Fucking idiot. Probably still has his lunch packed by his mother, every day.

"Oh, we let some friends stay over and they got a little carried away, I guess," Hannah lies, smoothly. "Really, you must go and see Aruba for yourself. It's truly magical." She beams, cheeks burning bright red. "There's this beautiful little villa we stayed at and they had these lizards—"

"Iguanas," I correct and Hannah shoots me a look behind her smile.

"*Iguanas*," she says dramatically. "Anyway, they climb everywhere, and I wanted to bring one home, but they wouldn't let me and it was a whole debacle that my sweet pookie bear, here, had to stop—"

"That's enough," the first guy says, looking back and forth between us while I try not to think of all the ways I'd fucking love to punish Hannah.

Fucking pookie bear?

"We've got another call, so long as you're clear."

"All clear," I murmur.

Stupid fucks.

He nods, not even second-guessing it.

"Have a good night. And try to make sure you enter the right code, next time. We might not be able to get here as fast if you actually need help if we're chasing after false alarms all night."

Jesus Christ.

"Of course. Thank you for keeping the streets safe, at night. You two be careful out there," Hannah waves, watching as they retreat down the stairs. As soon as the door shuts below, she lets out a deep breath, her hands shaking.

"Holy shit," she breathes.

"Pookie bear?" I cock a brow at her.

She chuckles, slipping her shirt back over her head. It's a shame.

"What? Would you prefer I call you Big Daddy like Puke and Ian?"

Lead fills my spine. "Try it. I'll have you screaming it by the time I'm done with you."

Her cheeks flame to a deep shade of scarlet.

Maybe she's better at this shit than I thought she was.

"Grab the purse and let's get the fuck out of here."

She bends down to grab it but stops short.

"Uh, Mason?"

I slip my shirt on over my head.

"What now?"

"Umm . . ." and I look at what she's holding up in her hand.

"Well, shit."

Melissa's phone.

"Hope you like it lukewarm."

Hannah comes back to the dining room table, setting a mug of sweet tea in front of me with *Barbie* on the side.

"The ice maker's broken," she grimaces, sliding into the seat beside me. "I plugged her phone in, so it should be on soon."

It's entirely too fucking close. My head's still spinning from the way she tasted. The way she felt under my fingertips. I've waited two years for that fucking kiss, and yet, now that I've had it, I'm disturbed to find the hunger's still there, glaring me in the face.

Maybe I need to fuck her. Get it out of both our systems so we can move on.

I know myself better than that, though, and I know *her*. As much as I'd want it to satiate the need for her, I know it would only fucking make it worse.

And that's the biggest joke of all, isn't it?

Fucking Hannah Gaines. Sister to my enemy. Daughter of the biggest crook in the state. Object of every single one of my fucking fantasies.

"This feels like an invasion of privacy," Hannah says, pulling Melissa's purse across the table in front of her. Gucci. Of course.

I fix her with a look and she blushes.

"Well, it is. A woman's purse is sacred."

"Should we go through yours first?"

"*No*."

I nod. "Then open the bag."

"Fine," she grumbles, unlatching the top and pulling the pamphlet for the Inner Sanctum out. "Sex club ticket. Check," she says as if she's mentally logging everything. "Chapstick—the nasty medicinal one, too—check." She pauses, look at me when I cock a brow at her. "Fine, sorry."

Lipstick, old makeup, a thong that Hannah quickly tosses to the side with the end of a pen, a wallet complete with every fucking credit card known to man.

"Could your sister be any more of a cliché?"

Hannah rolls her eyes.

"Right. I forgot. Mr. I hate the system and everything about it."

I chuckle darkly. "You're learning well. I'm glad you're finally catching on." She fixes me with a bored look that I would love to wipe off her face. "Credit cards will only lead to more debt. Why buy something if you can't afford it?"

"Credit cards help some, and for others they can be damaging, yes," Hannah concedes. "You have to know how to use them correctly. Knowing my sister, I don't think she did."

"Why didn't Melissa go to college?"

"She did," Hannah says. "She just flunked out a year in and after three tutors and a lot of special favors, Mom gave up on it."

"Doesn't seem like your mother. To give up on something."

The last two years have proven that.

"What was she going for?"

Hannah snickers, covering her mouth with the palm of her hand. "I shouldn't laugh. She was trying to get a degree in pop culture."

"Like a paparazzi?"

"I don't know," she shakes her head. "Something like that. Can you imagine Missy, though, trying to chase down a celebrity in Beverly Hills?"

I actually chuckle at the image of a deranged, naked Melissa running wild through the streets of Hollywood with a camera instead of a knife.

It's the little things in life.

"I'm not sure your sister would have stuck with any job, much less college. Everything she did or said was a façade. Fake."

"Not everything," Hannah chides and I cock a brow. "Her boobs were real. That counts, doesn't it?"

"And are yours?"

She nearly chokes on her drink.

"That is *not* a question you should be asking." She's flustered. "But if you *must* know. Yes. They are, but I don't think it should matter. Breast implants can be a good thing."

"They can also kill you."

"So can butter," she argues. "You're being vulgar."

"You're blushing."

She rolls her eyes, but the burn on her cheeks remains. She opens her mouth, but the sound of Melissa's phone chiming from the other side of the room causes her to jump.

She's awfully fucking jumpy now. Particularly when a phone rings. I thought it was just because her sister was missing, but now . . . I'm wondering if there's more to the story.

She gets up quietly and pads over to the phone on the counter. I try not to think about the red polish shining on her toes or the tan on her smooth, bare legs, but I'm also not blind, either. So, I find myself wondering what those same legs looked like wrapped around my waist earlier.

"Okay, it's on," Hannah murmurs, letting out a shaky breath as she takes her seat.

"Okay. You just going to stare at it?"

It sits on the table in front of her, her eyes locked on it as text messages and notifications pour through.

"I . . ." she starts, but it falls flat. Instantly, she grabs the phone and attempts to unlock it.

Wrong.

"Shit."

I cock a brow at her cursing because in the three years I've come to know little Hannah Gaines, she's never been anything but prim and proper. "Use the facial recognition."

She holds the phone up and it must be just alike enough to allow her in because, with a click, the phone opens.

"Seventy-five missed calls and one hundred and three texts," Hannah grimaces. "Who would want to talk to someone that much?"

"Who would want to talk to your sister that much?"

She nods cynically. "I guess you're not wrong."

"That might be the first time you've agreed with me," I point out.

"Well, don't get used to it."

She clicks on the calls first. *Parker. Parker. Parker.* Then, after his sentencing, *Prison, Prison, Prison.*

Something doesn't sit right.

"When was the last time you spoke to your sister?"

Hannah shrugs. "A year ago. Maybe a little more. She wouldn't return my calls or texts."

"Looks like you found your reason."

"There are a lot of calls to this number," Hannah grumbles. "It's not saved. Wait," she jumps, eyes going wide. "There was a call this evening . . . but it was made from this phone."

The air in the kitchen is suddenly thick in the shared silence between us.

Okay, now shit's getting really fucking weird.

"What time?"

"Just after nine . . . Mason, we got there at nine."

I scrub a hand over my face, willing this shit to start making sense. I'm almost thirty, and in all my life, I've never liked fucking puzzles. The mind games, the twists and clues you have to pick up on to put it all together. It's bullshit.

"Someone was in the house," Hannah whispers, looking around the room as if they might jump out from her pantry at any moment. "Do you think *they* tripped the alarm?"

"I think it's entirely possible."

She lets out a shaky breath, her face a shade paler.

"You sure you can handle this, little doe?"

Her eyes narrow and for a moment, I'm ready for her to snap at me, but the look fades, replaced by something deeper. A fear.

I fucking hate it.

"I have to," she shrugs, eyes sad. "No one else is going to."

"Have you ever thought about what you could find out?"

"Can't really think about it if I don't know what it'll be."

Jesus Christ. Ever the optimist.

"And if you stumble upon something you don't want to know?"

"Then . . . I guess I'll have to accept it."

She stares at me for a moment, her pretty green eyes meeting my dark ones. I could get lost in those fucking eyes. My cock swells in my jeans, despite myself, and my fingers burn where I touched her soft skin earlier.

Out of all the places. That's where I fucking got to taste her again.

The phone buzzes between us and Hannah jumps.

"A text," she says cautiously. She clicks on the icon. "It's unknown."

"Of course it is," I mutter under my breath.

"Thanks for sending those security guys away," she reads aloud. "I would have hated for them to have looked in the closet."

She freezes. Fuck, I freeze.

"They were there the entire time," she breathes, tears welling in her eyes.

"Give me the phone."

She pauses and I shoot her a look, daring her to argue. Begrudgingly, she places it in my hand, as if it's a ticking time bomb.

"Whoever this is has been sending weird shit like this to her phone for awhile," I murmur, scrolling through the list of deranged, cryptic messages. "Dating back to before she went missing."

"Do you think they took her? Whoever they are?"

"I wouldn't think they would kidnap her and then keep coming back to her house after."

"But who else could it be?"

"Look, Hannah." I set the phone down between us. "Parker had a lot of fucking enemies. Melissa would have, too, as his mistress. And I know you don't want to believe it, but she also fucked over a *lot* of people. People who wouldn't think twice if something bad happened to her."

"So, you're saying . . . it could be anyone."

"I'm saying these could be two different scenarios. Is there anyone you know of?"

Instantly, it's like a light bulb goes off behind her eyes. She jumps up, hurrying over to the counter and grabbing her own phone. She opens it and carefully sets it in between us, right next to Melissa's.

Unknown.

Now shit's getting serious.

Unknown: Roses are red, violets are blue. Your sister will be dead soon, how about you?

Unknown: There's only one way this will end.

Unknown: Stare at the darkness too long and eventually, the dark will stare back.

Texts upon texts of psychotic babble that doesn't make sense. Idle threats, disguised as nursery rhymes. A picture of the fucking finger found in Mom's mailbox, even a text asking about me.

"What the fuck is this?"

Hannah has the audacity to look startled by the anger thick in my voice. Like a child scolded. "They started a few months ago. It's what made me come here. Mom wasn't doing anything but covering Missy's disappearance up."

"And you just forgot to mention them?"

Her lips clamp shut and her eyes well with tears, but I don't care. I've been trying to keep her safe and yet, she's hiding this shit from me.

"Hannah, this shit is serious. People are fucking crazy. What if they come after you in the middle of the night?"

"I know," she bites. "But I've troubled you enough, I wasn't about to unload all that baggage onto you, too."

"And keeping it a secret is better?"

"I didn't want you involved. I thought it would be better for you to stay out of it."

"I'm already fucking in it, Hannah. I need to know this shit if I'm going to keep you safe."

Fuck.

I shouldn't have said that.

"I didn't ask you to keep me safe," she says softly, eyes narrowed on me as if I just told her I was a mass murderer.

I didn't ask for this gnawing obsession, either, but here we are.

"Yeah, well, shouldn't have been a question."

She's quiet for a moment, her gaze on Melissa's phone in front of her. She opens her mouth to speak multiple times, but each time, she slams it shut while I continue to read through the texts on her phone.

"Spit it out, Hannah."

She swallows a deep breath, her shoulders tight.

"Why didn't you . . . tell me about the finger?"

It's the elephant in the room, isn't it? I kept it from her and whoever is behind this ratted me out.

"Because I knew you would take it to heart."

I'm aware when she wipes a quiet tear off her cheek, even without looking at her. I fucking hate it.

"Pretty hard not to," she says softly, her hand shaking when she reaches for her glass.

I sit her phone down on the table between us. I've seen enough. Now, I just need to find a way for Logan to track down whoever sent these messages.

"Everyone thinks I'm crazy," she murmurs, drawing her knee up to her chest and resting her chin on it. "I think they're crazy for not bothering to even look."

I can't believe I'm fucking saying this.

"I don't think you're crazy."

Her eyes flash to mine and the tears there piss me off.

Fuck, I can't believe I'm saying this . . .

"If it were one of my sisters . . . I'd find them."

She doesn't say anything, but I can see that small flash of appreciation in her eyes. One that'll get me in trouble if I'm not careful.

"I'd do whatever I had to."

Slowly, she nods, wiping a tear that clings to her cheek on the back of her hand.

"Tomorrow we're going to the Inner Sanctum."

Her eyes widen to saucers.

"Tomorrow?"

"Yeah. So find something that screams, *I love sex clubs*."

I stand, chuckling internally. I'm not sure Hannah owns anything remotely sex-club-worthy.

Ironically, she's still the sexiest fucking woman I've ever seen.

"It's late. We have to work tomorrow. Go to bed." I stride toward the door, mostly because if I stay when she's soft and sweet, I'll never fucking leave. Unfortunately, the sound of her chair on the sparkly pink floor stops me at the door.

"Thank you," she says before I reach for the door handle. "For doing this. I know you've got a life to live and I know I'm taking a lot of your time."

Silly fucking girl. My life's revolved around hers for years.

She just doesn't know it.

"Goodnight, little doe."

I don't stick around to hear her reply.

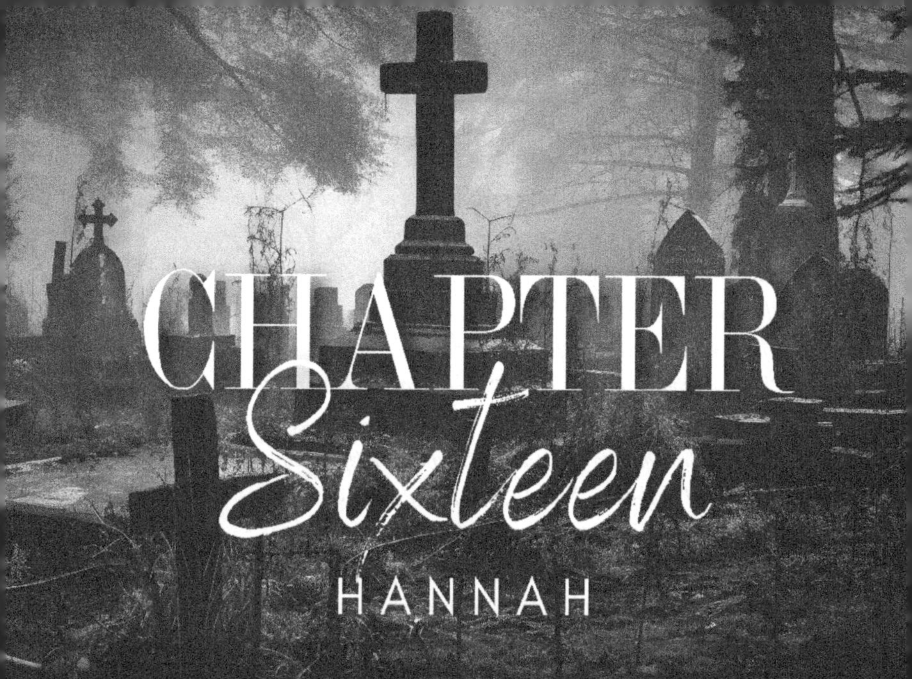

CHAPTER *Sixteen*

HANNAH

"That one looks like a crab."

Missy does an impersonation of a crab with her fingers and I can't help but laugh. This is our favorite place to come lately. The back of the house where no one really ventures to. There's a tall oak tree that shades the area, so it's perfect for cloud gazing.

I never took myself, nor Missy for cloud gazers, but it's simple and life has been anything but, recently.

"What do you think it would be like to be inside a cloud?"

"Wet," I joke and she chuckles, though halfheartedly.

"I don't like to think of clouds as water. I like to think of them like cotton or cotton candy. Big fluffy shapes just floating through the sky."

I try to imagine her world. "There would be little cherubs that lived on top?"

She nods. "And everything would be warm. Light shades of pink and baby blue or soft orange."

"What would the cherubs eat?"

Her face twists into a grimace and I cringe thinking about dinner last night.

"I'm sorry," I whisper when she doesn't answer. She shakes her head.

"There are worse things."

"It was pretty bad."

"Stop," she snaps, cutting me off. I fall back to the ground, looking up at the sky. The clouds are fusing, turning everything a dull shade of gray.

And so the fun stops.

"I hate her, Hannah . . ."

I believe her. Sometimes, I think I hate her, too.

"I hate her for what she is. For how she treats us. For what she did to Dad."

"She didn't do anything to Dad. He died of a heart attack."

"She pushed him to it," she murmurs darkly, pursing her lips. "All her stupid rules and ambition. She doesn't care about us. We're nothing more than pawns to her."

Worried, I look around us. No one's near. The gardener is on the other side of the house. Mom's gone for the week on vacation with her "friend" June, and the nanny she insists we keep on, even though Missy and I are nineteen, is inside, knitting.

We're completely alone.

"I . . . I hate her, too."

Missy's eyes, brown like chocolate, slip over my face, studying me. The face that mirrors her own, while looking nothing like it at the same time.

Yin and yang.

"For what she does to you," I whisper.

It feels like uttering a death threat against the king in Tudor England.

"And you."

Guilt washes through me. I've suffered Mom's punishments, but . . . never anything as bad as Missy.

"Yeah, me too. You get the worst of it, though."

She rolls her eyes, looking back at the clouds.

"It's because I'm different."

"You're too much alike," I correct, matter-of-fact. "Both intelligent. Both driven and brave."

She side-eyes me. "It's because I don't listen to her. You do. That makes you brave in my book. Smart. Doing stuff you don't want to so you don't have to live through whatever she dishes out. Hell, half the punishments you endure are because you take the fall for me."

I shake my head. "I'm just scared. Not brave."

Missy shakes her head. Sometimes, I wish I could be as brave as Missy. Stand up for myself and what I know is right. I wish I wasn't afraid of the dark. My own shadow. The sound of our mother's voice when she's angry.

"Why don't you come back to college with me? You can reapply. Pick a different major. Something you'll actually like."

"College isn't for me."

"But . . . what are you going to do?"

She shrugs, a small smile creeping onto her face. "Disappear." She sucks in a deep breath, letting it slip out slowly. "Maybe I'll turn into a bird and fly far, far away from sunny California. Maybe go somewhere frigid cold where no one would ever think to look."

"Please don't," I murmur. "At least not without saying goodbye, first."

She's quiet for a moment listening to the birds chirp and watching as the clouds darken overhead. I listen to the sounds of the neighborhood around us, someone mowing their grass down the road. The cars driving past, just outside the wall.

Our prison wall.

"You're so dramatic," Missy chuckles, brushing the moment off. "I'm not going anywhere."

"You sure?" I'm not sure I believe her. Missy doesn't make idle threats.

But . . . she lays her hand on top of mine and gives my fingers a soft squeeze.

"Of course. We're twins, remember?"

"What's that got to do with anything?"

She may think she's enigmatic, but I know her and I know when she's lying. She's going to leave someday and I'll have to make the choice to either go with her or stay and do as I'm told.

I close my eyes, letting the cool breeze quell the pressure behind my eyes. I refuse to cry because Missy wouldn't cry.

Distantly, thunder rumbles on the horizon and when I force my eyes open and look up at the sky, the clouds are dark . . . angry.

"What the hell?" I look around me because the leaves have changed. They're

brighter, more jagged. The hedgeline is unkempt and thorns protrude from between the leaves, daring me to touch them.

I reach for Missy's hand, but she's not there anymore. "Missy?"

"Hannah," she snickers from behind me and my heart nearly falls to my feet when I spin around and find her nestled among the thorns, a sinister smile on her lips that pulls her mouth into an inhuman grin. She holds out a little green bottle to me, the venomous liquid sloshing like syrup inside. "Just a little sip."

"No."

She takes a step toward me and I fall back, nausea pooling in my stomach as that grin widens even further.

"Are you awake, Hannah?"

"Come on . . ." Missy coos, the thorns digging through her flesh and tearing it until blood seeps out. She doesn't even seem to notice.

"Don't touch me," I snap, backing away from her. This isn't Missy. This is something else. My sister is gone, replaced with something cruel and violent and positively evil.

"Just a little sip and the demons will go away."

I scream when the voice sounds right behind me, and Missy steps toward me—

—And then a strong arm wraps around my waist and pulls me back.

"Hannah," a rough voice says in my ear, and a chill runs down my spine as I blink at the room around me. "Are you awake?"

I jump when a big hand grips my hip under the sheets.

That hand doesn't belong to me.

"You had a nightmare," Mason murmurs darkly, leaning forward and capturing my ear with his teeth. He releases it, presses soft kisses to the line of my jaw and though I struggle to understand just what the fuck is happening, I relax into him.

"Tell me about it," he murmurs darkly, continuing to nip and suck little pieces of my exposed flesh and I work to soothe my racing heart.

Unfortunately, waking up to find him in my bed does *not* make it easy.

"It was about—Wait, why are you here?"

I turn over onto my side to stare at him and I only realize the mistake I made after it's done. He's so handsome in this light, shrouded in the moonlight and the dim glow of the closet light I keep on every night. Like a Greek statue carved by a famous architect. Women would line the streets to stare at him for hours, begging the Gods to let their fantasies come to life.

"You texted me. Asked me to come back because you were scared. Remember?"

I swallow.

I did?

Listen, I had a glass of wine before bed and then that turned into half the bottle.

Conclusion—I'm a lightweight.

"Whatever's in your nightmares, little doe, I promise, I'm scarier," he murmurs, voice gruff. His hand slithers over my hip, down my thigh, and then, dangerously low below the hem of my nightgown. When his fingers find me, he hisses out through his teeth. "I'm going to fuck away your nightmares, Hannah."

I open my mouth, but I don't have a reply. My head says no. My body stomps her foot and *demands* that I say yes.

Still, as his thumb circles me, slipping my arousal over my clit, I find my head is a boring place to be, anyway.

Slowly, Mason slips down the bed, eyes flashing dangerously dark in the room before he presses my thighs apart with his shoulders, nestling between them and slipping my nightgown up over my hips.

"Keep your eyes on me."

"Holy shit!" I gasp, sitting bolt upright in bed.

I clutch a hand to my chest, my heart racing underneath my fingers as I look around my room.

Home. I'm home and . . . alone. I'm fucking alone.

On the nightstand, the bottle of wine I didn't even close up still sits.

That explains it.

It's with some annoyance I realize I'm incredibly hot . . . and turned on.

My nipples strain against my tank top, my panties are soaked and my skin is coated in a light sheen of perspiration.

Just like it would be if that dream was *actually* real.

Am I really that far gone that I'm having sex dreams now?

Growling under my breath, I reach for my phone, setting an alarm for three hours from now, when I'll have to get up for work. Still, as I lay down against the pillows, staring at the moonlight dancing across the wall in straight, perfect gashes from the blinds, I know I won't sleep a fucking wink.

Mason Carpenter's going to be the death of me.

If I thought going back to work was going to solve all my problems, I was dead wrong.

They're right there, glaring me in the face every time Mason's shirt hugs his broad shoulders a little too tight. Or the way he lifts the bottom to wipe the sweat off his brow, showcasing the chocolate syrup-worthy abs underneath.

It could also be the way his eyes follow me when I'm not watching.

The man either hates me . . . or he's having the same dirty thoughts I am. At this point, maybe both.

Either Mason enjoys the torture or he just likes to see me dirty, because when Puke and Ian are gone on lunch, he calls me out of the office to help him on a transmission because I'm "small enough to fit under the car".

I think it's just an excuse to torment me some more.

So . . . in the heat of the day, we circle each other in the garage, the only sound being the whir of a fan blowing hot around us. He's got me under the car—of course—while he gives instructions on how to do whatever it is I'm doing.

I'll be honest, I don't even know what it *is* that I'm supposed to be doing. I don't even know what a transmission does.

"I think I need a bigger size," I say annoyed, until I roll out from under the car and find him crouching down beside me, watching me like a psychopath.

Mason cocks a brow at me and my cheeks flame from that little implied nefarious smirk. Still . . . he doesn't move.

"You're quiet today."

"I was under the impression you enjoyed it when I was quiet." I'm finding it hard to keep the sarcastic tone out of my voice.

He's nearly dripping with enthusiasm.

"I didn't sleep well," I sigh. "Can I have a bigger socket?"

It's a wrench, but I've taken to calling different tools in the garage by the wrong names because I know it pisses him off.

"Why?" His eyes glint dangerously. I know he's thinking about the texts, but I don't have it in me to explain they come and go like a bad ex-boyfriend. You never know when they're going to show up, but when they do, you can bet they're going to make an ass out of themselves.

"I had a nightmare." Part of that is true. The part with Missy was definitely a nightmare. The part with Mason . . . *should* have been a nightmare because I haven't stopped thinking about it since I gave up on sleep around seven in the morning.

I'm playing with fire. Getting in over my head with a man who made it perfectly clear once, he wants a single shred of *nothing* to do with me. Not with any real substance, anyway.

Sure, he might want to fuck me, even though I *know* he hates it. He might even find he cares about me a little more than he would like to let on.

At the end of the day, I'm nothing more than a nuisance to him, and the day I let myself fall back into the swirling vortex that is Mason

Carpenter is the day I may as well give my women's rights card away.

I'm just another girl to him. Even *if* he makes me feel like I'm the only girl in the world when he looks at me.

"What was the nightmare about?"

I freeze, my entire body filling with ice despite the heat in the garage.

I'm not going *there* with Mason. About any of it.

"I'll get it myself," I grumble, stretching as far as I can to grab a bigger wrench. Mason makes no move to help me and I slide back under the car, hoping that maybe if I ignore him hard enough, he'll just give up.

Unfortunately, Mason's not the give-up type.

"Hannah." His voice is laced with a heavy darkness that sends a ripple of ice down my spine. I don't want to think about last night. How he said he can't protect me if I don't tell him everything. I didn't want to drag him into this in the first place, but I had to because he's the only freaking person on this planet willing to help me.

It's . . . dangerous. I know it. He has to, by this point.

As crude and grumpy as he can be, there's a soft side to Mason. I've seen it a few times. When he took me home after he watched my mother bust my lip. When he picked me up that very first time on the side of the road, soaking wet and crying.

When he kissed me like I was fragile, but his to break as he pleased.

"Why do you care?" I snap, using all my might to try and force the stubborn bolt I'm working on to move. Macho man must have put this bolt on the car because it's stuck like it's cemented in place. Or I'm just weak.

"I don't."

Okay, ouch.

"Rude. Why bother asking then?"

I roll my eyes, but before they even make a complete loop, the creeper is dragged out from under the car so fast, I drop the wrench to the concrete beside me. It clambers to the floor, the sound echoing in the air around us.

The asshole just *dragged* me out from under the car.

And consequently, right between his legs.

God . . . Universe . . . Mother nature? Whoever's out there, please don't let me make a fool of myself.

He leans forward, resting his hand on the side of the car, and for a split second, I thank God it's painted black. Otherwise . . . what was I rambling about, again?

"What was the nightmare about?"

This time, his voice is so low, I can barely hear him over the fan. His eyes are like the storm of the century, threatening destruction and I'm the idiot chasing it. His gaze travels over me, licking a line of heat from the center of my breasts in my tank top, all the way up to my eyes, before settling there.

His face is a few inches from mine, his breath warm on my skin and all I can think about is how that stubble on his cheeks would feel against my inner thighs.

My grandmother is probably rolling over in her grave.

"You," I whisper, and he doesn't move for a moment, save for the tick in his jaw.

He's thinking.

"What about me?"

Slowly, I shake my head. I will take that dream to the grave.

Unfortunately, Mason doesn't seem on board with that plan.

He leans closer, his lips hovering over mine. He's not even kissing me, more like stealing my breath away until all I can taste is the mint from his toothpaste, the smoke from the afternoon cigarette he sneaks every day, and something so uniquely him, it's addicting.

"Things I really shouldn't be thinking about you."

His small, amused smile is enough to make my stomach drop to my toes. His lips brush mine, just the smallest of touches. The lightest kiss I've ever had, yet, as soon as he touches me, the world lights on fire.

"You drive me fucking crazy," he murmurs against my lips and I can't tell if he meant to say it out loud or not.

I let out a shaky breath, completely resigning myself to the fact that I'm doing something I shouldn't.

So, since the damage is already done, I close the distance between us, kissing him lightly before pulling away. He doesn't let me, following me until my head falls back to the creeper, and his lips stay locked with mine.

Slowly, like he's savoring me, his tongue tangles with mine and my body melts into a puddle on the floor from the groan that reverberates through him.

There's no love in his kiss. It's pure sex. Uninhibited, volatile, soul-stealing sex.

"*Fuck*," he rasps and a shiver rolls through me.

And I want every bit of it.

Until a throat clears.

I jump, almost bashing my head into Mason's and he sits up on his knees, glowering at the person in the doorway.

I scramble away from him like we're forbidden lovers caught in the act as none other than Mila Carpenter steps further around the car.

Oh, shit.

"What?" Mason snaps and she rolls her eyes.

"You really forgot?"

My stomach sinks, the overwhelming emotion of guilt surfacing.

"Hi, I'm Mila," she greets, holding out her hand. I look down at my own greasy one and she chuckles, taking mine anyway and shaking it. "Mason's little sis—"

She stops. Her eyes go wide and her mouth clamps shut.

Awkward tension builds in the air and for a moment, I think about leaping out the window in the garage door.

She knows.

Of course, she knows.

"Mason," Mila says, voice higher than usual. She looks to Mason, who hangs like a dark cloud over my shoulder. "You didn't tell me you were dating Hannah."

"We aren't together," I say at the same time Mason says, "Didn't know I had to."

"Looked pretty together to me," Mila mumbles. "Sorry, Hannah. I just thought you were someone else for a moment."

Yeah, the woman who helped rip your family to shreds . . .

"It's okay. No worries."

Mila smiles, albeit a little tight-lipped, and turns back to her brother.

I can't blame her for being apprehensive. She has no reason to trust me or even to be nice to me. For all she knows, I could be the same as Missy, ready to tear into her brother the same way Missy and Marcus tore into each other. She doesn't know me.

"We need to leave. We have to be there in half an hour and you know traffic in the city's going to be hell."

"Just tell Mom I forgot. I've got a car to finish."

"I can finish," I volunteer, even though I have no idea what I'm doing. Mason shoots me a warning look. Somehow, he manages to pack more heat into the look than he could if he covered me in gasoline and lit a match.

"I'm not leaving you here."

He says it so quiet, I almost think I imagined it before Mila's eyes dart between us.

"Is there something going on?"

"Nothing that concerns you," Mason says before I can say anything.

He stalks to the shop sink to wash his hands and Mila follows him, hands on her hips. I stifle a laugh. She's feisty and she doesn't take Mason's shit.

I like her.

"You're coming because it will make Mom happy to see you. Even Bailey will be there. Well, in Zoom-form, but nonetheless."

I don't ask because I don't want to pry, so I busy myself with cleaning up some of the tools we've left out, my lips still burning from that kiss.

Well—my whole body burning.

I've kissed Mason Carpenter before. It was mind-blowing, but it cost me. This time, with no cameras around to catch us and nothing standing in the way . . . it was life-changing.

Or maybe I'm just being dramatic because he's hot.

Part of me wonders just how far it would have gone if Mila hadn't shown up. The other, more rational part is happy it didn't.

Want to kiss the only person willing to help you locate your sister goodbye? Sleep with them.

Mila shakes her head, stepping past me on her way to the door.

"So, Hannah, how long have you been in town?" she asks, leaning back against the shop cart.

"Uh—a couple weeks." I clear my throat, hoping she can't see the distress in my face.

"Oh, wow. Tired of Sacramento?"

"Yeah . . . just needed a change, I guess."

God, why did I say that?

"Well, I'm sure your mother misses you. You guys always seemed like such a close-knit family."

"Enough," Mason grits, rejoining us. His presence feels like electricity zapping at my skin. "Let's go."

"I was just speaking to her," Mila says innocently.

"Well, don't." He puts an arm on her shoulder and steers her toward the door.

She rolls her eyes but complies by marching toward the exit. "It was nice seeing you again, Hannah."

"You too," I call, but Mason hangs back.

He shakes his head before turning back to me. "Lock the door," he says, handing over a key. "And don't open it until Ian and Puke get back."

"Yes, Daddy."

His nostrils flare at my attempt at sarcasm and under different circumstances, I would laugh.

You know, if I hadn't been prepared not even ten minutes ago to have sex with him on the dirty garage floor.

"We're finishing this conversation later. I'll pick you up at nine."

Fuck. I forgot about the sex club.

I will *not* be finishing this conversation later, but I let him think that just so he'll leave. Having him around is fucking with my head.

With one last lingering glance, I watch him go, the closing door bringing about a finality that rattles me to my core.

Mason Carpenter just kissed me. Again. And for real this time.

Me . . . a sweaty, greasy mess and the sister to enemy number two.

And he kissed me like he was starved for a taste.

CHAPTER *Seventeen*

HANNAH

Rummie's looks like shit during the day.

Stepping out of my little yellow bug, it's easy to see the years of wear and tear on the old building that's not prevalent during the day. The iron bars are suddenly glaring you in the face, as is the group of thugs that stands off to the side of the building, talking in hushed tones.

This is the part of Inglewood everyone talks about. The rough part.

I've seen the rest of it. It's not bad. The people here are some of the nicest I've ever met and even with the evidence of poverty, no one has a problem helping each other out. There's a community around the garage and luckily, they've accepted Mason and his business as their own. No one bothers the shop.

Here, it's evident that people don't care as much. At least not the people hanging around a dingy bar on a Friday afternoon.

I slip inside, thanking the heavens it's not as crowded as it was the other night. There's no evidence of Bill and his gally of biker friends, no snobby women to belittle me, and no handsy men to grope my ass as I make my way through the dark bar toward the person I came to see.

"H—hello." I'm ashamed that my voice cracks, so I square my shoulders. I'm Hannah freaking Gaines. I've been speaking to people my entire life.

The brunette's chocolate-brown eyes narrow on me and a smirk pulls on her lips.

"Been wondering when you would be back, Red."

She nods to the stool in front of her and I slip into the seat while she grabs a glass, raising a brow expectantly.

"Um . . . just water, thanks."

She shoots me another look but concedes and slides a bottle of water across the scuffed wood bar at me.

"So, I take it you aren't here for the drinks, then?"

I take a drink, willing my nerves to calm down. No easy feat considering I just had the object of every single one of my dirty fantasies tongue down my throat an hour ago.

I'm afraid I'll have a permanent stutter in my voice for the rest of my life.

"No. I actually came to see you. I never caught your name the other night."

If suspicion were a physical thing, it would present itself as her twin.

"Britt," she murmurs, shaking my hand with the power of an ox. "Look, whatever business you came here for, I can't help you. I just work here."

"I know," I nod, hoping I give a gentle smile and not a garish grin. Judging by the way she eyeballs me, I'm guessing I don't succeed. "I actually came to ask a favor."

"I don't give out favors."

"This isn't anything extraneous."

"I don't know what that word means," she counters and I grit my teeth.

Okay, so maybe I'm not the best at making friends, but Britt? She's five thousand times worse than me.

"Okay . . . let's start again. Hi, I'm Hannah and I need help dressing for a particular type of party because I am in over my head. Is that better?"

She purses her lips, clearly not amused with me.

"What kind of party?"

Fuck. "A weird one."

"I take it you and Mason made up?"

"Uh, yes, I suppose so. We're just friends." I can't fight the blush on my cheeks any more than I can fight my stomach doing a back flip from remembering the way he growled against my lips. "You know him well?"

She shrugs, washing a glass in the miniature sink in front of her.

"I know of him. Can't say I've ever talked to him."

"Oh, I was under the impression you were all friends."

She looks at me like I've lost my mind.

"Can't say we are. Though, he has come in here a few times with his—" she looks me up and down with a dramatic pause, "—women."

Of course, he has. And now she thinks I'm just another groupie, pining after the famed Mason Carpenter. The kiss wasn't that good.

Okay, it was, but that doesn't mean he's the man of all men.

"Sorry. I must have assumed."

She shakes her head. "Mason's hot and all. Don't get me wrong, but I like a more . . . emotionally developed type of man."

I start to tell her that Mason *is* emotionally developed, but think better of it. I'll keep *that* to myself.

"Well, what about clubs, do you know anything about those?"

She gives me a bored look.

"Spit it out, Red."

I wince, adjusting on the barstool. The thing's ricketier than a one-legged rocking horse.

"What about . . . sex clubs?"

She stares at me for a beat, cocking her brow before a devious smirk pulls on her lips.

"*You*, in a *sex club*?"

My cheeks flame with embarrassment and I hastily search the room to make sure no one else heard us. "Keep it down, okay?"

Britt snickers, grabbing a towel from the counter behind her to start drying the glasses she just washed.

"Now *that*, I would pay to see."

I resist the urge to roll my eyes. "I'm not a nun."

Her lips quiver, but she doesn't laugh. "No, but I'd venture to say you've never even given a blow job in public before."

Never given a blow job, anywhere *before.*

Unfortunately, my poker face is that of a child. She sees right through me.

"You've never . . ." Luckily her voice trails off, and when she must realize the depth of my lack of sexual experience, she nods slowly, pursing her lips and mulling it over like the world just offered her the most peculiar problem. "So, how'd you do it?"

I pause, staring at her in confusion and bewilderment. Oh, embarrassment's here for the ride, too.

"Come on," she chuckles, leaning forward and pressing her hands on top of the counter. "Mason Carpenter's head over fucking heels with you," she says, lowering her voice. "Are you a witch?"

"No," I snap, appalled by her insinuation. "And Mason's not in love with me. He's helping me with something and I'm working for him as payment."

"So, like prostitution."

"No," I huff. "Look, I need something I can wear to a sex club and you're the only person I know around here besides three greasy mechanics."

She looks around her as if she's trying to decide if I'm worth it or not.

"Look, you're a nice girl, Red. Real sweet . . ." She says it like one would when speaking to a child.

"But . . ."

She sighs, leaning back and searching my face like a disappointed mother.

"You're sure about this?"

No.

"Yes."

She sighs, rolling her eyes. "Jerry, I'm heading upstairs for a minute." The man at the other end of the bar playing solitaire nods, not even looking at her.

"Come on, Red," she says, taking my hand and leading me toward the back where the entrance to the apartment upstairs is. "Let's go play dress up."

"Where do you buy all this leather?"

Britt chuckles under her breath, tossing a skirt on the bed beside me.

"Stores, Hannah. Here." She hands me a top that may as well be lingerie and I stare at her.

"I can't wear this."

"You're going to a sex club. With a sex god. Wear the damned top."

I swallow down past the lump in my throat, holding it up to inspect it.

My mother would shit herself if she saw me in this . . .

"You know what? You're right."

"Told you, Red."

I resume petting her cat, Chester, who purrs loudly on the top of Britt's comforter beside me.

It's strange. Being in someone else's room. I feel like I barely know her, but in a lot of ways, I could see Britt and I getting along.

We're from different sides of the world, yet, at the end of the day, we're the same.

I can tell by her demeanor, she's had a rough upbringing. Maybe not the same as mine, but it wasn't peaches and cream.

"What's Mommy going to say when she sees her perfect daughter in leather and heels?"

I cringe. "Probably start a nuclear war."

"Thank God she doesn't have the keys to the kingdom," Britt mumbles from her closet before turning back over her shoulder. "No offense."

"None taken."

"What's it like?" she asks, resuming her search through a never-ending array of clothing. "Having a mother who's the governor of the entire state?"

"Lonely."

I know by the way she pauses, she wasn't expecting that answer. Finally, she comes back out of the closet and moves to her dresser. Chester curls up against my leg to take a nap.

"Surrounded by a crowd of people, but yet you still feel like you're all alone."

"People who only know me as her daughter and not as a person on my own."

She mulls that over for a moment as she flips through a bottom drawer of pants.

"Like working at a bar in the middle of this shithole part of town, but studying medicine at night?"

Now, it's my turn to be surprised.

"Medicine?"

She turns back to me. "That hard to believe, huh?"

"No," I rush but fall flat. "I'm sorry. I just wasn't expecting you to say that."

She shrugs. "It's alright. People don't like to better themselves anymore. At least, not as much as they used to."

"No," I agree. "Doctor, then?"

She shakes her head, handing me a pair of what I can only assume are leather pants. I'm getting quite the collection.

"Nurse. They're the real backbone of the industry."

"I don't disagree with you."

"The doctors get all the credit, but it's the nurses that really save lives. Sure, you've got your special circumstances, but where would those doctors be without the men and women behind them?"

"Like politics," I blurt before I can even think, but luckily, she nods along. "Sorry, my mother has an entire team making sure none of us fuck up her perfect image."

"Your mother does that all on her own. She doesn't need you to add to it, so she makes sure you're perfect."

I roll my eyes. "My mother's a saint in the media's eyes."

"The media, sure, but what about the streets? People don't like the way shit's going. I hear about it every time she comes on TV down at the bar."

"What are they saying?"

"She's a con artist," she shrugs. "I know she's your mother, but I get the feeling she isn't a very good one."

"She's not," I admit. "But . . . she's the only one I've got."

"That's where we're different. I cut my family off because they were a bunch of sexist assholes who thought I would never be able to do better for myself than living in some rundown trailer in Mississippi with roaches climbing down the walls and a man who beats me every night."

"I'm sorry that happened to you," I say because what else is there to say when someone lets that out?

"Don't be. It may not be much, but I've got Chester. My job. Only a couple months left and I can get the nursing job I've always wanted. Shit's rough for everyone, no matter their plight."

Her phone buzzes on the bed beside me and she groans.

"Time's up," she grimaces. "Means Jerry's probably got all of three customers and has decided he can't handle it."

I chuckle as she slips her phone into her back pocket.

"Well, I can't thank you enough. I'll return these as soon as possible. Clean."

"Don't bother," she waves, holding out a hand and pulling me to stand. "I never wear the shit, anyway. Just don't go getting into trouble. Those clubs can be rough."

"I can imagine," I grimace. "I've never been to a real club before, so I don't know how this will go."

"Well, I may have lied a bit earlier. I don't know Mason well, but I know him well enough that he won't let anything bad happen. Especially not to you."

I shake my head, chuckling humorously. "There's really nothing there. We're just working together."

She smirks, pulling me toward the door.

"For now."

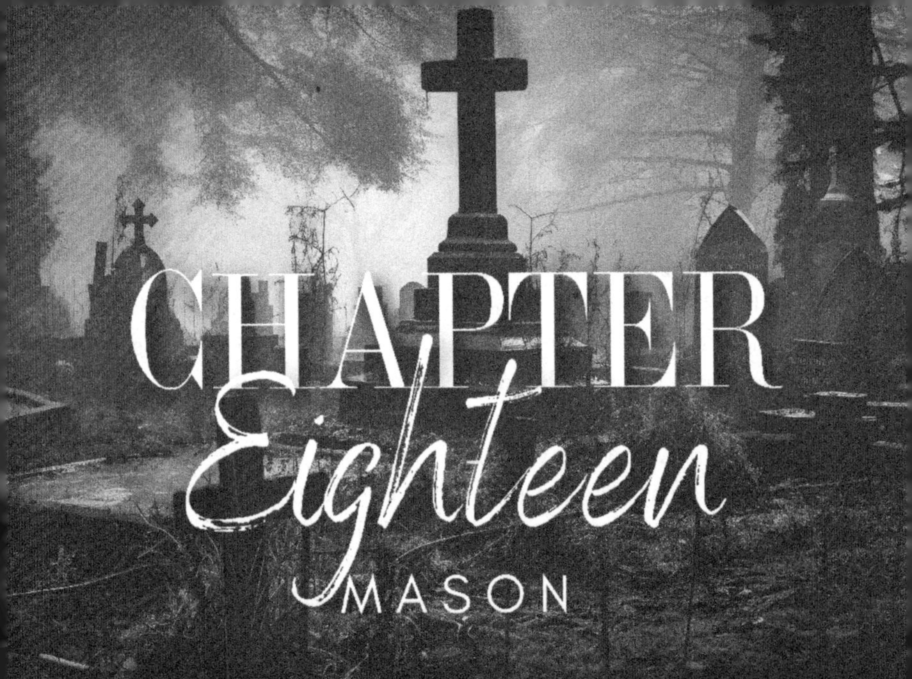

CHAPTER Eighteen

MASON

I think it's important for you all to remember you're a family, first. Your pasts can't erase that, but they *can* tear you apart."

Jesus. Fucking. Christ.

I've never been to therapy. Mom tried to force it on me because she thought it would help me after Dad's death, but I refused.

I mean, what's the point in paying some stranger to listen to my problems and give me the same regurgitated bullshit they do everyone else?

I only agreed to this because I know Mom's struggling. Since Parker went to prison, people have been showing up outside her new house; the press has been harassing her. Mila. Logan and Savannah even had a couple paparazzi show up, but Logan shut that shit down with a flash of his fancy FBI badge and a loaded 9mm.

No one's bothered me . . . yet. I'd like to keep it that way, so I keep my distance. I know it upsets Mom, but I knew Parker was bad news from the beginning.

If I had known what he was really into I would have killed him before he ever had the chance to hurt my sister.

Maybe that was my driving factor in helping Hannah. I could stop her from getting hurt. I could keep her safe and find Melissa Gaines in the process. Put an end to all of this.

At least . . . that's what I tell myself.

I shouldn't have kissed her. I shouldn't have touched her. I should have kept my distance like I'd planned, but once I got a taste of her, I couldn't stop.

Fuck . . . she's tastes like perfection. Sweet. Soft. Just like she always has.

I have no doubt in my mind shit would have spiraled out of control if Mila hadn't shown up. Out of all the stupid shit I've ever done, this obsession I seem to have with the governor's daughter is probably the most dangerous of all.

"Mason," Kenda, the therapist calls my name, staring me down across the room. "I haven't seen you for any of your one-on-one appointments."

"I don't need therapy."

"Mason," Mila grits quietly, but Kenda holds up her hand, silencing her.

"Can you tell me what goes through your mind when you think about coming to therapy?"

I shrug, leaning back in my chair. "A waste of money."

Kenda nods, scribbling something down on her pad.

I don't like it. I feel like I'm getting my brain picked over like a science experiment. And what the fuck is she writing, anyway?

"Perhaps you could give it a shot? One session, just to test the waters and if you don't like it, you can back out."

"Perhaps not."

Mom's eyes zero in on mine, but I ignore her. She's lucky I even came to her little family therapy session.

At a certain point, there's no repairing the damage that's been done. We've all been through fucking hell and survived. We should be celebrating. Not sitting here, talking about our *feelings* in a sterile office in the middle of a city built on false faces.

On the same side of that coin, just because Parker's out of the picture, it doesn't mean we're safe. My sisters are still being hunted. Mom's still getting unsettling letters. Fucking fingers in her damned mailbox.

Just because one snake's out of the garden, doesn't mean there isn't a whole fucking nest still laying in wait.

"Why don't Logan and Charlie have to be here?"

"While they've been impacted by your stepfather's actions, they haven't been in the direct line of fire," Kenda explains. "You and your sisters and mother have, so it's imperative that we discuss the negative ramifications of everything that transpired."

"Mason has never been comfortable speaking about his feelings," Savannah chimes. She's been relatively quiet through this whole session, even though, out of anyone, she was probably fucked over by Parker the worst.

"Don't see the need to. I know what I'm feeling."

"Do you?" Kenda asks, throwing it back at me in that professional manner that makes me feel like a damned kid again. "Your mother tells me you don't visit often."

"Or at all," Mila grumbles.

"I miss you, Mason," Mom whimpers, and I have to grit my teeth to keep from snapping at her and making it worse. "I just want to see you happy. Find a nice girl and settle down. Build a family. Get out of that dusty shop."

"Mom," Bailey warns from the tablet, but Mom can't be swayed.

"You don't have to live that life. You can do anything you want. You aren't tied to that place."

"I am."

"No, your father was and look where it got him."

"Dead?"

Everyone falls silent.

"Dead, Mom?" I challenge again. Tears brighten her eyes, but I don't care. I'm past caring. I cared for years when she left me with Gran because her husband didn't want me around. I cared when she missed my high school graduation. I cared when she tried to get Gran to sign Dad's garage away to her, so she could sell it, claiming it was a "poor investment".

Yeah, I'm way past fucking caring now.

"That's what you mean, right? Dad died and Parker's in prison, so now you want to control me? Where were you when I needed you? When Savannah needed you? Fucking Bailey, even? Too busy wallowing in your own self-pity because your husband was a sociopath and a cheater instead of doing something about it."

"Let's all take a breath," Kenda tries, but I'm done taking breaths in her little circle jerk of trauma.

"That shop is mine. Just like that house and just because you decided it wasn't enough for you, doesn't mean it isn't for me."

"If that's what you want," Mom says, voice cracking with emotion I'm really not in the mood to dive into.

"What I *want* is to get the fuck out of here," I snap, my temper right on the edge. I don't like being interrogated. I had enough of it when they arrested Parker.

"I think it's important we all remember why we're here," Kenda interjects when things grow tense. "To uncover that past trauma and dissolve it so we can have a happy union of family. This is good," she nods to me, offering me a gentle smile, even though I feel anything but right now. "There's obviously some tension here, dating back to childhood. I think that it would be worth exploring."

What the fuck does that even mean?

"Mason, what are your thoughts on Mr. Parker?"

"You don't want to ask that question."

No one says a word. If I had my way, Parker would have been skinned alive. He hurt my sister. My mother. I failed to protect them and there's that sick part of me that believes it's my fucking fault he was able to get to Savannah in the first place.

"I do want to hear your thoughts. It may give some insight into your stance on this situation."

"You really want to know?"

She nods.

I chuckle darkly, sitting forward. "I hope he rots in that jail cell until they have to scrape him up off the floor with a shovel."

She stares at me a beat, concern pooling in her eyes.

Funny. That's the only emotion I've seen from her all day.

Ting . . .

And just like that, time's up.

I stand before anyone can stop me. I need to get the fuck out of this stuffy little office before I say some shit that will get me locked in a padded room.

"Mason, wait!" Savannah calls as I exit the building Kenda's office is in. The heat of the day washes over me and sweat dots my brow as I search for my truck.

Then, I remember . . . Mila and Raul, one of Mom's drivers picked me up.

Fuck.

"Can you just stop running, you big asshole?" Savannah pants, catching up to me when I stop on the sidewalk.

I need a beer. Or to hit something. Or to fuck my pretty little receptionist.

Maybe all three.

"What, Savannah?"

While Bailey and I are close, Savannah and I couldn't be further apart. She's always been cold. I've always been colder. Where she's starting to open up after everything happened, I'm shutting everyone out because once they see what's inside my fucked-up head, they'll never want me around, anyway.

"Mom got another letter."

Of course, she did.

"What about this time?"

She shakes her head, watching a car pass us by on the road. "It was encrypted. Logan took it in to be cracked. But I think it has something to do with Melissa."

Prince didn't tell me that.

"Good. Maybe they'll kill her and save the rest of us some trouble."

"What about Parker?"

I whirl on her, the mention of his name like a shot of fire in my veins. "What about him?"

Savannah remains unfazed. "He's dying. He might have some inkling to where she's at, but he won't talk to Logan."

I shake my head. I know what she's asking. "No."

"He knows things, Mason. Things that could be useful. He won't talk to any of us, but maybe if you go, he'll let something slip."

"You sound like Prince."

"I *sound* like I'm right. We still don't have anything on the Brethren and if someone's got her, that must mean they're out to get Mom, too. We have to do something. Please just think about it."

"I said no."

"You could be putting a lot of people in danger."

"What do you want me to do, Savannah?" I snap and she falls back a step, her blue eyes filling with tears.

Goddammit.

"Look, whoever is doing this, I'm sure your fiancé will catch them. He found you, didn't he?"

"Are you still mad about that?"

"I'm not mad about shit. I'm glad he found you."

Her brow furrows and she takes that signature Savannah attitude stance. "But you're mad at yourself. Mason, you couldn't have stopped what happened any more than I could. It wasn't a playground bully. It was life or death."

I don't have a response for that.

"Look, I have to go. Call me if something comes up," I murmur and she pauses for a moment, clearly expecting me to say something else.

I can't.

I move toward the black Bentley when it pulls up to the curb, but before I can reach for the handle, Savannah wraps her arms around me from behind, hugging me.

"I'm not mad at you," she whispers.

And before I can even process what she said, she's gone.

"Spit it out, Mila."

She's been quiet since we left the therapist's and Mila quiet is never a good sign. Kid used to grumble in her sleep as a baby.

She turns to regard me, opens her mouth, closes it, opens it again, and takes a deep breath.

Jesus Christ.

"You going to tell Mom?"

"No . . ." she says after a long moment and turns back to the window beside her.

"She's different," I murmur. I can't tell if I'm talking to myself or her. "She's the polar opposite of Melissa—"

"*Don't* . . . say her name." She grimaces as if Melissa Gaines is Bloody Mary. Say her name three times and she pops out with a knife. "I'm not judging her."

"You're judging me, though, right?"

Mila cocks her head, shooting me a look.

"Not everything's about you, Mason," she snaps. It's the most un-Mila thing I've ever seen. She glares at me for a moment, but then her face crumples and she's back to that same resigned look of reproach. "I'm sorry. I didn't mean to yell at you."

"Talk to me. What's going on?"

She shakes her head, blonde waves falling around her shoulders.

"I don't know. I just . . . I have this bad feeling that something's going to happen and I can't . . . I can't stop thinking about how we all keep pretending everything's over."

"It's not," I murmur darkly. In fact, we've barely made it to halftime.

"She's with you because of Melissa . . . isn't she?"

I grit my teeth, back straightening against the leather seat of the Bentley.

"She is."

"She's trying to save her while you're trying to bring her down. Isn't that ironic?" Mila murmurs, brows furrowed. "Does she know?"

"About how deep this all goes?"

Mila nods in acquiescence.

"No. I want her to find out on her own."

"If it were me, I think I'd want a little head's up. Before I went through all the trouble of trying to find her."

I shake my head, staring at the black divider separating us from the front.

"Not Hannah. She'd save her just so she could turn her in the right way."

Mila smiles softly. "She's better than me. I wouldn't be able to call you my brother if you did any of those horrible things."

I can't say I disagree with her, though Hannah's always had a soft spot for damn near anyone. She'd try to rescue a worm if it meant it could do whatever worms do for another day.

"She knows the kind of person her sister is. She just doesn't want to believe it."

"You like her." It's not a question.

I clench my teeth because I can't deny there's some sick part of me that wants to claim Hannah for myself. Shatter her and put her back together so she'll never leave. Make her fall in love with me.

I'm a sick fuck, but . . . aren't we all a little obsessed with someone at the end of the day.

"If you're worried about what Mom or Savannah or even Bailey will think . . ." Her gray eyes flash with something I can't place. "Don't. They've all had their chance at happiness. We haven't."

Jesus. This is getting too much like a Hallmark movie for me.

"When it's all said and done, Mila, we'll just be two different people. I'll stay at my shop in Inglewood and Hannah Gaines will go back to being California's princess."

It tastes like fucking battery acid coming out of my mouth.

"Don't you ever get tired of pretending you don't care?"

"Don't you?" I challenge and she purses her lips.

"I'm not running from anything. Or anyone."

"And Bailey wasn't planning to go back to New Orleans just like Savannah wasn't falling in love with Prince. Just like *you* aren't hung up on Cross."

She narrows her gaze on me, cheeks flaming red. "Don't pretend like you understand me."

"I understand you better than you think because you're just like me."

She rolls her eyes. "I am not."

"Pretend all you want, Mila. You and I don't belong in their world any more than Hannah belongs in mine."

"What if she did, though? Belong in your world. You know her so well, what if she hates it as much as we do?"

I mull it over for a moment. Hannah in my world. Cooking dinner with me in my little kitchen every day. Watching movies on a rainy Saturday.

Curling up against me every night.

"She doesn't, though," I murmur as we pull up in front of my house. It doesn't escape me that in a couple hours, I have to meet Hannah to take her to the Inner Sanctum.

The last place on Earth I want her to see.

"You good to go home?"

She smiles softly. "I'll be fine."

I nod, climbing out of the back and stretching my legs. I'm too tall for the back of the Bentley. Another way I don't "fit" into this world.

"Mason," Mila calls before I shut the door. When I look back at her, her expression is guarded. "I trust your judgment. You always do the right thing."

She's wrong. I've tried to do the right thing my entire life, but this time . . . I'm not sure I want to. If giving Hannah up is the right thing, I don't know if I can.

If I'm toxic, she made me this way.

Now she gets to live with the consequences.

"Have a good night, Mila."

Hannah's house is pink.

Fucking pink. Like pink lemonade on a hot summer day.

My truck looks out of place up front, but as I stand on the little porch, knocking on her door, I realize, so do I.

I've always been out of place in her world, just as she is in mine. We weren't meant to meet. I know it. The fucking universe knows it and it reminds me every time I'm forced to remember she's Melissa Gaines' sister.

The forbidden fruit.

Thank fuck Mila didn't mention what she walked in on at the therapy session. I have a feeling Hannah would be the final nail in the coffin for Mom and me. She'd see it as a betrayal, even if Hannah wasn't the one who partook in the events that nearly destroyed us. She's related to Melissa, and that's enough in Mom's eyes.

I knock again when Hannah doesn't answer and finally, I hear footsteps on the other side of the door just before she opens it. I'm still tense from the gladiator-style family therapy session, and I'd rather be alone, but I gave her my word.

And I know she'd go by herself if I didn't go with her.

I have half a mind to tell her to hurry up, so we can get this over with, but when I see her . . . I stop dead in my fucking tracks.

Bare toes with red polish, tanned legs leading to a silky black robe that sits entirely too fucking high on her thighs. Lace from her bra at the center and finally, those fucking freckles that almost did me in years ago.

Fuck me.

"Hey," her cheeks flame, but she doesn't move to open the door.

"Are you going to let me in, Hannah?" My voice is just as dark as my mood, though I can't tell if it's lifted since she opened the door or gotten worse at the sight of what I can't have.

Probably a bit of both.

"Oh, sorry," she chuckles nervously, stepping out of the way to let me inside.

"Here," I murmur, holding out the bouquet of white daisies I felt the need to bring. Now that I'm here, I'm deciding I should have thrown them out the fucking window.

She pauses, cheeks brighter than I've ever seen them.

"I thought this wasn't romantic," she teases and I shrug.

"It's not."

"So you always show up at a girl's house with flowers and take her to kinky sex clubs?"

I swear to fucking God . . .

"You plan to go in that?"

I can't lie. The thought of anyone else seeing her like this pisses me off more than I'd like to admit.

I step closer, the scent of her perfume wafting over me and very lightly, reach out to rub the bottom hem of her robe, right over her thigh. Goosebumps raise on her skin from my fingers and I can practically hear her heartbeat hammering in her chest, but I don't step away.

Neither does she.

Her lips part slightly over a breath when my fingers dance across her bare skin, and her eyes go half-lidded. Hazy green in the late setting sun.

"Maybe I will."

"Go get dressed." *Before I spank your ass.*

Forcing myself back from her, I move into the living room. At least it's not entirely pink.

The house is warm, decorated in rich colors and all manner of different patterns. A stark contrast to the sterile mansion her mother owned in Bel Air and a hell of a lot smaller.

Funnily enough, it suits her better than the sprawling estate ever did.

Hannah moves into the kitchen to get a vase before coming back to set her flowers on the coffee table. There's a picture on the mantel, that catches my eye. Hannah and Melissa. Young, probably teenagers. It's easy to see their twins when they're right beside each other.

"I just wanted a reminder," Hannah says softly from behind me. The room shifts and the tension could be cut with a knife. She chuckles quietly, though it lacks amusement. "It's hard to forget she was that girl once. Happy . . . real."

"She's still real," I murmur, turning away from it. It's hard to look at the woman I've been obsessed with for years, standing next to the one I've wanted dead for a long fucking time. "She's just a murderer."

"She's still a person," Hannah says quietly. "She's still my sister."

"And she shouldn't be." I don't know what makes me say it, but it's true. No one as good as Hannah should ever be related to a monster like fucking Melissa Gaines. "She doesn't deserve to be."

Hannah watches me for a moment, biting the inside of her lip in thought.

"I'm not sure we're all that different. She just acted on her dark thoughts."

I shake my head, gritting my teeth. She's too fucking good for this world. Too fucking good for me.

"You don't have a dark bone in your body, Hannah," I murmur under my breath.

She's silent for a moment, watching me.

"And if I did? If I did those horrible things she's accused of."

Fuck.

I don't have an answer for her. In my mind, I want to say I'd kill her. In my chest I know I fucking couldn't.

Ironic, isn't it?

"I'll go get dressed now," she says quietly.

And then she goes to her room and shuts the door, leaving me with nothing to do but think.

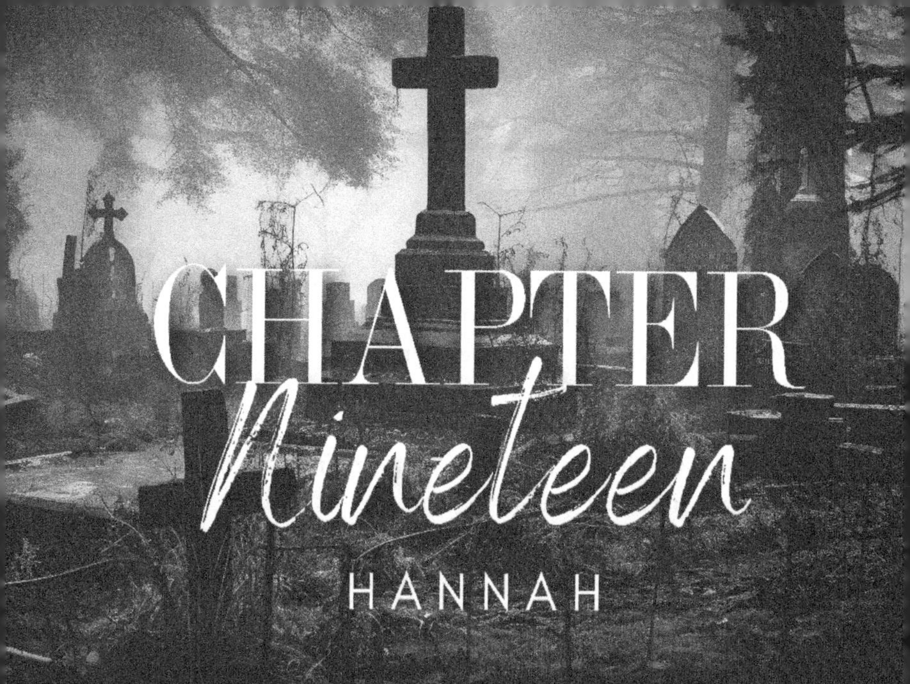

CHAPTER *Nineteen*

HANNAH

What does one even wear to a sex club?

Thank God for Brit, or this *Mission Impossible* trip wouldn't be happening. The clothes she lent me are strewn across the bed, but to be honest, I have no idea how I'm going to get any of them on.

Black leather, lace, chains, spikes for "flavor" as she'd said, though the spikes might not be a bad way to keep people away from me.

Get it together, Hannah.

I pull back to stare at myself in the full-length mirror in nothing but my black lacy bra and a leather skirt that hugs every. Single. Curve.

I feel . . . sexy? Alluring? Maybe there's something to be said about putting on the leather skirt, but I don't think my ass has ever looked this good. I slip on the black lacy corset top, but . . . like everything else in the pile, I need help to get it on.

Somehow, I feel like that was intentional.

Like I'm greeting a wild bear, I crack the door to my room.

"Mason, can you help me?"

There's a pause and then I hear the shuffling of his heavy boots on the hardwood floor.

God, help me.

He looks like sex incarnate tonight. Black button-up that showcases the tattoos on his forearms. Dark jeans. Dark eyes.

Right now, those eyes are aimed at the black corset top.

"I can't get the back hooked," I mumble, cheeks hotter than the sidewalk outside.

He doesn't reply save for a flash of something across his eyes, so I turn around. It's better than facing him.

Carefully, he steps forward, and I hold my breath while he hooks the small clasps together at my spine. His hands brush my bare skin and a shiver ghosts through me.

Goddamn body.

He makes a small sound and if I didn't know better, I'd say he was *chuckling*. Asshole.

He lingers longer than he should and both of us hold completely still, save for the buttoning of my top. Finally, when it's done, he steps back as if I'd burned him.

The top is tight. I know it's supposed to be, but I'm dangerously close to having the knock-off version of a Janet Jackson nip slip.

"Thank you," I breathe, my skin buzzing with electricity where he'd touched me.

He looks around the room and suddenly, I'm hyper-aware that Mason Carpenter is not only in my Malibu Barbie DreamHouse, but also in my bedroom. Like, where I sleep. With a bed. Where people have sex and do other naughty things.

Having him in this space feels too . . . intimate for Mason and me.

He's always been the unobtainable. The man I couldn't have and the one I could never get out of my head. I'm falling deeper and deeper into a hole I don't think I'll be able to climb out of.

Mason Carpenter is quicksand, sucking me in. My drowning is

inevitable.

I shake my head, forcing myself to slip on the black *Gianvito Rossi* boots that are higher than anything I've ever worn before. I bought them a year ago when I was feeling particularly rebellious before one of Mom's never-ending events that I was expected to attend.

I never got the chance to wear them because I chickened out before I left. Now, I imagine if my mother could see me, she would either disown me or lock me in the closet for a week.

I look like sex in a Sunday hat, but . . . when in Rome.

I turn around and find Mason leaning against the door frame. His gaze travels over me, down to the heeled boots on my feet, over the skin-tight leather, to the top, and finally, my eyes. His gaze burns a path in its wake and his jaw ticks, as if he's making note of something.

I don't know if I like the sound of that.

"Don't look at my ass," I grumble quietly when he helps me climb in the truck.

"Too late," he murmurs, and just when my mouth falls open, he shuts the door on me.

"Your feet are going to be killing you by the time this is over," he grumbles when he climbs in the driver's seat. I swear, now that we're forced to be in the small cab together, all my senses are on high alert. His scent, the way his button-up hugs his shoulders. The way those jeans look on his butt—I know, I know . . . hypocritical of me.

Heat washes through me and I find that even though I'm wearing less clothing than I have in a long, long time, I'm incredibly warm.

Maybe asking him to take me to a sex club was a bad idea.

"Hopefully this won't take long."

He peeks at me as he drives. It's then I notice the thick veins in his hands. How have I never noticed how hot Mason's hands are?

No. Stop it. We aren't that desperate, Hannah. They're just hands.

Big, rough, calloused, working man hands with sexy veins, but hands, all the same.

"Worried?"

"No. Why?"

"You look it."

"I think I look fine."

He peeks at me, his gaze traveling over the black lace at my midriff, but he doesn't say anything.

"Thank you, by the way. For taking me. And for bringing me flowers. And for not saying anything to your sister. At least in front of me."

That last part sucks because I know, without a doubt what was going through Mila's mind when she saw me. Everything Missy had done was my fault because I was the one present. I'm an extension of her and it sure doesn't help that we're twins.

He chuckles darkly, but he doesn't respond. The tension in the cab hangs thick in the air between us. So thick you could smear it on toast.

The buzz that's always there when he's around is suddenly tenfold. Maybe because of our kiss, but maybe because we're going to a sex club. Either way . . . my heart hammers against my chest at the way he looks at me.

Like he might swallow me whole.

"So what's the deal with this place? You act like you've been before."

"Once," he grits, fingers tightening on the wheel.

Uh-oh.

"And?"

"And, what?"

I roll my eyes, breathe out a sigh and lean back in the seat. Mason's eyes stay locked on the road, but I can tell he's tuned into my every move, just as I am his.

Interesting.

"How was it?"

He takes the highway, toward downtown, his tongue running

over his teeth.

"You'll see."

"I'm serious, Mason. Is there anything I need to know before we enter the lion's den?"

He cocks a brow. "Nothing is off-limits here. Piss, the illusion of rape, blood," he says roughly. "Don't touch anyone, you don't want to get hurt. Don't let anyone touch you, you don't want to get hurt. Don't drink the water. Good enough for you?"

"Why would it matter if anyone touches me? You said it yourself. This isn't a date."

He chuckles darkly, running a thumb across the stubble over his lips. I briefly, like a creep, wonder what it would feel like against my skin, again.

"Try it."

The Inner Sanctum is located in an old brick warehouse downtown. It's covered in graffiti, as are most buildings in the area, and from the outside, despite the bumping beat of music, you would think it was just a decrepit old warehouse.

Everything is dark in this area of LA. Bleak. Trash lines the sides of the road and some people sleep in the dark corners of businesses closed for the day. I want to help them because I know the charities Mom started are supposed to be helping people like this, but like most things government, it's all smoke and mirrors.

Unfortunately, I have a job to do.

And I need answers.

"Doesn't look like a club," I murmur while Mason pays to park across the street and pulls the truck into a spot in the dimly lit parking garage.

Now that we're here, my stomach is in knots. I don't want to go in, but I know I have to if I ever want a clue regarding my sister's whereabouts.

Why did she have to be so damned difficult? Why couldn't she enjoy cupcake parties? I've never heard of one, but I think it would be a hell of a lot more enjoyable than a bunch of sweaty bodies belonging to God only knows who.

I mean, think of the possible STDs.

Mason puts the truck in park and I notice the way his hand clenches around the steering wheel, his knuckles turning white.

He doesn't want to be here, either.

"Maybe we should just go home."

Mason eyes me with that damned bored look I wish I could slap off his face.

"You won't get answers that way."

"I don't have any idea that anyone here knows anything."

"Only one way to find out."

"And then . . . he's gone," I grumble when he climbs out, coming around to open my door before I can even extract myself from the seat belt. "A gentleman, even at fetish clubs."

His jaw ticks, but he doesn't respond. He starts toward the exit, but when I don't budge, he reaches back and intertwines our fingers. It's the most intimate, non-intimate thing that's ever happened to me.

"I don't know about this, Mason," I whisper when a car door down the line opens and a girl gets out, wearing only a pair of sky-high heels and a thin strap of material that looks like the female version of a banana hammock, covered by a fishnet dress. "I don't look like I belong here."

The muscles in his jaw feather and his eyes flare with a dangerous heat. Slowly, he steps toward me, his big chest backing me into the truck. He leans in and I think he's going to kiss me, but before his lips touch mine, he slips lower to murmur in my ear.

"You're the sexiest woman here, little doe." The scratch of his stubble against my jaw sends a shiver down my spine and for just a moment, I forget where we are. At least long enough to rest my hand on the muscles of his abs, which, might I add, are hard as hell underneath his button-up.

He pulls back enough to look at me, his gaze traveling from my eyes, down to my lips, and back. To anyone else, we'd look like any other couple. Really, I'm trying not to have a panic attack at the prospect of what we might find out inside.

"What if someone . . . I don't know. Touches me?" I feel selfish asking about myself, but the thought of someone else's hands on me makes my skin crawl.

I'll do damn near anything for my sister. I won't do that, though.

In the darkness of the parking garage, Mason looks like a romance novel mob boss. Tattoos, the dark glint in his eyes . . . the way that stare threatens to eat me alive.

"No one will be touching you."

He's so sure of it, I almost believe him.

"And you?"

He chuckles darkly, reaching up and brushing a loose strand of hair from my cheek. "I can assure you, little doe. Only one person here has anything I want."

My mouth clamps shut.

"Now. Let's get this shit over with."

He takes my hand in his again and leads me around the front to the line at the door. It's not long— from what Mason said, this place is invitation only.

We hand our ticket to the bouncer and he checks our IDs like he's doing background checks for the FBI before he lets us in. I suppose it's a good thing they're so careful, but I'm still embarrassed that he knows *I'm* coming to a sex club.

God, maybe Britt is right. I am a prude.

As soon as he opens the door for us and I step inside, I'm ready to step right back out.

The first thing to hit me is the scent. Sickly sweet perfume and cologne mixed with an underlying aroma of body odor and sex.

The first thing I see?

A dick, hanging freely in the wind surrounded by a pair of crotchless chaps and thick black pubes.

Ew.

Immediately, I spin around, covering my eyes and running smack into Mason's chest, who just chuckles and pulls me against him.

"You've got to move, Hannah," he murmurs, voice low in my ear. His hand presses at the center of my back and he steers me away from Free Willy toward a bar in the far corner and away from any wild penises that roam the rest of the room.

The lighting makes it look like Satan's bedroom, as does the added fog hanging in the air.

On a stage near the center, a man is bent over, his head and hands locked in a pillory while a woman stands behind him, whipping him. Even though I'm pretty sure he's bleeding, he still begs for more, the sounds of his cries being drowned out by the thumping music in the club.

A couple people are below them, watching with a weird look of sick pleasure and satisfaction on their faces and something uneasy stirs in my stomach.

Another stage shows a girl on a tarp getting peed on. That's it. Just two men peeing on her and groaning like they've been holding it for hours.

That explains the smell.

Despite the darkness, it's impossible not to see the various stages of sex happening all over the room. A threesome here. A foursome there. Bodies move together like any other club, only at this one, there are hardly any clothes.

"Spit on me" some guy in an actual cage demands when we pass him, but he takes one look at Mason at my back and the possessive way his arm bands around my stomach and falls back in the cage. "Nevermind."

Holy shit.

Mason leads me to a bar, ordering two drinks. I don't even hear what he says. I'm too busy staring around the room like a creep.

Drugs flow as freely as the alcohol.

I feel like a peeping Tom, watching people in their most intimate moments. While I have no problem with these clubs if everyone consents to what's happening to them, I have never once thought about coming to one.

Or coming in one.

Perhaps, that's how Missy and I are different.

We may look a lot alike, but she's far more adventurous than I am. I knew that. Now, I can see it.

"Here," Mason says, handing me a shot glass. "It'll help with the nerves."

I don't even ask what it is, I just swallow it whole, the smooth burn of vodka coating the length of my throat as it slides down. Mason watches me, keeping close. My brain is having a hard time remembering that he's doing this for show and not because he wants to. His comfort only goes skin-deep.

"You look like you're going to bolt at any moment, Hannah."

"I'm really thinking about it."

"Just try to blend in. You don't have to do anything."

"I don't *want* to do anything."

"Come on," he tugs my hand, leading me toward a dance floor that's filled with people dry humping. Not unusual at a club, save for the tits and dicks flying everywhere.

I let Mason pull me into the crowd of people. I let him circle his arms around me from behind and I let him force me to dance.

Yeah, I'm definitely glad I brought him because if I didn't, they wouldn't have even let me in.

"How are you so calm?" I ask him quietly, the sound of my voice impossible for anyone else to hear over their own, drug-induced sex craze. Well . . . and the music. "What did you do last time?"

I can feel him stiffen behind me and ice fills my stomach.

I move to turn toward him, but he grabs me by the hips, pulling me back into his hard chest.

"I didn't do anything," he murmurs low in my ear. A shiver moves through me from his stubble against my neck and I relent, letting him move me along to the music. "I came with an ex. I left after five minutes. This isn't my scene, Hannah."

"Well, that makes two of us," I grumble, putting on my best *I'm ready to get railed by strangers* face, so no one suspects that inside, I'm ready to bolt.

It's not that I'm against anyone getting off. I actually don't care what you like, so long as you aren't hurting someone or doing something you shouldn't.

It's the depravity for everyone to see that makes me uncomfortable.

"You've just got to blend in," Mason whispers, quietly.

"I don't know how."

"Feel my cock?" Mason's fingers on my hips tighten and he presses his erection against my back. A warmth envelopes me when his lips trail up the side of my neck and if I didn't know any better, he's enjoying this a little more than he would like to let on.

So maybe Mason Carpenter's *not* as indifferent to me as he'd like me to believe.

I bite my lip, hazily appalled at myself that I'm even thinking things like this in a room full of sweaty, sex-fueled people. It's not them, though . . . it's him and how he can turn me into a puddle of mush with just a few words.

"That's only for you, little doe. And you look so fucking pretty right now, grinding on it." I let out a shaky breath, my hand finding his on my hip as I arch into him. I don't know whether I'm trying to hold him there or pull him away, but when his hand slides up my stomach, all I can think about is what I want *him* to do to me.

Act like you want to be here, Hannah, I urge myself, but that anxiety still bubbles beneath the surface. People swallow us in the crowd, and between Mason's roaming my body and the thumping of the overhead music, my mind is maxed out.

He nips my ear and then he's spinning me in his arms and tugging me to him. I let myself follow his lead and lift my face to his. He obliges, pressing his lips to mine and drinking me in.

Someone presses up behind me and I realize it's a woman from her breasts when she pushes them into my back, her hands above Mason's on my hips and swaying me with the music.

"Easy. I have you." Mason breathes against my lips when I stiffen. My skin crawls, but I force myself to lean into him, even as another person comes up to wrap her arms around his back.

Forcing myself to breathe, I sink into him, wrapping my arms around his neck and pushing the stranger's hands on my body out of my mind. I knew coming here, I might have to kiss someone, at the very least. I'm glad it was Mason and not someone like *spit on me* man from the cage near the bar.

When the girl behind me slips her hand up to my top to cup my breasts, I jump, recoiling at the feeling, but Mason doesn't release me. Instead, he takes her hands and pulls them back to my hips, slipping his lips down my neck, like he's kissing me there, instead of speaking.

"Off the bathroom, there are private rooms."

"No," I breathe, forcing myself to stroke the side of his neck and hoping he can hear me over the music. I refuse to do *that* here.

"The same hallway leads to the dressing rooms in the back," he murmurs, so low I don't think anyone else could have heard him. "We buy a room and sneak into the dressing rooms when the guard's busy."

He slips back up to my lips, slipping his tongue between my lips and tangling with mine until my world rocks on its axis. The woman behind him reaches around, rubbing my ass and disgust fills me.

"Ladies," Mason says when he disentangles me from the two women trying to form a grind train on us. "My wife needs a break."

They both *boo* and I can't stop myself from rolling my eyes. One of them—a beautiful brunette wraps her arms around his waist and tries to grope him through his jeans. Luckily, he catches her hand and pries her away before she does, but the sickening feeling of both jealousy and revulsion rise inside me.

Mason steps away from them and wraps his arm around my waist. He pulls me toward the back where, sure enough, there's a booth and someone handing out room vouchers.

Mason pays the person, while I struggle to catch my breath and take in the depravity around me. To my left, a girl has one man thrusting above her, another below her. She looks like she's in pain, judging by the grimace on her face, but no one stops. To my right, two men are tangled up together and the sounds of their grunts feel like they're battering the edges of my brain.

God, this place gives me a headache.

Finally, Mason's pulling me toward the doors, as if he can't wait to get me alone.

As soon as our room door is shut, I break down.

Mason locks the door and I sink onto a cool leather couch that's probably covered in half the city's bodily fluids and try to catch my breath.

"Hannah."

Mason is in front of me, sinking to his haunches and taking my chin.

"Breathe."

"That is the most joyless excuse for sex I've ever seen," I stammer, chest aching painfully. "Call me old-fashioned, but I have to actually know and *like* someone, before I let them grope me."

Mason chuckles, brushing a hair out of my face.

"You did good."

I roll my eyes.

"You're just saying that because those girls were hanging all over us."

His eyes flare and before I can react, he's wrapping his fingers around the back of my neck and pulling my lips to his with a harsh, rough kiss that heats me from the inside out.

When he breaks it, his eyes are wild.

"I have no intention of fucking anyone here but you, little doe."

He stands, pulling me off the dirty couch and stepping back toward the door while I gawk at him. He peeks his head out, motions me forward and we slip back out into the hall.

While the club is dark, the hallway is nearly pitch-black save for the few red lights overhead. Doors line the corridor, but none of them are open save for a crack in the very last one.

All kinds of sounds come from behind those other doors. Someone sounds like they're getting whipped in one. Another sounds like a woman is being murdered. Mason's hand tightens around mine when he feels me tense, but he doesn't say anything as we near the end.

Light streams from inside, but when he pushes the door open, it doesn't lead backstage, at all.

It's a fucking office.

A wall of security cameras sits behind the desk, each with a display of live-action porn playing from various areas of the club. The private rooms. The stages. The bathrooms. There's not a square inch of the place that isn't covered.

Ew.

"Look what the cat dragged in."

I was so preoccupied with all the laws the club is breaking that I hadn't even noticed the man sitting at the desk. My gaze flits to him and he's smiling wickedly, like a cartoon villain.

"I was wondering when we were going to see you."

Drew Marshall. I hadn't heard of him since he and Bailey's engagement ended, let alone seen him. I would have thought he would have skipped town, knowing Mason and all, but here he is, creepy smile and all.

Time hasn't been good to him. His good looks have waned, and he no longer looks like a Disney prince. His once-perfect skin is now aging, the stubble on his jaw holding little flecks of gray despite his young age of thirty-three. His hair, once glorious and full is now thinning on top of his head. But it's the scar . . . circling his eye and leading down into his cheek that really alters his appearance.

I pause because Drew's looking at me. Mason stiffens, putting himself between me and Drew, but I can still see the purple-hued glasses covering his eyes.

"Should have known you were behind this shit, Marshall."

"It's Mr. Hollywood, now, actually." Drew smiles widely, spreading his arms out as if to say *ta-da*. "And this is my house. Funny how that works out, huh?"

"I don't really give a shit who you are now. You'll always be the same spineless little shit who pissed his pants when I came after him." I step closer to Mason because honestly, Drew Marshall gives me the creeps, but mostly because I feel like I'm going to be snatched from behind at any second. I could totally take him if I needed to . . . I hope. "We came for information."

"Well, all information comes at a price and I don't disclose the identities of my patrons." He looks past Mason and directly at me. "Even your sister."

I could vomit.

"You know, Hannah Gaines, this is a poor place for someone who wishes to remain hidden. I bought this club and made it my own because I like to watch. It's fun for me and fun for them." He stands, walking around the desk as if he's giving a college lecture on literature. "What I don't like, is people showing up snooping around."

Fuck.

"Please . . ." I push away from Mason and slip under his arm. His arm bands around my waist to prevent me from getting any closer—something that doesn't go unnoticed by Drew. "My sister is missing. I know she used to come here. We need information about where she could have gone."

Drew chuckles as if I'd said I'd like to speak to the Pillsbury Doughboy.

"I know she came here. *Religiously*. I'm afraid she's in danger."

"Well, you're all in danger, aren't you? What with Mommy trying to eradicate small business and all."

"Drugs," I correct. I may not like my mother, but one thing I find admirable from her time in office is her fight against the drug problems of California. "She is eradicating drugs."

Drew just smiles wickedly from his side of the desk.

"How bold of you to come here, expecting me to give you information on Melissa Gaines." He sits down in his chair and leans forward until the lamp in front of him reflects off the purple lenses of his glasses. "Melissa Gaines is a dead woman. If she's not already. She fucked me over."

Surprise, surprise.

"And . . . I'm afraid, I just don't care."

My heart drops to my toes. So many people want my sister dead. And for what? I've only just scratched the surface of her mental health crisis, but already, I'm beginning to wonder if she doesn't deserve it. After everyone she's hurt. The drugs. The poison.

When does it end?

"You'd care if the FBI found out about your cameras, wouldn't you?"

Mason steps forward, placing me behind him, again as he watches Drew with pure, unadulterated hatred.

"Savannah settles for a lowly FBI agent and now you're going to throw him around whenever you like? Oh, don't *tell* me you've never dreamed of being the one creeping in the shadows, Carpenter," Drew laughs sardonically.

"No, but I have dreamed about finishing what I started the night you tied my sister to your bed and left her to die."

Drew's jaw tenses, right underneath the scar rippling on his face.

Something tells me Mason knows exactly where he got that scar.

"How about I make you a deal, Carpenter? You can have all the information you want. The girl stays."

Horror washes through me. I would rather chew off each of my toenails than spend another second inside this delusional club. Much less with Drew Marshall and his rapidly receding hairline and dirty fingernails.

"The girl goes where I go. You won't be touching her."

"I could just call security? I can assure you my men aren't police. We don't handle things the way you might be accustomed to."

Mason shrugs. "Call them," he murmurs darkly, reaching back under his shirt to pull something from the waistband of his jeans. The glint of a pistol shines in the light when he presses the hard steel down against the table. "That is if you think they can get here before I can finish what I started three years ago.

Suddenly, Mr. Hollywood isn't so cheerfully delusional.

He looks back and forth between Mason and the gun, his eyes flashing warily. If he knows Mason, he knows not to poke the bear, and right now, Mason's looking more like a grizzly than any cuddly teddy bear I've ever seen.

"I think I'll take that information now."

Slowly, Drew swallows over the lump in his throat. Then he nods.

Carefully leaning forward, he grabs a pen and pad of paper and scribbles an address on it before handing it to Mason with a look of bleeding fear in his eyes.

I find myself wondering what Mason did to him years ago, but I hope it was everything he deserved.

"Thank you," Mason replies with fake politeness. His voice is little more than a hum. Like a vampire in the night, right before he leaves his victim on the brink of death. "Now, if you'll excuse us, we'll be leaving. Smells like come and piss in here."

Mason grabs me around the waist and steers me toward the door, but before we reach it, he stops.

"Oh, and I don't think I need to remind you, you didn't see us tonight."

A slow, quiet nod from Drew.

"Good."

CHAPTER *Twenty*

MASON

Fucking Drew Marshall.

I should have known he'd be involved in this shit, somehow.

It's like my family gets rid of one venomous snake and another falls from the fucking sky.

Now, I'm involved, too and there's no way in hell I'm letting him near my family again, let alone Hannah. Not after what he did to Bailey.

The fear in his eyes wasn't undeserving. A couple years ago, when he tied my sister to the bed and left her to go on vacation, Drew found himself with a few shattered ribs, a broken nose, and in need of a whole hell of a lot of stitches to fix the damage I'd done to his pretty face.

Drew's the kind of man who likes to watch others bleed. He likes their pain—he gets off on it. The women he fucks always end up bruised and battered when he's finished and my sister was no exception.

I'll be damned if he gets so much as a whiff of Hannah's perfume after tonight.

Sex has always been at the forefront of Marshall's mind. Deranged sex, bordering on depravity. Humiliation, blood, welts that don't heal for a week. It's what makes the Inner Sanctum so . . . exclusive. You don't get in without an invite. You don't get out without scars.

It was a mistake to bring Hannah here, but it would have been an even bigger one to let her come alone. If I hadn't been with her, I'm not sure she would have made it back to her little pink cottage, much less gotten the information she needs.

That is, without losing that light that makes her Hannah fucking Gaines.

Perfection in a little five-foot-five redhead.

"Mason?" she breathes, damn near running to keep up with me as I tug her through the crowded club and toward the exit. There are no rules at the Inner Sanctum and it's evident as we make our way through. Thank fuck, Hannah didn't notice half the shit I did. I'm not sure she'd be able to stomach some of the very . . . unusual tastes of some of the patrons.

Finally, when we reach the door, I push her in front of me and lead her out, the tension radiating through me, volatile.

In the dark streets outside the club, I take a breath, slowing my pace. It's cooler now that the sun has set, and it feels good after the inferno of hell that is the Inner Sanctum.

I fucking hate sex clubs. I hate clubs in general, but the Inner Sanctum is a cesspool for the self-righteous. The people that think they're entitled to get off on whatever they want and in a lot of ways, they are—just not at the expense of others.

I've seen the other side of that coin and when there's no one drawing a line in the sand, things become . . . hazy. Horrific.

I was twenty-three the last time I came here, coincidentally the same age Hannah is now.

"Mason, *slow down*," she grits and when I don't immediately stop, she jerks her hand out of my grasp. I spin, but she's already storming past me and to the truck.

"What's your problem?" I grit, voice strained with the irritation coiling through me. I brought her here. I went above and beyond. I fucking threatened a man at gunpoint to get information about her maggot of a sister.

All for fucking her. Because I can't stop and I for damn sure can't help myself.

"What is wrong with you?" she snaps, whirling on me when she reaches the truck. I step right into her until her ass is pressed into the cool door behind her, both my hands on the truck window on either side of her head.

"I think I should be asking you that very same question."

"You could have gotten us killed," she snaps, tears glowing under the dim fluorescent lights overhead. "A fucking gun, Mason?"

"Would you have rather I let him keep you? I'm sure you've heard the stories." She glowers at me, but she doesn't argue. She knows I'm right. "Like it or not, princess, you're in this with me and me alone. No one else is going to help you because your sister fucked over every single person she came into contact with, including you. You're just too damned proud to see it."

Her lips purse in anger and then she's placing her hands on my chest and shoving me as hard as she can. I take a step back because my cock's rock fucking hard in my jeans and fucking her right now is the last thing I want to do.

Well, it's actually the *only* thing I want to do, but not after the Inner Sanctum. Not after Drew Marshall and his perverted lair of cameras. When I fuck her, I want her needy and begging for me, spread out in my bed with not a fucking shred of fabric between us.

Not here, in a dingy parking garage.

"You think I don't *know* my sister was an awful person?" she challenges, biting back tears in her eyes even as they stream down her cheeks. "You don't think there's not a part of me that hates her as much as everyone else does? As much as you do?"

"What I can't figure out is if you're just a masochist or just a fucking idiot."

Shock pools on her face and then, as if the universe wants to make *sure* I know I'm the asshole here, tears well in her eyes.

"Fuck *you*, Mason. Take me home," she demands, tugging on the truck door handle.

"Gladly," I bite, letting her struggle for just a moment longer before she glares at me over her shoulder and I finally unlock it.

She gets in and I slam the door, a little harder than I mean to and she jumps, scowling out the front window.

The ride to the little pink house in West Los Angeles is a tense one, both of us pissed off. Both of us high off the adrenaline of the club. I want to rip something to shreds after Marshall threatened her and right now, it's that fucking top she's wearing.

I need to get her home. I need to take a cold fucking shower.

I need to go back to the club and take care of the cockroach that is Drew Marshall before he ever gets the chance to get close to her again.

When I pull to a stop in front of her house, she starts to rifle through her little shoulder bag.

"Stop."

"Nope. I don't want to owe you a single thing," she replies cooly, rifling through hundreds in her wallet.

Jesus fucking Christ.

She's pissed. I get it, but so the fuck am I.

"Go inside, Hannah."

She throws a hundred at me like my truck has become some kind of aggressive strip club.

I throw it back.

She moves to throw it again and this time, she stomps out of the truck and up the sidewalk toward the house before I can reciprocate.

Fucking hell.

"Hannah," I bark, sliding out and following her, even as she gets out her keys.

She shakes her head. "Take it and go. I should have known this was never going to work out."

"Do tell, little doe. I'd love to hear your reasoning why you think you can get rid of me."

"I'm not playing these games, anymore. Being punished for something I didn't do. For caring about my twin sister. Yes, she was terrible to me in the last couple years, but it was *your* stepfather's fault and no one's holding you accountable for what he did."

Fuck me.

"Is that what you think we're doing?" I bite, gripping her under the chin to force her to look at me. "Playing games?"

"I don't care what you want to call it. I'm not doing it anymore. I—" Her resolve wavers for a moment. "I don't want to see you again."

"Say it again," I dare her, taking a solitary step toward her.

I give her another moment. Time for her to tell me to release her again.

I cock a brow when she doesn't.

"You want me gone, say it, Hannah."

Her lip wobbles with the tremor that moves through her. I can't tell if she's terrified or if she wants me as much as I want her.

"No."

There's a moment— a cacophony of ringing silence and the roar of the pissed off animal in my head that refuses to let her go.

This shit has gone on far too long.

You know what?

"Fuck it."

The moment her lips meet mine, her startled gasp turns into a soft moan. Her hands go to my hair, instantly fisting the roots, but she's not pulling me away. She's tugging me closer.

It's rough, impatient, and anything but romantic, but fuck, I need to feel her.

She deepens the kiss, slipping her tongue against mine and I growl, low in my throat at the taste of her. Fucking sweetness and honey and everything I've been craving since I left her in the garage this afternoon.

I nip her bottom lip when her fingers slide lower, blunt nails digging into the muscles of my back and it's then I decide this obsession has gone too far and now, I have no intention of turning back.

I want her.

Isn't that fucking ironic?

Her legs lock around my hips and I lift her to straddle me, crashing back against the wall with a hand behind her head. She pulls away, just an inch, and her teeth chatter as she moves against me, grinding her pussy on the length of my cock.

Carefully, I step toward the wicker couch on the patio. This wasn't my intention for tonight, but now that we're here, uninterrupted, with those little moans rolling off her tongue like Hail Mary's, I'll be damned if I stop.

I'm going to show her what it means to be mine.

"You make me so goddamned crazy," I bite, falling back on the couch with her over me, her hands raking up the back of my neck and a heat in her eyes that steals my next breath.

"Mason," she breathes, a shudder rolling through her when I pull her against my chest and nip the pulse point below her ear, before sucking it between my lips.

"You don't want me?" I taunt, hands sliding down to cup her ass through the same fucking skirt that's kept me both pissed off and preoccupied most of the night.

"I hate you," she grinds out, but the threat is lost on me when I move lower, kissing the hollow of her throat, then her chest. I slip down, running my tongue over the seam where the lace of the corset meets her breasts, and fist her hair to tug her head back and give me more room. She melts, giving me a little roll of her hips, eliciting a sharp intake of breath when her pussy grinds against my cock.

"Your pussy says otherwise, little doe."

I slip my hand under the hem of her skirt and use my palm on her ass to move her against me again. Her skin is soft, perfect under my fingers and I'm both thankful and pissed off I didn't take her inside where I could spread her out on the bed and fucking feast on her.

"Tell me what's in your nightmares."

Her eyes screw shut and a soft moan leaves her when I meet her next thrust, kneading the flesh of her ass while I move her against me. I'll get my answers, one way or the fucking other.

"You," she pants, a tremble moving through her when I slip a finger into the top of her corset and peel it down.

Fucking finally.

"And what about me?" I kiss the swell of her breast, swirl my tongue over the soft skin above her nipple, suck on the underside.

Fucking perfection.

She whimpers, back arching when my teeth graze her skin, her voice coming out rushed and desperate.

"You kissing me. Your tongue."

Sweetheart, my tongue's not the only thing I'd use on you. "You dream of me, little doe?"

She nods, pinching her eyes shut, and lets out a cry that I'm sure will be the last nail in the coffin to finally send me straight to the insane asylum.

Joke's on them. I'm not going without her.

She did this to me and I'll drag her to hell right behind me if it means I won't have to give her up again.

"Turn around."

She pauses when I still her hips, green eyes glowing in the moonlight overhead.

"Turn. Around."

Awkwardly she does, a startled gasp leaving her when I tug her back into my front. I smile against the side of her neck. I don't think I'll ever get enough of her little sounds.

She trembles in my lap when my hand slips down her stomach, to the fishnets covering her thighs that I will definitely be burning later. "This fucking outfit," I grit, moving higher, under the folds of the skirt to where the fishnets meet right at the apex of her thighs.

"What if someone sees?" she breathes, but in that moment when she wiggles against me, I don't think she much cares.

"Do you want me to stop?"

"No."

"My little exhibitionist." I seize her by the throat, tugging her head back to whisper in her ear. "And if anyone does see, I'll let them die a slow, painful death while they watch me fuck you."

"Mason," she gasps, a shiver running down her spine, though I'm not sure if it's from my dark words or the way I fist the fishnets and rip a hole right in the center of them. "I thought you couldn't stand me?"

She shakes her head, but before she can speak, I slip her panties to the side and run a finger through her folds. Soaking fucking wet.

"This better all be for me." My cock aches to be let free, but this is one of those moments where I need to control it because fucking her here is not in the cards right now. I don't have it in me to be gentle tonight. Not like she deserves. "Place your feet on either side of the ottoman."

"But—"

"You want to come?"

I'm nearly blind with the need to sink inside her, but if she wanted me to, I'd let her go. Even if my cock feels like it would go on strike because of it.

Begrudgingly, she places each foot on either side of my legs, effectively spreading herself open for me. I pull the skirt down farther, thanking fucking God, the universe, mother fucking nature, that it still covers her. I'm not lying when I say I'll fucking gut anyone who sees her.

"You listen so well when you're aching for me, little doe. Maybe I should piss you off more often."

"Fuck you" she bites, though it lacks any real enthusiasm with the quiet gasp that slips free when my finger enters her.

"Soon . . ." I grit. *So fucking tight.* "Tell me what's going through that pretty little head."

I suck on the flesh of her neck, marking her for myself while I move that finger in and out of her at a painstakingly slow pace. She's tight, fitting snug around me and so fucking perfect, my hand fucking shakes.

It pisses me off.

"*Hannah.*"

"You," she breathes, arching into me. "How much I can't stand you. How much I can't stand that I *want* you."

"That makes two of us."

I rub my palm against her clit, the sounds of her wetness filling the room and mixing with the harshness of my breath.

"Mason . . ." she moans, biting her bottom lip between her teeth and just like that, I'm ready to sign my own death warrant hearing my name like that on her tongue.

Shit can get addicting.

Her fingernails dig into my hand at her throat and then the one buried in her panties, whimpering as I adjust my hold to grind against her clit. Heat builds at the base of my spine, my balls tightening with the force of her ass rubbing my cock, but I ignore it.

I shift, forcing her to widen her legs and give me all her weight, I tug her flush against my front, lift her leg to the railing of the porch, and bring her right to the cusp, quivering and nearly shattered.

"Fuck," I hiss through my teeth, her arousal slipping down my fingers. "So fucking perfect."

I grip her throat in my hands, tightening until it muffles the sounds of her cries while her body tightens around my fingers.

"These are for me and me alone."

"I'm going to—" she pants, voice strained for oxygen.

Then I pull out.

"I thought you hated me?" I chuckle darkly, letting her orgasm fade before slipping back inside her. She whimpers the moment she's in my hands again.

"You're such an asshole," she grits, breathing as ragged as mine. Her fingernails leave little half-moon crescents in the skin of my wrist, the sting of pain turning into lust. The pain keeps me grounded, staving off the need to feel her tightening around my cock instead.

"And you're a fucking brat."

She moans and it's the sexiest fucking sound I've ever heard. I can feel her tightening, her movements growing choppier. The need to watch her come isn't one I'd anticipated, but now, it's all I fucking want. To watch the prim and proper California princess fall apart from my doing.

"You want to come, Hannah?"

She nods her head, lost in the pleasure as her movements become choppy against my hand. She grinds her pussy into my palm, while I thrust inside her with my fingers until the sounds of my hand meeting her flesh fill the air around us.

"Use your words," I rasp low in her ear as I draw out my motions, keeping her right on the precipice of losing control.

"Please," she whimpers, voice soft and breathless. "Please, Mason."

"Please what?"

"Please make me come."

She lets out a strangled sound when I quicken my pace, aligning to hit her at the perfect spot and tightening my grip on her throat to steal some of that fight left in her voice.

"Show me how pretty you can come for me, Hannah," I rasp and this is what pushes her over the edge.

With a shrill cry, her pussy clamps down on me to the point of nearly pushing my fingers out of her. The sound reverberates through me, even as she collapses against my chest, writhing above me like she's in the middle of receiving an exorcism.

I'm not sure how much time passes as we both pant, breathless and hot, before she speaks.

"Holy shit," she breathes, chest heaving to match my own.

Fuck, that was intense.

A shudder moves through her and slowly, carefully, I remove my hand from under her skirt, running up her side and drawing shivers out of her.

My cock still aches for her, but I can see the moment the postcoital clarity sinks in. Her cheeks flame and she shifts above me when I withdraw my fingers from her, my hand shaking like I'd just lost my fucking virginity.

Jesus Christ.

"Still want to get rid of me?" I ask when a tremble rolls through her, though even I can hear the darkness winding its way through my voice. The barely caged desire to carry her inside and make her moan my name like that until her voice is hoarse.

"Shut up," she groans under her breath. "Please."

I chuckle, shaking my head.

Fuck, I need to get her out of here. I need to take a ride. Clear my head of all things Hannah.

I need to find her damned sister so she can go back to her side of the state and I can stay here, in mine.

"Mason . . ." she starts, voice small and I know that this is the moment that follows obtaining the obtainable. I slip the hundred back in her purse while lead fills my veins.

"Go inside, Hannah."

Carefully, she nods her head, her green eyes looking anywhere but at me as she climbs off my lap. Unfortunately, her scent lingers.

Without a word, she nods carefully and moves toward the door, the sounds of her pretty little moans echoing in my ears and I watch her.

I get it. Now that she's come there's that doubt there, slowly trickling back in like the poison her sister loved.

I'm not the man of her dreams. I'm not her knight in shining armor. I'm a goddamned mechanic. My house has three bedrooms, none of which are in a huge mansion. There's no staff to clean up. No one to cook. No one to protect her but me.

It's wrong for her to want me.

I'm a monster, hiding in the dark, waiting to strike when she least expects it.

And now, I'm fucking attached.

She wouldn't get it. Kenda the "world-renowned" therapist wouldn't get it.

Fuck, I'm not even sure I get it.

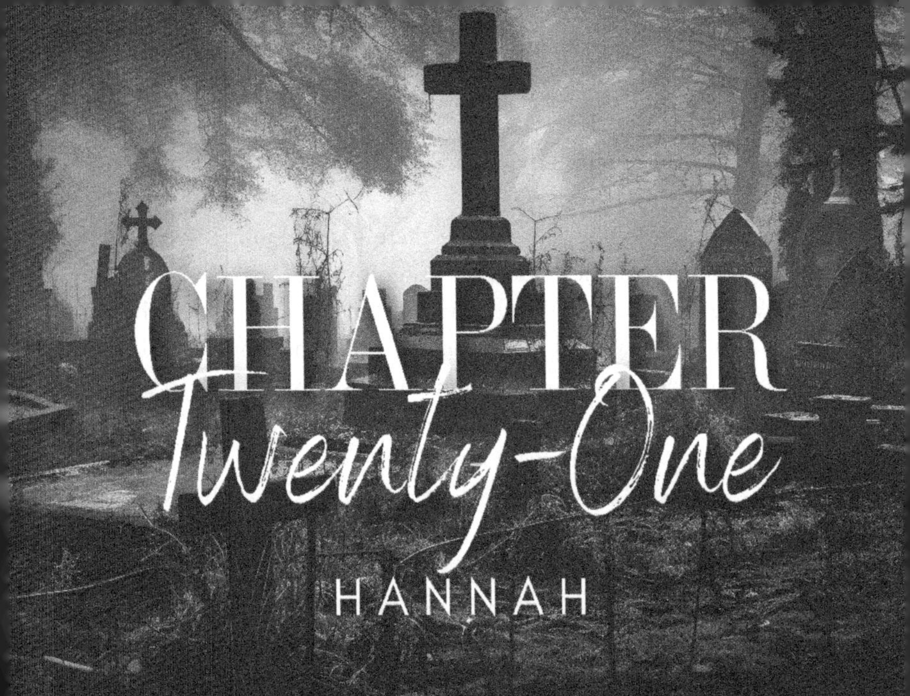

CHAPTER Twenty-One

HANNAH

Picture this.

You're sound asleep, dreaming of the way your boss's shirt clings to his biceps when he's working under a car (hot right?) when a sharp rap drags you out of your dream and into the darkness of the room around you.

My eyes feel like they're full of sand when I blink against the blackness surrounding me.

My first thought is a panicked *why is it fucking dark?*

My second thought?

Who the fuck is knocking at my door?

Slowly, I sit upright in bed. Did I hear that or was I imagining it?

As if to confirm my suspicion, the sound of three, quick heart-stopping knocks sound from the darkness beyond my bedroom door.

Oh, fuck.

My chest feels like someone's injected me with lead as every hair on my body stands straight up.

Swallowing a shaky breath, I force my legs to carry me out into the pitch-black void that is my living room. Remember my thing with the dark? Well, it's here in full force and I can feel the invisible hands grabbing at me from the shadows, even as the threat outside knocks again.

Three quick, harsh taps.

That's not a normal knock.

Slowly, so as not to alert the person I'm here, I peel back the curtain the smallest bit to peek out to the front porch.

I have to crane my neck, but I can just barely make out the back and shoulders of a man pressing into the front door.

Instantly, I fall back, slapping a hand over my mouth to silence my squeak.

"Let me in . . . *please* . . ."

My heart drops to my stomach as the sick, almost childlike voice sounds through the door.

I don't know who the hell that is.

"Hannah . . ." He whimpers my name like a prayer and it feels like the weight of the world comes crashing down on top of my chest.

How the hell does he know my name?

Three more taps sound, followed by silence. I back up until I run into the wall, like if I press my body into the plaster hard enough, I'll slip inside and out of sight.

The silent ringing in the air is louder than anything I've ever heard before.

That is . . . until those taps start from my bedroom window.

I bolt for the room, just as the man tries to tug the window open and fall back, watching the shadow through the thin white curtain as if there's a spotlight on me.

Diving for my phone on the bed, I start to dial the cops, but what the hell are they going to do? Show up in an hour after the man has either murdered me or wandered off and tell me to lock my doors?

I know how our justice system works and there's no charge for knocking on someone's house.

So, I do one better and dial the only person I know that's scarier than anything knocking on the window at two in the morning.

"Hannah." Mason's voice is gruff and full of sleep, but he answers on the second ring. Under different circumstances, it would make my stomach do a little backflip, *especially* after Friday night. But right now, in the face of whatever psychopath is outside my window, I don't have room for much else but fear.

"Mason," I whisper, working to keep my voice low, even though it shakes when the man pounds his fist against the window pane.

One.

Two.

Three.

What's stopping him from breaking the glass? From getting in if that's what he really wants?

"What the fuck was that?" There's rustling on the other end of the line and I imagine him slipping out of bed.

"Someone's trying to break in."

"Who?"

"I don't know," I whisper, my voice choked as fear slips through my veins like ice. "He knows my name."

The shadow steps away, a hand remaining and I watch that hand as it slowly, deafeningly slips across the window until it too disappears. I

"Hannah . . ." the man cries, banging the glass of the small bathroom window next.

"Grab a knife from the kitchen and get to the bathroom. Lock the door. Don't come out until I call for you, okay?"

The rush of thoughts spiraling through my head drown out the sound of his voice. Like what if he gets in? Is he connected to *unknown*? Missy? What if they sent him?

What if they hurt Mason?

"Hannah."

"Okay," I whisper, letting out a squeak when the man bangs somewhere near the back of the house. Then . . . everything goes silent, again.

"I'm on my way."

"Okay."

The taps start again, louder now. More deranged and uneven. Desperate.

"*Hannah.*"

I open my mouth to speak but nothing comes out but a breath of air.

"Breathe."

I nod as if he can see me and tiptoe toward the kitchen.

"Where is he?" Mason's voice is sharp, demanding my attention while I struggle to listen for the intruder.

"I—I don't know,' I stammer, tiptoeing into the kitchen and slinking along the counters to peek out the window in the backyard. Nothing. "It's dar—"

Another bang sounds, this one only a couple feet from where I stand at the knife block and I let out a squeak in terror before I can stop myself. Immediately, I look toward the back door and with the sinking feeling of full-body dread, everything in me runs cold.

"Hannah. Get to the fucking bathroom," Mason growls, practically feral on the other end of the line.

"The back door's unlock—"

Just as I rush for the door, the knob twists in my hands and the man hurtles through, slamming into me and knocking me to my ass on the kitchen floor.

I scream as he topples over me, but all the breath leaves me with the weight of his body. He claws at me in the darkness and my phone skitters along the floor under the table.

That time with Missy flashes back to my mind, when she attacked me in her bedroom all those years ago.

"*Help. Me,*" he roars, his face looming over mine in the darkness. I can't see much, but I can smell him. The powerful scent of either ammonia or cat urine on his skin. His breath washes over me, a nasty combination of decay and poor hygiene as I fight against his hold. "*You* did this to me!"

I don't know who *she* is, but I manage to knee him in the groin and roll when he cries out in pain. I try to scramble to my feet, but before I can, he grabs my hips and drags me back, a feral sound leaving his lips.

"You did this," he snarls, tugging at my hair until I feel strands rip free. "You made them do this to me."

I twist in his hold, throwing my head back as hard as I can and despite the pain, the sickening crunch of his nose is what rattles my brain. He screams in agony, his hold lessening just enough for me to try to escape, hair be damned, but whatever he's on either dulls the pain or makes him impervious to rage. He grabs me, pinning me down with his body weight at my back.

Deathly cold fingers clamp around my throat when I scream and it comes out a sputtering choke as he forces the breath from my lungs, cutting off my air supply. Tears leak from my eyes, and my skin burns from the lack of oxygen, but he doesn't stop.

He's going to kill me.

I croak, clutching at the linoleum, his fingers around my throat—clawing him, but he won't budge. My vision blurs and then the edges start to grow dark, peppering like an old film when suddenly, the fingers are gone and I'm sucking in air like I just swam from the bottom of the Pacific.

I cough, gasping for breath as I try to come to in the commotion of the darkness surrounding me.

There are the cries of my attacker, but there's also the feral animalistic growl of a very pissed off, very *big* Mason Carpenter, as he beats him into the floor on what used to be the table not even five feet away from me.

When the man's cries turn to quiet whimpers, something big and dark skids across the floor with a metallic *thunk*.

Holy shit.

A tire iron.

"Hannah . . ." Mason murmurs, flipping on the light by the back door.

In this light, everything lacks its usual cheeriness. The man is alive, but he's going to be in a world of pain when he comes down from whatever he's on. His face is a bloody, beaten mess. His clothes are tattered, though I suspect they were like that when he arrived.

He looks like he's on the brink of death. Sweat dots his brow, mixing with the blood in his thinning hair. His eyes are sunken and his teeth are yellowed and broken. I don't know how much is Mason, but it's clear the man is very, very sick.

It's not until Mason drops down on his haunches in front of me that I realize I'm shaking like a leaf.

"Come here." Mason's voice is rough and strained, whether from the fight or something else, I don't know.

He gently helps me sit up and then tugs me into his chest. I can't look away from the man, though, whining in a puddle of his own urine on my kitchen floor.

"Little doe. Look at me." It's not a question. It's a command. Gently, he lifts my chin to inspect my neck, his nostrils flaring at whatever he sees. I wince from the soreness, my eyes locking with his dark and stormy gray ones as shivers rack through me from head to toe. He searches my face, but he looks away before I can understand that look in his eyes.

Protectiveness? Possessiveness? Murderous?

All three?

"You've got to help me . . ." the man whimpers from behind Mason, seemingly not even on this planet anymore.

Instinctively, Mason's grip on my waist tightens when he peers back to the man.

"What's your name?"

"Help . . . Me . . ." he wheezes in response and Mason shakes his head. "They left me here."

"Who?"

"Them . . . them, them, them, them . . ." He repeats the word over and over rocking back and forth on the ground. "It hurts so bad."

"Going to hurt a lot more in a bit, don't you worry."

I jump, scrambling back into the kitchen island and Mason's grip on my waist tightens, steadying me. The dark fed I saw at the shop a couple weeks ago is here, standing at the back door and staring down at the man on my floor with a look of quiet anger and disgust.

"You just had to let him piss himself, didn't you?"

Mason's jaw ticks, but he doesn't respond. Instead, he slips his arms under me and stands, hoisting me up like a toddler being carted to bed. He carries me away from the man and the handsome FBI agent and into the living room before carefully depositing me on the couch. He reaches behind me, his shoulders tense and his face unreadable before he covers me up with a bright pink afghan from the back of the couch.

"I'll be right back," he says quietly, and before he straightens, he wipes a thumb gently under my eye to collect a stray tear that escaped.

Is this Mason Carpenter . . . comforting me? Is this the soft side he claims he doesn't have? Hidden away behind the harsh, handsome exterior that he shows to the rest of the world?

He gives me one last look before he heads to the kitchen. I watch him go, gingerly laying my head back on the couch.

"Ew."

Savannah Carpenter, looking like she just stepped off a runway, stands in the back doorway, looking down at the man on the floor with the same look the agent had.

"I told you to wait in the car," the dark fed says and she just shrugs.

"I got bored."

He shakes his head, turning back to whoever he's on the phone with. I get the feeling they do this a lot.

So the FBI agent and the princess of LA . . . are an item? That doesn't seem fair. They're too pretty to reproduce together. Their kids will be gods among men.

It's then, her blue eyes ghost over me.

And . . . I forgot she hates my family.

"Jesus, Mason . . ." she breathes, but he doesn't say anything, stepping past her and bringing me a glass of water.

Come to think of it. Almost getting strangled to death *did* make me thirsty. It could also be the animosity in the room.

"Is that . . .?" Savannah starts, but when Mason fixes her with a hard stare, her lips clamp shut.

Oh. So his family *really* doesn't like me.

Way to fuck it up for the rest of us, Missy.

"Drink. " Mason hands me the water and I take a sip, wincing as it slips down my sore throat.

"Thank you . . ." I'm so surprised by my own raspy voice that I shut down completely. Mason lifts a finger to my lips, silencing me before stepping back. Two new people step through the back door— I guess my house is just the place to be at two in the morning on a Saturday night— and they make their way over to me.

"These people are going to look at your throat. I need to have a conversation with Prince, but I'll be back in a minute."

I nod, wincing when I realize it freaking hurts and he goes, leaving me alone with Savannah, Thing One, and Thing Two, the first of which looks at me like I am the cause of all that is wrong in the world.

Fuck. So much for making peace.

She's quiet while the two . . . I don't know, secret service EMTs check me over, watching me from across the room. Savannah has always been known to be cold and ruthless, but I've always admired her and assumed they were just rumors. That stare, though . . . she and Mason may as well be twins.

Finally, once they've given me a clean bill of health and told me

I'll be sore for a few days, the two fancy EMTs say goodbye, leaving me alone with just Savannah. The crazy guy is gone—more people in black, unmarked uniforms came and carted him off ten minutes ago—and Mason stepped out with Logan, as I've learned, to talk about God only knows what.

Is he cautioning Mason away from me? Warning him that I'm just like my sister and I'm just as much to blame for all the crimes she's committed as she is? People see twins and don't think that they can be polar opposites.

Well, Missy and I, as much as everyone wants to omit that fact, have grown to be polar opposites. I could never sit by and watch innocent people be hurt. Raped. Murdered. I couldn't turn a blind eye for love because love shouldn't make you have to hide it from the rest of the world. It shouldn't tear apart families. It shouldn't breed addiction and dementedness.

It should be warm. A place where you can go when the world is threatening to swallow you whole. Where everything makes sense and you don't have to worry about the consequences of giving your all to another person and praying they hold it as closely to their heart as you do with theirs.

There are good parts of Missy and even if they can't erase the bad, they're still there and they're what I think about when I get sick to my stomach with hate at all the terrible things she's done.

Missy's strong. Really strong. She could handle Mom's CIA-like punishments in stride where I nearly had a mental breakdown. She's powerful, sure of herself, and most importantly, she's determined. Determined to get away from Mom and start a life of her own, no matter how much I disagree with how she did it.

I'm nowhere near as tough as she is.

"What do you want with my brother?"

I pause, my entire body freezing under the weight of Savannah Carpenter's blue-steel stare.

"I don't want anything from him."

She regards me coldly, crossing her arms over her chest and leaning back against the wall.

"I remember you, you know?" she says after a long moment. "Always side by side with your sister, two peas in a pod. Hard to believe the apple fell far from the tree."

"Yes," I mutter, just as frigidly. I don't have the will to be polite. Not tonight and certainly not here. This is my house. "Very hard to believe, isn't it?"

Her eyes narrow and she takes a step forward, stopping just in front of my coffee table.

"Mason may, but I don't trust you. Your sister ripped our family apart and we're just now putting it back together."

"Did it ever occur to you that your family *also* ripped your family to shreds? Or did that not come to you somewhere in between your self-righteousness and pity party?"

I stand, albeit unsteadily from the couch, biting back the grimace from the tenderness in my neck. It's not as bad as it was, but it's sore and right now, all I want to do is go to bed, but I can't.

I can't stay here.

"You know," I start. The plan was to walk away before I said something heinous, but she's pissed me off. In my own home. Where I didn't invite her. "I always admired you, Savannah. We never really spoke, but I thought you could see the good in people and not hold people accountable for the actions of their families. My sister may be a bad person, but she's my sister." She doesn't say anything, but there's this little moment when her eyes get wider where I know the reality of what I'd said sinks in.

Checkmate.

I turn to go to my room, but she can't let it go.

"If you love him, or even *care* for him, you'll let him go. He's had a hard enough time. He doesn't need to be mixed up in your problems, too. This family loves him."

"Yeah, well—" *I do, too.* I stop myself.

Fuck, that's not true.

Shit. Shit, shit, shit.

My heart swells and I curse myself internally for not seeing the signs before. I'm an idiot. Plain and simple.

And I'm falling in love with Mason Carpenter.

"Mason's a grown man," I say after a moment. "He's welcome to do whatever he pleases. If he wants to walk away, I won't stop him."

It tastes like battery acid as soon as it leaves my tongue. My chest burns, my eyes grow watery, and for a moment, I think about crying.

But I won't. Not tonight.

I need to leave.

"Have a good night, Savannah."

And I turn to go pack my bags.

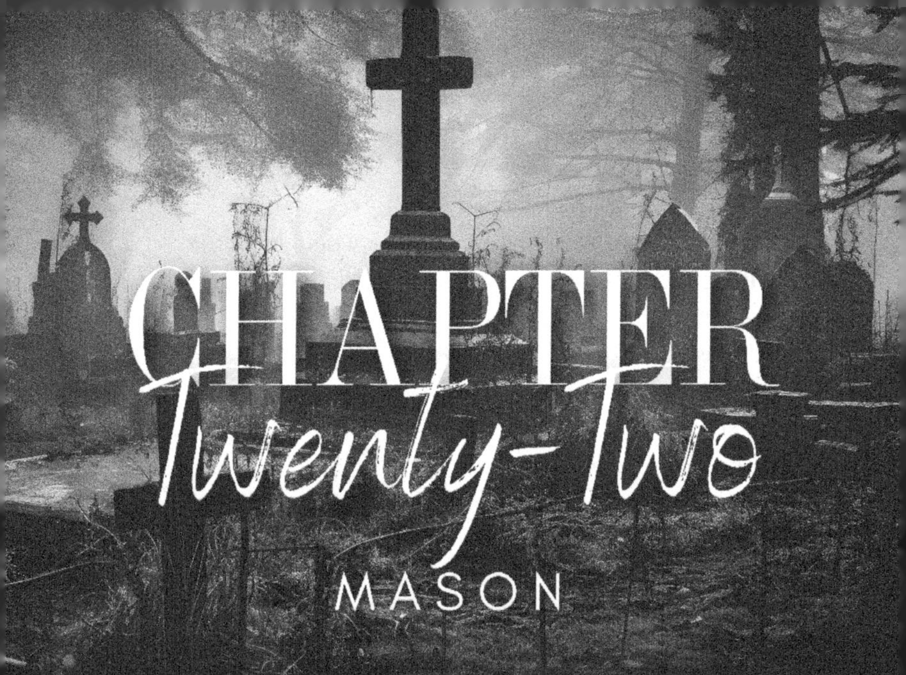

CHAPTER Twenty-Two

MASON

"There's no chance? How well do you really know her?"

That's the problem, isn't it? That I've come to know her better than the back of my fucking hand and now I can't walk away.

Somewhere along the line, this stopped being about bringing Melissa to justice and morphed into something far more dangerous. If Hannah's in this shit, then I am, too, whether she likes it or not.

"She's not helping her."

Logan nods, waving to one of his unnamed workers as they leave for the night. The little prick that broke into Hannah's house was hauled away ten minutes ago, leaving behind nothing but a pool of his own blood and piss and a broken kitchen table on the linoleum floor.

I should have killed him.

I want to. For what it's worth. When I arrived and saw his hands wrapped around Hannah's throat, the gun at my back seemed too kind an execution for him. I wanted to use my bare hands. Wring the life from him for daring to touch her.

Now . . . I'm struggling to remember all the reasons I said she could never be mine.

And that's a real fucking problem.

"What I can't figure out, is why they would let her go." I know he's talking about Melissa from the cold, dark hate in his eyes and the call Hannah got the other night. I can't say I blame him, though, Parker's just as much to blame for Melissa Gaines's issues as her Mother, but there's something dark about her that wasn't put there by anyone else.

"She can be very . . . persuasive."

"We need her to talk, Mason. I need to know what the fuck she brought with her," Logan says so quietly, Savannah can't hear.

"I'll handle it."

"None of that sob story shit, either. I need the full story. This affects more than just you."

"I said, I'll handle it."

Logan's eyes glint black in the light while he watches Savannah step up to the back door. There's a scowl on my sister's face as she looks back and forth between the two of us.

I know what she's thinking. I don't care.

She hates that I'm here with Hannah as much as Mila did. They don't trust her and while I understand why, I also don't give a fuck. I've seen the differences between the two Gaines daughters. I can understand wanting to save your sister from a gruesome death, even if it means putting them behind bars for the rest of their lives for the horrible shit they've done.

"Just know," Logan says, eyes glinting black in the moonlight. "I'll do what I have to. No matter the cost." He looks at Savannah grimly. "Antonio's men will watch your house. I'll send you his number, in case you need anything."

And then he walks away, pressing a kiss to Savannah's forehead.

I can't fault him for loving my sister—for being willing to do anything to protect her, no matter the cost. He'd put a bullet in anyone if it meant she'd be safe.

I also can't shake the dark anger that comes with thinking about that gun being pointed at Hannah and because of that, I know I'd do the same fucking thing.

"We need to talk," Savannah says cooly when I step up to the back door. Logan, who murmurs quietly into the phone on the other side of the kitchen, eyes us carefully.

"It can wait." I need to find Hannah. Of course, she's not where I left her because the girl can't follow simple instructions.

"No," Savannah snaps. "Right now. What were you thinking?"

"Right now, Savannah? I'm thinking you need to get the fuck out of my way." I move to step past her, but of course, she crosses her arms, her blue eyes flaring angrily.

"Mom's going to be hurt."

"When is she not?"

She doesn't like that answer, because she falls back like I'd slapped her. I take the opportunity to step into the house and leave her glaring at me in the kitchen.

Mom can be hurt. Savannah can throw a tantrum. They can tell me it's not safe. It won't change the fact that the one girl I've never fucking been able to get out of my head is the one who was almost strangled to death tonight. Or that she's directly related to one of the two people that ripped my family apart.

Anxiety-riddled tension slips down my spine as I make my way down the hall. It's not safe here anymore, and while the thought of having her in my home makes every fucking nerve ending in my body feel like a live wire, I'll be damned if she's staying here.

Hannah's bedroom door stands ajar and I step into the doorway, finding her scurrying around the room. Three suitcases sit on the bed, open with clothes strewn haphazardly inside.

My muscles feel like someone injected them with concrete. Packing in a hurry can only mean one thing.

She's running.

She doesn't notice me until I step up behind her and when she spins around, she collides with my chest, letting out a startled gasp. I take the small duffle bag from her hand, peering inside.

Cash. A fuck ton of it.

"Mason—" she starts, but I drop the bag on the bed and silence her by taking her chin in my hand. Her breath catches in her throat, but she doesn't pull away when gently, I lift her chin to look at the marks on her throat.

The bruises staining her skin set my blood at a low, molten boil.

And from that moment forward, my mind's made up.

"You aren't running."

She swallows hard, her breath coming out shakily when I release her chin.

"I have to," she says, so quiet, I almost can't hear her.

"Why?"

The thought of her leaving and never coming back pisses me off. That anger at her being gone *also* pisses me off.

I don't get attached. I've *never* gotten attached. Not until her.

And there will never be another like her.

She's my addiction. Letting her walk away, not knowing if she's safe is like asking to take a bullet to the foot.

—Fucking stupid.

"Who was that, Hannah?"

"I don't know," she breathes. I can see it in her eyes that she doesn't, but I had to be sure.

"Who's after you?"

"I don't know," she repeats, and I can tell by the look in her eyes, she means it.

Part of me wants to accept that answer. The other half wants to drag her to the bed and not come up until she's putty in my hands and willing to tell me the secret of life if I ask for it.

"Then, I'll tell you this. You run; they follow. You aren't in any less danger on the road than you are right here." Her green eyes flash in the dim lighting of the room, but she still shakes her head.

"I . . . I can't bring this to you. Your family," she glances around, dropping her voice. "I can't stay here."

"You aren't." Grabbing one of the suitcases around her, I zip it shut. "Get anything you need."

Immediately, she's shaking her head. "That's a horrible idea."

"Why?" I grit, my teeth clanking together, and she goes silent, her cheeks flaming and tears brimming in the corners of her eyes. "Did Savannah say something to you?"

"It's nothing. Really. She's just worried about you and I can understand," she rushes, placing a hand on my chest to try and stop me from moving toward the door. "You have a family, Mason. People who care about you. I . . . don't."

"What the fuck did you just say to me?"

Her lips clamp shut at the anger seething in my voice.

I step into her and she steps back, her eyes on my chest until her back hits the wall behind her. I close the distance between us, reaching up to cradle her cheek in my hand because I fucking need to.

She doesn't stop me when I brush a loose curl behind her ear. She doesn't stop me when I gently raise her chin to not hurt her. She definitely doesn't stop me when I lean in, sealing my lips over hers and stealing a kiss, just like I'm planning to steal the governor's daughter.

She's mine.

It's not the harsh, erratic kiss we shared in the truck, but my cock aches in my jeans with the need to slip inside her. Feel her clenching around me like a fist.

She makes a little breathy sound, letting me slip my tongue lazily along hers, drinking her in like she's my last breath.

When I break the kiss, her eyes pop open, cloudy and the brightest fucking green I've ever seen.

"Little doe, if it were that easy to walk away from you, I would have done it years ago."

Her mouth parts and I know she wants to know more, but she

doesn't ask. Good.

I couldn't escape her when she was just working for me and I was helping her find her sister.

Now . . . she'll be everywhere.

Something about that is unsettling.

Logan's words drift back through my brain.

How well do you really know her?

Unfortunately, like the back of my fucking hand.

Her eyes are soft when she lifts her head. She's scared. I can see it. Fuck, I can feel it in the little way her hands shake against my chest. Still, she raises up on her tiptoes and softly, presses her lips not to my mouth, like my body craves, but my cheek.

"Thank you," she whispers.

It's the most heartfelt thank you I've ever received.

It also pisses me off.

"It's final."

I release her, grabbing one of the suitcases and heading toward the door. Savannah's eyes follow me when I pass them out the front to throw the bag in my truck, but she doesn't say a word.

Good for her.

Logan's right. She's running, but from what? Her past? A ghost? This *unknown* motherfucker? I'm not even sure she knows.

I need to get to the bottom of it—fast, if I plan on keeping her.

The only problem is I've got secrets, too.

Secrets far darker than anything she could imagine.

"I still feel like I smell like him," Hannah grumbles, stepping out of the bathroom. The marks on her neck have turned an angry purple against her skin and she looks exhausted. I'm exhausted, too, but I know I won't sleep a wink. Not after everything that's happened tonight.

"You don't," I murmur darkly, polishing off the rest of my beer. Listen—sometimes, you just need one. I'm no alcoholic, but I feel like it, having Hannah in my space. I don't invite people into my house. It's the only place I can come and be alone and now . . . it's full of her scent.

Her bare feet pad across the floor and she stops and I realize I've got a newfound foot fetish.

No.

A fucking *Hannah* fetish.

This was a shit idea.

"Do you have an extra blanket?"

"You're in my room for the night. I'll set up the spare tomorrow."

Also a bad idea, but I'm not having her sleep on my old couch while I sleep in the bed and the spare may as well be a warzone right now. No one's slept in there for years, so there aren't any sheets on the bed. Not to mention, it's full of boxes of Mom's shit I removed from the house when my grandmother signed it over to me. I just didn't know what to do with it and she didn't seem to care.

Hannah's eyes go wide for a moment and I almost laugh.

"No, really," she protests. "I'll sleep out here. I can listen in case anyone tries to get in."

The thought of Hannah on the floor, the man from earlier on top of her as he chokes her fills my veins with venom.

I'm still pissed off he's alive.

"Hannah."

"Mason."

"Go to bed."

"No, I don't want to put you out any more than I already have."

I grit my teeth, standing from the couch and carrying my empty beer bottle to the trash.

"It's temporary," I agree, my back to her, so she can't see the agitation winding through me. "You help keep the house clean. Help with dinner. Groceries. Don't bug me and don't bring anyone over. I don't care what else you do."

I know I'm being harsh, but ask me if I give a fuck.

Not with the tension winding through me.

The need to break the man that tried to steal from me, steal *her* from me sets my blood on a low simmer. Especially when I turn back and take in that soft, sleepy face and throat covered in his bruises.

I find the reason I'm so pissed off is because try as I might, I can't get her out of my fucking head. Whether she's in my house or not, she's always been there. Like a pest that's impossible to irradicate.

She probably always will be.

Instead of arguing, Hannah bites her tongue for once.

I don't fucking like it.

"Well, I'll still take the couch. I just need a blanket."

And so, we're back to this.

"No."

She groans, sitting down on the sofa and crossing her arms over her chest and, for a moment, I actually debate on spanking her ass. My patience is holding on by a single thread at this point.

"I'll sleep here without a blanket, then."

Jesus Christ.

Stooping down, I reach for her, slip my arms under her when she tries to scramble back, and haul her up against my chest to carry her wedding-style.

"You asshole," she grits between clenched teeth and I can't resist the chuckle that claws up my throat before laying her on the bed.

With some dismay, I realize I wasn't counting on having her face to face with me when I brought her into my very large, very available bed. So close, I can taste the toothpaste on her breath, smell my scent in her hair.

Yeah . . . this is a big fucking problem.

She's inches away and like there's a magnet pulling her in against her will, she leans forward, her lips an inch from mine.

My cock begs me to fucking kiss her again. Pull her in, drink her like the last drop of water on the planet. My head tells me to get the fuck out of there.

"Go to sleep, Hannah."

Forcing my legs to move, I pull back from her and make my way to the door, only pausing when she gives me a soft reply from the bed.

"Goodnight, asshole."

I shake the little voice out of the back of my head, telling me to stay. That fucker never knows what's good for him.

"Goodnight, brat."

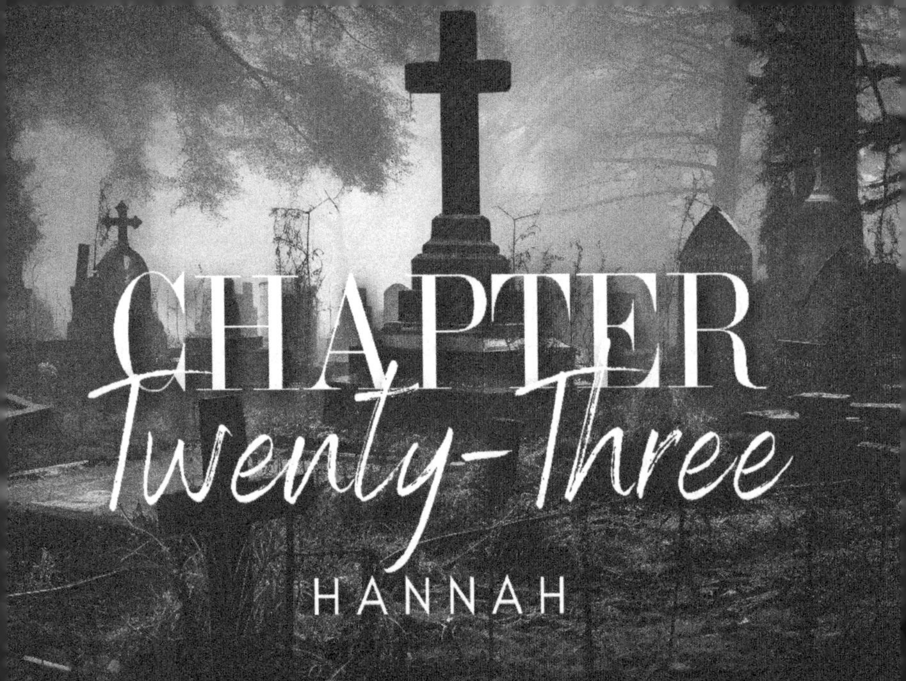

CHAPTER Twenty-Three

HANNAH

You know that heat that makes you feel like your limbs weigh a thousand pounds? The kind that makes it hard to breathe? To take a drink even though you obviously need it because, with the sweltering sun overhead, you sweat it all back out within the hour?

Yeah, that's the kind of heat that settles over LA the day after my attack.

The concealer I'd put on this morning to cover the dark blue and purple bruises vanishes without a trace by eleven. The mascara I'd vainly worn is all but gone, having dripped off my face to find cooler weather by the time noon rolls around.

By one, I'm nearly exhausted and I'm sure the guys in the garage aren't feeling any better. Ian and Puke have already come to interrogate me about my throat and though I gave them the cliff notes version, between them and Mason peering through the garage window all day to check on me, I'm mentally exhausted, as well.

This morning, Mason tried to tell me to stay home, but being in his house, surrounded by his . . . *everything* all day just didn't seem like a good idea.

So, I trudged to work behind him—half an hour late, I might add because he wouldn't let me walk across the alleyway behind his little bungalow by myself to the garage.

After last night, I could barely sleep. I don't think I dozed off until the sun was starting to crest on the horizon and even then, it was fitful.

I know there are men stationed around to watch the place. The house, the garage. It's all secure. I just . . .

Who was that guy?

How does he know Missy and how does he know where I live? More importantly, why is he showing up to kill me in the dead of night?

One thing about having a sister on the run from the law and whoever else is after her, is that I am sure to be expected to carry the blame for some of that. While I'm accustomed to taking the fall for Missy, I'm *not* used to people being so blatantly hateful toward me. Like Savannah last night. She hates me. I can feel it. The damned pope can feel it.

I'm sure Mason can.

Why he's letting me crash at his place, I'll never begin to understand, but I'm grateful, all the same.

When I was lying awake last night, desperately trying to fall asleep, I thought that when I woke up, I was going to realize it was all one long, fucked-up dream.

But . . . no cigar.

Instead, I woke up surrounded by *his* scent in *his* bed in *his* house.

Now, it's messing with my head.

Try as I might, I can't deny this . . . attraction to Mason. Maybe it's because, to everyone else, he's dangerous. But to me, he means safety.

I don't want to read too much into it, but that's exactly what I laid awake last night and did. How sweet he was when he carried me to the couch. How he brought me water, even though I hadn't thought of it myself. How he'd all but forced me to intrude on his space because he wanted me to be safe.

There's something there. Just not something that will ever end well.

But damned if I don't daydream about it.

I spend my lunch break getting slushies from the corner store down the road for everyone because, let's face it, there's only so much you can do in an office and Mason only lets me out to play with the big kids when it's just him and I.

I know I'll probably be in trouble, even before I make it back to the shop. When I walk in the front door and find Mason standing at the counter, talking on his phone and looking like he's going to pop a blood vessel in his neck, I know without a doubt.

"She's here."

He ends the call, setting his phone on the counter a little too hard.

"You're going to break that," I tell him, handing him a cherry slushie. I know he likes cherry because he said it once, a long time ago.

Hopefully, that's still the case.

He takes the slushie, albeit a little too roughly.

"If the lid pops off, I'm not mopping it up," I grumble.

He looks like he's either going to kill me or fuck me. Maybe both, knowing him.

I set my bag back in its spot, wincing before I stand because I know he's pissed.

"I'm sorry," I breathe, before I even look at him. "It's hot. I needed some air and I knew you guys would be boiling out there."

He takes a step forward and I step back.

God, he really is tall, isn't he?

My back hits the counter and I have to arch my neck to look at him. It's a mistake. I should have just looked at his nipples because his eyes tell a different story to what's really going on in his head.

He's pissed off because I made him worry. And Mason Carpenter doesn't worry.

He places both hands on the counter on either side of me, caging me in. My heart stutters in my chest at his proximity. I don't know if it's the grease on his arms, the way he smells, or the dark timbre of his voice, but my body reacts in ways I know I should feel ashamed about, but I don't.

Heat pools in my core at his closeness, my clit vibrating with every second that passes.

Maybe I just like it when he gets all dark and dangerous on me. Maybe it's just him.

"What part of you almost died last night didn't you understand?"

Okay, valid.

"You said it yourself. There's security up and down this block. I was okay."

"You put your faith in those men? They get paid to watch you. You really think they're willing to take a bullet for you if something happens?"

"And you are?" I challenge. When he doesn't say anything, my heart skips a beat. He's absolutely crazy if that's the case. He's said it himself a million times. He can't stand me.

After a beat, I have to do something. So, I reach up and smooth down the collar of his shirt, only for him to catch my fingers in a flash. He steps forward, even closer, his body pressing against mine and I can feel his hardness digging into my stomach.

Holding my gaze, his other hand lifts my chin to inspect the marks on my neck, his gaze caustic while he looks them over.

Finally, he removes his hand and leans forward. His nose runs up the side of my face, and my skin tingles from his breath. My nipples tighten, pressing into his chest and the irrational thought that I'd let him do whatever he wanted to me, right here, for anyone to see, startles me.

God, who am I?

From prude to exhibitionist. Missy would be proud.

"The next time you leave this office without me, I'll spank your ass," he murmurs in my ear. "And I'll make you beg for it."

And finally, he steps away, grabbing his slushie and the two for the guys and shooting me a look before the garage door shuts behind

---

him.

I clean the office because I don't know what else to do. The guys have been busy for most of the afternoon, though both Ian and Puke stepped inside to thank me for their drinks and to debate if it was hotter in the garage or the office.

Mason says he's got errands to run and warns me not to leave the building in that growly voice of his before disappearing out the back door.

Even the phone barely rings.

I debate on clearing out a spot in Mason's mini-fridge to hide in, but it's too small. Instead, I settle on looking into private security, which I'm surprised is a whole buttload of money I don't really have.

I'm not struggling. Mom still sends money to my account every month, but I refuse to touch it because doing so would be accepting everything she did and turning a blind eye. I've got plenty saved up and I'm only adding to it working for Mason, but I certainly don't have thirty grand a month for a single guard.

So, I settle and look at guns, instead. Maybe if I ask really nicely, I can get Mason to teach me. If not, I'll wing it like everything else.

By four, I'm so bored I've reverted back to thinking about last night. About Missy and the crazy man and what it all means. Mom's involvement and . . . surprisingly, my father's death.

Missy and I were so young when he died. Around seven or eight. I don't remember much except for how the house just seemed empty after he passed. Mom cried a lot. Missy and I took to being quiet because she'd get headaches.

Then, one day, like nothing had happened, she was better.

And we never spoke about my father again.

Seems so long ago now.

Dad was a good man. At least I thought he was. Mom said he'd had a heart attack, but he was only in his thirties. Mom seemed better with him around. She was a young woman in politics—no easy feat in Virginia at the time. It's why she moved us to California. She swore it was a more progressive state that would accept her as a leader.

I guess, looking back, she wasn't wrong, though I don't really think it has anything to do with the state of California. I think she's just a good liar and that sweet southern accent sure doesn't hurt.

Finally, when the clock strikes a quarter to five and Mason's still not back, I'm about to start cleaning up for the day when the door chimes and a familiar face steps in.

Well, shit.

Busted.

"Michael?"

Tension roils through me at the darkness in his eyes. I don't know that I've ever seen Michael angry before.

At least not with me.

"Hannah Marie," he murmurs, shaking his head. "What the hell are you doing here?"

"Well . . . it's a long story . . ." I pause. "Wait, what are you doing here?"

"The charity coordinator called to ask me if you were still coming. Apparently, you never showed."

Backstabbing asshole.

"Well, I had other business to attend to," I say, attempting to act as detached as possible and wrap my arms over my chest.

He sighs in defeat, his head hanging low.

"Come here."

Letting out a deep breath, I concede, allowing him to wrap me in a hug.

"I was worried about you," he murmurs quietly and something in my chest pangs with guilt.

Of course, he was. You know who he's not worried about, though? My sister.

I step back, forcing some space between us because I still remember what we spoke about before I "left for the mission". That *it's time to seriously consider getting married* talk that always comes when one friend catches feelings and the other doesn't.

And that's what I get for drinking a little too much wine on a lonely Friday night three years ago.

"What the fuck happened to your neck?" Michael snaps, eyes glaring at the angry bruises on my skin.

"It's nothing," I reply, but he cuts me off, taking my chin and lifting my head. While he's a little too rough and it hurts, I don't move because I don't want to give in to the fact that it's still painful.

"Who the fuck did that? Carpenter?"

"No!" I snap, appalled that he would even suggest such a thing. "Mason actually stopped the guy from killing me, so be respectful. Especially in his shop."

"Yeah, and you're sure he didn't set it up in the first place? Send you running back to him?"

"You're being gross," I grimace, disgust pooling through me as visions of the man's face, beaten to nearly unrecognizable pieces, flash through my mind. "It was some psycho who was looking for Missy. He broke into my house in the middle of the night. I called Mason and he saved me."

He shakes his head, his jaw feathering as he looks around the lobby. "Yeah, always there to save the day." He steps away from me, his shoulders tight and his three-piece suit extremely out of place in the office of a mechanic. I'm not even sure Michael's ever stepped foot in a garage. "And he's got you working here."

"I like it," I shrug.

"It's too hot in here."

I roll my eyes.

"I'm not an infant, Mike. It's fun. The guys are all nice and it's not bad work. Mason pays me well."

"And when he's done with you?"

I glare at him. "Is this why you came here? To make me feel like shit?"

"Of course not," he grits, brown eyes flaring with aggravation. "I've come to take you home."

The room falls silent. Even the garage is silent as ice fills my veins.

Home.

"What?"

He sighs, rubbing a hand over his face. When he surfaces, he shoots me that Dad look that makes me feel like a petulant teenager and not a capable grown woman. An adult making her own choices, despite what everyone seems to believe.

"It's not safe for you to be out on the streets. Not with who your mother is."

"My *mother* is part of the problem. She won't look for Missy."

He takes my hand, a look of desperation flashing quickly across his face. "Let the cops handle Missy."

"Missy's my sister," I snap, tugging my hand free of his. "And I'm not giving up on her. I'm perfectly capable of taking care of myself."

"Yeah, your neck proves that." he grits angrily, attempting to reach for me, again. He only misses because I stumble back into the counter. "While it's admirable that you feel like you need to save her, Missy made her own bed, Hannah. I can't protect you here."

"She doesn't need your protection."

Both Michael and I fall silent as I turn to see Mason crowding the frame of the garage. It shuts behind him with a deafening metallic thud that seems to echo throughout the room. He looks at me only once, his stormy gaze searching my face like he can read me like a book before his eyes lock with Michael.

"Jesus Christ, Hannah," Michael mutters, gaze sinister as Mason steps up behind me. I can *feel* the volatile rage seeping off him like black smoke. Michael looks about as thrilled as Mason does and the two do their little dick measuring showdown right over my head. I wish I could see Mason's face, but I can practically feel the possessiveness radiating against my back.

Jesus. *Men.*

I've read about moments like these in romance novels. The two love interests face off for the main female character. I've always found it alluring, but this is not that and I don't want to be stuck in a romance novel love triangle. Especially since Mason barely tolerates me and Michael's just my best friend. Nothing more.

"So, you'd rather stay here than come home, Hannah Marie?"

I *hate* when Michael takes that fatherly tone. As if I didn't watch him eat a bug when we were nine years old because I dared him to. As if we didn't grow up side by side all these years.

"Don't call me that and *yes*. He's actually been *helping* me look for Missy instead of just telling me to sit back and let the men handle it." I cross my arms over my chest because I'm angry, then quickly uncross them because I realize, maybe I really do look like an angry teenager.

"I didn't say that."

"No, but you implied it," I bite.

Michael's jaw hardens as if he has the right to be angry. I'm the one that keeps getting blindsided. I'm the one who's standing in between two men who act like I'm the favorite toy at a preschool.

"I won't go back to Sacramento," I tell him quietly. He knows my reasons. I'm surprised he even thought to try. "It's final."

Michael stares at me for a long moment, as if he's memorizing my face. As if he knows something I don't. If I know Michael, though, he won't tell me. Not unless he thinks I'm in real danger.

"Hannah, I need to take you home—"

"She said, no."

"I didn't ask you," Michael grits.

"You didn't ask her, either."

Mason's voice is cool and indifferent, though I can feel the simmering rage seeping off him. I can't pretend to understand it. I know Michael's only looking out for me, but I also can't believe he doesn't know me better than that.

"Go. I'll text you," I say, working to keep my voice amicable. I know he's just worried about me. He's just going about it the wrong way.

Truth be told, Mason's is the safest place I've felt in a long, long time.

I step forward and give him another hug, just something to try and mend things between us, but the tension wound through him doesn't budge.

"I'll be fine."

Michael searches my face for a moment too long and for some reason, I feel sick. Uncomfortable.

I've never been uncomfortable around Michael. He's been my rock for fifteen years.

So, why do I now?

I pull away, backing up until I almost run into Mason and Michael gives me one lingering look before he heads toward the door with a shake of his head.

"I'll be back to check on you."

And then he's gone.

Mason doesn't say anything, but he doesn't need to. He doesn't like Michael. Michael doesn't like him.

Somehow, I'm still the one caught in the middle.

CHAPTER Twenty-Four

MASON

"You want *me*. To get on *there*."

It's not a question.

"Scared, little doe?"

Hannah looks distraught.

"No," she lies, swallowing past a lump in her throat. "I just don't like the thought of my head hitting the sweltering pavement."

"Sounds like an excuse."

Pretty green eyes narrow on me and she takes that as a challenge. It's almost too easy at this point. Determination flashes through her gaze and she steps up beside the bike.

"It's just a motorcycle, Hannah. I ride it every day."

She stares at the back seat and I know she's trying to determine a way to get on without touching me.

Funnily enough, it's the same reason I decided to drive it. Because she'd have to.

"I don't know how to get on." Her voice is small, as if admitting defeat doesn't come easy.

"Place your hand on my shoulder and your foot on the peg,

there."

Begrudgingly, she does as I tell her, her cheeks flaming as she climbs up on the back. I've had a passenger before, that's not the problem. The problem stems from having my little obsession on the back.

And now my dick's painfully hard.

"Put this on." I hand her a helmet. I don't always wear one, but Hannah will if she's going to be on the back of my bike.

"How many heads have been in this helmet?" she grumbles, wincing when she slips it over her hair.

"None," I murmur, cranking the engine and she pauses. "I bought it today."

"You . . . bought me a helmet?"

Jesus Christ.

"Tighten the strap," I answer, twisting around to make sure the damned thing is secure. "When I move, you move. We lean into the corners together and your hands don't leave me. Understood?"

She blinks back at me.

"Like, you want me to touch you?"

Unfortunately, in more ways than this.

"Yes."

I reach down, taking each of her knees and fastening them securely around my hips.

Fuck me.

Maybe this was a bad idea.

Hannah clears her throat heavily from behind me. "Now what?"

"Wrap your arms around me." I'm pissed off at the huskiness in my own voice.

"Like . . ."

"Around my stomach, Hannah."

Carefully, she wraps her arms around me, doing this uncomfortable dance behind me to not get too close, but still follow directions.

"All the way, Hannah."

"I think you're just doing this because you're yearning for a hug, but you're too afraid to ask," she murmurs under her breath, finally pressing against me.

My cock presses painfully against the zipper of my jeans. This shit's working out to be foreplay.

I grip her wrists, making sure they're wrapped tightly around me before I put the bike in gear.

"Remember what I said. Lean with me. On the bike, we're one. You go where I go."

"Sounds a little like a Hallmark movie," she breathes in my ear.

"Little doe, nothing about what I'm going to do to you would be in a Hallmark movie. Now, hold on."

We take off and the second the bike moves, Hannah's arms are tightening around me. I chuckle under my breath. We're not going that fast, but to Hannah, we're flying.

I remember my first time on a bike. I was eight on a dirt bike Dad used to own. There was no one with me, just Dad from the sidewalk, urging me to try again when I dumped the fucking thing over.

So, I got back up and rode for the rest of the day until I figured it out.

Now, taking Hannah out feels like Dad's still here, urging me to keep trying.

We pull to a stop at a red light and I reach down, running my fingers over Hannah's thigh and smirking under my helmet when she stiffens.

Her hand tightens on my stomach, just as a car pulls up beside us.

A couple girls sit in the front seat, giggling and waving at me. I don't pay any attention to them, but I can feel Hannah stiffen under my fingers.

So . . . I reach up, take her hand on my stomach and slide it down to my cock. Hannah doesn't move, save for a tremor that slips through her. I, on the other hand, chuckle behind the tinted shield of my helmet and take off as soon as the light hits green.

By the time we reach the gun range, Hannah's a fucking natural on the back of the bike. Not that I thought she wouldn't be. She picks shit up quicker than most, but by the time we pull to a stop, her body's molding with mine like it was fucking made to.

Perfection.

Her hands are shaking when she places them on my shoulder to climb down and I stifle a laugh.

"What was that?" she challenges as soon as I slip the helmet over her head.

For the first time in my life, I'm finding something adorable. From the disturbed hair to the flush in her cheeks.

I shrug. "They insulted you."

She rolls her eyes and my hand snaps out, catching under her jaw. She tenses, a quiet gasp leaving her lips when I gently pull her to me and press my lips to hers. Not kissing, just breathing her air.

"You're on the back of my bike. Not them."

I nip her lip, but I don't kiss her. Pulling away when it's not enough because I want her as starved for me as I am for her.

A delicate tremor rolls through her, but, again, she doesn't argue.

"Come on," I murmur, tightening the helmets on top of the bike. "Time for your first lesson."

Hannah jumps the moment a gun goes off near us, her eyes going wide as she searches around the gun range.

I've got guns. Plenty, but we can't shoot in Inglewood, so I brought her to a range.

I need to be sure she can handle herself if I'm not there and this is the best way to do that. Giving her some of the power back that her mother stole from her for all those years.

"Insert the mag."

"What?" she asks, jumping again when another shot rings off.

"Little doe, the mag. Inset it into the pistol." I take my own gun—a .9mm that I carry every day—and slide the mag up in place with a metallic click, showing her.

She stares at my hands, repeating the motion.

"Now—now what?" she stammers, her gaze slipping over the room.

"Hannah, am I going to have to *make* you pay attention to me?" I cock a brow.

"Sorry," she mumbles. "It's loud."

"It is. But there's nothing to worry about if you know what you're doing."

"But, I don't know what I'm doing."

"Yet; you will. Now, pull the slide back."

"What's the slide?"

"The piece on top," I demonstrate.

She does and then I motion for her to punch it forward.

"You're loaded, so don't point it at anything you don't want to kill."

"What if I don't want to kill anything?"

Jesus, this girl's going to make me go gray.

"Point it at the target." I nod down the range. "Ignore everyone else here and focus on that mark in the center."

She swallows, following my gaze to the bright pink target down at the other end of the room.

"Lift your arms and point exactly where you want to shoot. Keep your fingers off the trigger until you're ready to shoot."

She swallows, a flush rising in her cheeks when she lifts the gun.

"Straighten your arms."

"Am I going to hit myself in the face?"

"No."

"Feels like it," she murmurs, voice tight with anxiety. She pauses, sucking in a deep breath.

Then, her shoulders drop.

"I can't do this."

"Are you helpless?"

She gawks at me, her brows quickly furrowing together.

"What?"

I shrug. "You want to be helpless, there's nothing I can do for you."

"You can't force me to be okay with guns."

She purses her lips, cheeks flaming to match her lips. I step behind her and take her round hips in my hands, jerking her until she's facing straight down the line toward the target.

"Are you afraid of them? Or what you can do with them?"

Her mouth snaps shut, breath hitching from my lips at her ear. I run my nose up the column of her throat and though she'd deny it, a shiver rolls through her.

"I . . . I don't want to hurt anyone," she breathes, voice soft just like her skin when I slip my hand under her shirt.

I brush my thumb over her belly button, then higher until the cotton falls over to cover my hand. Hannah jerks in my grasp when I run my hands over the underside of her bra, her body molding perfectly against mine when I tug her back to me.

"You know how it feels on the bike?" I ask, voice low and dark in her ear, her heartbeat racing under my fingertips. Goosebumps pebble on the flesh under my lips, but she doesn't move away.

"Someone might see us," she whispers when my other hand slips lower, grazing over the smooth planes of her stomach to slip beneath the waistband of her jeans.

"If I slip my fingers in your panties right now, will you be wet?"

"Mason," she growls under her breath, but she fails to realize, there are no cameras here. Not in the range, or at least, none that can see us beyond the divider separating us from the other shooters. It's why I come here. I don't need anyone else in my way.

"Answer me, Hannah." I nip the shell of her ear and her eyes close of their own volition.

"Yes," she bites and I almost chuckle at the bitterness in her tone.

I can relate.

If I thought having her in my space would be a problem before I moved her in, I was wrong.

It's a goddamn nightmare.

She's everywhere and she did it all in less than twenty-four hours. Not that I'm surprised. She's always been a walking hard-on waiting to happen and having her scent around me constantly is like dangling a steak in front of a hungry lion.

Now she can see what it feels like.

"Does holding the power to protect yourself in your hands feel good, little doe?"

Her reply catches in her throat when I work the button of her jeans loose and very carefully slip my hand inside.

Fucking soaked.

I press my face into her neck, slipping her arousal around her clit.

Fuck, she's going to drive me insane.

"Hannah?"

"Yes." Even through the earplugs in my ears, I can hear the desire in her voice, carefully muted under a guise of sweetness.

I smirk, my fingers finding her clit, and withdraw my hand from under her shirt to lift her arm.

"Arms up."

She does as I say, letting me hold her arm up until her fingers are underneath mine on the gun. I hold her steady, growling softly in her ear when I let her choose the mark on our target.

"Let go of everything, little doe. Breathe and pull."

"Pretty hard to do that with your hand in my pants," she

whispers, so quiet, no one else could hear her over the sound of other shooters firing down the range.

"You have until that mag's empty to come. If you don't, I'll spank your ass when we get home."

That gets her going, and her pussy blooms under my fingers, her arousal leaking down my palm. I bite back a groan, circling her, and when the first shot rings off, she lets out a shaky breath, her thighs clenching on either side of my hand.

"That's my good girl," I murmur, low in her ear and she almost forgets what she's doing. "Nine left. Make them count."

She takes aim, again, and this time, she doesn't jump when she fires, instead biting her lip to silence a moan that threatens to claw its way from her lips.

She fires another, this time managing to hit the target off to the left.

"Does it make you wet that anyone could catch us right now?" I tease in her ear, and she nods softly, her ass pressing into my cock. I clench my eyes shut as heat builds at the base of my spine and she fires another shot.

If the bike was foreplay, this may as well be fucking.

She fires another, and then another after that until only a few remain. Her eyes pinch shut and I still my hand until they open.

"Always keep your eye on your attacker, little doe."

She growls under her breath, but listens, firing two more while her pussy clenches under my fingers.

"Fuck," I bite in her ear and a tremor rolls through her. "You going to come in my hand?"

She nods but doesn't speak while I circle her clit faster.

"Mason," she breathes unsteadily, pulse thrumming from where I reach up to take her tiny throat in my hands. I know she's right on the cusp of breaking, shattering under my fingers, and fuck do I want to hear her moans right now.

I also don't want to have to shoot anyone else who hears them, either.

“Come for me, Hannah. Now.”

I strum my fingers across her and she shudders in my grasp, her knees nearly buckling until I have to hold her up. She places the gun down on the counter in front of us, her eyes screwing shut and I force her lips back to mine to swallow her moans.

Fucking hell.

“Good girl,” I murmur, reaching around her and taking the gun before emptying the last two rounds into the target.

They hit right of center, by about an inch and I know it’s from the fucking shake in my hands.

“Someone could have seen us,” she bites, voice quiet, despite the gunfire around us and I chuckle, placing the empty gun on the table again.

“You’re under the impression I would *allow* anyone else to see you come for me, little doe.”

Her lips part, her cheeks flushed, but before she can say anything, I hand her the box I picked up this morning.

Can’t have anyone finding her, so I took the liberty of getting something for her myself.

“You . . .”

I cut her off with a finger to her lips and she falls silent.

“That stays with you at all times.” I step closer, pressing into her until her ass is resting against the table.

“What happens if someone finds out?”

I shrug and just because I feel like I need to, I nip the flesh of her jaw in my teeth.

“Don’t get caught.”

“Wow, these are really good,” Hannah says, surprised as she

takes her first-ever bite of cheeseburger.

I cock a brow at her, and she flushes.

"Are you sure you're an American?"

"Very funny," she deadpans and I stifle a laugh. "Mom preferred . . . extravagant dinners over simple ones and by the time I got to college, I guess I just forgot to try this. I've never had a hot dog before, either."

She pauses, mid-bite. "What's your favorite food?"

"Lasagna." I wait and she looks afraid to admit it. "You've never had it, either."

"Yes, I've had lasagna," she rolls her eyes. "Just . . . probably not the way you have."

"We're going to need to broaden your horizons if we're going to be working together, little doe."

"Hey, I've done three new things today. Four if you count the getting fingered in public part."

My eyes flash wickedly and she blushes, looking anywhere but at me.

"It's not the first time I've had my fingers inside you in public."

"Okay, we are *not* going there." She bites into a homemade fry. "Tell me about tonight."

I smirk, letting her change the subject, because as much as I love making her blush—and come—we have a job to do as soon as night falls.

"We go, park the truck a few blocks away and sneak in."

"Do you even know where we're going?"

"Do you?" I challenge and she purses her lips. "It's downtown. A few blocks from the Inner Sanctum. We'll park the truck there."

"What if someone sees us and follows?"

"Drew?"

She nods her head warily.

"Drew Marshall won't be a problem anymore."

"One down, fifteen to go," she murmurs. "And what about once we get there?"

I shrug. "We'll cross that bridge when we get to it."

"I don't like this plan."

"Do you have a better one?"

"No," she admits. "What about the Nightstalker wannabe? Heard anything about him?"

"Nothing that would interest you."

In fact, I haven't heard jack shit. Logan's been MIA all day and I'd rather chop my dick off than reach out to my sister right now. Especially with her looming threat that we need to speak about Hannah.

"I keep thinking about it," Hannah murmurs, shaking her head. "I haven't told anyone I was here. How did Michael know where to look for me?"

I lean back in my chair, pushing my empty plate away from me.

It's almost easy to forget she's the governor's daughter when she's sitting in my little kitchen, eating a cheeseburger for the first time in her life. It's . . . normal. Comfortable. And that's why it's a problem.

I'm happy to see that since she's been working with me, she doesn't cover the freckles on her cheeks and nose anymore. In fact, she's forgone most of her makeup, the expensive clothes, the taming of the wild waves in her hair. The late evening sun shines through the window over the sink in front of her, painting her in shades of gold and orange and, for a second, my chest aches. She looks like a fucking angel.

Temptation never looked so fucking sweet.

Then, I shove that shit down.

"I've always wondered if they have a tracker in my phone or something." She rolls her eyes as if this violation of her privacy is something all parents do. My mother did it. Yeah, it saved Savannah's life when she was kidnapped last year, but my sisters are all still wary of gifts from her for that reason.

"He shows up at my shop threatening you again, it'll be the last thing he ever does. Mark my words, Hannah."

Fucking prick. I should have gotten rid of him when I had the chance. The first time I had Hannah's sweet mouth on mine and caught him watching us from the shadows should have been the last. Now, he knows where she is, so it's only a matter of time before *they* show up next.

Truth be told, his involvement now pisses me off. Showing up at my garage to play hero after the job was done. He had his chance to put an end to this when Melissa first went off the deep end. He did nothing, in lieu of staying in good with Mommy dearest.

There was something more to his visit today than what I've told Hannah. He's planning something and while she may think he's only looking out for her, I could see through that shit. She wants to believe everyone's good and that a little evil doesn't lurk in all of us. I know better.

Especially with that fucking smirk he shot me over Hannah's shoulder when he had his arms around her.

"You two. Why do you hate him so much?" She's not accusing. Merely asking, but I don't like her defending him. He doesn't deserve it.

I eye her for a moment, taking a drink of my beer.

"Because he wants to fuck you."

Her eyes widen and I almost laugh, but then I remember the way he tried to wrap his arms around her today, as if he could hide her from me, and I'm pissed off all over again.

"And . . . why doesn't Michael like you?"

Because you're mine.

"Because you want me to fuck you."

Her cheeks flame and she looks anywhere in the room but at me. It's . . . cute and I can't believe that word is something I would ever use. *Cute* and *me* sounds like a fucking joke.

"You're awfully presumptuous," she says, clearing her throat before swallowing half her sweet tea in one go.

"Am I wrong?" I know I'm not.

She cocks a brow, studying me for a moment.

"I think you're attractive," she concedes. "But . . . you and I can barely get along unless some part of me is touching some part of you. Or if someone's trying to kill me."

"We're getting along right now."

Her lips purse. Got her with that one.

"You make it sound like this is one-sided. We both know it's not."

I shrug. "It's not. I'm also not holding my dick, hoping you'll choose me. You want to go with Michael, I won't stop you."

Something about my answer doesn't sit well with her. The amusement in her eyes drifts away and it's replaced with the same melancholy distrust I saw when I first met her.

Something about it . . . makes me feel like I've swallowed battery acid.

"Right," she says as if she's trying to solidify it for herself. Abruptly, she stands, taking both our plates over to the sink.

Instinctively, I reach for her because that stupid fucking voice in the back of my head panics at the thought of her leaving.

Jesus Christ. Who knew my life would hinge on a little five-foot, four-inch firecracker?

Certainly not fucking I.

I manage to catch her hand and I can see the way she purses her lips.

"Hannah—" I start, but she cuts me off.

"We have a job to do," she says quietly, tugging her hand away from me and going to the sink to clean up.

Men like me ruin pretty little girls like you, little doe.

If I had known that night almost three years ago how everything would change, would I have done something differently? Driven right past her before I got too sucked in? Before she became the focal point of my world, even if she isn't a part of it?

I know the answer. I'm not a fucking idiot. I also know dwelling on the problem at hand won't change the outcome.

I'll help her find her sister, make sure she's safe, and then send her on her way. She can go back to her mother if that's what she wants and I'll go back to pretending she's not mine.

"You're upset."

"I'm not," she grits, though she and I both know that's a lie. "I don't fit into your world. You've said it a thousand times."

Yet, I'd burn the fucking world to the ground if it means she'd stay.

And then I shake myself.

It's better she realizes now that this thing between us is volatile. It'll only end one of two ways, neither of which ends with me and her riding off into the sunset together.

I want her.

It's dangerous, but . . . I can't tell her that.

Hannah places the plates in the dishwasher and dries her hands before turning back to me. Her expression is guarded, closed off and that fucking fake smile I've always hated threatens to tug on the corners of her lips.

"I'm going to go get ready for tonight. Thank you for dinner."

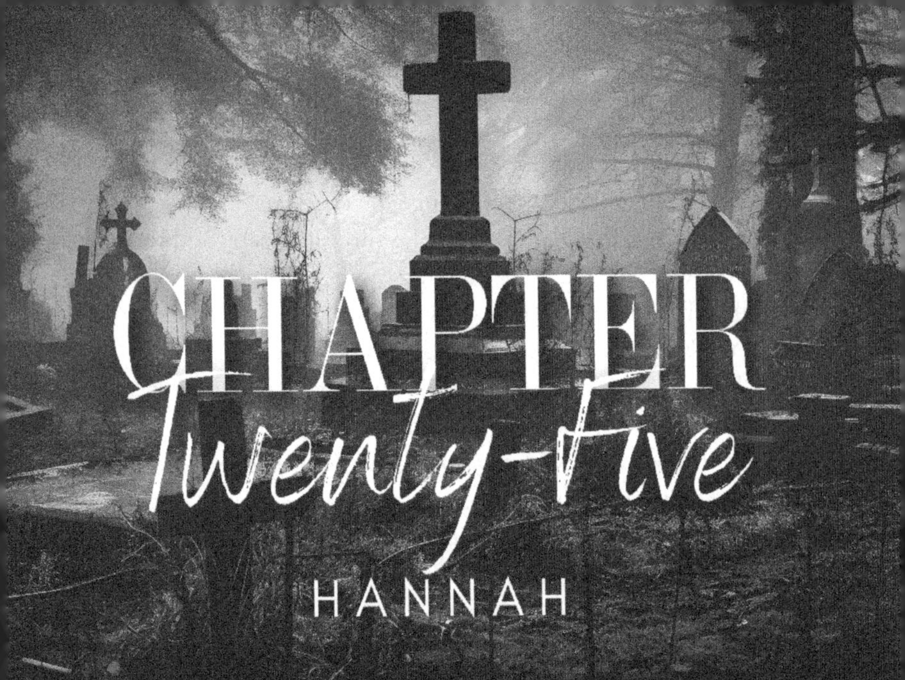

CHAPTER *Twenty-Five*

HANNAH

"It stinks here."

Mason cocks a brow at me, but otherwise, doesn't say anything.

I have to admit, the truck ride from Inglewood to the heart of downtown was . . . tense. To say the least.

Neither of us is acknowledging dinner. The gun range. His fingering me *at* the gun range. It's like there was this big elephant sitting in the back seat, just looking between the two of us and waiting. To be honest, I thought about faking sick tonight.

But . . . like always, Missy popped into my mind, making me feel guilty for abandoning her, so I put my big girl panties on—literally, I wore a thong in case another "situation" occurred—and joined Mason in his truck after the sun went down.

Now, we're standing in front of what looks to be an abandoned warehouse, right outside the fashion district.

This area of town isn't great. The poverty and crime rates are high, and while those two things don't go hand in hand, theft and violence do. Mason parked the truck a couple blocks away, in a garage, and we had to hike here, so I'm glad I wore my old sneakers.

At least I'm not in a leather skirt, heels, and a corset tonight. I'd opted for a black T-shirt, black pants, and black shoes, so I at least *look* the part of a ninja in the night, even if I don't feel like one.

To be honest, my stomach is cramping because I have no idea what we're walking into.

"How the fuck do we get in?" Mason murmurs. The place is huge and if whoever has Missy is using this as some kind of base of operations, I'm willing to bet they have the place rigged to know when someone's here.

I scan the building, though, in the dark alleyway, it's more than difficult.

"There."

He follows my line of sight to a busted window a couple stories up. There's an old, teetering fire escape that I could reach with a little boost.

"Lift me up there."

"Hannah."

I roll my eyes. "Like you can't pick me up?"

"It's dangerous."

"Do you have a better idea?"

He looks like the ladder personally wronged his grandmother.

And then it dawns on me . . .

"Are you afraid of heights?"

"Did I say that?"

I suppress a chuckle. Mason Carpenter being afraid of *anything* is astounding to me.

"It'll be fine," I assure him and he shoots me a dark look. "It's not even that high. You probably—*definitely* wouldn't die from a three-story fall. And this thing was built back when stuff was made to last. It's not falling off from us." *I hope.*

Okay, you definitely would die, especially on the hard concrete alleyway below, but I don't tell him that.

"Look. I don't need scared of heights Mason, right now. I need fearless, hot, big-muscled Mason who makes me feel like I'm safe for the first time in my life."

His jaw ticks and despite the heat burning on my cheeks, I feel triumphant at the subtle shift in his demeanor.

I got him.

With a deep sigh, he steps up behind me and I turn away so he can't see my triumphant smile.

He places his hands around my waist and if we were anywhere besides a dirty alley that looks like rats have raised entire family trees of their offspring here, it would be hot. It still makes me blush, though mostly because when he lifts me up, my ass is nearly eye level with his face and I can't stop thinking about this afternoon.

I grab the ladder and he hoists me higher to reach my foot to the bottom rung, slipping and almost crashing to the ground below. Mason, in his precarious position, puts a hand firmly on my ass to steady me.

"Jesus fucking Christ," Mason grits under his breath and I can't decide if it's because he's worried about me or because he just really doesn't want to do this.

I'm going with the latter. Seems safer.

Hauling myself up—no easy feat because I'm not strong—I manage to make it to the first level of the fire escape, albeit, completely out of breath.

"Are you coming?"

He glares up at me but doesn't say anything. I watch him do a little hop and reach the bottom of the ladder easily—asshole— before he's climbing up.

"What?" he asks when he reaches the top and I just shake my head. The bastard's not even winded. "We need to work on your stamina, little doe."

Rude.

"My stamina was just fine this afternoon, thank you."

He chuckles darkly but follows me as I climb the rickety stairs as quietly as I can to the third floor. We're high up and Mason moves slower the higher we go. It's almost sweet, seeing the big, dark, and dangerous man afraid of heights. Makes him seem more human, rather than some unobtainable god.

I crouch down in front of the busted window and work on prying the lock inside open so we can slip through. Meanwhile, Mason crouches behind me, *way* too close for me to focus.

"Can you back up? You're clouding my judgment."

"Little doe," he says, voice rough. "Get the fucking lock open."

I stare at him for a beat, and then it dawns on me.

And now, I'm softening for him. Honestly, who am I?

"Okay. It's okay," I start and as if it wants to spite me, the fire escape makes a quiet metallic groan.

I pry at the lock inside with all my might, hurting my fingers until finally, the old metal latch clicks, and I can slip the window open.

I climb through, hastily moving out of the way so Mason can join me. It's amusing to me that his shoulders are so broad, he barely fits through the old window, but soon, he's standing on the old concrete floor beside me.

"That wasn't so bad, was it?"

His jaw ticks.

"Just looks like an old office to me," I whisper, keeping my voice low and aiming the flashlight in my hand around the room. Papers for a printing company lay scattered on the old desks and the floor, none of which are any help to us.

"Hannah," Mason murmurs from across the room. He motions for me to join him, so I do, being careful to step over the stuff on the floor that could give us away.

"What?" I follow his flashlight. Stairs. He steps down and I follow him, keeping close behind him as we descend because even though we're on the hunt for rogue people, *ghosts* are still a concern of mine and I don't care who knows it. There's more than just people who go bump in the night and while a person can be dealt with, a ghost, you can't shoot.

The second floor leads to a rickety skywalk over what used to be the printing factory below, so I don't even bother. I barely got Mason up the fire escape.

Finally, he stops at the doorway to the first floor, keeping his flashlight off and watching.

I peek under his arm and pause. Empty.

Well, shit.

There's nothing here. The inside of the factory is completely devoid of anything, including equipment. Water sits on the low parts of the ground and some debris from the crumbling walls litters the ground, but, apart from that, there's nothing that could lead us to Missy.

"That asshole lied to us," I whisper, but just as I do, a thud sounds from somewhere . . . else.

Mason clicks his flashlight on the dimmest setting and points it down another set of stairs, directly behind me. My foot teeters on the edge. If I would have stepped back, I would have fallen.

I scramble away, my irrational fear of the dark taking hold for a moment and sending a shot of panic through me. Mason catches me, an arm around my waist, and aims his flashlight down.

"Come on."

"Are you sure?"

He pauses at the top of the stairs, raising a brow. "Don't tell me, you're afraid of the dark."

Asshole.

"Maybe we really are a match made in heaven," I grumble stepping past him while he chuckles quietly.

The basement is where dreams come to die. A demon would be afraid to lurk in the dark down here, much less me. Mason is scary and all, but the never-ending darkness that seems as thick as maple syrup is next level.

"Breathe, little doe," Mason murmurs softly as we step into what appears to be a long hallway. I say *long hallway* because we can only see right in front of us with the flashlight on dim.

"I'm breathing." Barely.

"You're shaking."

"Yeah, well, maybe I don't like the dark."

"Relax," he says, so close to my ear I nearly jump out of my skin. I hadn't realized he was that close. "I'm scarier than anything lurking in the dark."

God, I hope he's right. I open my mouth to speak, but stop when I see a door looming just out of range of the flashlight. Surprisingly . . . stupidly, the door is partially open and a light shines dimly in the crack. Mason peeks his head around the corner before pulling back and opening the door.

"Holy fucking shit," Mason murmurs, stepping inside.

I follow him and for a moment, my eyes struggle to adjust.

Then I see the cages.

Cages line the walls. Thick, metal cages with iron padlocks like what they use in old cartoons to transport animals. They're empty,

The room *stinks*. Like mold and decay and . . . death. I cover my nose with my hand and my eyes water at the stench. In the center of the room sits an old incinerator, probably used to burn the old papers that were either messed up or weren't sold and it burns brightly, lighting up the room.

"What do you think they kept in these?" I ask quietly, though I know the answer.

Mason's eyes are hard as he scans the room, taking in the cages and the incinerator. It's not hard to decipher what happened here.

"Definitely not animals," he murmurs darkly.

"Mason . . ." I grab his hand because I feel like I'm going to be sick. In the darkness beside the incinerator is a long tarp. On top of that tarp, are the bodies of four dead women.

"Fuck," he murmurs and I gag as the scent of murder fills my nostrils and mouth. "Turn away."

"What if it's her?" Tears burn in my eyes, clouding my vision, but for once, I don't see the hate on his face at the mention of Missy.

"Turn away. I'll check."

Forcefully, he turns me around to face the door and I hear his heavy bootfalls as he makes his way over to the corpses.

A laugh sounds above us and I freeze, all the hair on my arms standing straight up.

"*Fuck*," Mason curses under his breath, rejoining me in the center of the room. He tugs his gun out of the back of his jeans, aiming it at the door.

"*No*," I growl. I don't think I could stomach him getting shot tonight. "We have to hide."

Reluctantly, he shoves the gun back in its holster and steers me with a hand on the small of my back. I move toward the door, but he hauls me back to a small closet that I'm not sure both of us can fit in.

Mason opens the door and climbs inside and before I can react, he's reaching forward, wrapping his arms around my waist and pulling me in on top of him. He's so large he barely fits, but he pulls me down onto his lap and locks me against his chest with an arm around my stomach.

Just as he shuts the door most of the way, heavy bootfalls sound from the dirty concrete floor outside.

"Why does Martinez always get to go first?" a male voice whines. Three men pass by the small crack in our door, but none of them look our way.

"Because Martinez shows up for his watch on time," an older man retorts, pushing a cigar between his lips and lighting it with a match.

"You always rough them up too much. No one else wants them after you," another guy says and Mason's arms tighten around me to the point that I think he might squeeze me to death.

They all snicker and the second man opens the door of the incinerator. Fire blazes from inside, filling the already hot room with heat. A bead of sweat travels down my neck, between my breasts, but still, I don't move.

"What are they doing?" I breathe, when the guy who complained about Martinez moves toward the women on the tarp.

Mason presses his lips against my ear, his voice so low, even I can barely hear it. "She's not here."

Trembles rack through me and Mason takes my hand in his, holding it firmly against my stomach as I watch in horror while two of the men lift up one of the women and carry her over to the incinerator.

They can't be . . .

"How much longer do we have to do this shit? This one stinks."

"You've left her down here too long," the older man says, still smoking his cigar and watching from a distance. "You've got to know when to throw your toys away."

The other guy chuckles as they toss the woman into the flames. Just like she's trash.

"Until boss says to stop."

"Well, when the fuck is that going to be?"

"You know how the government works. Everything happens on their time."

I freeze. The government?

"Just be happy they aren't throwing us in the furnace after that shit Beck pulled."

"Governor's daughter. Man, I would have loved to take a slice of that pie."

"Nah. That bitch was crazy. He did us a favor letting her go. Her sister, though . . ."

Mason's hand tightens around mine to near-bruising strength, but he doesn't move. I can feel the tension radiating through him when they toss another body in the incinerator, not a care in the world that these were real people. People with families and moms and dads. Probably even kids.

"Good luck getting that one," the older man says. "Mommy's little princess."

"We need to get out of here," I breathe, saliva pooling in my mouth. That would be something, wouldn't it? My vomiting giving us away?

"We will," Mason murmurs in my ear. "I've got you."

"She's spoken for."

They all fall silent as a new voice comes into the room from somewhere we can't see. They've just thrown the fourth woman in the fire. It sounds familiar, but I can't make it out.

"Oh, is she now?" the older man chuckles. "Mommy dearest promise you a little piece of that cherry pie if you keep an eye on us?"

"Something like that."

Ew.

Double ew.

My skin feels itchy. Like there are ants crawling on me at the thought of whoever this mystery man is getting a piece of my *anything.*

"Got room for another?"

"Jesus Christ. You fucking killed her already?" the guy who hates Martinez asks.

"She bit Martinez in the dick. He put a bullet through her head," the new guy answers. "Just get her out of here. Place stinks enough as it is."

Mason's hand comes over my mouth and he pulls my head back against his chest to keep me quiet. I know that voice.

I stare as hard as I can through the crack in the door, and finally, I catch a good look at the new guy's face.

Michael.

Tremors begin to slide through my body, the harsh reality of what I've been blind to for years running rampant through my mind.

If Michael's in on this . . . does that mean my mother is, too?

"A moment of silence for the best pussy we've had all week," the old man says as they all place their hands on their hearts.

"And may we get another soon," another laughs.

"Amen."

They're silent for a single second before the old man shrugs. "Toss her in. I'm tired."

I lurch for the door, but Mason's arms won't let me move even a single inch. Tears burn in my eyes, but it's nothing compared to the gut-wrenching sickness in my stomach for the women they've killed. Raped. Tortured.

Michael chuckles, helping another guy throw the young woman in the flames.

Michael. The boy who wouldn't hurt a fly.

"Still think he's a good guy, little doe?" Mason murmurs quietly in my ear.

The men in the room are talking, but I can't make out what they're saying. My head's spinning from the revelation that my best friend, and possibly even my mother, is a part of this.

"That's the last of them. Let them bake for a while and we'll be good to go."

"I say we call it a night."

"Got a bottle of whiskey upstairs," the old man says, stepping out of view. Their voices drift toward the door and then down the hall, but all the while I can't stop staring at the incinerator in the center of the room.

The scent is awful. Different than the decay and while that still lingers, this is . . . stomach turning. Like sulfur and rotten meat and everything else you don't want to smell when you think of another person.

Mason and I sit there for God knows how long. Long enough for my legs to hurt from being cramped and long enough for the incinerator to die down enough that the heat isn't scorching.

Finally, he wakes me from my haze, slowly opening the door to our cabinet, so it doesn't make a sound.

"Hannah."

Carefully, I climb off his lap, watching the incinerator, as if it's going to reach out and grab me. Mason said none of the women on the floor were Missy and the men had mentioned someone let her go, but . . . where *did* she go? She hadn't come to me. Parker's in jail. Mom would have sent her right back here.

Even as Mason wraps his fingers around mine and tugs me toward a small door that leads outside to the alley where everything started tonight, I can't get the simple question out of my head.

Where in the world is Melissa Gaines?

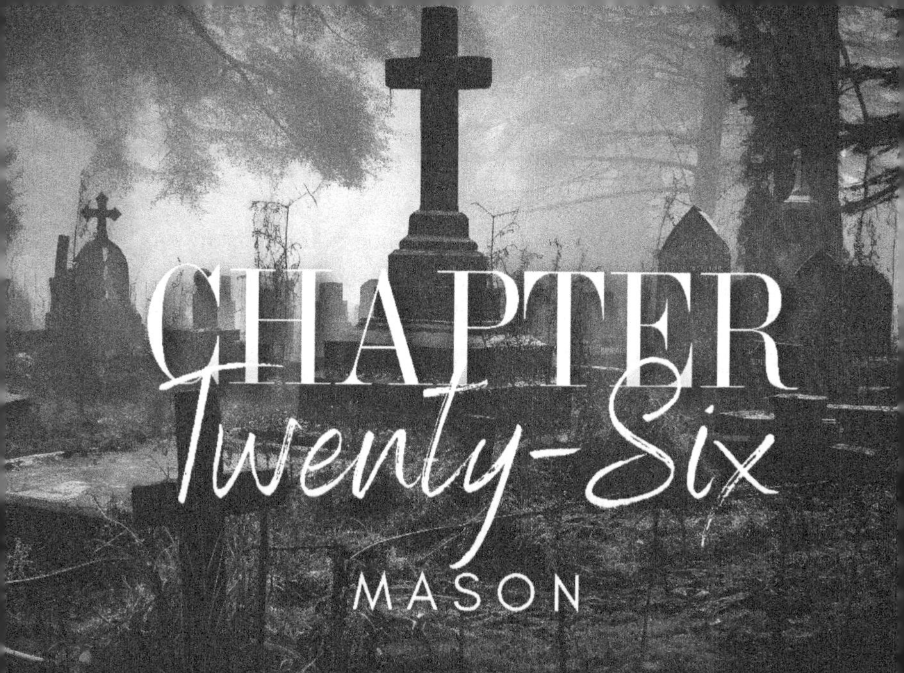

CHAPTER Twenty-Six

MASON

"It wasn't her, Hannah."

She's been quiet on the car ride home. After everything we found tonight, I don't blame her. I regret bringing her here. I should have come alone. Or with Prince. She shouldn't have to see the destruction her mother is causing. The mess her "best friend" is at the centerfold of.

She needed to know, though, and she never would have believed me if she hadn't seen for herself.

I knew they were trafficking people. What I didn't expect is the *who*.

"I believe you," she says quietly, looking out the window. I wish I could read her mind. Pick up on whatever the hell's going on in that pretty little fucked-up head of hers, but I can't.

"Those girls . . . I recognized two of them as people that hung around in Parker's circles. Rich girls."

She looks at me as if I've lost my mind.

"Are you saying my mother is trafficking rich kids?"

"I'm saying they're hunting down the children of Parker's

friends."

She falls silent.

"That would explain why they continue to torment my mother. Mila lives with her so, she's no better off. Savannah has Prince. Bailey is all the way in New Orleans and has Charlie. And . . . someone attacked you."

"Why would they do that?"

I shrug. "Isn't it obvious? They know too much. Shit that could upend everything."

"My mother wasn't Parker's friend—"

It dawns on us at the same time.

"Parker was one of your mother's biggest sponsors."

"And Michael . . ." I can feel her watching me from the corner of her eye. Honestly, I knew he was up to something and now that I know what it is, I'm wishing I had gone with my original plan of killing him when he showed up at my shop and demanded Hannah go with him. I have no doubt in my mind he was planning on taking her for himself to God only knows where. "Do you think he has anything to do with the attack?"

I grip the steering wheel until my knuckles turn white. "Little doe, I think he has everything to do with the attack."

She lets out a shaky breath. "Why would he do that? We've been friends since we were kids."

"You heard him. Your mother promised him you in exchange for tying up her loose ends. If he scared you enough . . ."

"I'd run right into his arms."

She shakes her head, leaning back in the seat. I can tell she's tired. I'm fucking tired. I'm also pissed off at the prospect of Michael touching her with the same hands he touched those dead girls with. Murder and rape one to go home to another?

Hannah's too fucking good for me. I know it . . . but Michael makes me look like a fucking saint. I'll kill him before he gets his hands on her. I'll make it hurt.

"Is there anywhere else your sister would go?"

"No."

"Anywhere—"

"I said, *no.*"

"Hannah, we have to find her, one way or the other—"

"Can we just drop it for now?" she snaps.

I want to fight with her. Fuck, I really do. I want that fire back in her eyes that was there before Michael and her mother snuffed it out. Before she saw all that shit tonight.

I want her.

So, I do the only fucking thing I know how to and reach across the center console to take her hand. She lets me slip my fingers through hers. So I do.

Is this how you do it? Comfort and romance and shit? Her hand feels small in mine, the simplest of touches feeling like electric shocks to my dick.

"Thank you," she says quietly, and I don't have to look over to know she's crying.

We ride in silence the rest of the way home. I don't bother pushing her tonight and she doesn't offer any thoughts.

What I can't get out of my head is how easy it was for them to desecrate those women. How mundane it had gotten for them that throwing the bodies of their victims in the incinerator was just an everyday job.

It's not until I pull to a stop in the driveway that I realize she's asleep in the passenger seat. She looks so damned peaceful. After the heat of today, the attack last night, and now, everything that we've just learned, I don't want to wake her.

She doesn't stir until I'm laying her in her bed.

"Mason . . ." she grumbles, eyes still shut when I undo the knots on her shoelaces. I've never done this before. Not without sex involved. I don't like it. It feels too . . . intimate. Too much for me to think about later when I can't sleep.

I remove her shoes and place them by the old vanity I set up for her when I ran my errands today. It was Mom's, but I knew Hannah would like it. It's been sitting in storage, anyway. "Little doe, sit up so I can take your jeans off."

She blinks one bloodshot eye open at me, burning in the dim light of the nightstand lamp. She complies though, lifting her hips, so I can slide her jeans down her legs and toss them in the hamper. Finally, I slip her into the center of the bed and she rolls over, quickly falling back to sleep.

It hurts to look at her. She's too fucking perfect and in my head, I know I can't keep her.

We're too different. Too close to enemies to be anything else, but . . . as I cover her up with the comforter and step from her room . . .

Suddenly, I wish I could.

"You get information about where Melissa Gaines could be hiding out and you don't think to tell me?"

I didn't want to come here. It's late and there's a storm raging outside. Savannah's already in bed, but I knew I needed to alert Logan of the warehouse before Michael and his band of merry traffickers had the chance to move.

Besides, the conversation Savannah wants to have is the last one I do after tonight.

Places like that don't stay in one place. They shift, jumping from building to building so they can avoid being caught. Michael's not an idiot. Well . . . at least not in that sense.

"I'm telling you now. And she wasn't there."

"Jesus fucking Christ," Logan grumbles, scrubbing a hand across his face. "And you took Hannah, of all people. Her damned sister."

"You wouldn't have that information if it weren't for her."

He shakes his head. "Look, I don't give a shit about whatever Romeo and Juliet situation you've got going on. But do you really think if she's going to this length to find her sister, that she'll just turn right around and give her to the cops?"

"Yeah, I do." In fact, I know she would. Logan eyes me, his dark gaze reproachful. "They're hunting the kids of the Brethren, Logan."

He seems to understand the gravity of my statement after a moment.

"Don't tell Savannah."

"Not a smart move. She finds out, she'll be pissed."

"I know she will, but . . . your sister's learning how to feel safe. I don't want this fucking everything up. She's got security. She's got me. She'll be protected."

"You don't sound so sure."

Logan eyes me, calculating.

"When your sister went missing, I fucking lost my mind. Destroyed my house. Threw some kid through a wall. All because I failed her. Because I let her be taken." He leans forward, lowering his voice. "That won't happen again."

"Then you'll understand when I tell you I'm going to kill the governor of California."

The room falls silent, only the sound of the AC whirring in the background.

"And I suppose you want immunity."

I shrug. "Whatever you see fit."

"All this for her?" He cocks a brow at me and tension slips into my shoulders.

"You know how you said Savannah's learning to be safe. Hannah will never be safe, so long as her mother's alive. No matter what I or anyone else does."

"I wanted Parker dead. All the shit he'd done to your sister and to others. He doesn't deserve a fair trial. He also doesn't deserve the ultimate kindness, either. I want to watch him rot."

"I want to watch Laura Gaines choke in a pool of her own blood."

Logan ponders this for a moment, before sitting forward.

"We can use her."

"No."

"Well, do you want her safe, or not?"

"I want her safe. Not sacrificed."

"Well, sometimes, you've got to sacrifice a little to get what you need. There's a charity ball next week. Take her. She can keep up appearances with her mother and she'll know where she's at."

"So she can kidnap her? Not fucking happening."

"No . . . so she can see that there's someone standing in her way. She won't touch her with you connected to Parker. She won't want to get involved."

"Sounds like a shit plan."

Logan shrugs. "You have a better one?"

I shake my head, chuckling bitterly.

"Almost a year later and Parker's still fucking with us."

"Fucking tell me about it."

"So, I take her to this thing, then what?"

"Then, we wait. It's like playing chess. You don't move all your pieces at once. Just keep Hannah safe, make sure she doesn't go wandering off. Whatever you've got to do."

"No."

Both Logan and I turn toward the doorway to the kitchen. Savannah stands there, eyes full of tears and glistening in the light overhead. I grit my teeth, steeling myself for what I know she wants to say.

"Don't do this," she bites and Logan scrubs a hand over his face.

"Savannah—" he starts, but she cuts him off.

"*No.* You said it yourself. Having her around is dangerous. We just went through hell, Mason."

"Yeah, well, you're not the only one and just because you're safe and sound in your little Santa Monica mansion doesn't mean everyone else is."

While Logan sits staring back and forth between the two of us, my sister is not so easily perturbed.

"I want to put all of that behind me. Parker, Melissa Gaines. The Brethren. I want a life, Mason."

"What would you do, Savannah?"

Her lips clamp shut and she pauses, glaring at me.

"What would you do if Bailey was Melissa Gaines? Mila?"

"That's a ridiculous thing to say."

"Answer the question."

"I would let justice take its course," she says quietly.

"Bullshit. You and I both know you'd fight tooth and nail to save either one of them."

"Why does she need you?"

"Why?" Jesus fucking Christ. I should have left when I had the chance. "Because of people like you that blame her for what her sister did."

"Jesus Christ," Logan grumbles, standing up and going for the bar in the corner of the room. Right now, I can't blame him.

"She knew what was happening—"

"Did I?" I wait for her to answer, but it doesn't come. "Did Mila? Mom?"

I've backed her into a corner. She knows it and I know it.

We stand there, seething for a moment. Both of us pissed off because Hannah exists and me pissed off because Melissa does. Without her, maybe shit would be different and I wouldn't be having this conversation right now. Maybe I wouldn't even know Hannah.

She'd be married off to some rich kid. Raising spoiled children and attending business parties in some high-dollar gown that probably costs more than what I make in a month, not asleep at home—*my* home.

I can't lie, the thought of her with someone else feels like I swallowed battery acid.

"You're in love with her . . ." Savannah says softly, eyes shining with unshed tears in the light. "Aren't you?"

I grit my teeth, something like electricity shooting down my spine. I'm not in love with her. I'm obsessed with her and the difference is clear. I can't stand her, but I won't give her up, either.

"Oh my God," Savannah shakes her head, sitting down in a chair beside the door. You would have thought I'd just told her someone was dead.

I don't fully understand, and maybe I never will, but I can't justify hatred by blaming someone else for their family member's actions. Mom was married to Parker and while we've got our shit, I don't blame her for everything he did. Bailey almost married Drew and I don't blame her for the nasty shit he does. Hannah may be Melissa's sister, twin even, but she didn't help Parker traffic those girls. In my eyes . . . trying to stop it. Trying to save someone who hurt you in ways I can't imagine. Hannah's a fucking saint.

"She'll ruin you, you know?"

"And if she does, I'll let her."

Savannah's eyes widen in shock. I wasn't lying when I said I don't get attached.

I need to get the fuck out of here.

I head toward the door, but Savannah's voice rings out from the dining room when my hand touches the knob.

"Why her? Out of everyone else in the world?"

I think about lying, but this time, I can't. I need her to understand, I'm not walking away from this fight.

"Because she exists."

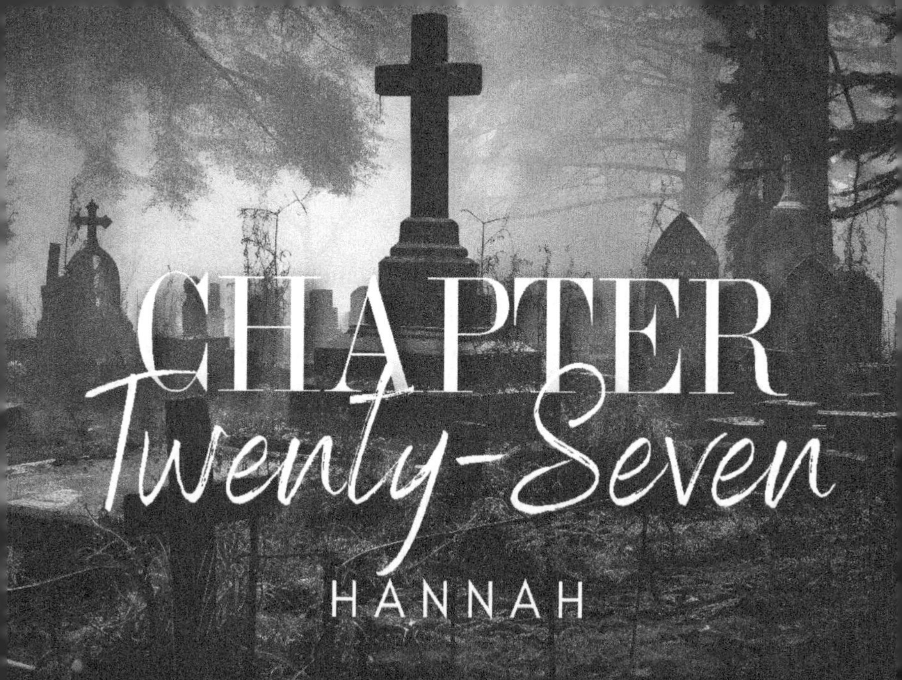

CHAPTER Twenty-Seven

HANNAH

I can't sleep.

I woke shortly after Mason left and forced myself to shower because I could feel the sickness of that place on my skin. I was still awake even when I heard him come home. I listened to his footsteps on the hardwood floor outside my door, before they retreated quietly to his room.

The rain pounding against my window is, to put it lightly, the least of my worries.

My sister is still missing. Fact.

My best friend is helping to traffic men and women and facilitating their deaths as well as rapes. Fact.

Mason Carpenter is the only person I feel like I can really trust in this world.

Unfortunately, fact.

I can't help but feel like this is only borrowed time with him. Like he'll wake up tomorrow and decide I'm not worth the trouble. That Missy's only going to get what she deserves because, let's face it, she's an asshole. Even if the rumors aren't true, she still wouldn't be a good person underneath it all, and for most people that's enough to give up.

I'm not that smart.

I should walk away. Count my losses and cut contact with the entire state of California. Maybe somewhere across the world. Maybe somewhere tropical. Somewhere no one would think to look for me so I could live out my days in undefined peace. Away from my mother. My sister. Michael.

Mason . . .

For some odd reason, Mason hurts.

Maybe it's just the way he can make me come like he was born to do it or maybe it's because, try as I might, I can't stop the tightening in my chest when I see him. Or the way I could listen to him talk in that deep voice for hours. Or the way his eyes make me feel like I'm the only woman he's ever seen.

Either way, it can only end one way. He ghosted me once and even then I thought maybe he was just afraid of his own feelings. Maybe my mother scared him off or maybe he was just busy when he didn't show up the day he said he would.

The next day came and went, though. Then the next and eventually, I started to understand in the back of my mind that he *wasn't* going to come back because I was nothing more than a passing moment for him.

A girl with baggage and a dangerous sister.

Mom was right.

He doesn't even like you. He just wants what's between your legs."

And that's the big joke, isn't it?

Girl likes a guy. Guy decides she's not good enough or is too boring. Maybe she won't let him try anal with her or maybe she's not into whatever the next girl is.

Next girl is exciting. Next girl is carefree and fun. Next girl won't complain or ever have a normal human emotion because *next girl* is perfect.

Next girl isn't real.

Still . . . Current girl loses. Next girl always wins.

It's smart to stay unattached. Uncommitted.

I just wish I could follow my own advice.

Thunder rolls off in the distance as I watch the window beside me light up with lightning.

I hate storms. I always have.

They remind me of that dark place.

Unease stirs in my chest, but I ignore it, closing my eyes and forcing myself to try and fall asleep. I have to work tomorrow and after our late night, I'm betting I'm going to be exhausted by the time Mason and I get home.

I'm almost asleep when another strike of lightning hits, this one a lot closer. My eyes pop open with the thunder that rumbles the house and I stare around my room as if it will manifest into my darkest fears.

And then . . .

The fucking power goes out.

The house is thrown into darkness and for a moment, I just lay there, heart beating loudly in my ears.

No.

I squeeze my eyes shut, waiting for the lights to flicker back on and forcing deep breaths past my lips that may as well be wheezes at this point.

One, two, three.

I open my eyes, my throat seizing when I realize the lights are most definitely *not* back on.

Okay, Hannah. You've been here before. You've spent plenty of time in the dark. It's not a big deal.

Then the voices start to trickle in.

"Hannahhhhh . . ."

Tap, tap, tap . . .

I spin around as if I might catch someone standing behind me, but there's no one there. At least no one I can see in the pitch black of my room.

"M—"

I start to call out for Mason, but I *know* as soon as I do, I'll feel like an idiot. Like a scared child, calling for her father to scare away the monster that lives under her bed.

"Whore."

"I'm doing this for your own good."

"Just a sip and the demons will go away."

Fear wraps around my lungs, squeezing tightly until I feel like I'm either going to suffocate or explode from my racing heart.

Shame envelopes me, but even so, the storm rages on outside, a bolt of lightning shooting across the sky and then the rumbling crack of thunder shaking the house.

Terror crawls up my spine at the sinister voice playing in my ear, repeating over and over like a broken record until I swear I'm losing my mind.

Whore.

I tear from the bed, imagining cold fingers wrapping around my throat and sucking the life from me while I fight helplessly. I almost face-plant on the floor before I make it to the door and rip it open, and rush to the one across from mine. I bang on his door, my other hand clutching at my chest as the sickening feeling of dread washes over me.

I don't want him to see me like this. Panicked because the lights went out. Afraid of the dark like a child.

I also feel like my heart's going to explode if I spend even another *second* in this hell by myself.

His door opens, just as I raise my hand to knock again and he stands, shrouded in the shadows. Over his shoulder, a candle is perched on the top of his dresser, casting a soft warm glow behind him.

I know it's him from the scent of his skin. Something woodsy, deep, and . . . safe.

"I'm here." His voice is soft when he wraps his arms around me. He lifts me against his chest and I straddle his waist, burying my face in the side of his neck as a quiet sob tears from my throat. "Breathe." I hadn't even realized I was shaking, but with his body pressed against mine, tremors move through me. "Slow."

I force a deep breath past my lips, my lungs aching and my throat dry. Mason carries me to the bed and instead of depositing me on top of it, he sits down, cradling me against him.

"Keep breathing." I don't think about it at first, but the way he says it almost feels like it has a deeper meaning. Like a warning that if I stop altogether, the outcome will be disastrous.

So . . . I repeat the motion, sucking air into my lungs and slowly letting it back out until my throat begins to loosen and the ache in my chest dies down.

Now that the panic attack has subsided, I'm exhausted and the comfort of his shoulder, mixed with the way he runs his hand from the top of my head down to the small of my back over and over makes me want to fall back asleep, right here, where the demons of my childhood can't get to me and the dark is just a simple time of night.

Thunder rolls in the distance, the lightning slowly moving further and further away until the only sound is rain.

We don't get storms often in Southern California, but when we do, they can be treacherous. Harsh and unpredictable. Suddenly, I'm wondering what would have happened if I had been home tonight, in my own house, completely alone.

Neither of us moves for a long time as he strokes the ends of my hair. I listen to the sound of his heartbeat and let my mind slowly calm down until I'm just memorizing the sound. Call me crazy, but I don't want to forget.

"What did she do, Hannah?" Mason asks after a long, long time. He says it so quietly, I think I imagined it at first.

What didn't she do?

I swallow past the lump in my throat, willing myself to form the words. I've never told anyone out loud just how bad my mother could be, but I don't have the fight in me to keep it from him. Not anymore. Not when he'd risked his life multiple times to help me.

"She would . . . lock me in the darkness."

I can't decide if it feels good to get that off my chest or not.

"Why?"

Mason's body is riddled with tension, but he doesn't stop stroking my hair with the same gentle softness he did before. He smells so good, all I want to do is climb under the sheets with him and let him hold me, but I know that's not what Mason Carpenter and I are. We're not softness and comfort and that feeling of home you get when you find your person. We're harsh and demanding. Two peas in a pod when there's a job to do, but at each other's throats when there's nothing else to focus on but us.

He still hates me for that night. I still hate him for walking away.

"Whenever we were bad, she would lock us in this closet she had specially fitted to be light-tight. It started when we were kids, but it carried on when we moved to Sacramento." Absentmindedly, I run my finger over a tattooed snake where it ends on his shoulder, thick muscles rippling under my finger. "She thought she could lock us away and it would set us straight. The darkness was just another punishment."

"And Missy?"

I chuckle, though it lacks any real humor.

"Missy got the worst of Mom's punishments. Eventually, she started doing everything she could to piss Mom off because the closet didn't work on her anymore. I started doing everything I could to stay out of it. She locked me in the closet for hours when she found out I'd kissed you."

Sickness pools in my stomach at the dark memories resurfacing. Something tapping on the other side of the door. My fists sore from trying to beat it open and my throat scratchy from begging for someone to let me out when I could swear something was lurking in the dark, waiting to drag me to hell.

Something evil and pitch-black with blood-red eyes staring from the void. Just like my mother's soul.

"Look at me, Hannah."

Carefully, I raise my gaze to his. Even in the darkness, he's so handsome, it hurts to look at him. Stormy gaze. Hard jawline. Broad, bare shoulders, dark tattoos over strong muscles holding me steady.

"I've never told anyone that before. You must think I'm an idiot," I half chuckle, though I feel like I'm going to be sick. If I look at him and see pity, I'll shatter. I can't.

I move to get up, but his hand on my back hardens, holding me there.

"No."

His other hand comes up, gripping my chin to turn my gaze to his. When I meet it, something inside me burns hotter than the candle on the dresser behind me.

"The only thing here that's going to hurt you, little doe, is me. And I plan on making it feel like fucking heaven when I do."

My core warms at the dark vehemence in his voice. As if he's a knight vowing to protect me with his life and I'm the princess reigning over a stolen castle. Perhaps he could be a knight. In shiny black armor with chinks and scuffs and a knack for making me feel steady when the ground is falling out from under my feet.

"Mason . . ." I whisper. Don't ask me why. Maybe because of what he just said or maybe because my knees are starting to hurt from kneeling over him for so long. Hell, maybe I just want to say his name because it feels like I've been starved for him, even though I've barely had a taste.

Still . . . when his eyes lock with mine, heat floods my core and my demons seem to drift away.

And then I realize why I'm so drawn to Mason Carpenter, of all people.

It's because when he looks at me, I feel like he'd burn the world to the ground just to watch me spit on the ashes.

Heat burns in my core, my clit thrumming with the beat of my heart. My hand rests on his bare shoulder and I'm suddenly acutely aware that I'm just in a baggy T-shirt and lacey panties that leave nothing to the imagination while he's in a set of boxers.

His jaw ticks when I lean into him, but he doesn't stop me.

I close the distance between us, my pulse thrumming between my legs. I don't know whether I'm seeking him or his comfort or maybe even just the way he makes me forget, but when my lips hover over his, my chest suddenly feels tight again.

Gently, I brush my lips over his, tasting him. Drinking him in. He doesn't kiss me back, but a low groan rumbles up his throat, filling me with heat that spreads through me like wildfire.

I kiss him again and this time, I don't stop. He lets me for a moment, before finally, he meets my kiss with a harsh one of his own. As if he's punishing me for wanting him. For making him want me. When I pull back, he catches me around the waist and pulls me back into him. When my hands slide up into his hair to deepen the kiss, his slide under my shirt and over my bare hips until he cups my ass in his hands. He tugs me closer until the notch in his boxers lines up perfectly with my clit.

I slip my tongue into his mouth, tasting the peppermint on his breath and letting out a soft moan, rolling my hips over the length of his erection.

A sharp sound of anger rumbles through his chest and he fists my hair to tug my head back.

"I'm not fucking you tonight, Hannah."

Something pangs in my chest and despite the hand in my hair, I repeat the motion of my hips, drawing a hiss from between his lips.

"Why?" I challenge. He obviously wants me. I want to get lost in him. Forget about the darkness. Stop fighting my desire for him and just let this man consume me like I've dreamed about for years.

His hand on my ass slides up to grip my hip and he stops me, pulling my gaze to meet his forcefully. When he lets go of my hair and raises his hand, instinctively, I turn my head.

But the pain doesn't come.

Instead, his thumb, gentle as ever, swipes a tear from under my eye.

"Because there are still tears on your face from a panic attack."

Rejection burns like acid in my throat, just as bad as any panic attack.

I must look pathetic.

"I'm sorry," I murmur, tears burning in the backs of my eyes. Thank God it's dark in here. I'm sure in the light, I would look pitiful. "I just . . . I don't want to remember that anymore. Every time it's dark. I want . . . something else. Something good."

Even in the dim light of the candle, I can see his jaw clench. The intensity in his eyes burns me, full of possessiveness and sizzling heat and . . . something else I'm not sure I want to understand.

"And you think I'm the one to do that?"

"I trust you," I admit, though now that I've said it, I regret it. It's true. I trust him with my life. Do I trust him not to rip my heart to shreds when this is all done, though? I'll get back to you on that.

"Bad idea, little doe."

I open my mouth to speak, but he shuts me up by bringing my face back to his with a rough kiss and a deep growl that settles between my legs. Before he pulls away, he nips my bottom lip between his teeth before sucking the marred skin into his mouth.

"I'm not going to fuck you," he rasps, peppering kisses along my jaw and down to my throat. "Not tonight. But soon."

My stomach clenches at the thought, but I don't have time to react before he flips me onto my back on the bed, the comforter cool against my skin, despite the heat blazing through me.

"But I will make you forget."

My stomach tightens at the look in his eyes. He's never looked at me like this before. With soft, all-consuming desire. Like he has to touch me or he'll lose his mind. Like I'm the only woman in the world.

Like I'm his.

It's fucking terrifying.

Placing a hand on either side of me, he hovers over me, his cock pressing into my core. He captures my lips with a rough, quick kiss, before slipping my shirt over my head. He tosses it into the abyss surrounding us and slips a hand up my stomach to knead my breast.

With the candle at his back, he looks like the devil, come to steal my soul in the dead of night.

With the way my body tightens when he leans down and sucks my nipple into his mouth, circling the bud with his tongue, I wouldn't be surprised.

Electricity zaps against my skin where he touches me and all I can think about is how badly I want to please this man. The fear is gone, replaced with something hungry. Something warm and new and completely lost to me.

"Fucking perfect," he murmurs and my heart flutters at the way he grumbles it, like it pisses him off. Like he wants me, even if he hates himself for it.

He grabs my other breast, nipping it before sucking my nipple with a deep groan. My back arches underneath him, the heat inside me liquefying in my veins.

Releasing me, he slips lower, running his tongue down my stomach, past my navel, and then lower, to nip the inside of my thigh. I yelp from the pain, but it quickly dissolves into a moan when he soothes the sting with his tongue.

"Mason," I breathe when he makes a quiet, dark sound, slipping my panties to the side. I've never . . . done this. I don't know how to tell him that as a new kind of heat floods my cheeks.

He eyes me darkly, slipping from the bed and yanking me forward until my ass rests on the edge. Even on the floor, he still has to hunch over to reach me.

"I've never—*ah* . . ." The most erotic sound I think I've ever made tears from my throat when he leans down and runs his tongue from my ass to my clit. I surge off the bed, jumping at the new sensation and he bands a hand over my stomach with a raw possessiveness in his eyes.

The growl of satisfaction that rumbles through him goes right to my core.

"I've waited years for this," he murmurs, almost to himself, before he's using his other hand to spread me open. He circles my entrance with his tongue before he slips it inside.

I watch him between my legs, my hand fisting the comforter below me as he moves his tongue in and out, slipping through my folds, but completely ignoring my clit. His eyes lock with mine as if he's daring me to stop him when he spreads my legs wider, hooking one over his shoulder.

He's never looked so . . . dangerous.

"You're fucking soaked, Hannah," he murmurs against my skin, circling the area around my clit, but not touching me where I need him. "This little cunt has always begged for me."

My body tightens, my legs shaking as my orgasm already threatens to tear through me. It's always been harder for me to come, but with Mason, it's like a walk in the park. A few touches, a couple growled words, and I'm barreling toward ecstasy faster than I could have ever thought imaginable.

"Mason, please," I whimper, my eyes screwed shut as he continues to deny me what I want. He's trying to prolong this where I feel like I'm going crazy with the need for release.

A sharp sting startles me and I gawk at him.

"Did you just bite my clit?"

"Did you just tell me what to do?"

"Asshole," I snap, though it lacks its usual bite.

"Brat," he rasps, nipping me again and drawing out the pain. "Want me to stop?"

He's daring me. He raises a brow, hovering on the edge of insanity. I'm right there with him because I actually shake my head no.

"Good girl."

God, if this is the devil . . . you better never drag me to heaven.

Though it's slightly twisted and probably degrading, heat floods my core. So much so that my arousal leaks down my inner thighs which would be embarrassing if Mason didn't slip a finger inside me and finally, finally draw my clit into his mouth.

My back arches off the bed and I cry out, not bothering to be quiet. I don't care who hears me now. I just want this man inside me.

Why didn't I do this sooner? The sight of Mason Carpenter with his head between my legs is a sight I'm sure most girls would sell their right arm to see. I didn't think I would. But that was before. Now, I feel like I've been let into some secret club where it's just me and all my dirty fantasies are coming to life, right before my eyes.

"Fuck, Hannah," Mason rasps, his eyes locked on mine when I roll my hips into his mouth. "That's it." Using his free hand, he spreads my pussy, diving back between my folds and feasting on me like I'm his last meal. I writhe underneath him, grip his sheets so hard I distantly worry that I may rip them, and tug on the strands of his short hair until I'm sure I've given him a bald spot.

Something tells me he'd wear it with pride.

Sealing his lips around my clit with a deep sound of satisfaction, he flutters it back and forth, his fingers curling up to rub over a spot that I didn't even know existed.

My entire body feels like it's been dipped in a vat of lava and then finally, everything explodes, sending me catapulting into an orgasm that I'm sure will be my last. I scream—yes, scream—out his name, tugging the strands of his hair, the bed, anything I can get my hands on while the pleasure rips through me. He says something, but I can't hear him. I can't even see him through the blurriness in my gaze.

He rips his mouth away when the orgasm starts to fade, but his fingers stay buried inside me, drawing out the little aftershocks of my orgasm. A soft whimper tears through me because the pressure is building again and I don't know if I can survive another orgasm like that.

He crushes his lips against mine and I moan into his mouth when he curls his fingers up again to stroke over that spot that only he seems to know about. Tears leak from the corners of my eyes, but he doesn't stop and I don't want him to.

Time stops, balancing on the edge of a pit that will send me straight down to hell. He kisses me until my lips are bruised. Until my body is engrained with him and I'm not sure I ever want to leave his bed. Until I need him.

He fingers me through another orgasm, this time swallowing my cries with a deep groan before withdrawing his fingers. I reach between us to wrap my hand around his cock, startled at the sheer size of the thing. He groans, a feral sound, and catches my wrists, pinning them to the bed above my head.

He kisses me until the heat returns. Until our grinding becomes too much and before I'm on the edge of telling him I don't care how I'll feel later, I just want him to fuck me. When he rips his lips away, a shudder rolls through him that's both the hottest and most terrifying thing I've ever seen.

I can feel the desire radiating through him. The tension. The hunger. He wants me, but he won't fuck me tonight. I'm not even sure I could handle it, but I want to, and that's the most dangerous thing of all.

Maybe that's why I find him so . . . alluring. He's bad for all the right reasons. Dangerous and safe, at the same time. He's a rocky island in the middle of a hurricane at sea.

My darkness and his aren't the same, but they go hand in hand.

He doesn't say anything when he picks me up and deposits me on a pillow at the head of the bed. He still doesn't say anything when he covers me up and slips in behind me.

Neither of us acknowledges it, but when he slips his arms around me and pulls me back into his chest, pressing a rough kiss to my cheek with a quiet, "Sleep," something's shifted between us. Some new understanding I'm not sure either of us wants to know the meaning of.

So, I let him hold me. In the dark. Even when I hear the power kick back on while my mind is teetering on the edge of my consciousness, I don't move.

Because right here is where I want to be.

Safe and exhausted in the arms of a man who should hate me but can't bring himself to do so.

CHAPTER Twenty-Eight

MASON

The first thing that wakes me up in the morning is my phone ringing.

The second is Hannah's ass grinding against my cock.

"Mmm . . ." she moans, soft and sweet. I hiss out a breath through my teeth, my cock already rock fucking hard and she's barely touched me.

She shifts against me and I damn near go cross-eyed.

"Little doe," I bite in her ear and she goes still. I roll my hips into her ass, my fingers tightening on her waist and her breath hitches. "What were you dreaming about?"

She doesn't open her eyes, but she chuckles lightly, her cheeks flaming in the pale glow emanating from the window. It's raining still, and the sounds of water pattering against the house cast everything in shades of blue and gray.

"I'm not telling you that."

"So, now you're awake." I shift against her again, aligning my hips to run my cock over the seam of her panties. I could snap them and sink inside her. With only two layers between us, she's warm and sweet and I can feel her wetness coating me through my boxers.

Fuck this.

Leaning down, I use my arm under her to tug her to me until her back is pressed into my front. A soft moan slips free when I kiss the inside of her neck and slip my hand down her stomach.

I don't know what time it is, but I never sleep more than a few hours at a time. Call it what you will, but I'm used to a couple hours a night.

What I'm not used to is waking up to my pretty little obsession wet and wanting.

I knew moving her in would be a bad idea.

I roll my hips into her ass, stroking the head of my cock over her pussy until her nails dig into the skin of my wrist. I chuckle, repeating the motion, and this time, she arches back to meet my thrusts.

"*Fuck* . . ." I grit. I fist the lacy strap of her panties, toying with the idea of decimating them. They're in my way.

"Mason . . ." she breathes, my name a plea on her lips and that's all I need to lose every ounce of fucking self-control I have.

Rolling onto my back, I tug her over me. She comes, breathless as she straddles me, her cheeks burning brightly.

"I have morning breath."

I shake my head. "I don't give a fuck."

She cocks her head at me defiantly. "Well, I *do*."

She slips down my legs and my fist tightens in her hair, holding her there.

"I swear to God, Hannah, if you leave this bed—" I growl, but she reaches up, pressing a finger to my lips to silence me. If I weren't so fucking surprised, I'd bite her.

"We're uneven," she says as if that's supposed to mean something to me, but with a flush in her cheeks of shy embarrassment, she slips even lower, between my legs.

Fuck. Me.

"Hannah," I warn when she tucks a strand of hair behind her ear and grips me through my boxers. It's not confident. It's nervous and self-conscious.

It's the hottest fucking thing I've ever seen.

"Are you going to keep talking or are you going to let me do this?" She cocks a brow at me.

Little fucking brat.

My spine stiffens when she slips my boxers down, a breath hissing out through my teeth when she wraps her palm around me for the first fucking time.

Fuck, I've waited years to feel her hand wrapped around my cock.

"Fine, little doe," I grit, leaning back against the pillows and tucking my arm behind my head to watch her. "You win."

A small, mischievous smile tugs at her lips and she repeats the motion and I swear every fucking muscle in my body tightens.

Carefully, she leans down as if the task of taking me in her mouth is daunting and runs her tongue along the head of my cock.

"Fuck," I bite, a groan rumbling through my chest from the simple little motion. Hannah squirms, readjusting on the bed and moving lower to run her tongue up the underside of my shaft and it's all I can do not to fist her hair and pry that pretty little mouth open. "Stop playing with it," I rasp when she runs her lips over me, and her cheeks flame.

"Are you always this moody about your blow jobs? Maybe you're not in the right mood." If she knew what her taunting did to me, she'd be singing a different tune.

"When I've been waiting years, yeah, I fucking am."

She eyes me cynically, wrapping her palm around me again.

"You honestly expect me to believe you haven't slept with anyone else in years?"

Reaching down, I grip her hair in a fist, tugging her gaze up to meet mine when she tries to swirl her tongue around my tip.

"Let me make myself clear, little doe. I've waited years to see that pretty mouth choking on my cock. Suck."

Her lip trembles, a shaky sigh leaving her throat when I release my hold. She lowers back down, her eyes half-lidded and hazy because that's what Hannah and I are.

Fucking toxic. Fucking broken. Pieced together by the same tragedy and fear.

My roughness should make her run. Unfortunately for her, it only makes her want me more.

The moment she slips her lips around me, it feels like coming home. My head falls back and I let out a growl, my hand resting on top of her cinnamon-colored waves tightening, but not moving her. I'll let her set the pace, for now.

"That's it," I rumble, my body tight with the need to feel her taking all of me. She moans in response, the vibrations sending a shot of fire down my spine. "All of it."

She slips me deeper, her hand wrapping around the bottom of my cock to feed my length between her lips. It's fucking intoxicating, seeing my pretty little doe on her knees in front of me, her lips wrapped around my cock. I ball my other fist behind my head to keep from winding it through her hair and making her swallow the rest of me.

"Such a fucking good girl," I grit through my teeth when she manages to slip more than half my length into her mouth. "You look so fucking pretty taking my cock."

She moans in acquiescence, lashes fluttering softly against her cheeks. My phone buzzes again, from the nightstand, but I ignore it.

I don't give a fuck who's dying. They can wait.

"You like being my whore?"

She glares up at me, but I see the way her thighs clench, perfect ass in the air I would love nothing more than to take a bite of. She can deny it all she wants. She likes my filthy words almost as much as she likes sucking my cock.

Slowly, torturously, she works my cock into the back of her

throat, bottoming out before she's sliding back up. This madness goes on for what feels like both a lifetime and a millisecond. The need to come and fill her pretty throat sends a lance of fire down my spine and I pump my hips up into her once.

Fuck, I'm being gentle, but it's not enough. I need more of her. I need her fast and hard. Fucking rough.

I need all of her.

I stroke the top of her head, slowly guiding her over my length as she works to swallow me. Her hand strokes the bottom of my shaft as she takes me faster until drool drips down her chin and soaks my cock.

Fucking perfection.

She chokes, pulling back and I damn near cry from the loss of her.

"Sorry," she whispers, wiping her chin, before moving back to my cock. "I'm not used to this."

I still. "Is this your first time, Hannah?"

She looks embarrassed. "Yes," she breathes.

Fuck. Me.

"Little doe, I'm going to ruin you."

She nods slowly before pulling me back between her lips. The knowledge that I'm the first man to have her mouth sets a new fire in my veins. The need to consume her. Own her.

Keep her.

"Keep sucking, just like that," I rasp, using my hands to guide her down on my cock. I don't push her as far as I'd like—until she's got more of me than air in her lungs, but I get damn near close when my phone buzzes again.

"Jesus fucking Christ," I grit under my breath, stilling my hand on her head. She pauses while I reach for it, checking the screen. "Holy shit."

It's past noon. We slept in.

"Hello?"

"Hey, boss . . ." Ian starts awkwardly. "You guys coming to work today?"

My gaze flicks down the bed to Hannah who cocks her head, a devious look glistening in her eyes. I shake my head in warning, daring her, but she still lowers, swallowing me again and I have to bite back the groan that threatens to tear free from my lips.

"We're on our way."

"Hannah, too?"

I grit my teeth. It wasn't my intention to clue the guys in that Hannah would be staying with me for the foreseeable future but fuck it.

"Yeah," I growl when Hannah moans around my cock, sending a shudder through me. I'm going to fucking come soon and I for damn sure don't want Ian on the line, distracting me when I do. "Some shit happened last night. We'll be there soon."

"You got it."

I hang up the phone before he can say anything else and toss it to the bed beside me to take Hannah's face in my hands.

"Reach down and rub that perfect little cunt. I want you coming when I do," I grit and she obliges, slipping her hands into the front of her panties and swirling them around her clit. She shivers when she does and I use my hands on her head to guide her over me, forcing myself to hold back from fucking her mouth like I want. "That's it, baby."

She whimpers, the sound a pleading grip on my balls as they tighten with my impending orgasm.

"You have five seconds to come, Hannah. Show me your tongue."

She meets my gaze and in a second, she's shuddering over me as the pleasure wracks through her, her eyes fluttering. I pull out at the last second, groaning with the force of my orgasm rushing through me. I shoot, coating her tongue and lips, her cheek until the world feels like it's going to fall off its fucking axis.

Jesus fucking Christ.

I've never come that hard before in my life.

Hannah coughs, and somehow, watching her swallow everything I gave her is the sexiest fucking thing she's done yet.

"Come here," I murmur, pissed off at the tremor rolling through my hands when I reach for her.

Carefully, she slips back up the bed when I sit up, grabbing her shirt from last night to clean the come off her cheek. Tears stream from the corners of her eyes and run down her face and I wipe them with my thumbs. "These are the only tears I want to see."

Fuck, I could look at her for hours.

"What did Ian want?" she asks, her cheeks burning.

"It's noon."

Her eyes go wide.

"We have to go."

"We do."

Still, I don't release her.

"Why are you staring at me like that?" She actually sounds offended. Like my looking at her and wondering how the fuck I found her is something bad.

"Wondering how long it would take to make you come again," I lie and she rolls her eyes, attempting to pull away from me. I grab her around the waist before she can leave the bed and back into my chest. "Was I really your first, little doe?"

She bites her lip, refusing to look at me.

"Was it that obvious?"

I press my lips to her ear, nipping the lobe and drawing a startled gasp from her lips. She shivers at my stubble against her soft skin, but she doesn't pull away.

"Someday, I'm going to ruin you, Hannah Gaines, and when I do, you won't ever ask an idiotic question like that again. You may hate me, but my cock, my fingers, my tongue will be the only ones that make this perfect little cunt sing."

She swallows over the lump in her throat, releasing a shaky breath. I can tell she wants to ask what that means, but I don't give her the option, tightening my hand in her hair and turning her face around toward mine.

This kiss is rough, on the precipice of turning into something more, and fuck if I don't want to bury myself in her and tie her to my bed so she'll never leave.

I have no control when it comes to her.

"Get dressed," I murmur darkly and finally, I release her. "Before I do something stupid."

She doesn't ask before quietly slipping from the bed. She pauses a foot away and turns back to stare at me, her green eyes flashing with something new before it's quickly replaced with a mask of indifference.

"For the record," she says softly. "I could never hate you."

And then she exits through the door, quietly shutting it behind her without another word.

The rain from last night decides to continue most of the day. I'm not complaining. It keeps the heat out of the air and sends a nice cool breeze through the garage with the fan. Besides, SoCal rarely gets enough rain to make a difference and after the summer we've had, we can fucking use it.

Hannah and I arrive at exactly twelve-thirty and Ian and Puke pretend they don't notice the hickey I left on Hannah's neck. It's humorous, actually, seeing them squirm, but fortunately, both of them keep a respectable distance from her.

I've been up in the office a few times today. Each time, she's so engrossed in her work that she *pretends* to pay no attention to me. I'm not an idiot, though and I can see the way her shoulders tense when I come in the room and I almost laugh.

So this morning got to her, too.

You want the truth? I'm fucking reeling. Having her lips wrapped around my cock has been a personal fantasy for years, but seeing the real thing?

Fucking nirvana.

If I'd thought I could wipe this addiction away by dosing myself with her until I was tired of her, I was dead fucking wrong.

Now, I only want more.

I meant what I said earlier. Someday she'll learn the truth, but before that happens, I plan to have her so fucking addicted to me, that she won't even think about leaving.

Is it right?

No.

Do I give a fuck?

Also no.

Drying her tears last night solidified that, but then I've always been in this deeper than her.

By five, I let Ian and Puke cut out early, but Hannah's not done in the office, so I stay back, cleaning up, organizing shit. I'm not used to this new domestic reality we've taken on in the last seventy-two hours, so I have no fucking idea what I'm doing.

It's not until I'm contemplating throwing Hannah over my shoulder and carrying her home to finish what we started this morning that my phone buzzes in my pocket.

Ian.

Odd.

"Hello?

"They're coming."

I don't have to ask to know who the fuck *they* are.

"*Fuck*," I bite, tossing the wrench I'm holding onto the tool cart. It rattles with a deafening clang, but it does nothing to drown out the roar of blood in my ears. "Where?"

"A couple blocks away. You need to get Hannah out of there,"

Ian says and my entire body goes on alert.

Fuck.

Fuck.

And then, before I can even fucking react, the rumble from multiple engines sounds down the street.

Shit.

"They're already here."

"I'm coming back," Ian declares.

"No. Go home." I'm already heading toward the office door.

"Mason—"

"Go home, Ian."

I end the call, tossing my phone on the counter as soon as I enter. Hannah who was singing softly to the radio on the desk as she organizes the last of tonight's invoices, jumps like I'd fired a shot. Under different circumstances, I would almost feel guilty for scaring her after the other night. Right now, we don't have time to care.

Not with the cartel on our doorstep.

"You need to go."

Her brows knit together in confusion when I grab her bag and wrap an arm around her waist, forcefully tugging her from her spot behind the counter and toward the door to the garage.

"What's wrong?" she demands, surprise coloring her voice. Worry pools in those fucking eyes and my chest clenches with something sharp and ugly. I need her out of the shop. Out of sight. Out of fucking danger. My chest feels ridiculously tight at the thought of them finding her. Possessive. Murderous.

This has got to be my fucking karma.

"No time. Go through the back and right across to the house." I don't want her walking home alone, but I also don't want her here when Cortez gets here. "I'll explain later."

"Mason," she snaps, tugging a hand free and my palms are just sweaty enough that she manages. "You can't keep—"

I don't know what she was going to say and quite frankly, I don't care. I tug her against my chest, grip her chin, and silence her with a rough kiss.

That shuts her up.

"You said you trust me. Well, now's the time to prove it, little doe." My voice is rough and her eyes widen with concern. "Go home and don't leave the house until I come for you."

"Are we in danger?"

Fucking always, it seems.

"Go," I push her toward the garage door and follow her out. "Back door."

"Going somewhere?"

Everything in my body fills with cement.

Hannah freezes, her mouth falling open at the group of men in the room around us.

Fuck. Me.

As far as bad shit goes, this pretty much takes the cake.

Cortez. I don't know his first name. Probably evil motherfucker, if I had to guess. He stands in the center of the garage—*my* garage—with a devilish smirk on his face.

He knows exactly what my plan was.

And now he knows my weakness.

He chuckles, that same sinister grin flashing a set of bright, white teeth. "You're a dead man."

I step in front of Hannah. No need to stand on formality. Unfortunately, my shielding her doesn't mean much, and now that he's seen her, I can tell by the black glint in his eyes . . . he's going to use her against me.

"We're closed, Cortez."

Cortez smiles brightly, though there's a sinister glint to the way he bares his teeth. As if he wouldn't hesitate to rip your throat out if you pushed him to it.

"Well, I think the owner would make an exception for me, don't you?" He chuckles and a couple of his men follow suit. Fucking sheep.

"Of course, the customer's always right."

Another round of laughter.

"If you've come to check up on us, we're good," I grit. Hannah's hand rests on my lower back and I can feel the tremors move through her. "Everything's been done as it was agreed upon."

Of course, I didn't agree on shit, but we don't need to get into the details.

Cortez continues to smile, the wicked glint in his eyes unfaltering.

"Yes, I suppose, though, we are going to have to start ramping up production here, soon. We're expanding."

"I don't have the room. I have a business to run."

"And you'll run it," he growls aggressively, his eyes flashing black, "however I tell you to run it."

He walks back and forth in front of me, his steps slow like a cat. Calculated to hide his next move. Cortez is a loose cannon. In the two years they've been showing up at my garage, forcing me to do their fucking bidding, he's only been here once. The first night.

The night everything changed.

"You see, Mr. Carpenter," Cortez wraps an arm around my shoulders and though he's considerably shorter than me, I let him because it's better to go with it and fight when needed than to fight now That is and risk him hurting Hannah. "It appears someone broke into one of my warehouses the other night and fucked around inside . . . you wouldn't happen to know anything about that?" He pauses, gauging the reaction on my face. I keep my expression neutral, but inside, my blood is boiling just beneath the surface. "Would you?"

"Can't say I do."

He chuckles, patting me on the back.

"*Sostenlo.*"

He shoves me as hard as he can and I stumble forward a step, only to be grabbed around the shoulders by two of his men. I rip against their hold, managing to break free for only a moment before the deafening click of a pistol sounds in the air and cold steel presses to my temple.

"No!" Hannah lurches forward, panic in her eyes, but I meet her gaze and she falls back a step.

Cortez chuckles while my heartbeat pounds from the struggle. The bastard loves to scare people. Namely women. He steps right in front of me and now that I'm restrained, he thinks he's safe. Too bad it took four of his men and a gun to hold me.

"You'll receive your first shipment within the next couple weeks and you'll make sure nothing happens to them until they're ready to be moved. Understood?"

No. Fuck that.

"No."

He smiles brightly.

"*Uno.*"

The pistol aimed at my head bashes into the back of my skull, but I don't feel it, save for the blood in my mouth from biting my tongue.

"Let me say it, again," he purrs, voice sickly sweet. "You'll hide them, and you aren't going to say a word to your lovely brother-in-law. That is . . . unless you want to find your sisters in the cage next to them."

"Go fuck yourself," I bite between ragged breaths.

He chuckles darkly, shaking his head.

"You're a big boy, Mason. But you're not unkillable. You think you can hide behind your ego and I'm just going to tuck tail and run?"

"I don't care what you do. You're not bringing them here."

He runs his tongue over his teeth and gives a final shrug. "Have it your way."

In a flash, he whirls around and the same gun he used to bust my lip is now pointed directly in the center of Hannah's forehead.

I'll fucking kill him.

"Say, does *Mama* know you've got her precious little angel holed up here in this dusty little shack?" Cortez chuckles. I snarl, the sound reverberating through me. Hannah looks past him, at me, then back to him, shivers rolling through her. Her eyes shine with tears and black, all-consuming rage pours through me in waves. I struggle against the men holding me, but another thud of steel connects with the back of my head.

"Well, hello there, *beautiful*."

Cortez's eyes rake over Hannah and he whistles through his teeth.

"Awful lot of people are looking for your sister. You know, she's pretty and all. Got this beautiful dark, glossy hair." He reaches out, brushing a lock of hair from Hannah's face with the end of his pistol. "But you . . . you're something else."

Everything in my body recoils; my eyes running red with rage. I want to fucking kill him. I want to break those fingers off and feed them to him, one by one until he's choking on his own blood for daring to touch her.

For daring to touch what's *mine*.

"Mason, you didn't tell me the governor's daughter was such a fine little piece of ass."

Hannah meets my gaze, her lips wobbling when he steps around her, slowly stalking her. A predator. I give her a small, subtle nod that only she would be able to notice. Cortez can sense fear like a shark to blood in the ocean. I need her detached.

"So, you've got your cake and you're eating it, too . . ." He smiles at me over her shoulder, wrapping his arms around her waist and pulling her back into him. "Can't say I blame you," he smirks, the cocky grin on his face the one that will remain burned in my brain the entire time I'm ringing the life from him. His hands roam down her body until his fingers rest just above the waistband of her jeans. "Tell me . . . when you're fucking her, does it ever cross your mind that she's what got you into this mess in the first place?"

Fuck.

Hannah's eyes widen and it's then she figures it out.

"No?" he presses a kiss to the top of her head. "Well, consider this a warning. The next time I have to come here and make sure you're keeping in line, I'll kill her. And if you think I need *Mama's* permission, it's already been granted."

"*Sueltenlo.*"

He shoves Hannah toward me at the same time the men holding me let me go. I catch her and hold her against my chest while Cortez's men laugh and Cortez heads toward the door of the garage.

"Oh, and Carpenter," Cortez stops just before the door, turning back to us as Hannah buries her face in my chest. "Tell your *mama* I said hello."

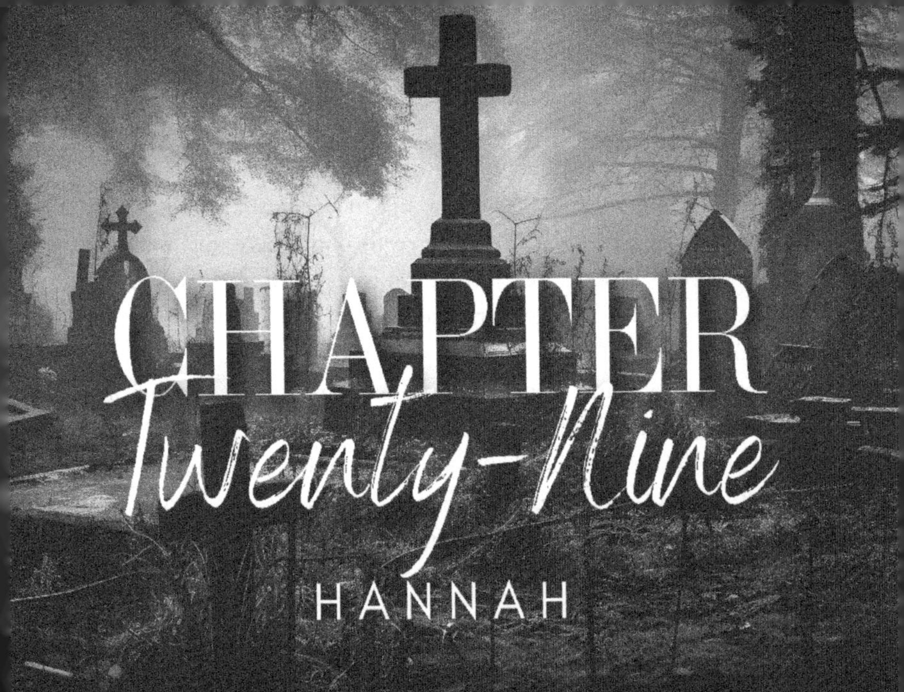

CHAPTER Twenty-Nine

HANNAH

The door to the garage slams shut and after a few moments, the rumble of engines sounds outside as the cartel packs up to leave. We stand in silence, listening to them until their engines are drowned out by the sound of the rain and I'm sure they're gone.

This is all my fault.

I push away from Mason, storming toward the office.

"Hannah," he bites, locking the door and following after me. The adrenaline coursing through my body is enough to make me sick to my stomach. All these lies. All these secrets I have to find out through weird texts and near-death experiences.

Mason had a gun pointed at his head.

A fucking gun.

"Hannah."

His voice is laced with rage, but I'm angrier.

"You lied!" I bellow, whirling on him. I stop just inside his office.

I need to get the fuck out of here. Betrayal burns hot and disgusted in my chest, making me nauseous. Even then, it's nothing compared to the sickness that comes from the image of Cortez pointing a gun to his head.

I'm so angry I could kill him.

I shove at his chest with all my might, but he doesn't budge.

In fact, he just steps closer, eyes flashing with venom.

"I didn't lie. *You* didn't listen," he growls, voice deeper than I've ever heard it before. My heart bottoms out in my chest at the rage in his voice and the darkness in his eyes.

"They could have killed you! And you're a part of it? *Trafficking* Mason?"

"They forced me into a chop shop, Hannah. Not trafficking." His gaze darkens. "Not until now. I'm as much a part of it as you are," he bites. "And you can thank your mother for that."

My mother . . . "All these years, you've been dealing with the cartel and now you're trying to say it's because of *my* mother? The governor of California? Why would she do that?" There's no way.

You also thought there was no way she would open up a trafficking ring, either . . .

Mason doesn't say anything, though his eyes burn with an intensity I've never seen before.

I fall back a step.

Everything makes sense now.

"Because of me."

He chuckles, though it lacks any humor. "Imagine her surprise when you ran right back to me."

I shake my head. There's no way. The. Fucking. Cartel.

My mother sent the fucking cartel after Mason because I . . .

Mason's eyes flash with a caustic black glint, his jaw tight and his muscles tense. Something violent radiates just beneath the surface of his icy exterior. It's then I realize why Mason Carpenter has tried so damned hard—and failed—to keep me at arm's length. Why he disappeared.

He cares. Way more than he or I will ever be willing to admit.

I thought I had problems. Now, I'm seeing he's being haunted by ghosts, too. Only his are a lot bigger and a lot more dangerous than just my psycho sister.

. . . And now they know about me.

The ground shakes with the force of the thunder rumbling outside and then, like the sun got sucked away from the Earth, all the lights in the garage go out, plunging us into near-darkness. Shadows lurk in every corner, the only light a pale green glow that shines through the windows.

Mason looks like a mercenary in this light. A bioweapon sent to drag me back to hell with him. Dark. Huge. Devastating in this light.

My body hums in the heavy silence that follows, my heartbeat the only sound despite the rain and our heavy breathing. Only now, for the first time in God knows how long, my pulse is fluttering for an entirely different reason than what could be hiding in the shadows.

It's him.

"You're being harassed by the cartel because of me," I breathe. "Because you won't walk away from me."

He doesn't say anything, but his jaw ticks.

"Why . . . why would you do that?"

"Because you're mine."

My chest tightens with something harsh and ugly and sweet and beautiful.

Then it crashes to the floor at my feet.

My mother will kill him.

"We . . . we can't do this anymore." I'm not even sure if I'm speaking to him or myself at this point. Still, it tastes like I swallowed bleach the moment the words leave my mouth.

Mason's nostrils flare, his eyes caustic. "What?"

I suck in a deep breath, willing my voice to find the words. "It's not safe. You and me. This is a dangerous game."

Tears well in my eyes, but I refuse to cry. Not here. Not right in front of him.

"You think this is a game?" My heart drops to my stomach when he steps forward, closing the distance between us until his front is barely touching mine. Then, he presses closer until my back hits the wall and I'm trapped. Distantly, I'm aware of his cock pressing against my stomach and it stokes a fire in my core, low and indomitable.

Slowly, like he's calculating his next move, he places his hands on the wall on either side of my head until we're at eye level.

"You think I didn't try?" He dips his head until his lips are pressed against my ear. The stubble on his cheeks against the soft skin of my neck sends a shiver down my spine.

One that doesn't go unnoticed by him.

"You think I didn't try to cut you out of me? That I didn't try to walk away?"

He leans back enough so I can see the sneer pull on his lips. His hand slips into the loose strands of my hair, sliding up to fist the roots in his fingers and drag my head back to look up at him. At this angle, all I can see is him, consuming me. His gaze rakes over me, from my eyes down to my lips, like a caress. His jaw ticks when he tears his face back to mine and there's no denying it.

He's gotten attached, too.

"You and I will never be done, Hannah. You know why?" His fingers flex in my hair, pulling me closer until his lips hover over mine and I shiver. Like he's trying to steal my dying breath. It's just the lightest of touches, but I want more. I *need* more. I try to move closer, to kiss him, *feel* him, but he holds me in place, forcing me to face my demons head-on, rather than run from them as I always have.

His thumb runs over my lips, like he's memorizing them. Like he's ingraining them in his brain for later.

"Because as much as you'd prefer to tell me you hate me, little doe, you're as obsessed with me as I am with you."

Holy shit.

Warmth pools in my core and the dull ache that centered between my thighs turns to an incessant throb. His eyes are darker than I've ever seen them. Like the stormy gray had turned to night.

Like a man on the brink of losing control.

Suddenly, I want to see what it looks like when that control snaps.

"I would take a bullet to keep you safe, Hannah, but I can't do anything if you don't listen to me."

"Mason . . ." I breathe, my voice shaky when he stoops down, nipping the line of my jaw.

I shouldn't let myself get sucked in. It's dangerous. For *both* of us. Mom will kill him when she finds out and the cartel may as well be bloodhounds out for my scent. Still . . . I tell myself all of this while I wrap my arms around his neck and arch my own to give him more access. I tell myself I don't like him while I whimper at the feeling of his teeth grazing my skin. I tell myself this has gone too far, even as I beg for more.

Every nerve ending in my body goes live when he presses his face to my neck, inhaling and letting out a low sound of satisfaction.

"Tell me you hate me, little doe," he rasps against my ear. "Tell me to let you leave."

I *should* do as he tells me. I *should* go back home so we can both cool off. I *should* do a lot of things, none of them involving this man, but, even as he says it, I know it's not true. I can't hate Mason Carpenter any more than I can stop myself from falling for him.

I know I should. I should back away before this gets too far, save that heartache for later . . . but, when his hand on my back slips lower, cupping the bottom of my ass under the hem of my shorts, I lose track of that rational side of my brain.

"Fuck me," I breathe, so quiet, I'm not even sure he heard it over the storm raging outside.

He pulls back to look at me, his gaze dark. "If I fuck you, Hannah, there's no going back from this."

I swallow over the lump in my throat at those words.

They should be enough to scare me off, but . . . for some disturbing reason, my stomach tightens at the thought.

So, I do what any sane woman would do— repeat myself.

"Fuck me, Mason."

He leans forward, his thumb tracing the pulse point where I'm sure he can feel my heart racing. I stir under his heavy gaze. He's looking at me in a way I've never been looked at before. With such soft, soul-consuming desire.

Like I'm his.

Abruptly, he leans down, nipping my bottom lip and making a low sound. Almost like he's angry with himself for losing a hard-fought battle.

"You have no idea what you just asked for."

His hand on my ass clenches and then he's lifting me into his arms as if it's easy. It's fucking terrifying.

He carries me to the desk, depositing me on top and swiping papers and folders I know I'll have to figure out come tomorrow morning, but I couldn't care less. Not when he fists my hair, bringing his lips crashing against mine with a deep groan.

In a flash, he's tugging my shirt over my head until I'm in nothing but the old bra I put on this morning. Of course, I would pick the most unsexy undergarment I own on a day like today, but he doesn't seem to care, expertly unhooking it and tossing it to the old computer chair with the rest of my clothes.

My breasts sit heavy and tight, my nipples hardening under his gaze and even in the darkness of the office, with nothing but the pale glow from outside and the strike of lightning, my skin burns under those eyes.

"So fucking perfect," he grumbles under his breath, like he hates it, right before he cups one of my breasts in his hand and seals his lips over the hardened peak.

The second his lips touch my nipple, I lose every last strand of my moral dignity.

And just like that, I'm willing to let this man do whatever he wants to me.

His groan reverberates against my skin, sending sharp tingles of pleasure straight between my thighs and I arch into his tongue. He switches sides, feasting on my other breast and rolling the first with his fingers until the pleasure radiating in my clit threatens to send me into orbit.

Is it possible to come from just nipple play? Is that even a thing?

Somehow, I know Mason is the one that could do it, even if it's not.

"Is this what you wanted?" he rasps against my neck where he bites the pulse point over my fluttering heartbeat. "You wanted my hands on you again? My cock?"

"Yes," I breathe. What I actually want is for him to fuck me until the racing thoughts in my head drift away. Until all I can feel is him and the anxiety swirling in my stomach is snuffed out and I can just be free for once. Free of the worry. Free of the guilt.

Dropping to his haunches, his hands slip up my thighs to the button of my shorts. He pops them open, tugging the denim and my panties down my legs.

When I'm completely naked, his heavy gaze centers on the apex of my thighs, his nostrils flaring.

His eyes drop almost unwillingly over the length of my body. Raking from the polish on my toes, up my legs and over my clit, then my breasts, before finally, his eyes meet mine.

Something about the unhinged look in his eyes has me swallowing in fear.

"There's no going back from this, Hannah."

"Are you telling me to back out?"

He chuckles dryly, dropping to his knees and nudging my legs apart with his shoulders. "If you want to watch Los Angeles burn to the ground tonight, go ahead."

What's wrong with me? I should be running for the hills, but instead, I'm reveling in the fact that I can get *this* man as unhinged as he makes me feel. Like I've tamed a grizzly bear and now it's prepared to lay its life on the line for me.

His palm on my leg is a warning. It's him saying: *You're mine. Every fucking inch of you.*

Right now, I don't think I could argue if I tried.

He nips the skin of my knee with a rough growl, then his tongue darts out to lick a path up to my inner thigh.

"Mason . . ." I warn, but he just turns that dark look on me, stopping my heart in its tracks. "Just fuck me."

I can't believe those words just came out of my mouth.

"Not yet," he rasps, his teeth grazing the flesh of my mound. "You're not ready yet."

"I can't get any readier," I protest, tugging at the short strands of his hair and desperately trying to urge him back up my body.

"Do you want me to stop?"

No. Please, God, no, but also yes because everything in me is screaming that I need to be perfect for him.

In a rush, he grabs my hips, spreading my legs wide and completely exposing me to him. Instant shame fills me, my legs trying to snap shut on their own volition.

"No," I breathe. "But—"

"You have the tightest fucking cunt, little doe. I'll bruise you if I don't work you up to take me."

I swallow over the lump in my throat.

"I need a shower for that," I protest, though it sounds meek, even to my ears.

"Stop."

I never knew how much credence that little word could have until now.

His dark gaze on mine, he dips his head, holding my eyes as he runs his tongue from my opening to my clit.

I gasp at the sensation of his velvety tongue slipping along my folds. He groans as if he's been dreaming of this moment all his life.

"*Fuck*," he rasps, slipping his tongue in and out of me.

A moan escapes me when his fingers find me, sliding through my slick folds. "Mason," I whimper, arching my back when he seals his lips around my clit.

He flutters his tongue and when he growls in satisfaction, all the shame and humility vanish from my body. This man wants me.

My hand goes to his hair and he eyes me while his tongue circles my clit. His finger pumps in and out of me, matching the rhythm of his tongue as he feasts on me. I've never felt so completely open to a man before and after everything I've just found out, it should stop me in my tracks.

But . . . it only makes me want him more.

"Mason, please," I whimper when the first waves of my orgasm start to roll in, full force. His eyes glint in the darkness and a strike of lightning outside paints his face in shades of blue and white.

"So fucking sweet," he grunts, reaching under me and gripping the backs of my thighs until my knees are by my breasts.

I stammer, clambering for something to grab onto, but all I find is him. I don't have time to catch a single breath before he slips his tongue back between my folds. A moan claws its way up my throat, and I fist his hair until I'm sure strands break free.

"Fuck, I've been craving that sound," he grits against my skin, swirling his tongue higher until he's circling my clit.

My back arches off the desk, my hips seeking his mouth while he works me like I've never been worked before. Moisture clings to every inch of my skin as the pleasure shoots through me. But . . . because Mason gets off on my pain, he pulls back just before I come.

"Asshole," I growl, my hand smacking the desk as I'm denied a third time.

My fingers claw at his hair, desperately trying to drag him back to where I need him, but a sharp sting shoots through me that has me bucking under his hold, a strangled moan escaping.

He just bit my clit, again.

"You'll come when I say you can. Not a second sooner."

I collapse back with a groan, my eyes rolling so hard I fear they may fall out when his tongue soothes the sting, drawing out a new, unspeakable part of me that I never knew existed until he came along. Heat floods my body and the pain mixes with the pleasure, leaving me a moaning puddle of need underneath him.

"Please, Mason." I'm beyond caring about begging, at this point. I'd pray at his feet if he let me come right now.

"Fuck, Hannah," he grits against my skin, sucking in a sharp breath. "This cunt's so fucking greedy for me."

I try to focus on anything else other than the orgasm threatening to ruin me as he continues his torture. The price of gasoline. Unwanted religious visitors. Taxes.

None of it helps, though and my legs shake with anticipation as pleasure races through me.

"Come for me, little doe." Burying his face in my sex like a man starved, he seals his lips around my clit, fluttering his tongue back and forth until I'm writhing underneath him.

That's all it takes for the orgasm to rip through me, sending me hurtling toward another dimension where I don't even know my own name. My vision goes blurry, a guttural moan falling from my lips I'm sure sounds more like an exorcism than an orgasm.

"That's it," Mason grits, but he doesn't stop his assault on my body. Not when I'm pushing him back and not when my legs clamp down on his head. He eats me straight into another orgasm, this one leaving my heart racing until I'm sure the Grim Reaper will show up at any moment to set me free.

What a way to go.

I float back to earth, my body shaking with little aftershocks as Mason kisses his way up my stomach, nipping the flesh above my navel and then circling my nipple with his tongue.

Abruptly he stands, tugging his shirt over his head. He lowers the zipper of his jeans and I finally get a chance to ogle him. His tattoos shift over his muscles in the darkness, each one intricately carved out in his skin. I've never cared much about tattoos, but now that he's standing in front of me in all his glory . . . I get it.

He fists his cock, unceremoniously gripping my hips to tug me to the very edge of the desk.

The second he enters me my body erupts in tremors. He, however, lets out a growl that can only be described as feral.

"Fucking hell, Hannah," he grits, the moment he pushes inside me. His head falls back, his eyes clenched and he groans, a deep, animalistic sound that settles right between my legs, even if it feels like he's splitting me in half. "So fucking tight, baby."

I've never been called *baby* before. I know it's stupid, but I can't escape the way my heart flutters at the way he grounds it out. Like he has no choice. Like he needs to say it.

"It's too big," I gasp, the pain of taking him too much and I shake my head, my nails digging into his shoulders as my body struggles to adjust to him. I think it would be more comfortable fucking a tree at this point. Or a light post.

"You can take it." He moves slow, only pushing in an inch before pulling back to surge forward again. Tremors move through him, his teeth clenched so hard I worry they'll crack. Little by little, he fills me until I feel like, surely, he'll break me. "You feel how wet you are, soaking my cock?"

Wetness drips down my leg and I want to be embarrassed, but with the way he fills me, I can't think of anything but him.

"You pussy begs for me, Hannah."

Fucking traitorous bitch.

Despite his size, my body blossoms at the rough sound of his voice and the way his hands shake on my hips. He's trembling . . . a man on the brink of his control, but he's holding back so he doesn't hurt me.

It's oddly touching, even as he does the dirtiest things to me.

Reaching under me, he lifts me, my breasts pressing against his chest as he carries me to the old armchair in the corner of the room.

He deposits me on his lap and I straddle him. I reach between us, taking him in my fist and aligning him with my entrance. I allow myself to slip down slowly, filling myself with him with a whimper and a prayer.

"Fuck, I should have known you'd be fucking perfect," he grinds out, his fingers tightening on my hips until I know I'll have bruises tomorrow.

"Careful," I muse, my voice breathier than usual as his groin grinds against my clit. "You keep saying such sweet things to me, I might get the wrong idea."

The slap to my ass is not something I was prepared for.

"What's the matter?" he purrs when I yelp from the sudden bite of pain. Still . . . the sting morphs completely, liquefying into something else. Something I never thought I would enjoy.

"You are such an asshole," I grit, though it doesn't stop me from moaning when the next one hits.

"And it turns you on. Ride my cock."

He does it again and heat floods my body, my arousal slipping down my inner thigh. He curses under his breath, gripping my hips and pulling me down the rest of the way on his length.

I gasp from the intrusion, but I can feel my body bending to him, even as he damns my soul with each thrust of his cock inside me.

"Fuck, Mason . . . " He uses my hips to move me over him, thrusting into me until the sounds of our bodies moving together fill the room. It's both the most erotic and most disturbing sound I've ever heard.

"I'm going to ruin you, little doe. This tight little cunt was made for my cock and after I'm done, you won't be able to come without me."

With what he's doing to me, I actually believe him.

Impossibly, my body relaxes, greedily sucking him in until I'm rocking my hips to meet his thrusts. His groin grinds against my clit, drawing a whimper from my lips. It's too much. It's all too much, but if he stopped, I'm afraid they would have to commit me.

He shudders, rolling his neck as he moves me over him. I bury my face in his shoulder, my nails gripping his shoulders so hard, I fear I might leave marks.

Good. Maybe he can think about those the next time he's pissed off at me.

"Harder," I dare, knowing I'm playing with fire.

"Hannah," he warns, his fingers flexing on my hips.

"I want more," I breathe, leaning forward to press my lips to his. He nips my bottom lip between his teeth with a groan and his hand snaps to my throat, his fingers tensing and robbing me of air.

He runs his tongue over his teeth, sweat dotting his brow. "Are you adjusted?"

"Yes," I breathe, my pussy clenching around him as the onslaught of pleasure threatens to send me into a third orgasm.

In a rush, he tugs me against his chest and locks his arms around my waist. He bounces me on his cock, hard and fast until I couldn't stop myself from coming if my life depended on it.

A cry leaves my lips and I come so hard I see stars, clinging to him like a life raft at sea as he doesn't slow his pace.

"Fuck, that's it, Hannah," he grits, powering into me with a punishing rhythm. "Fucking come for me."

With a final thrust, he spills inside me with a shuddering groan. I collapse into him, my body spent and shaking.

I'm not even sure I can walk, now, let alone move.

Our heavy breaths fill the silence as we both float back to earth. I sigh in contentment, riding the high of post-coital bliss as he brushes the ends of my hair from my damp face.

"Fuck," he breathes, relaxing back in the chair.

Fuck is right.

That was the most intense sexual experience I've ever had. Not that I've had a lot of them, but I have a feeling that one will be at the top of the list.

Somewhere in all of that, the storm outside subsided and a ray of sunshine beams through the window above us, entirely too bright for after-sex clarity, so I bury my face in his neck and shut my eyes. If I can just stay like this with him for a few minutes longer, I can forget all the thoughts racing in my head.

"I'm hungry," I breathe.

Mason pauses for a moment, then he laughs.

I pull back to stare at him. He's lost his mind.

"Did you just laugh?" I reach out with the palm of my hand, placing it on his damp forehead. "Are you alright?"

He catches my hand, bringing it to his lips to nip the flesh over my pulse point. Despite everything, my body still reacts.

"Rest up, little doe. I've been waiting years for this."

My heart swells, but before I can say anything, something warm and wet slips down my leg.

Oh no.

Oh, this is bad.

Scrambling, I climb off his lap, wincing at the loss of him. He stills for a moment, watching me confused until I reach for my clothes.

"Hannah."

"Condom, Mason," I grit, tears welling in my eyes.

God, I'm so stupid. I can't bring a baby into this. Savannah's words echo through my mind, warning me that I'll only destroy Mason.

Seems like she was more right than even she knew.

He stares at me for a moment, calculating in his mind.

"You're not on the pill."

It's not a question.

"Fuck," he grumbles, scrubbing a hand through his hair, and for some reason, though his reaction is valid, something in my chest stings.

"That's all you can say?" Tears burn in my eyes and I hate them.

I hate him. Most importantly, I hate myself for getting into this dumb situation.

He reaches for me, but I step back out of his grasp. His jaw ticks, but he doesn't push me.

"We'll get a pill," he murmurs, carefully lifting his hand to brush away a tear on my cheek. Though he's trying to comfort me, there's a distance that wasn't there before. An icy coldness that fills my veins from the way he looks at me.

Like it was a mistake.

Whore.

Mortification coils through me and I stumble to the bathroom, refusing to look at him again.

Once the door is shut, I lean back against it, letting the tears quietly fall.

I'm an idiot. A liar. A girl with baggage. I can't blame him for regretting what happened any more than I blame myself.

I always knew something would send this whole thing crashing to the ground.

I just didn't think I'd care this much.

CHAPTER *Thirty*

MASON

I'm a fucking idiot.

I know it. Hannah knows it. The fucking teenage clerk at the local drugstore knows it, judging by the grimace on her face when she rings up my shitty *Plan B* pill.

I shouldn't have fucked her. I definitely shouldn't have slid inside her bare. In the moment, though, when she was begging for my cock, I really didn't give a shit.

I still wouldn't. And that's a dangerous fucking thing.

I can still feel her fingers in my hair. Hear her moans echoing in my ear while I was buried inside her. From the scratches on my back to the taste of her on my tongue, she's engrained in me.

I fucking hate it.

Her crying at the thought of the two of us being tied together solidified it. She couldn't have made it any more clear that the thought of having a kid with me horrified her.

Those tears burned like acid in my chest when I watched them roll down her cheeks.

Still . . . I know she's too fucking good for me. She always has been and maybe that's why I crave her so much. Like an invasive species, I want to take her. Make her mine. No matter what she's done, it pales in comparison to the terrible shit I have. The people I've let down. She's a fucking saint where I'm concerned and touching her is like an act of defiance toward God.

If you believe in that shit.

I've never been religious, but watching her come for me, hearing her cry out my name like it's a Hail Mary? That's the closest I've ever felt to fucking heaven.

She was so fucking beautiful riding my cock . . . and now, she hates me.

The clerk finishes ringing me up and I take my bag, not bothering to mumble my thanks. She won't hear me over the headphone jammed in her ear, anyway.

I make my way home in silence, taking my time because I just don't have it in me to pretend I'm not still fucking reeling.

I've always been in this deeper than her. I've come to accept it. Where she can move on and forget about me, I wouldn't be able to breathe in a world without her in it.

Isn't that fucking poetic?

My hands shake as I drive. Jesus Christ. You'd think I just lost my fucking virginity.

I laugh bitterly in the silence of the cab. I was a dumbass to think she'd react differently. She's still holding onto that hope that life is just going to magically be what she wants it to be tomorrow, when in reality, it's ugly, cruel, and demeaning.

I'm not an idiot. I know a pregnancy with everything going on right now would be the worst thing either one of us could do.

Even so, the sick and twisted part of me didn't care about coming inside her. Knocking her up would finally put an end to this. I'd marry her in a fucking heartbeat and finally give her a reason to stick around. To think of me as more than just the asshole helping her find her sister.

This *obsession* in me has this idea— a perfect fantasy where I'd find her in my bed, every night. I'd fuck her every morning and put a smile on that pretty face. Give her everything she could ever want so she'd never leave. She'd be mine, fully and neither heaven nor hell would be able to drag her away from me.

In reality, I can't give her the life she wants. Parties and diamonds and too much wealth for any one person to spend in a lifetime. I make a comfortable living, but nothing near what she's used to. My house isn't a castle and I'm definitely not her fucking knight in shining armor.

She'll leave when this is done. I need to accept that.

She's got me by the balls and there isn't shit I can do about it.

With the cartel knowing where she is, it's only a matter of time before her mother shows up. Now they're sucking me into their trafficking bullshit.

I won't do it.

I'll die before I ever let Dad's garage get turned into that same shit the old paper mill was.

I scrub a hand over my face, a plan forming. I need to see Logan. I need to get every single ounce of information out of the little prick that broke into Hannah's house to see if we can fix this because right now . . . shit's looking pretty fucking bleak.

There's a car I recognize in my drive as soon as I pull in and I groan in frustration.

"Jesus Christ, Savannah," I grit, ready to break apart whatever bullshit fight she's come to start now.

I force my legs to carry me inside, the sound of their voices ringing out from the living room.

Both freeze when I step into the doorway, Hannah's gaze wary while Savannah's is tense.

"I just came to speak with Hannah."

"Wonderful."

I look to Hannah

I nod to the kitchen and Hannah swallows, face bleak as she follows me. As soon as we've stepped inside, I hand her the bag and she takes it like it weighs a thousand pounds.

"Mason—" she starts, but I cut her off.

"No."

Her eyes flick to mine and I can see she's been crying. I expect her to argue, but she doesn't push, popping the pill in her mouth and swallowing it down without water.

I nod. It's done.

"Do I need to stay?"

She shakes her head softly, though she doesn't look at me. My chest aches to take her chin in my hand, but if I touch her right now, I won't want to stop until she agrees to be mine.

"I'll be back later," I murmur, heading for the door. I don't want to look at her. See the fucking disappointment in those pretty green eyes.

I grab the bike keys on the way because I need to clear my head before I meet Logan. "Don't wait up."

Maybe if I drive fast enough, I'll forget all about Hannah Gaines and her pretty fucking eyes.

But I'm betting I won't.

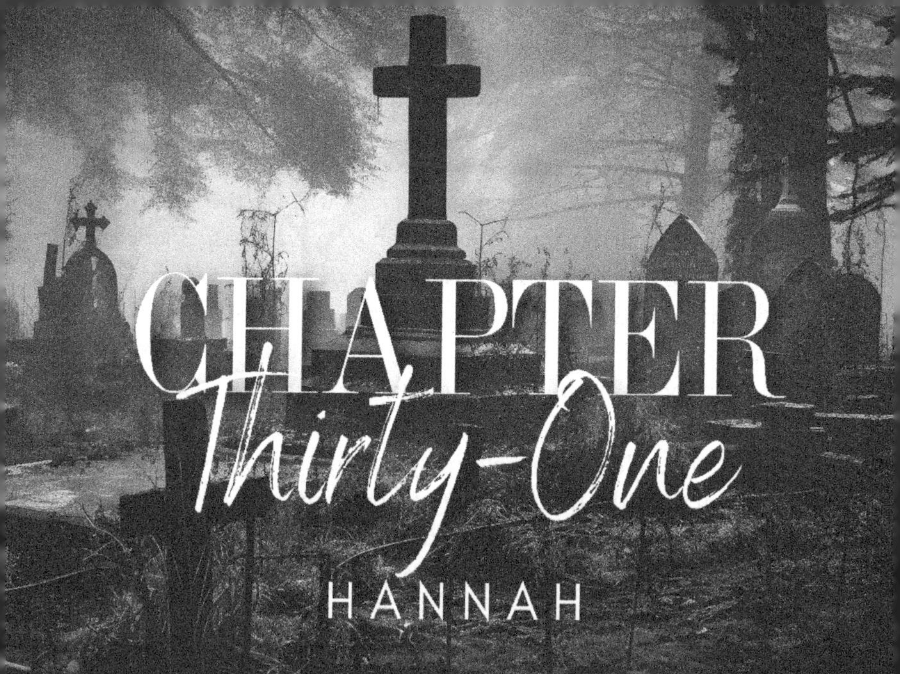

CHAPTER Thirty-One

HANNAH

"That was awkward," Savannah chimes, coming into the kitchen after Mason leaves. She sits down at the kitchen table, watching me through a guarded gaze.

Savannah freaking Carpenter. You know, I'm starting to think the cold, indifferent Carpenter smolder should be patented. God knows they've all got it down to a T.

I wipe the corner of my eye, hoping foolishly, that she can't see that I've been crying.

"Things seem . . . tense," Savannah chimes when I step to the fridge.

"What was your first clue?"

She chuckles, but it's lacking in any real humor.

"You know, your sister could learn a thing or two from you. She never did have a sense of humor."

"Nope," I agree, pouring two glasses of lemonade. I only put one ice cube in hers, though, because screw her and her high and mighty attitude. "That why you came to speak to me? About Missy?"

"*Melissa* is the furthest thing from my mind right now."

"Let me guess," I sit the glass down in front of her and slip into a chair on the other side of the table, wincing when at the slide of the denim against the marks from Mason's fingers on my ass. "I am?"

"No," she replies coolly. "Though you are there. Festering."

"I've been told I have that effect on people." I keep my voice as sweet as possible, the venom-laced pretty words rolling off my tongue easily now. There's no use trying to win her over. She's already said what she needed to.

Which doesn't explain why she's here now.

"If you want the truth," she starts, her tone clipped. "I came to apologize. It wasn't my place to say those things the other night."

I blink, though her apology doesn't really mean much because I can tell she doesn't mean it.

But . . . there's that voice in the back of my mind, practically forcing me to play devil's advocate.

"No," I sigh, relaxing back in the chair. "It was. I can understand."

"You can't."

"No? My sister became addicted to drugs because of *your* stepfather."

"So, perhaps both our families are assholes."

I pause, staring at her.

"So, you're here because . . ."

"Because Mason enlightened me on a few issues the other night and I'm finding it hard to hate you as much as I want to."

Wow. Can't accuse her of beating around the bush.

"So you came to tell me you didn't hate me?"

"Mason's a good man and he cares about you. Regardless of how I feel, I want him to be happy."

"Savannah, I know my sister hurt your family. I know she did some really *awful, horrible* things. I'm not excusing that, nor am I trying to hide her from that."

Her blue eyes narrow on me. "So, why are you trying to help

her?"

I suck in a deep breath, wiping my clammy hands on my jeans. "Because as bad as she is, she's my sister. Her death would solve nothing and it wouldn't make anyone feel better. Prison is the best place for her if she really did what they're saying she did."

"You would rather her rot away in a jail cell than take a bullet to the brain?"

"None of us are innocent," I murmur, forcing myself to take a drink of my lemonade. "Some of us just have bigger sins to pay for."

Savannah regards me coldly, and I can read every expression on her face as the thoughts flash through her mind.

"You and I are a lot alike," she murmurs eventually.

She's right. We both have scars. Deep wounds that have since scabbed over, but that still haunt us every day. Though I don't know what hers are, I'm willing to bet those knives cut just as deep.

"Yeah, we are."

"So how did you turn out normal? Mommy dearest, succubus sister . . ."

I shrug. "What's normal?"

She smirks. "Yeah, I guess you're right."

I pause because I've wanted to ask this for a long time, but I've never had the courage to.

"Do you think . . . do you think Mason blames himself for whatever happened with Marcus."

Her eyes fill with disgust at the name, as if saying it three times will cause him to *poof* magically into the air.

"He does," she bites, but that anger dissipates as her eyes fill with tears. "I hate that he went to live with our grandmother because Marcus didn't want him at home. I hate that he's built all this by himself when we should have been there to help him. He's been on his own for a long time. Until . . . now. He's hard on himself. I hate it, but . . . we've never been that close."

"There's still time," I offer and she nods slowly, gaze trained on her hands.

"Yeah, I guess so. We're working on it. Slowly." She clears her throat, finishing her lemonade. "Hannah, I want to ask you something."

"Of course," I answer, though I'm not sure if I really want to.

"Do you love Mason?"

I nearly choke on an ice cube, coughing and sputtering as it slides down my throat.

"I'm sorry?"

"Do you love him?" she repeats.

"Love isn't the end of pain," I explain, though my chest aches because, of course, I can't stop thinking about the disgust on his face when he found out we'd forgotten a condom. "If I loved him, it wouldn't change anything."

She actually chuckles this time.

Rude.

"Wow," she breathes, shaking her head. "We really are alike."

"What does that mean?"

For the first time since I've met her, a smile tugs on her lips, but she pushes it down.

"You'll see."

She gets up from the table, crosses to the sink, and rinses her cup out.

"Well, I've got to go. I wasn't supposed to be out today, with everything happening, but I nearly forced Antonio to bring me over because I needed to get this off my mind."

She pauses on the way back, stooping down to pick up the little box on top of the trash.

"This is going to fuck you up."

"Wonderful." I'm not bitter or anything.

"While it grosses me out to think about my brother having sex with *anyone*," she sighs dramatically, chucking the box back in the can. "I can't say I haven't been there myself. Shitty ex-boyfriend," she winks.

"Savannah?" I call when she starts to walk away and she stops turning back to me. "How did you and Logan figure it all out?"

She smiles softly and it's the most emotion I've seen since she arrived. There's real love there. Love I'm not used to.

"He saved my life," she answers quietly. "In return, I gave him my soul."

And then, without another word, she leaves.

CHAPTER *Thirty-Two*

MASON

I find myself in the garage out behind the house when I return. I don't bother with dinner because doing so would mean pretending like I'm not still pissed off from earlier and I can't.

Not when she's right fucking there.

After I left on the bike, I took a drive past the old Parker estate. The fucking thing's empty, sitting against the sun like Dracula's forgotten castle. Sure as fuck had enough darkness in it. I circled back around, waiting until I was sure Savannah would be gone before I came home. Luckily, Hannah was in the shower, so I was able to sneak quietly out here without having to face her.

Dad and I spent whole summers out here in this little shack, working on cars. Motors. Lawn mowers. Whatever we could. At the time, I didn't understand why we did it. Now, I'm glad we did because they're some of the best fucking memories I have with him.

I wish I could talk to him. Ask him what the fuck I'm supposed to do. How I'm supposed to keep all this shit going. What to do about the cartel. Hannah. Governor Gaines and her disturbed daughter. All of it.

He'd know. At least, that's what I tell myself while I angrily pull the parts off that need to be replaced.

Tomorrow, I've got something to do. I won't be around, but Logan's men will be, as well as Ian and Puke and I know they'd never let anything happen to her.

Not if they enjoy breathing, anyway.

At some point, I notice all the lights in the house are off. Good. That means she's gone to bed and I can get the fuck out of here without having to face her and deal with the bullshit that happened earlier.

My head's still reeling; my cock still rock fucking hard remembering the way she felt wrapped around me, milking me.

Don't even get me started on the fucking fantasies.

Fuck.

She was perfection.

I close up the shop and head inside, stepping quietly through the house to grab the keys to my bike. I'm about to head out when I notice the empty *Plan B* box in the trash and the plate covered in foil on the stove.

Fuck me.

And now, I feel like a dick.

Despite being hungry. I shove the plate in the fridge and head for the door. I grab my bike, rolling it out to the road so I don't wake her, only to look back at the house and see the glow of the lamp emanating from her room. She stands in the glow, messy red hair and soft eyes.

It's the worry in them that makes my heart stutter awkwardly in my chest.

I don't know why. We both got what we wanted. Or at least, that's what she thinks. What I thought I needed to end this obsession so I could finally let her go. But . . . looking up at her, my chest burns with something possessive and violent.

Growling under my breath, I turn away, climbing on my bike

before I do something stupid.

And I don't look back.

I have never been a needy man.

It's why Mom and I never got along when I was a kid. At the end of the day, I didn't need her and I was content to keep myself occupied whereas my sisters needed her constantly.

I suppose that's partially to blame for the large gap separating us now that I'm an adult, but . . . it could also be the man sliding into the stool in front of me through the scuffed and damaged bulletproof glass.

The California State Prison smells like cheap government cleaner with an underlying aroma of piss.

Good.

I hope Parker gags on it as he rots away in his cell.

"You look like shit," I murmur into the receiver and his eyes flash with displeasure before he picks up the phone.

"Funny," he murmurs, a small smirk tugging at the corners of his lips. "Seems the tables are reversed."

He's referring to the few days I did down in county for beating the smug smirk off Drew Marshall when he hurt my sister. An offense Parker himself had me cleared of.

"Orange suits you," I remark coldly, regarding the bright pumpkin-orange jumpsuit he's wearing. "Cancer, huh?"

Though his eyes are sunken in and rimmed in dark circles, they still hold the same discontent for me they always have. A superiority that he created in his own head.

"If you came to ask about my diagnosis," Parker starts, leaning back in his chair and crossing his arms over his chest. "I will be dead by the end of the year."

"While I would love to think about you dying a slow painful

death due to the tumor in your brain, I can't help but feel it's too kind for you."

He smirks.

"Let's get to the point," he says, looking over his shoulder. There's a guard standing back, pretending to not pay attention, but we all know he's going through every word we say with a fine-tooth comb. "I don't have all day, you know?"

"Yes, I would hate to distract you from counting the cinderblocks in your cell," I murmur, gripping the phone tighter. I've always fucking hated this guy. Even when I didn't know the extent of his depravity, I found him dangerous.

Now that I know what he's done to Savannah, he's lucky there's a bulletproof shield protecting him.

"Tell me what your mistress's mother is doing rounding up all the kids of the members of your private club?"

His eyes flash with something, but it's quickly replaced with a look of indifference.

"Can't say I know."

"Can't say I believe you."

"You know, I never liked you," he murmurs, so matter of fact, you'd think he was talking about the weather.

Can't say I disagree with him though.

"You always had this pathetic savior's complex. As if you were God or some shit."

"Funnily enough, I didn't care for you or your perverted glances toward my ten-year-old sister, either."

His eyes zero in on me. "What do you want Carpenter?"

"You dead," I murmur, holding up a finger. "That's the first thing. Unfortunately, before you go, I need some information on your mistress."

That gets a rise out of him. For the first time since I've sat down, something more than contempt flashes across his gaze.

"Melly and I are no longer together."

"Shame. You two seemed so perfect for each other."

"If this is about her, I haven't heard from her in months."

"No, but you have attempted to call her. Several times, from the looks of it." I hold up Melissa's cell phone, showcasing just how many times he's called since he's been locked up. The look of disgust on his face is almost humorous.

"I have things I need to discuss with her. My house, for one."

"It's a shithole, really," I interject before he can finish and his jaw twitches.

Fuck, why didn't I do this sooner? Fucking with Parker is the most fun I've had in a very, very long time.

"So you've been."

"I have."

"And?"

So, he does still care.

Funny.

"Seems she either flew the coop or someone did it for her."

"And you care because?"

"Because she's a criminal. She should be charged, just as you are."

"Her sister's looking for her, isn't she?"

Silence falls between us.

Hannah is off the table for this conversation. The moment Parker catches wind that Hannah's involved, she'll be on his radar and I'll be damned if he sends his thugs after her next.

I'm no stranger to death. I'm prepared to put someone in the ground if it means protecting what's mine because, make no fucking mistake about, Hannah's mine, just as much as I'm hers.

She just needs to accept it.

I can see by the hard set of Parker's jaw, he wishes I would have died a year ago when he sent his men after me in the middle of the night in a last-ditch effort to silence the family. That was the night he hired Johnson to try and murder my mother and sisters on live television.

Unfortunately, for him, it's not so easy to kill me. If that were the case, I would have been dead a long fucking time ago.

"A word of advice—"

"I didn't ask."

"I'm giving it anyway," he grits, wiping a hand over his forehead. Dark purple bruises mark the hand as the veins protrude from the skin.

The cancer's eating him alive.

"I was led into my . . . charges by a very conniving offer. I was to work alongside Laura to create this business and then, when shit hit the fan, I was sold out. She cannot be trusted. Laura will turn in the blink of an eye and if you think your pet is safe from her just because she's her flesh and blood, you're a bigger fool than I thought you were."

It doesn't surprise me that he'd pass the blame to Governor Gaines. Setting him up, forcing him to rule over the Brethren as if the status and immeasurable wealth were all just the negative side effects of his plight.

Parker is simple. Selfish. Rude. Arrogant. Disgusting.

A wet napkin is more complex.

"So, no indication as to where Melissa could have gone?" I cock a brow at him.

"No," he grits through his teeth, sweat dotting his brow. I imagine, in his state, sitting up for this long is no easy task, though forgive me if I just don't give a shit.

"Great, then I'll be off." I move to stand and he opens his mouth, but it's not until I go to hang up the phone that he stops me.

"Wait."

The sinister motherfucker in my head can't help but chuckle.

See? Simple.

"She went to her mother for help."

I wait for him to add something, but he doesn't.

"And?"

His jaw feathers and he sucks his teeth. My biggest fucking pet peeve.

"Shortly after I was apprehended, they started hunting Melly out like sharks to blood. She went to her mother. Though . . . her mother never turned her in, did she?"

"She was sent to the warehouse. I already know this."

I move to hang up for the second time, but again, he stops me in a rush.

"But who helped her out of there?" When I don't answer, he continues. "Ask yourself this," he starts, dropping his voice so low, I can barely hear him. "Would I have sacrificed myself, my career, my fortune, to save your mother? Your sisters?"

No. The answer is no.

"I think you'll find Laura is a lot closer to Cortez than she lets on. Same with her lap dog."

"Five minutes," the guard barks, looking directly at me.

So the Cartel is working for the governor. I've known that. Michael, too. All for the prize of Hannah.

"You've not told me anything useful."

"No one trusts the government, Carpenter."

"They double-crossed her. How?"

"Melissa was addicted to the black dahlia. I couldn't stop her, of course . . . I wasn't able to stop myself, either."

"If you're trying to justify years worth of crimes against humanity with a drug you created, this conversation is finished."

"No. Only, explaining. Six years ago when they first approached me about the black dahlia, I thought they were insane. But . . . when it came into fruition and we started sampling it, we found it could take you to new heights. Sexual, astral, that profound thinking that only comes from a real, good high. We used it countless times at our events without any issues. You want to know who owns it?"

I cock a brow and wait for his answer.

"Cortez."

"And you think . . . Cortez has Melissa."

His eyes glint wickedly.

"I know it."

"Time's up, Parker."

Parker stiffens when the guard's hand lands on him, trying to mask the wince of pain.

"Get her out of there. Hannah, too, and leave."

That's exactly what I'm afraid of. Turning a blind eye to the deaths of dozens to save Hannah sounds heroic and all, but Hannah's not that kind of person.

She'd turn herself in if it meant saving those people and that's exactly what I'm afraid of.

One thing I've grown to loathe in my adult life is my vivid imagination.

If she turns herself into the cartel to save her sister, I know exactly what will follow.

Parker is hauled from his chair and escorted toward the exit and with the deafening slam that follows, those visions of what they would do to Hannah—to my fucking girl—plague my mind.

Fuck, I need to get out of here. I need to see her.

I need to bury myself inside her until she forgets about that fucking plague of a sister of hers and accepts that she can't do anything to save her.

I need *her*.

As I said, I've never been a needy person.

Looks like that's changed now.

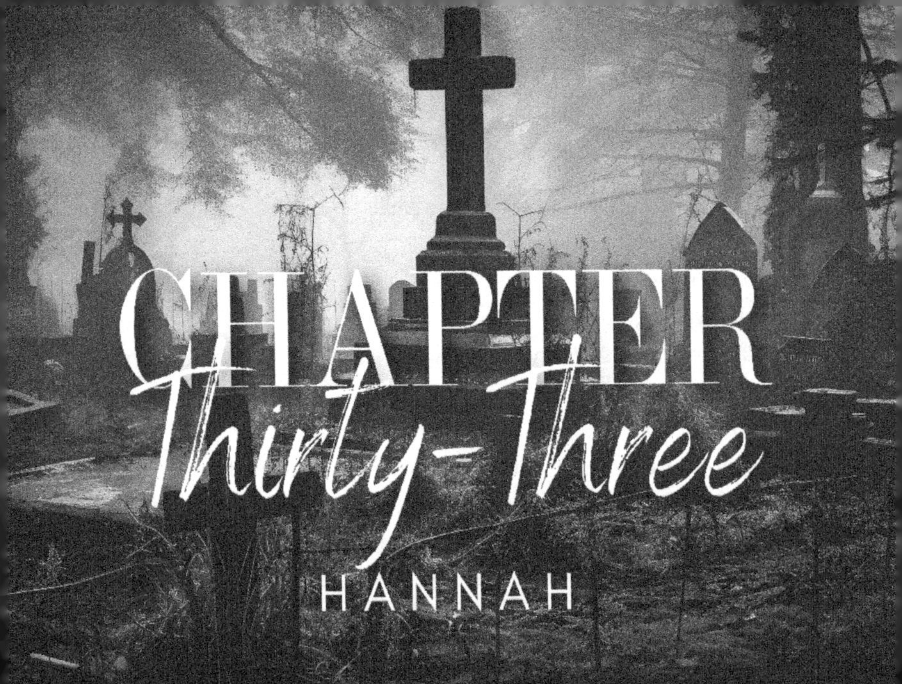

CHAPTER Thirty-Three

HANNAH

Expectations are fickle things.

For example, I expect the *Plan B* to work and not make me feel like I'm either going to vomit or pass out at any second.

I expect Mason to be at home this morning like he always is. For things to go back to some form of normalcy when I was just the annoying sister of the woman he detested.

I *expect* not to care when he's not at work the next morning when in reality, my heart is aching to see him, even if he won't speak to me.

As I said . . . fickle things.

I've screwed up a lot of things in life, but this one has to take the cake. I've never not remembered condoms. Not until I got his hands on me.

Neither of us spoke after the pill. He asked if I'd taken my "medicine" and I said yes before he disappeared out to the garage. That's been the extent of our conversation in the last twenty-four hours.

Something about the cold indifference in his eyes stung.

And for that, I hate myself.

I shouldn't care. He doesn't, but yesterday was both the best sex I've ever had and the most connected I've ever felt to another human being. Like we were a part of one another. One person.

Like he knew every piece of me.

I guess I've been reading too many romance novels. Shit like that doesn't happen in the real world.

I stay up at my desk most of the day. My body aches. My limbs feel like I ran a mile last night and there's a soreness I'm not accustomed to between my thighs.

Like I'd been ridden hard and put away wet.

I guess that's the truth.

Every time I sit, see the light purple bruise on my neck from his teeth nipping that pulse point, *look* at the empty office door and see that damned chair, I'm reminded he was *there*, and the feeling of rejection comes full circle.

Mason doesn't want to be tied to me by a child. I get it. Kids are a big commitment, especially with someone you really aren't supposed to like.

But did he have to act so . . . disgusted by the idea?

He wouldn't even look at me and it stings to know he detested the idea so much, even if it would be the worst possible decision either of us could make at this point in our lives.

The cartel. My sister. My mother . . . my secrets.

No. I can't bring a baby into that mess. Nor do I *want* to. I'm just saying . . . I don't know what I'm saying.

What's worse is now that I know he actually cares, at least to some degree, the sickening feeling in my stomach can only mean one thing.

I've fallen for him.

Mason didn't come home last night, or if he did, I didn't see him. His door was closed, but his truck wasn't in the drive. With a bitter resentment that surprised even me, I found I hated the thoughts of where else he could be. Another woman's house. A bar. Anywhere I wasn't so he wouldn't have to deal with me.

Because that's what I am to him. A problem he doesn't know how to solve.

Throughout the day, I find myself creating the perfect woman for him in my head, because it's better than allowing myself to worry about things that can never happen, anyway. She'd be gentle and sweet. Probably a schoolteacher or a nurse. She'd be someone who helps people and she'd probably have a cat or a cute little dog. She'd wear sundresses and vanilla-scented perfume and she'd give him her all because she wouldn't have anything to hide.

I name her Sabrina, in my head, because I once knew a Sabrina that was as sweet as sugar on the outside, but a vindictive snake underneath.

Seems fitting.

Guess you can say I'm bitter.

By the end of the day, Mason's still not shown up and I've given up hope.

It's around four when a bright blue cupcake is sat down on the counter in front of me.

"Puke's mom made them for his birthday," Ian smiles proudly.

"Is it his birthday?"

"No, tomorrow is. A bunch of us are going out for drinks since he's turning twenty-one." He leans back against the counter beside me. "You should come out with us."

"Sorry, I can't. Responsibilities and all that."

The thought of going out makes my skin crawl. Especially after everything that's happened recently. Even though . . . I can't help but wonder if Mason will be joining them.

Ian chuckles, shaking his head. "Right. I just thought you'd like to have some fun . . ."

"Yeah."

An air of awkwardness hangs between us now. After I moved in *temporarily* with Mason, I feel like both he and Puke have been keeping their distance. Not that I blame them, but it just adds to the air of *Hannah's a whore* that's been hanging around in my head all day.

"Ian, about—"

"You deserve a night out, though . . . every now and then," he says, cutting me off without regard. I pause, a strange, unease settling over me. It's nothing. I know I'm just emotional, but . . . it's still there. "Even if it's not with a bunch of greasy mechanics."

Okay . . .

"I get out." It's totally a lie. My first— and last— time I'd been out in months had been when Mason took me to the Inner Sanctum and we all know how that went.

Ian stares at me for a beat, boredom clouding his chocolate gaze as if he doesn't believe me. He's entirely too close for comfort, but with the edge of the desk behind me and the counter in front of me, I have nowhere to go.

Plus . . . this is *Ian*. My *friend*. He's been nothing but kind to me since I started and better yet, he was the *only* person that spoke to me here for days. At least with any kind of humanity.

And so I'm reminded of Mason again and everything that happened between us yesterday. Maybe the *Plan B* isn't what's making me sick. Maybe it's just his absence.

"You and I both know that's a lie," Ian goads. "When was the last time you did something for yourself?"

Well, every time I *do* something for myself, I also do something stupid. Like forgetting condoms or locking the back door.

"I do," I stammer, skin burning from being put on the spot like there's a military-grade spotlight shining down on me. "I read. I . . . I go visit friends." *Used* to visit friends. "I do a lot of things. Plus, I *like* being independent."

Ian inches closer, his gaze burning into mine. My heartbeat quickens, pounding in my ears, but it's not for anything good. It's a sick, uneasy feeling in my stomach and though I know I'm overreacting, I still don't like the insinuation in this conversation.

"You need to take time for yourself." He reaches up, surprising me when he pushes a strand of hair back from the hickey on my neck with a brush of his fingers. Fingers that don't feel like the ones ingrained on my skin. "Did he hurt you?" he asks, so quiet, I'm almost sure I missed it.

I arch away from him and open my mouth to snap at him to stop touching me, but before I can . . .

A throat clears in the doorway. Ian leaps away from me like he's been poked with a cattle prod and nervously runs a hand over his short hair.

Oh. Shit.

If I thought things were bad before . . . they're about to be fucking awful.

Mason stands in the doorway from the garage, flowers in his hand and murder in his eyes. Violence seeps off him in waves. Only that gaze isn't aimed at me.

It's aimed at Ian.

Suddenly, my heartbeat is racing for a different reason.

Mason doesn't even say anything before Ian's making off toward the door, his head hung low and a mumbled apology falling from his lips. He points to the cupcake, dejected on the counter. "I just thought Hannah might enjoy a cup—"

He stops talking when Mason's gaze flashes with venom. Honestly? I would, too.

Ian disappears out the shop door without another word, scooting past Mason who doesn't move even the slightest inch. Part of me wishes he would stay. I don't think I've ever seen Mason so thoroughly pissed off. Not even when I cleaned the office. The other half is glad to watch him go. Things were just getting way too weird.

Mason doesn't speak to me, nor does he look my way as he strides past, tossing the flowers on the counter in front of me. Daisies. My favorite.

"He just brought me a cupcake," I snap, trailing after him. "You don't need to be rude to him." How dare he bring me my favorite flowers, throw them at me, and then *leave.*

Mason whirls on me so fast I stumble back under that wild gaze. Like a hurricane on the horizon. "In case you forgot, they're my employees. Fucking me doesn't mean you get a say in how I handle them."

Ouch.

Tears burn in my eyes for the second time today, only this time, they manage to break free, slipping down my cheeks and burning like acid.

"Yeah, and I wish I never had."

His jaw ticks, his nostrils flaring with heat before it's quickly masked by something else. Something dark and pissed off and bleeding.

Did I . . . did I hurt him, too?

The eye contact sears, burning me from somewhere within. Still, I can't fight the anger and rejection pouring through me. The bitter resentment I've been shoving back at all day coiling like a snake, ready to strike.

It's already ruined between us. Why not burn it to the ground?

"You can bring me flowers." *My favorites.* "You can carry me to bed when I fall asleep." *Like I'm the most precious thing in the world.* "You can tell me I'm beautiful." *Look at me like I'm the only woman you've ever seen.* "None of it means anything if you don't actually care and I'm not willing to get my hopes up and wait around until you decide you're done with me."

I turn to leave, angry and ready to fight. Ready to cry. Ready to apologize because I know I just took everything he did for me and threw it back in his face and I hate myself for it, but I don't stop.

Not until his voice comes out, barely above a whisper, and I freeze in my tracks.

"I don't care." He chuckles sardonically and slowly, I turn back around to see him shaking his head. "You want to know where I went last night? This morning?"

I pause, a mixture of harsh words and hurried apologies on my tongue.

"I was with Prince, interrogating the asshole that tried to kill you because even if I wanted to, I can't fucking walk away. I need Prince because I'll be damned if your mother takes you away from me. Not because of *you*," he bites. "But because I'm selfish enough that I can't stand the fucking thought of losing you. I visited Parker this morning to get whatever information he has on your missing cockroach of a sister." He shakes his head as if the thought of doing all that for the likes of me is despicable. "I've dealt with the fucking cartel for two years because it meant you were safe. Still . . . every other day you try to find a reason why I'm not worth sticking around for."

My chest cracks at his words, but still, the venom burns inside me. I'm in love with him and it fucking sucks.

"I waited for you. Two years ago and you *never* showed. You made me feel like I meant nothing to you."

Cocking a brow, he chuckles darkly, stepping forward to get in my face. His eyes like midnight only amplify the icy darkness rolling off him in waves and a shiver rolls through me at his proximity.

This Mason is fucking terrifying.

Tears stream freely down my cheeks now, but I don't stop them. I don't have it in me. "I brought you flowers because I knew they would make you smile. I carry you to bed because I just need some fucking excuse to hold you. And beautiful? You were fucking made for me. You just can't see it."

He can't mean that.

"So, yeah, you can preach at me about treating Ian kindly. He and I both know he touched something that's mine and I *really* don't like people touching my things."

His words cut internally, wrapping my heart in cold steel and constricting my lungs to the point of pain.

My heartbeat slows at the angry vulnerability he let me see. While I've been cowering behind my fear of abandonment and my feelings of inadequacy, I failed to realize he shared the same fears.

My throat tightens at the thought that I'm the source for those feelings. Whoever had left him in the past . . . I was no better, demanding perfection when I am *far* from it.

He's silent for a moment, watching me with what he's trying to play off as indifference, only I can see through it now, to the man beneath. He's not as cold-hearted as he'd like me to believe.

Please kiss me.

He turns away.

"Go," he murmurs coldly. Like ice slipping through my veins. "Go home. I have stuff to finish here."

"Mason—" He cuts me off, dismissing me completely by turning his back to me. I want to go to him. Apologize. Just freaking be near him for the first time in nearly twenty-four hours.

But he doesn't want that. Not right now.

"Hannah." His voice is so quiet, so calm, I know he just wants to be alone.

I take in the strong lines of his shoulders where he stands at the desk, back to me, and accept that sometimes, even the people you want most need time away from you.

So, I don't say another word and slowly back out of the office, shutting the door behind me with a final *click*.

Mason's father was handsome. Not nearly as handsome as his son, but a good close second. It's easy to see where the hurricane eyes come from, as his father had the same ones. He smiles back at me from the picture in Mason's home office, surrounded by his three older children while holding Mila.

They looked so happy.

Even Monica grins from the side of the picture, her arm around Mason's shoulders.

Funny how things change.

I came in here a little over an hour ago because I ran out of things to do. I cleaned the house when I got home, even scrubbing the baseboards. While Mason's tidy, you can tell those hadn't been done in a long time. I made dinner, picked at it, and opted to put it away, leaving a plate for Mason in case he decided to come home.

I tried watching TV, but nothing could hold my attention, so, I started cleaning again.

I'm beginning to think it's become a nervous habit.

Now, I'm in his office, sitting at his big desk in his giant chair and thinking about all the things I said and staring at the single text he sent me when I asked if he was coming home.

Mason: With Prince.

The little girl in me wanted a Hallmark movie ending. Where he would come home, we would kiss and make up and I could profess everything I felt about him.

But . . . Mason and I aren't a Hallmark movie. We never have been.

We're darkness and lust and seething passion that threatens to drown me in a pool of my own making. I've been standing at the edge of that pool, afraid to jump in, but now that I've had that glistening moment of Mason's affection, I find I'm fucking destroyed without it.

I want to go to him. I want to help. I want to apologize and wrap myself around him, but the knowledge that his refusal could end me keeps me pacing the floor in the living room until I worry the carpet is going to wear down.

He can't just leave me here. Wondering what the hell's going on. It's my right to know why that man tried to kill me as much as it is anyone else's. I've been good, thus far. Listening. I've stayed inside. I've avoided all contact with my mother or Michael.

"It's bullshit," I murmur angrily to the picture of Mason's family on his desk. "I should be there."

They don't reply, but I have a feeling his father would agree if he were here.

And then it dawns on me when my gaze catches on a young Savannah.

Fortunately, she answers.

I'm going to be in so much trouble.

"Hello?"

"Savannah, I need your help."

"I know why you're calling Hannah, and trust me, it's not a good idea."

"Why?"

"Because I've been there. Sneaking out when I'm someone's out to kill me. I was nearly murdered again."

I shake my head. "The man who wanted me dead is being interrogated and I would like to know what he's saying."

She lets out a sigh.

"Mason's already pissed off at me."

"He's pissed off at me, too, but he's not in control of me."

"And what are you going to do when you get over there? Just barge in?"

I hadn't thought that far ahead.

"I'll handle that when the time comes."

"Hannah . . ." she growls, soft voice riddled with anxiety. "If I tell you, Logan's going to have my head."

"Nonsense. I won't tell him you gave me the address."

"And what's your big plan there? Did you think of that one?"

"No," I admit, scrubbing a hand over my face. "But I'll think of something on the way."

She's silent for a moment, contemplating.

"Look, Savannah. You were right, the other day. I do care about your brother. I think I might even be in love with him." I suck in a deep breath, my chest aching. "You were also right when you told me I'm putting him in danger. If this is about me, I want to be involved."

"God," she grumbles. "You really know how to drive a hard bargain."

"Politics," I explain and she chuckles humorlessly.

My phone pings against my cheek and I pull it back to check it, in case it's Mason.

But it's not. It's the address.

"It's a house in Compton. Doesn't look like much from the outside, but inside is where they're interrogating him."

"Thank you," I rush, climbing to my feet and moving toward my room. "I'm indebted to you."

"Yeah," she murmurs. "Especially after Logan finds out I gave you the address."

"Forgive me for saying this, but he seems a little harsh."

"No," she chimes. "He's fair. Goodnight, Hannah."

"Goodnight, Savannah."

The driver of my clandestine Uber is on her phone when I climb into the back of the car.

Good. She doesn't pay an ounce of attention to me as he starts back down the road and I sink back into the seats. The windows are tinted, but I still feel like at any moment, one of the guards is going to sniff out my scent like a bloodhound and drag me back into the house to sit and wait some more.

I'm not a waiter.

I'm also not a runner. Not anymore.

Absentmindedly, I play with a loose thread on the bottom of my T-shirt while the driver talks about something her kid did at school to whoever's on the line.

My stomach is in knots. This is either a really bad idea or a really bad idea.

There is no other option.

Still . . . if this concerns me, I refuse to be put on ice. Mason may care, but he's not going to keep secrets from me.

He can't hide anymore.

When we pull to a stop in front of the building, I tip the driver, who doesn't even notice, and climb out in front of the dingy little house. From the outside, it looks like any other house in Compton. Still, Mason's truck is outside and all the windows are dark, so I stride right up to the front door.

Locked.

Should have known.

"Who the fuck are you?" a voice growls behind me.

Well, shit.

Busted.

I raise my hands in surrender when the click of a gun at my back sounds in the night air.

This is the second time someone's held a gun to my head in forty-eight hours. It's getting quite old.

"Hannah."

"Hannah who?"

"*Mason's* Hannah."

"ID."

Rolling my eyes at the front door, I slip my hand into my bag and hand him my wallet over my shoulder. He wastes no time checking my ID and scanning me as if I'm wearing a skin mask of the *real* Hannah's face.

"Inside."

That's what I was trying to do, I think darkly, then scold myself.

He's just doing his job. I'm the one sneaking around in the dark like a maniac.

He pushes forward, waving his hand over a card reader next to the door that looks like one of those doorbell cameras and the door clicks, unlocking.

He opens it and pushes me inside before quietly shutting the door behind us, again.

"You aren't supposed to be here."

He's a young guy, no older than his twenties and I can tell by the disgruntled look on his face, he's not happy about my appearance.

"Would you like me to walk back home?"

His jaw tightens and he pushes me forward with a sigh.

That's what I thought.

He leads me through an empty living room, down a hallway, and to a kitchen. It's not until he stops at a door that surely leads down to a basement that my stomach does a somersault.

"They're going to be pissed, you know?" he murmurs, opening the door. Voices drift from downstairs, followed by the disgusting smell of blood and ammonia.

Okay . . . this was definitely a bad idea.

"Have fun, *Mason's* Hannah."

Dick.

He shoves me onto the landing and closes the door behind me, sending me into the dim lighting of the basement stairs. Slowly, quietly, I descend, making my way toward the bottom when I hear the gut-wrenching sound of flesh on flesh.

The painful kind.

Mason shakes his hand when I reach the bottom of the stairs, having just punched the guy who tried to kill me so hard, his head fell back. His back is to me, but the strong lines of his shoulders are tense under his T-shirt.

They've been at this a while.

A two-way mirror separates this room and that, but the small intercom on the wall lets me hear every word as if they're wearing microphones.

Mason's voice drifts through the speaker, cool and deadly and unlike anything I've ever heard from him before.

Ice fills my chest. This isn't Mason. This is the devil.

"Do you like choking women, Montclair?"

"No," the man whimpers, clenching his eyes against the blood and sweat streaming down from his forehead. "I don't know what you're talking about."

"I don't believe you," Mason murmurs, voice like a purr.

There's a strange soft hum and then the man in the chair—Montclair—is screaming in agony, his back bowing off the harsh metal.

"This is madness," I whisper to my own reflection shining back at me in the mirror.

The hum cuts and Montclair falls forward, his chin resting on his chest as violent shivers rack through his body.

Still, Mason's voice comes out low and concise.

"You attempted to murder her, in turn attempting to steal from me."

"I didn't want to hurt anybody."

Oh, fuck. He can't possibly be—

Mason hushes him and Logan lands another shot to the man's face, cracking his knuckles after, but it's what's under the chair that really makes my stomach turn.

A battery. Two long jumper cables.

A lack of . . . pants.

"Oh my God," I breathe, panic surging through me.

The room smells awful. Like body odor, blood, and urine. But it's the sickening heat that really takes its toll, turning everything tenfold.

"You won't answer our questions," Logan Prince chimes from beside Mason. Other people I recognize from that night at my house stand around, but no one notices me as I stand in the shadows for a moment longer. "You say you don't remember what happened to you or how you got *this* in your stomach." He holds up a plastic baggy with something small and reflective inside. "I for one am tired of asking.

I'm going to start cutting things off soon."

The man whimpers as fear takes hold, sliding down over the bruises covering his face.

Jesus. It's a wonder he's still alive.

Guilt washes through me, despite the knowledge that this is the man who tried to kill me.

They're torturing him . . . for me.

"Can I ask him some questions?"

All eyes in the room turn to lock with me and suddenly, I feel a tad out of place. A set of stormy gray ones, in particular, bore into mine with the intensity of a thousand hurricanes from across the room.

Mason's *pissed.*

My cheeks flame as I take in the other people. All people I don't recognize. Some I do. The two that checked out my throat the night of the attack are here, but neither shows any expression on their faces. Logan Prince, sans the suit, stands in front of the man, little flecks of blood on his white dress shirt. Other people I don't know, but who all seem to know me as they look amongst themselves.

"And what do you need to ask him, Ms. Gaines?" Logan sneers. You know, for as handsome as he is, he really is an ass sometimes. Must be the FBI in him.

I shrug. "That's for him to know."

Mason looks like he's ready to either kill me or fuck me into oblivion. I can't decide which. Maybe a bit of both.

"Look, he attacked me, not you guys and he's pretty well tied to that table, so I don't think it's going to happen again. You can stand right outside, but I don't think torturing him is the best course of action."

"You know we have guards who should have shot you for coming in here?" Logan challenges, completely glossing over the fact that I just asked to speak to the man he's currently torturing.

"Well, they didn't." When he stares at me some more, I roll my eyes. "Look, that's between you and your agents. I just want to get to the bottom of this and you don't seem to be doing a very good job, considering there's a battery hooked up to his, um, bits."

Logan stares at me for a moment and I have to admit, he's fucking terrifying. It could be the dark, dark-gray eyes, but there's also this unkillable energy. Like he could walk through the fires of hell and come out with a light tan.

"You have ten minutes."

He stalks toward the door and with a wave of his fingers, the others follow like he's a king in a room of peasants. I resist the urge to roll my eyes again. Mason, on the other hand, hangs back, staring at me darkly from across the room.

"I'll be fine," I assure him, but he doesn't seem convinced, looking back at the man who stares between us like if he moves a single muscle, he might get ripped to shreds. Hell, he's probably still scared of Mason and his diabolical crowbar swing.

He points a finger at the man, his eyes flashing dangerously. "You touch her, it's your life."

Mason shoots me a look that tells me I'll have hell to pay for this later. Then he stalks toward the door and shuts it with a harsh slam.

I'm now completely alone with the man who tried to murder me.

Now that I'm seeing him in this light, I can tell he's young. Younger than me. He's practically shaking when I approach, stepping gingerly over the puddle of bodily fluids mixed on the floor.

He hisses through his teeth when I very cautiously kneel down beside him, gingerly removing the battery cables from his balls.

"I'm sorry they did this to you," I murmur softly and he doesn't respond as I very quickly drop the cables from whatever they could have on them.

Ew.

I take the chair in front of me and move it around to sit next to him, away from the urine and blood staining the floor.

"You don't need to be afraid of me."

"I'm not. I'm afraid of them." He looks behind me and I follow his gaze to the two-way mirror.

"Yeah," I agree, turning back to him. "I imagine I would be, too, in your shoes."

Finally, the kid's gaze turns to mine.

"My name is Hannah, but I'm assuming you already know that?"

He pauses for a moment, searching my face. "I don't know what I know." He breaks down, a tear slipping down his cheek. Under different circumstances, I would feel bad for him and, in a way, I guess I still do. He's too young to end up in this life. He can't be more than nineteen or twenty.

"What's your name?"

"Dawson," he says through tears.

Sucking in a deep breath, I reach into my bag and pull out a tissue. When I reach forward to dab at the blood oozing from his nose, he flinches, but he doesn't move.

"Why did you try to kill me, Dawson?"

He shakes his head. "I don't know. I can't remember much. Just that they dropped me at your house and said you had the cure."

"The cure for what?"

"Poison. Whatever they were giving me."

Black Dahlia.

"And who's they?"

My line of questioning runs short because I can see in his eyes, he doesn't know.

"Where did you come from, Dawson?"

"Bel Air." He pauses, looking back at the two-way mirror. "I really don't remember anything. I swear. It's all just pictures."

I move to the cut on his lip next, dabbing at that and he seems to relax when he realizes I'm not going to hurt him.

"What's in those pictures?"

He takes a shuddering breath and I realize his mouth is bloody, too. I reach into my bag and grab the bottle of water I'd brought from home—Mason's home, I guess—and hand it to him.

"Why are you being nice to me?"

He's suspicious. I would be too in his situation.

"Because I've seen enough people die and I get the feeling you didn't actually want to kill me,"

He shakes his head. "No. I'm sorry I did that to you." He nods to the faded bruises on my neck and takes a drink of water. They're so much lighter now, I'd almost forgotten they were there.

"I survived," I murmur. "So did you. Now, tell me about those pictures."

He shakes his head, confusion on his face.

"My . . . sister. They took my sister. I can't remember why, but I just know they had her and they made me agree to meet them or they wouldn't give her back."

"And what happened after that?"

He pauses, wracking his brain.

"Dawson, they won't stop hurting you if you don't tell them what you saw."

He shivers as if the memories are haunting him, even if he can't remember them.

"I remember a warehouse. Some dusty dirty place. I remember my sister lying on the floor. Her eyes—" He waves a hand in front of his face "—they were glassy. Reflecting some kind of fire. She didn't look like her, though. Pieces of her were missing." He looks up at me, his eyes wide with horror as an uneasiness settles in my stomach. "I think she was dead."

Tears burn in the backs of my eyes as one slips down his cheek to mix with the dried blood under his nose.

"Fuck . . . my sister's dead."

"I'm sorry that happened to you, Dawson. Is there anything else you can remember? One of the people? What they looked like?"

"No," he murmurs as another shiver wracks through him. "Wait! There was a man who was in control of everything. He and another woman had sex in the cell next to mine."

I pause. That can't be true.

"He had dark hair. Dark eyes. Looked like he had a lot of money."

"And this woman . . . what did she look like?"

He stops, staring at me as if he's just seeing my face for the first time.

"You. She looked like you."

Horror breaches his face and then he launches himself back from me, crashing to the ground with a scream of terror.

I don't hear anyone come in the room, but seconds later, big, strong arms are wrapping around me and hauling me away from Dawson who scrambles to cower in a corner as Logan's men go to calm him.

"Don't hurt him!" I screech, but I'm still hauled away.

"Stop," Mason growls low in my ear when I fight at his hold, arms tightening like thick bands around my stomach. He drags me back from the room and to the area behind the two-way mirror before he releases me as if I'd burnt him.

My heart pounds in my chest as I suck in air, that night on my pink kitchen floor coming back full-force.

"Please don't kill him," I beg, uncaring if Mason doesn't want anything to do with me. I can't allow them to hurt this man because of me. It's wrong.

Logan just shakes his head, tutting under his breath as he watches them carry the man back to the chair and tighten his bindings.

Mason's jaw ticks, but still, his gaze remains locked on the man in the room.

"Please, Mason?" I beg, shaking from the tears and shivering as the iciness from the distance between Mason and me bleeds into my veins.

He won't even look at me.

"Find someone to take her home," he murmurs darkly, but not

to me. "I don't want her here."

And then he strides back in the room without another glance in my direction.

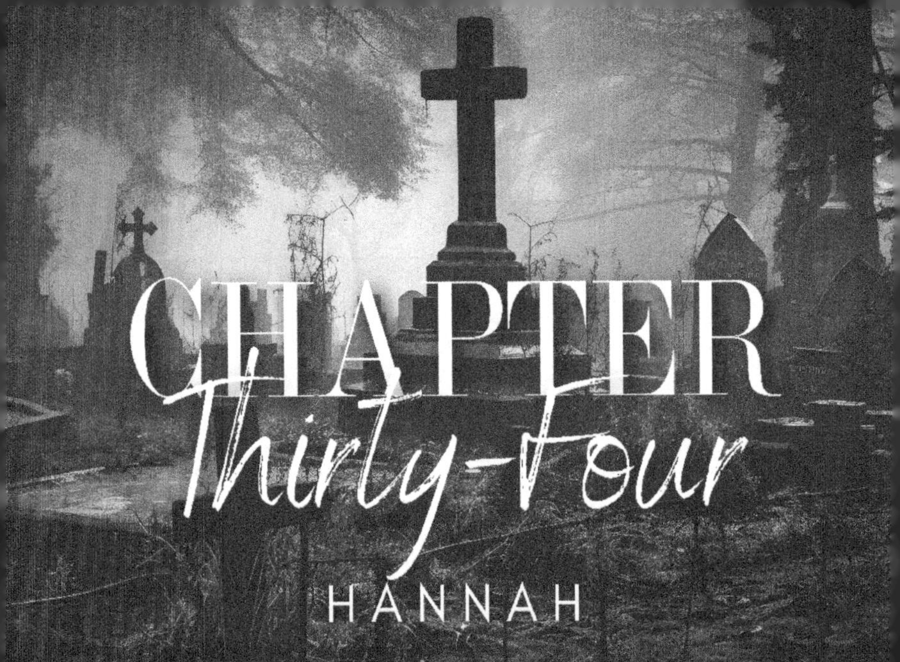

CHAPTER Thirty-Four

HANNAH

I'm falling for Mason Carpenter.

As much as I hate it. As much as I try to fight it . . . I know it's true.

Underneath his cold, hard exterior, is a man who cares. Who wants to see the people around him happy. Who wants to save his family so much, he's willing to go to family therapy to make his mother happy.

Some distant part of me feels like I've known him my entire life. Or maybe in a previous one. Either way, there's a connection there that's as deep as it is troubling.

I must drift off to sleep on the couch after I'm brought home because it's not until after one in the morning when the door closes that I wake up with a start. I jump from the soft click of the lock, sitting bolt upright on the couch and meeting Mason's gaze.

He stares at me for a moment in the dim lighting, his eyes impossible to read. It's not indifference, this time, but something else. Acceptance?

My stomach flutters when his jaw ticks and suddenly, our fight means nothing to me anymore.

I miss him.

"It's late," he murmurs, voice rougher than usual and I nod. I can tell he took a shower. His clothes are changed and he smells clean.

Not like he's been torturing someone all evening.

"Can we talk?"

It's a stupid question, I know. What is there to say? We laid it all out earlier. Well . . . he did, at least. I know I'm setting myself up for rejection when his jaw clenches, eyes flaring darkly.

"I don't want to talk."

Oh . . .

His eyes coast the length of my body, over the pajama shorts on my legs to the thin tank top. Heat sears my skin and a shiver rolls through me.

"Bed."

Oh . . .

He must realize I understand because that's all he says before he turns around and disappears into his room.

Carefully, I extract myself from the blanket and stand on shaky legs. This is either a really bad idea or exactly what we need, judging by the pressure building between my thighs.

Slowly, I follow him to his room, like I'm coming to meet the executioner and not the man watching me like I'm the only woman in the world.

Like I'm his.

I shut the door softly behind me, locking it with a deafening click, and then watch as he tugs his shirt over his head. Thick bands of muscles ripple under the movement of his tattoos and that ache inside me turns to a full-on throb. Quietly, he leans back against the dresser, his eyes boring into my freaking soul.

I spent the rest of the day wondering how we would navigate this. Going over the terrible things I'd said in my head because I was angry and hurt.

Shame feels heavy when it's staring you in the face.

Especially when it's got hurricane eyes and a jawline that could slice through your jugular.

Mason's silence is palpable. His gaze dark and hot. Everything in my body stirs until a shiver ghosts up my spine. Slowly, I make my way toward him, like a lamb approaching a seriously pissed-off lion.

His hand raises and for a second, I flinch. I guess old habits die hard. But instead of pain, his rough palm caresses my cheek.

My heart melts into a puddle at his feet.

Tears burn in the backs of my eyes and instinctively, I step into him. It's more intimate than we've ever been. Mason doesn't hold me, but with a quiet growl, he tugs me closer until my face is pressed into his chest.

"I'm sorry," I breathe, sucking in a shaky breath and he makes a rough sound of satisfaction, his fingers sliding from my cheek and back into my hair.

He lets out a breath of amusement and disbelief. "And finally, the sweet side comes out."

He's so warm, his body folding into mine perfectly. Like we're two puzzle pieces meant to fit. I can't help but sink into him, wrap my arms around him and steal his warmth. Maybe hide it away for a time when he's not here. When I'm alone with nothing but the memories.

"Thank you," I whisper, because I feel like it needs to be said. "For the flowers. And for helping me. And for every—"

"Stop."

The words hang on my tongue, but I can't figure out what to say. Thank you for protecting me. For saving me. For everything. But he doesn't want to talk and I'm in no state to profess my feelings.

So, I carefully extract myself from him, even when his hand tightens in my hair painfully to tug my head back.

"Hannah."

I shake my head, pulling on the strands as I attempt to drop to my knees.

"I don't want to talk either."

His gaze goes from hard to hungry and *hot* in the blink of an eye. He keeps his grip on my hair for a moment as if he's reading my thoughts and trying to decide if this is a trap.

But finally, he relents, and I drop down in front of him.

I'll admit, the prospect of having to fit Mason in my mouth again is daunting, to say the least. It hurt to have him inside me. What if my jaw gets stuck wide open or what if I choke to death?

But when I undo the button of his jeans and pull him out and find he's harder than I've ever felt him, I find I don't much care.

"I take it you've decided," he murmurs, cocking a brow at me as if he's testing me. Still, I can feel the way his abs tighten when I stroke him from root to tip. His gaze sears.

"It was never a question."

Nerves twist my stomach, my knees shaking as I force all the thoughts out of my head but the man in front of me.

Somehow, I think that's more terrifying.

Leaning forward, I run the tip of my tongue over the underside of his shaft, from his balls to the very tip.

Mason's jaw clenches tightly as he watches. He looks like a king, standing before me, demanding my loyalty with a touch of his gaze.

I bend my neck, running his cock over my lips, and circling his heavy sac with my tongue. I feel his muscles tighten underneath my hands and his hands grip the dresser so hard, his knuckles turn white.

"Hannah." I flick my gaze up to his, sucking his sac between my lips. His eyes flare, his Adam's apple bobbing with a heavy swallow.

And just like last time, power consumes me at my effect on this dark god of a man.

"Suck my cock."

My legs press together, the throbbing in my core begging for me to release some of the pressure. Lifting my head, I tongue my way up his shaft, stopping to swirl my tongue around the head. And when he's about to say something else, I slip him in my mouth.

"*Fucking hell*," he hisses through his teeth, his head falling back and his eyes clenching shut. I hum my approval at the taste of him and he pulls in a strained breath. "That's it, little doe. Show me how sweet you can be."

His voice is rough and unhinged, his hand resting on top of my head, guiding me. I'll admit, Mason Carpenter growling out curse words under his breath because of something *I'm* doing to him is an aphrodisiac. Heat travels from my stomach down to my pussy and I can feel my own wetness coating my thighs.

And I've barely gotten my hands on him.

I slide him down halfway, using my fist to pump him in and out of my mouth slowly, savoring him. When I pull back and lathe my tongue around the tip, his eyes grow dark and hazy.

His hand tightens in my hair and I suck him further, tears streaming from my eyes and I choke when he hits the back of my throat, pulling back.

"Are you done?" he challenges, his eyes full of twisted amusement. He fists my hair, tugging my head back to meet his gaze roughly. He's testing me and while it should turn me off, it only makes me more determined to watch him come from what I can do to him.

So, I shake my head, running my tongue over him from his heavy sac all the way to the tip.

"Fuck, Hannah," he grits, his hand coming down to grip my chin. "Open your mouth."

I do and he leans down, spitting on my tongue. Heat consumes me as my pussy clenches with need at the dark violence in his gaze. Then that hand is sliding into my hair as well, only instead of fucking my face like I think he's going to, his thumb caresses my cheek. "I want to fuck your mouth."

I nod, my heart fluttering in my chest, but the fire burning between us keeps me going, sucking him. I want to see this god crumble underneath my fingers, just as he'd done to me.

Holding my face, he slowly slides in deeper, his cock pressing past the constrictions of my throat until I'm gagging for breath.

"All of it, baby," he rasps, slipping back, allowing me to suck in a breath before sliding back in. My heartbeat pulses in my clit when I choke, having more of him in my mouth than room to breathe. "Fuck, you sound so pretty when you're choking on my cock."

This is what it feels like to be completely owned by Mason Carpenter. Fully and completely possessed. My head spins at the thought of giving my everything to this man.

Or maybe it's the lack of oxygen.

Either way, I don't want him to stop.

He pulls back, fucking my face and watching me with an air of angry adoration. Like he's obsessed with me, but he fucking hates it and for some reason, that makes me warm all over.

Tears stream down my face, my cheeks growing red from the lack of oxygen, but I still don't ask him to stop because I'm too lost in him now.

"That's it, little doe . . ." he grunts, his cock slipping between my lips and over my tongue. His chest heaves with heavy pants, his forehead shining in the light from the exertion. "You going to swallow my come like a good girl?"

I moan, sealing my lips around him and he curses under his breath, his fingers tightening in my hair. Biting back on a growl, he comes, shooting thick loads down my throat until I'm sputtering and so desperate for him to touch me, I'd sell my firstborn.

"So fucking perfect," he murmurs, his hands still shaking with the aftershocks of his orgasm. "Now, strip."

He pulls me to my feet, tugging my shirt over my head. My breasts fall out, heavy and tight, but he doesn't touch me anymore, standing back to watch as I slip my cotton pajama shorts down my legs.

His gaze flares and his eyes travel the length of my body, from my nipples to my glistening sex.

Eyes like midnight, he nods to the bed.

I go, sitting on the end, but he shakes his head.

"On your stomach."

My chest tightens, but I do, laying on my stomach and kicking my feet up in the air behind me.

He takes his time, stalking behind me like a predator, on the hunt for blood. His heavy bootfalls fill the room, and my heartbeat mimics each one as he steps behind me.

Oh, no . . .

Somehow, I have a feeling I might not make it out of this in one piece.

Sex in the garage was one thing. We were limited as to what we could do. Sex in his soft, comfortable, oversized bed?

I might have a permanent stutter by the time this is over.

"Are you still angry with me?" I ask and he pauses behind me. I move to turn around, but he steps out of my line of view.

"And if I am?"

My heart drops. I should just get up and leave, right now. Finish myself off with my vibrator, but something keeps me here. Maybe it's the way his voice is dripping in lust. Or maybe it's because I know, no matter what I use, it'll be nothing compared to the man behind me.

I'm giving myself to him. And whether that's good or bad, I don't think the outcome will be any different.

"You think you can walk away?" he murmurs darkly, his voice caressing my bare back and bringing goosebumps to the surface. "As if I wouldn't hunt you down."

"I don't want to leave," I breathe, my breath hitching when his finger softly glides up my calf.

"You push me to the point I don't know whether I want to fuck you or hate you. Unfortunately, your hatred is so fucking sweet, I'm addicted to it as much as I am your sweetness."

"I don't hate you." I want to. I want to despise him because it would be safer than allowing myself to fall into his darkness.

"This ass . . ." he murmurs quietly, his hands light as a feather and the slip over my curves. "Is fucking perfection."

I let out a breathy sigh, closing my eyes and surrendering to his touch.

Then he bites my ass.

The fucking bastard bit me.

I jerk on the bed and his palm comes out, resting at the center of my back. His tongue soothes the sting from his teeth and he chuckles darkly.

"I'm not angry, little doe." I hear shuffling and then both his hands are reaching under me, gripping my hips and pulling me to kneel on the bed in front of him. He pushes my front down until my ass and pussy are completely exposed to him, God, or anyone else who might walk in the room. "But fuck if punishing you isn't going to feel good."

Thank God for modern door locks.

He presses each of his hands to the backs of my thighs, using his thumbs to spread my pussy open.

"Try not to scream."

Then, he's running his tongue through my folds.

I gasp, choking on the sound and burying my head in the comforter to let out a heavy breath. "You're soaked. Is this from getting me off?"

I nod, anticipating the next stroke of his tongue.

"Words, Hannah."

"Yes," I breathe.

"Good girl."

Then he's slipping his tongue inside me. I need him on my clit, but his tongue inside me feels so good, I don't want him to stop.

"So goddamned sweet," he grits like it pisses him off as he nips and sucks a line from my pussy to my clit. Only he stops, right before he reaches the sensitive bundle of nerves practically begging for his attention. "Are you going to be my good little whore?"

"Yes," I pant, my clit throbbing even as he avoids it completely.

"Yes."

This is his revenge. His vengeance on me for all the nasty things I said earlier. Call me crazy, but I'd be committing a lot more crimes if Mason Carpenter was the one doling out punishments.

"You make me so fucking insane." He slips higher, sucking the flesh around my clit until I'm whimpering on the bed. "Sometimes you piss me off so bad, I want to fuck you until you can't run off."

"Mason," I groan, my head spinning when he denies me again. I try to move my hips against him and position him exactly where I need but his fingers tighten to near-bruising strength.

"My own little brand of poison," he hisses, nipping my inner thigh. I jerk up the bed, but he just chuckles darkly, soothing the sting with his tongue and not allowing me to run away. "You keep running, but like a sick fuck, I keep coming back whenever you want me. What does that make me, little doe?"

I can't form words into a sentence. I can't even form a coherent thought. My arousal drips down my thighs, his words sending electric shocks straight through my body.

"Show me how it looks when you stay . . ." he murmurs, biting the globe of my ass again. His fingers slide underneath me, toying with my nipple and my pussy clenches on nothing.

"Mason, I need you."

He lets out a dry, unamused laugh. "Do you need me, Hannah? Or do you just want me because I make this tight cunt feel better than it's ever felt?"

Holy shit.

I wrack my mind for an answer, all number of thoughts careening through my head like a pinball machine.

"I need you," I admit, finally. "For sex and for . . . everything else. I l—"

His hand slaps my ass hard and the sting liquifies in my veins.

"Don't finish that sentence, Hannah," he rasps. "Not until you're ready to prove it."

His voice is darker than I've ever heard it before. Menacing. World-ending. Like he's prepared to rip civilizations down if I'm lying to him.

In my chest, I know I'm not.

I'm falling in love with Mason Carpenter and there's not a damn thing I can do to stop it.

"I'll stay," I breathe, arching my hips when his tongue slips into the tight ring of muscles above my entrance. I gasp, my eyes screwed shut as a sensation I've never felt before surfaces.

I feel dirty. Used. Cherished. Fucking adored. All at the same time.

"I don't believe you," he murmurs and my heart threatens to shatter like glass. "Don't scream," he reminds me.

Then his lips seal over my clit and his tongue flutters across me, sending me into the most intense orgasm I've ever had. I bury my head into the comforter, biting the material to keep from screaming. My body shakes with the force of the waves, but I don't have time to react before he's grabs me and flips me over. He drags my hips to the edge of the bed, tonguing me straight through into another orgasm while I bite my own palm to stay quiet.

"I need inside you," he grits, voice huskier than usual when he flips me over. He stands, wiping my arousal on the back of his hand and it's the sexiest thing I've ever seen.

He removes the rest of his clothes, his body rippling in the light from his bedside lamp. I watch him walk to the dresser, his ass as devastating as the rest of him.

Mason's butt could end a war.

He opens the top drawer and pulls something out, before coming back to the bed and holding it up in the light.

A condom.

My stomach clenches when he hands it to me.

"I've never . . . put one of these on," I whisper, my cheeks flaming with embarrassment.

He doesn't let me back out that easily.

"Guess it's time to learn."

He's challenging me. Pride wells inside me and I rip the packet open and pull the condom out. His eyes flare when I place it over him, sliding it down his length and making sure to stroke him in the process until his jaw tenses.

Two can play at that game.

Mason looks like a man possessed when he climbs on the mattress above me.

"While knocking you up would have its fucking day, I agree we aren't bringing a child into this mess. Not yet." My stomach dips at his words and when his hand runs over my stomach. The dark glint in his eyes as he looks up my body at me sends a shiver down my spine. "But make no mistake. I will be fucking you raw again."

I shiver, the darkness seeping off him palpable when his hands come to my hips, but he doesn't waste any time pushing inside me in one full roll.

I bite down on his shoulder to keep from screaming and he curses under his breath, eyes wild.

"Oh my god . . ." I pant, my head falling back and my eyes screwing shut from the pain and pleasure of having him so deep, so fast. My nails dig into his shoulders, but he doesn't pull back. "Please, Mason. Move."

"Too much for you, little doe?" he sneers, but then he reaches up, brushing the hair out of my face with a soft caress. "You can always tell me to stop, Hannah. Give me a word."

"What?" I stammer, my pussy still pulsing around him from my last orgasm.

"Give me a word and that will be your safe word. Whatever you want to say to let me know you've had enough."

I roll the words around in my head, but only one comes to mind. "Hurricane."

He pauses for a moment, but he doesn't bother asking.

"Hurricane," he reminds me. "Now, fight me or fuck me, little doe. Your choice."

He pulls back before slamming inside me and he doesn't stop. He fucks me hard, grinding his hips into mine like he's trying to carve out his spot on my body. Like he's trying to imprint himself on my soul so that everyone will know I'm his.

I mean, at this point, I'd shout it from the rooftops.

His hands come up, capturing mine and holding them above my head. I'm sure I've left marks on his shoulder, but he also bit my ass, and for that, he deserves it, no matter how hot it was.

"This pussy was made for my cock, Hannah," he murmurs, voice low and quiet. "You feel how you're squeezing me, begging for more?"

I whimper, my eyes rolling back in my head. My body tightens to a near fever pitch, but the orgasm remains just out of reach.

The asshole is keeping it from me.

"Does it scare you that I would torture for you?" he grinds out, voice rough and animalistic in my ear. "Kill for you?"

"Yes," I breathe because it's true.

"And yet, you want me anyway?"

"Yes. *Mason*," I grit through my teeth and he chuckles darkly, shifting and stretching my arms all the way out above me before centering himself between my legs.

At this angle, his groin brushes against my clit and I swear I go cross-eyed from the sharp bite of pleasure that shoots through me.

"He tried to kill me when he tried to murder *you*. I don't take lightly to that, little doe, because whatever's good in me rests in your hands." He enunciates each word with a thrust of his hips until everything in me seizes. His lips crash against mine and my heart feels like it's going to explode.

"You're such a fucking good girl," he growls against my lips. I arch into him, my body on the brink of either breaking in half from the size of him above me, covering me, or coming. At this point, maybe both. "You look so fucking pretty taking all of me, sweetheart."

My tongue glides against his and he sucks on the tip, sending shivers through me until I think I'm going to pass out.

"Mason, I'm going to come," I whimper, rolling my hips to meet his.

"Did I say you could come?" He changes his angle, fucking me until the sound of skin on skin fills the space between us. The head of his cock brushes the most sensitive spot inside me.

"Please?"

"Fuck, Hannah," he rasps, a tremor rolling through him. He's on the edge, too, and the list of things I'd do to see him come undone from *me* is longer than the list of things I wouldn't do.

"Your cock feels so good," I whisper and his nostrils flare. He fucks me harder, punishing me for my dirty words. I bite back at the cries that threaten to leave my lips, but I don't stop. "Harder, Mason. Please, I need you."

He growls between his teeth, his hand coming up to wrap around my throat. He squeezes, just enough to shut me up, but the combination of what he's doing to me and the unsteady beat of my heart drown out the need for oxygen anyway.

"Come for me, little doe."

And I explode. My body goes rigid, wrapping as tightly around him as I can while his hand comes up and clamps over my mouth. I bite his palm, tasting blood in the process of not screaming to God. The devil. The men outside. Whoever will hear my prayer because I swear this orgasm will be my last.

He lets out an animalistic growl, burying his face in my neck when he comes. He pulls me so tightly against him, I think I might break, his body shuddering over mine in the most delicious way.

"Fuck," he pants, rolling his neck. "Fuck."

He brushes the hair out of my face, absentmindedly moving his hips as our bodies tremble with aftershocks from our orgasms.

"You're going to fucking kill me," he murmurs, pressing his lips against my damp forehead. “No more running.”

I open my mouth to argue, but when I catch sight of the sincerity in his gaze, something in me crumbles.

I’ve been running from my problems my entire life. Yet, every time I’ve tried since I met him, he’s always there to catch me and put me back together again.

God, save me if he ever doesn’t.

“No more running,” I repeat and this time I mean it.

CHAPTER *Thirty-Five*

MASON

Why are you looking at me like that?"

"I cock a brow. "Like what?"

"Like you want to take a bite out of me."

Funnily enough, that's exactly what I was thinking when Hannah stepped out of the room in her little green evening gown that matches the hue in her eyes. The shoulders tie, leaving thin straps of material hanging down her back and I can't think of anything other than how I'll be pulling those ties apart tonight and fucking her with the damned thing bunched around her waist.

"The thought crossed my mind."

She blushes, the pretty shade of pink matching the mark from my teeth on her ass. Fuck . . . I wonder if it's still there?

Carefully, I reach for her, my hand sliding into her hair to pull her to me. I press a kiss to her lips that has my cock swelling in my jeans despite being buried inside her most of the night. Even though my balls ache from how many times I made her come, punishing her with either my fingers, my mouth, or my cock, I still want more.

I'll always want

Wonder what Kenda would have to say about that?

"You aren't so bad yourself," she purrs, gaze raking over me. I rarely wear a suit. In fact, I fucking hate it because it's hot, but I can't very well show up in jeans for tonight's endeavor.

"I'm going to destroy this dress later," I murmur, fingering the small bow at her shoulder. "I hope you're not attached."

"If it's anything like last night, you can destroy anything you want."

Last night was a blur. My little doe on her knees, big green eyes wide and innocent even as she took my cock down her throat is enough to put a permanent shake in my hands. I can't get her out of my fucking head.

Not that she hasn't always been there.

With a nag of pain in my chest, I realize I'd give my left fucking arm if it meant giving her the life of peace she deserves. Now that she's chosen me—no, *given* herself to me—I'll take a bullet if it means I can keep her.

Kenda would say I'm toxic. I prefer the term loyal.

As much as I tried to fight it, I couldn't. Hannah Gaines is mine whether she likes it or not.

I don't know what my family will say. I don't even know what the future has in store for us. I also don't give a fuck. I feel like I've found something forbidden that I didn't even want, but now that I have it, I'll be damned if anyone's prying it from my grasp.

She's too good for me. Still doesn't mean I'm giving her up.

"You look beautiful."

She blushes, placing her hand over mine on her cheek. I can see the worry in her gaze. It's not misplaced. Tonight could go very, very badly, but we can't miss this opportunity.

The benefit is being held downtown, only a couple blocks away from the warehouse where they burned and desecrated those women. We park Dad's Challenger and I almost laugh at how out of place it is amongst the wealth in the parking garage.

It's like a sick fucking joke as Hannah and I arrive, stepping up to the front doors surrounded by people in their fancy fucking clothes and jewelry that cost more than my house.

Parker always made my sisters go to these. Benefits. Galas. Misplaced charity functions. He could never force me and I hated them, so I stayed far away in my "dusty" garage. I don't belong here. Not with the engine grease stained under my fingernails and the tattoos under my dress shirt.

Hannah does; though, judging by the way she's cowering into my side, holding onto my arm like I might slip away from her if she loosens her grip even an inch, I'm starting to think maybe she doesn't.

Maybe neither of us belong anywhere. Maybe we've just created our own little paradise in the midst of a warzone.

As soon as we step inside, I can feel her stiffen. She's on high alert, scanning the room around her. Even as people approach us, welcoming her and consequently me, I can feel the tension radiating through her.

I would fucking hate to be in her shoes. Greeting people who think they know you. Who know your name, just because of who your mother is. I would rather remain nameless in a crowd. A mystery, instead of someone everyone thinks they've got figured out.

Being part of the governor's family makes you California royalty. You bleed purple and Versace and no one ever questions if you're okay because you have to be, right? You've got more money than God, so why wouldn't you be okay?

I used to think that, too. I used to believe money solved every rich motherfucker's problems, but really, the problems just get more complex because now there's no simple fix.

Give me a simple life, budgeting to make ends meet over a mansion with a whole vault full of hundred-dollar bills any day.

"Hannah."

The voice is tightly laced and filled with something like apathy from behind us.

I know that fucking voice. Hannah's fingers tense on my arm, but she still turns around and plasters a fake smile on her face. To the outside looking in, it probably looks normal. I can see through it though.

"You haven't called," Michael grumbles, stepping up to us, his own date on his arm. He doesn't look at me, but he does look at her hand on my arm with a disdain I know all too well.

Still holding onto hope that Mommy dearest is going to hand Hannah over like a prized pig.

"I apologize, Michael. I've been busy." She nods to the blonde on his arm, who watches her with a carefully concealed look of venomous envy. "Beatrice."

God, what is it with rich people and weird fucking names?"

"Hannah." Beatrice looks at me.

"This is Mason Carpenter. Mason, Beatrice Porter," Hannah says. She slinks further into my side and something strange passes between the two women. I almost laugh. My little doe is territorial.

"I've been worried about you," Michael says, completely oblivious to the fact that no one gives a shit about what he's been worried about.

"Well, I'm sorry for worrying you, but as I said, I've been busy."

"Yes, I'm sure working in a hot and dirty garage is keeping you very well strapped for time to pick up the phone."

Hannah's eyes narrow. "Funnily enough, it is."

"Well, your mother will want to see you." Michael dares to look toward me. "I can take you."

"That won't be necessary," Hannah says at the same time I say, "She'll go with me."

Michael seems to think about saying something before those words fall flat. Realization crosses his features and I think it's then he realizes, we know.

"Come, Beatrice," he says after a moment, smoothing the lines down in his suit. "I believe dinner is about to start."

"Yes," Hannah chimes, and he pauses. "Wouldn't want you to miss your slice of the pie."

"Hannah?"

Hannah stiffens.

"How wonderful," her mother croons, stepping up to her and attempting to pull her into a hug. She hangs back, that plastered smile on her face falling.

"Mother."

"Oh, come now. Don't tell me you're still upset with me. That was a real stunt you pulled lying about the charity. They were expecting you."

She doesn't answer. It's then she must notice me standing beside her. Her eyes go wide for a moment, then they darken, a nearly imperceivable hatred slipping through her gaze before it's replaced with coldness.

"Carpenter," she greets, holding out a hand. I shake it, hard enough that her eye twitches. "I didn't think a suit was in your attire."

"It wasn't," I reply coldly.

She nods, chuckling darkly. Another woman—her campaign manager from what I remember—joins us and slips close to her.

"Hannah, how lovely to see you," she says, voice laced with tightly wound tension.

It seems our presence has caused a bit of a disturbance for them.

"June."

"Hannah, June and I haven't gotten the chance to tell you, yet, but we've recently gotten engaged. We will be the first lesbian couple in the governor's seat in California."

June flashes a gaudy ring that would probably cause her to sink, should she be thrown into the Pacific.

"Well, congratulations," Hannah chimes, voice aloof. "I guess."

"Hannah—" Laura Gaines starts, but she cuts her off.

"Sending Michael to do your bidding? Seems a little rich, doesn't it?"

She's speaking outwardly about Michael's attempt to get her to come home, but there's an underlying tension I'm sure she picks up on. I see her scan Hannah's face for a moment, trying to decide what she knows. Little does she know, we know fucking everything.

"You and Michael used to be so close. He cares about you."

"Yes, well, it seems you don't always know people as well as you thought."

"Dinner will be starting soon," June says, attempting to change the subject. "We're having salmon. One of your favorites."

"I hate salmon," Hannah replies coldly and pride swells in my chest at the venom in her tone.

That's my fucking girl.

"Well, you'll learn to love it."

"Have you found my sister?"

"Now is not the time," she bites and June scans the crowd around us. Luckily for them, people are making their way to their dinner seats, not paying an ounce of attention to the verbal standoff in the center of the room.

"No. Only when it's convenient for the polls, right?"

"Come, Laura. Your speech will be starting soon."

Hannah's mother stares at her for a moment and she stares back. I'm prepared to step in if needed, but she needs to do this. It's the only way she'll ever break free from Laura Gaines' clutches.

"So, it seems," Laura murmurs coldly, and I have a feeling she's not speaking to June.

She steers June away, but not before shooting one long glance at me. I return it, matching the same cold clarity that shines in her eyes, hoping she can read the thought echoing over and over in my head.

I'm going to kill you.

She must see something that scares her because her eye twitches again. Then she leaves.

"I hate fish," Hannah grumbles, picking at the food on her plate. "And asparagus. It makes your pee smell weird."

I chuckle, though I'm starting to get that itch to get the fuck out of here. Fortunately, we were sat at a random table and not with her mother and Michael. I'm not sure her knife would have stayed on her plate, should we be forced to dine with them.

Guess we have Prince to thank for that.

Not that I blame her. Hell, I might even reward her for it, but that's provided I could get her home after the cops arrest her for murder.

"I'll make you a cheeseburger when we get home," I murmur quietly and she relaxes, placing her fork on her plate.

The room quiets and before she can respond, her mother takes center stage, as everyone looks on. It's moments like these where I wonder why the hell we listen to people like Laura Gaines. A woman who's involved with the cartel. Who traffics young women and men. Facilitates their rape, murder, and torture. All for her political gain.

She beat her kids. Subjected them to years of psychological abuse, yet, we still vote for her because we *think* she's a good person.

People are different behind closed doors. I don't care what anyone says. No one's good one hundred percent of the time.

We've all got a little evil in us. Just . . . how much?

"I want to thank everyone for coming tonight," Laura says into the microphone and the whole room quiets. "You know, I'll admit, I never knew how big of a problem human trafficking was until I took office. I thought, oh, there's no way it could happen here."

Hannah squeezes my hand tightly under the table, so I squeeze back, shooting her a look.

It'll be over soon.

"So, imagine my surprise when I found out it was right there. Right in my backyard." Laura Gaines looks around the room, her eyes landing on Hannah. "I have two *beautiful* daughters and I couldn't imagine what I would do if they were taken from me."

I stiffen. A threat is still a threat, even if it's said in front of a thousand people.

She's threatening her.

"My heart goes out to all the families affected by these heinous acts. And that's why I'm here tonight to ask for you to lend a hand. Help these people find their babies. Their sisters, mothers, brothers, and fathers." She pauses for dramatic effect. "Let's bring them home."

And then, in the most theatrical sense, a woman falls from the second-story balcony behind the governor to hang right in front of the American flag. A noose around her neck, even though the decay on her skin indicates she's been gone for a while.

Screams erupt around the room and chaos ensues. I grab Hannah, tugging her from the table and into my chest, holding her as people pass us by, running from an armed gunman as he takes the balcony and starts firing off shots.

Fuck.

"Hannah," I bite, pushing her in front of me, our backs to the gunman. We crouch through the crowd of people toward the back rooms. "Get down."

She hunkers down, and I stay right behind her, shoving people back as we make our way toward an open door.

My blood roars in my ears, my ears ringing from the assault rifle above our heads, but I don't stop. I need to get her out of here.

A loud pop rings through the air and then blood coats the side of Hannah's dress and something wet hits my face.

A woman falls dead at our feet. I don't recognize her, but her black dress shirt tells me she was a worker at the benefit.

Hannah lets out a startled gasp, but the bullet wound in the center of her forehead tells me there's nothing we can do for the woman now, so I push her past and we finally reach the back hallway.

Hannah turns to run toward the exit, but I grab her, tugging her back the other way.

"Mason," she pants, breathless as she almost runs to keep up with me.

"We need to find out who that is."

"We *need* to get out of here."

"In time," I bite, locating the stairs to the balcony and tugging on the door. Locked.

Hannah growls behind me. "Here."

She shoves me out of the way and reaches up under her hair, pulling out a pin.

My little fucking safe-cracker.

"What? I've been practicing." I shake my head, pulling her toward me and crushing my lips against hers with a growl, blood droplets on her cheek and all.

When I break away, her cheeks are burning.

She shakes her head after a moment to clear her thoughts. "We don't have time for this."

We don't, but my cock still hardens from the stutter on her tongue.

"Come on." I take her hand, pulling her toward the stairs. "Stay behind me."

The gunfire stops as we make our way up the stairs and right as we reach the top, so does the guy that opened fire on the crowd of the benefit.

So, I stick my arm out, clotheslining him to the ground.

He falls with a thud, assault rifle falling to the floor beside him. I nod to Hannah and she grabs it, pointing it down into his face.

The guy just chuckles.

"It's fucking empty, dumb bitch."

"This isn't."

His eyes widen when I point my pistol at the center of his forehead.

"You're the governor's daughter," he clucks, eyes zooming back and forth between the gun in my hand and Hannah.

"He's one of the men from the warehouse," Hannah says,

completely ignoring the bastard on the floor.

"Yeah, he is. He's the one that kept pissing and moaning because he didn't get a chance to rape a woman before she was brutally murdered."

"Come to think of it," Hannah adds, "You said I was a fine piece of ass. How does it look now that there's a gun pointed at your head?"

That's my fucking girl.

"Still fine as fuck, though all you Gaines girls are danger whores."

Hannah blinks at him, unmoving. He seems to take that as a sign to keep fucking talking.

"Yeah . . . I know all about you two. I bet your pussy's soaking wet right now. How about it, princess? Wanna show me."

I cock the gun and he jumps, but Hannah does one better.

She aims the assault rifle at his leg and fires and miraculously, it's still got one in the chamber. She stumbles back, eyes going wide as the idiot beneath us roars in pain. Blood runs from the hole in his leg, soaking the marble floor.

"Where is she?" I bite, kneeling down beside him.

"Who?" he grinds through clenched teeth.

"Melissa Gaines. I know she was at the warehouse. Where the fuck is she now?"

He spits in my face. Hannah raises the gun again and he jerks back in fear.

"Where?"

"Cortez!" he rushes, squeezing his eyes shut. "She was working with Cortez."

Hannah and I meet each other's gazes.

This is bad. Really fucking bad.

A commotion sounds downstairs as the cops finally arrive.

"Time to go," I tell her, standing and wrapping an arm around his waist.

"What are we going to do with him?" Hannah asks, eyes flashing angrily. I know what she's thinking about. The women, the incinerator. Her sister.

I shrug. "You really think he needs his dick?"

Without a second thought, she shoots him, right in the balls and I've got to say, I don't envy him.

Serves his dumb ass right.

"Good job, baby," I take her hand. "Let's go."

I tug her back down the staircase and toward the back exit while the man upstairs screams out in pain. There's a good chance he'll bleed out before he ever makes it to the hospital. I'm just sorry his time in agony is so short.

We head out into the night and don't look back as cops begin to swarm the place. I pull her right to our car in the parking garage and we're gone in less than a minute, the venue vanishing in the distance behind us.

I start the trip home, my heartbeat fucking pounding in my chest, but I don't want to wait any longer. I pull to a stop on a darkened street, locking the doors and pulling Hannah to me. She slips into my lap and we barely fit in the front seat of the old Challenger, but neither of us stops.

Our breathing is harsh and ragged as she works on the button of my jeans and I fist the material of her panties, snapping them off and drawing a sharp hiss through her teeth that only seems to spur her on more.

She reaches between us, wrapping her hand around my cock and lining me up with her entrance, her breathing ragged against my lips.

And then I'm pushing her down on me.

"Fuck!" I bite, my head falling back against the seat as she envelopes me in her tight, wet heat. "*Fuck*, Hannah."

She shudders over me, rolling her hips to meet my thrusts and working me inside her. Her eyes screw shut and she bites her lip, wrapping her arms around my neck and riding me. The burn of her pussy opening for me only drives me to roll her hips faster, working her over my cock until she's tightening around me greedily.

"That's it, little doe," I growl against the flesh of her throat, using my hand on her ass to move her faster over me, working more of my cock inside her. "You were so fucking sexy back there, baby."

"Mason . . ." she whimpers, her nails digging into the flesh at the back of my neck as her hips move faster. Shakier. "No condom," she breathes, but she makes no move to get off me.

"I'll pull out."

"Okay," she nods, even though both of us know that's not going to stop anything.

Reaching up, I tug the straps loose on her dress and her tits fall out, heavy and bouncing in my face. I capture one with my lips, nipping her nipple before sucking it into my mouth to soothe the sting with my tongue. She cries out, her body shivering over mine and I can feel her walls closing in on me already.

Good, because, right now, I don't know that I have the self-control to stop myself from coming.

I bounce her over me, reaching between us and stroking her clit with my thumb until she's nearly screaming from the pleasure. Her fingers bite into my shoulders, spurring me on, but she doesn't say the safe word and she doesn't ask me to stop.

"That's it, Hannah. Come for me."

I enunciate each word with a thrust of my hips and power into her until she unravels in my arms, my name a breathless plea on her lips.

Two more strokes is all it takes before my cock is exploding. At just the last second, I pull out, coming on her pussy and damn near going blind from the intensity of my orgasm.

When we come to, she's spent, resting her head on my shoulder as little tremors move through both of us. I take her face in my hands, pushing her hair back and pressing a kiss to her lips, drinking her in.

"You're mine," she whispers against my lips and I resist the urge to smile.

Finally, she fucking gets it.

"I'm yours."
Her stomach rumbles loudly between us.
"Can I get that cheeseburger now?"
I can't help but chuckle.
"Anything you want, little doe."

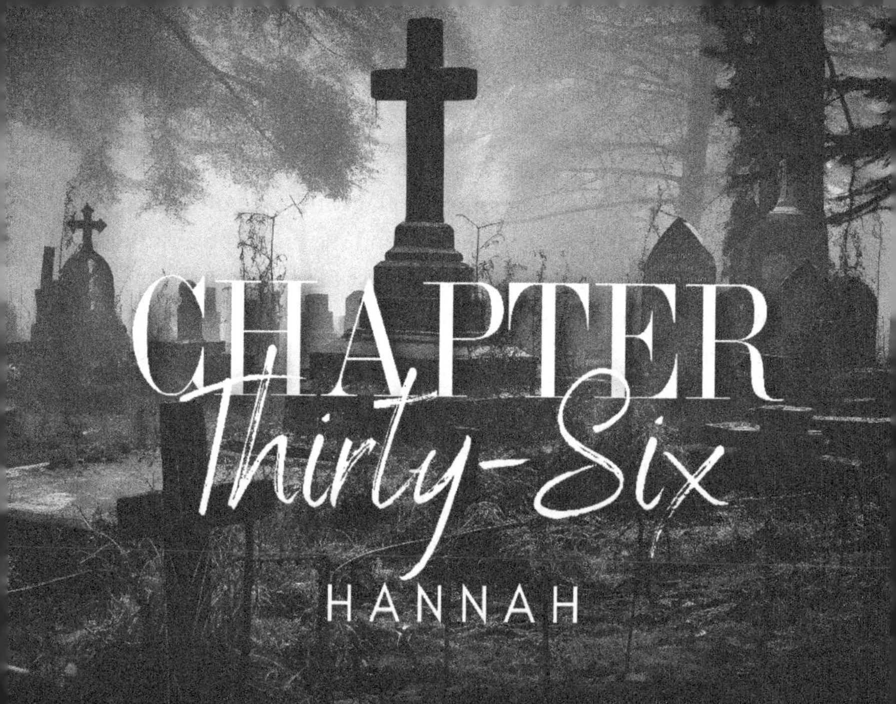

CHAPTER Thirty-Six

HANNAH

So this is what it feels like to be without a home.

It's strange. I thought I'd feel empty, but really, I just feel numb.

All the secrets I've learned in the past few weeks. The people I thought I'd once known like the back of my hand.

The death.

Death brings about a sense of clarity in times like these.

For example. My mother is not a good person. Everyone knew that—fuck, even I knew that, deep down—but it wasn't until it was laid out in front of me that I realized just how . . . evil she is.

Michael is not my friend. He may have been at one time, but now, friendship isn't enough for him. He wants to own me and I'm no genius, but I don't think love bred out of bartering is the real deal.

And Missy. Or Melissa. I've conceded to the fact that Missy Gaines, my twin, best friend, sister . . . is dead. Missy and Melissa are two different people. Missy would braid my hair while we watched old reruns of *Buffy: The Vampire Slayer*. She'd bake Christmas cookies with me every year and she always let me do the decorating.

In a lot of really messed up ways, Missy and I were like each other's mothers. We took care of each other when one of us was sad. I made her hot soup when she was sick and she made the best flu tea I've ever tasted. She'd dry my eyes over whatever stupid boy had broken my heart and I'd stick up for her at school when the girls in our class tried to tease her about the gap she used to have in her two front teeth.

Missy was loving, kind, and caring.

Melissa is vile.

Say it was all for love. Seems like a pretty fucked-up excuse to me, for helping kidnap people. Helping rape them. Sell them into the sex trade.

She drank the poison and that poison wasn't some illegal absinthe, imported from overseas. It was Marcus Parker. Pure evil Marcus Parker.

The stepfather of the man I'm helplessly in love with.

Sure, he has his faults, but so do I. I can be rash. I can be cruel if I'm angry or hurt. I can even be stupid and walk to the convenience store for slushies when someone tried to kill me the night before.

I know he hid the nature of his long nights in the garage from me. I know he wants to see my mother dead. I know he hates my sister with everything in him.

I also know a man who's still willing to help me find said sister, even though doing so could literally mean death for him . . . is not a man I want to give up.

My chest constricts at the thought of losing him. Of what will happen when this is over.

Can we survive in the mundane after our relationship was built on destruction? Will he still look at me like he did tonight when I shot a rapist in the dick? Like I was the only other person in the world. Like I was handpicked by God, just for him?

I convince myself it's water slipping down my cheeks, even as quiet sobs rack through my shoulders. I scrub my skin, even though the blood of that poor woman is long gone, until it's red and stinging under the hot water.

I move to the other arm with my washcloth, but a big hand stops me, another pulling me back into a solid chest.

Mason's voice is rough and quiet in my ear.

"Let me," he murmurs gruffly. I hadn't even heard him come in.

Disaster looms in the distance, but I push it from my mind, forcing myself to focus on him under the heavy flow of the shower. I lean into him, soaking in his warmth because my mother made it clear tonight. He's going to show up and when he does, he won't leave without me.

And then my mother's going to sell me to Michael, in the most barbaric, public sex trade she can.

Sometimes Mason can be rough, but right now, he's gentle. Tender. In a lot of ways, it feels like a sin—maybe if those girls had a Mason Carpenter on their side, they would still be alive.

Maybe if I could walk away, he'd be safe.

"You're so pretty, it hurts to look at you," he murmurs in my ear while he washes the tiny flakes of blood off my skin.

And then I know it's not just water on my face.

"You should moonlight as a hairstylist. Or a cheeseburger chef."

Mason's cheeseburgers are among some of the best food I've ever tasted.

"You're saying I should work at McDonald's?"

I shake my head.

"No. This is high quality. At least a Wendy's."

That earns me a chuckle.

He takes my empty plate and his, carrying them to the sink. "Well, I'm happy to see you like cheeseburgers better than fish."

"I hate fish," I grumble, taking a drink of the sweet red wine he'd poured me before dinner. Well, midnight dinner, I guess.

It's past one now and though I'm exhausted, I'm not ready to sleep yet. I don't know if I can, even if I tried. My nerves have been all over the place since we got home. I'm either calm and tired or so high-strung, I feel like I'm going to bounce my leg off.

There is no in-between.

"Why do you go?" he asks suddenly, turning back to look at me from the sink. I pause for a second. He should really start wearing a shirt if he's going to be asking me questions.

"Because . . ." I stammer. I don't really have a good reason. "I just have to. Or had to, I guess. I don't think I'll be going to another one."

"Why go at all? You don't like the food. You don't believe in politics. You definitely don't like the people."

I'm ashamed to admit, I never thought of *not* going. It was never an option.

"It's just what was expected of us. You never had to go to any functions for Parker?"

He takes his seat, downing half his beer in one drink.

So I've struck a nerve . . .

"Parker didn't own me. He couldn't control me like he could my sisters."

And then it dawns on me. I want to know everything about him.

"Mason . . . why did you choose to go live with your grandma over your family?"

He's quiet for a moment, calculating.

"My grandmother was a good woman. You would have liked her."

"She took you in."

He shakes his head. "She gave me everything. This house. The garage. She made sure it stayed with the family. And she made sure Dad wasn't forgotten."

"How did your sisters feel about that?"

He chuckles bitterly.

"They went to live with Mom and Parker. They had no need for this place anymore."

"And you were . . . left behind." Tears well in my eyes, but I don't let them fall. Not right now when he's finally opening up to me.

"You want to know why Savannah was so against you when she first met you?"

My heart bottoms out in my chest. Of course, I always thought it was because my sister had an illicit affair with her stepfather, but it never occurred to me that there could be something deeper.

"Parker was a part of a club," he murmurs darkly. "Some fucked-up, high society sex club. I'm talking politicians, people you see on TV, CEOs. It was invitation-only and the best-kept secret in LA until last year."

"Like the Inner Sanctum?"

"Worse."

I suck in a deep breath, reaching for the bottle of wine.

"I have a feeling I'm going to need another glass."

"Probably."

While I pour myself another glass of wine, Mason continues.

"One of the requirements of long-standing members was to bring someone to auction. Called party favors. Most of the time, they were brought in like slaves. It wasn't consensual and the things they'd do to people were horrific. Like a cattle trade. They'd pay big money to fuck whoever was auctioned and the auctioneer, or whatever the fuck you want to call it, would keep that money."

"Please don't tell me Savannah was one of the party favors."

His jaw ticks and he doesn't say it, but I can tell from the stiffness in his shoulders that's exactly what happened.

Though my stomach feels queasy, I reach for the bottle of wine. Turns out, I need the whole damned thing.

"The Brethren, more importantly, the children of anyone

associated with the Brethren, are who your mother is trafficking."

"And . . . I suppose my sister fits in here somewhere, as well," I murmur slowly and he nods.

"Hannah . . ." he starts, letting out a deep sigh. Like he doesn't want to say whatever's on his mind. "I'm sure your sister was good. Once. But once Parker got to her . . ."

"Was she a party favor, as you called it? Or something else?"

"She was a member."

My chest cracks at the thought.

"And that's why my mother gave her up."

Neither of us has spoken it out loud, yet, but it's evident my mother is solely responsible for my sister's disappearance. As well as countless others.

I feel like I'm drowning.

"I don't want to tell you this, little doe, but I need to. Prince told me this morning," Mason murmurs gruffly, scrubbing a hand over his face. "They found a body washed up on the beach down in Huntington last night. It was unrecognizable, but . . . it was a woman."

I swallow over the lump in my throat, staring at a bead of wine that slips down the inside of my glass.

"And . . . was it missing a finger?"

"It was."

Silence is loud. Especially when there's a ringing voice in the back of your head telling you it's finally over. This part of your search is done and there's nothing left for you to do.

"I expected tears, not silence," Mason says, as though the absence of my tears disturbs him. "What's going on in your head, little doe?"

I grimace, scrubbing a hand over my face. I'm suddenly very, very tired.

"I . . . I don't know what's going on in my head. I feel like we're dodging bullets left and right with no end in sight. I want to be relieved the mystery with Missy is over, but I don't want to be relieved because

. . ." I suck in a deep, shivering breath. "That makes me a bad person."

Mason's gaze is caustic, glinting in the light overhead. "You're the best fucking person I know, Hannah, and I don't say that lightly."

I stare at him for a long moment, studying his face for any sign that he himself doesn't believe it. Nothing. Not even a glimmer of doubt, but . . .

"I wish I could believe that."

"What are you afraid of, little doe?"

I suck in a deep breath, my chest aching. A heavy heart, my mother would say.

"I'm wondering when it will all end. How it will end. What happened to Melissa . . . What's going to happen between us if we make it out of this alive."

Now that I've said it out loud, I wish I could take it back. How stupid is it that despite everything we've been through together, coming off as clingy and lovestruck makes me want to cry in shame? Perhaps it's the way women have been conditioned to always let the men come to them. Maybe I'm just emotional after tonight.

"I don't get attached," Mason says after a long moment. He stares at his fingers on the empty beer bottle in his hand as if it'll tell him the secrets of life if he stares hard enough. "To anyone besides my family."

Oh . . .

I nod, ashamed at the warmth that pools behind my eyes.

"Until you."

I pause, daring to raise my gaze to his, my heart stopping in my chest when I see the look in his eyes. Possessiveness. Warmth. Adoration. Affection. And something else, burning so hot, I have to look away for a moment.

Oh . . .

"Your family hates me."

"They don't. And if they did," he shrugs. "It wouldn't change anything."

"My mother is going to try to kill you."

"I'm not afraid of death."

"I come with a lot of baggage," I say, almost whispering. Giving him any reason to find an out.

"I'll carry it."

My heart stops.

"Come here."

I stay frozen.

He cocks a brow.

"Little doe, don't make me come over there."

Fine. Slowly, I stand, stepping around the table to stop in front of him. He turns to face me, leaning back in his chair and pulling me between his legs.

And then he does something so unlike Mason Carpenter, I think I might melt into a puddle on the floor.

Leaning forward, he wraps his arms around my waist and lays his head on my stomach. Holding me gently, as if I might shatter.

Right now, I feel like I might.

Gingerly, I reach up, stroking through the short strands of his hair, forcing myself to see him in full. He's not just a powerful man, a dark and dangerous protector, or even an asshole. He's also kind, loving, caring, and the best damned cheeseburger maker in the state. I'd put money on it.

A shudder rolls through him and he peers up at me for a moment, before tugging me forward to sit on his lap. And then he presses his lips to mine while my heart threatens to bruise my chest with how hard it's racing. He kisses me like he needs to. Like it's his last breath.

When he breaks away, our breath is ragged. "You can call me your boyfriend, Hannah. Your person. Your lover. Your fucking husband." My heart bottoms out at the mention of husband and the rough way he growls it. "Just fucking stay."

Carefully, I lean forward, pressing my lips to his gently. "I'll stay,"

I murmur against them. Is it even a question?

He rolls his hips against me and I wince, still sore from last night and the car this evening. Still, my body warms at its center, as if no matter how much I get of him, it'll never be enough.

"I'm sore," I breathe into his mouth.

He chuckles darkly, carefully lifting me and standing from the chair.

"Do you want me to stop?"

"No." I'm surer about that than anything else in life, right now.

"Little doe, I think I've ruined you."

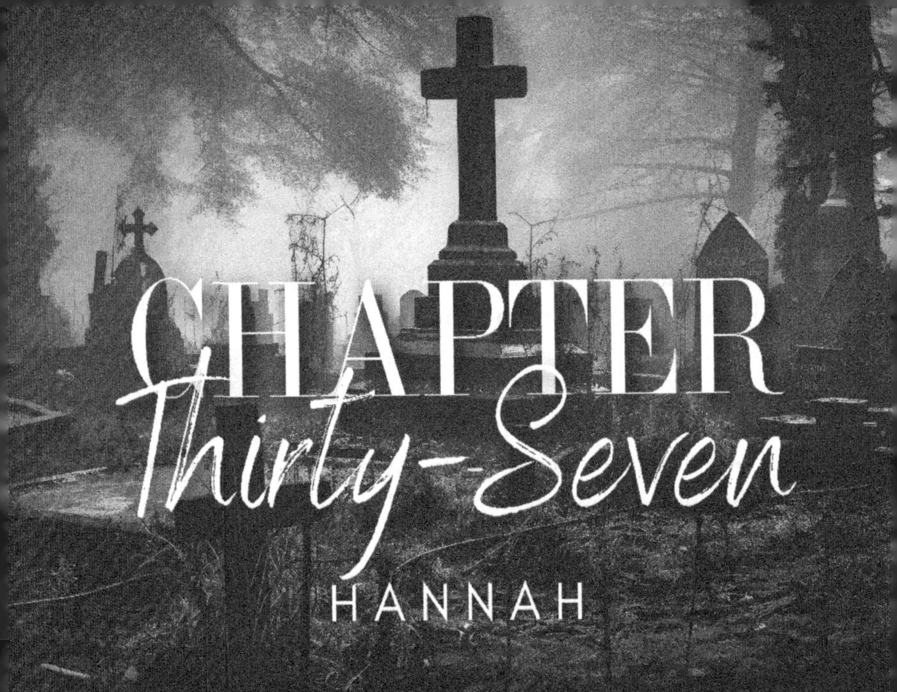

CHAPTER Thirty-Seven

HANNAH

"You look beautiful," Mason murmurs roughly when he opens my door to the truck.

I wish that were enough to quell my nerves.

My stomach is in knots, standing outside of the daunting Monica Parker's house. The Santa Monica mansion is huge, though not nearly as big as the old Paker estate.

When Mason asked me to come with him to a family get-together, I'd thought surely, he'd lost his fucking mind.

I mean, his mother. The dowager queen of the *I hate Hannah club*.

He helps me down and I teeter from the anxiety rushing through me, as I try to keep my pale green sundress from showing everyone, *including* his mother, my ass and the very prominent bite mark on it. Suddenly, I feel stupid in my dress covered in daisies. I mean, these are the Carpenters. The epitome of Los Angeles fashion.

I may as well have worn a paper bag.

"Are you sure this is a good idea?"

Mason stops, stepping forward and taking my face between his hands.

"It's you and me, right?"

"It's a big step," I whisper and he chuckles softly, his rough calloused thumb stroking over my cheek. Normally, I'd be a puddle at his feet, but right now, it barely takes the edge off.

"It is."

"It could create a big rift between you and your family."

"It could."

"And you're sure you want to do this?"

"Yep."

I work my brain to come up with any excuse that could get me the hell away from Monica Parker's swanky mansion and cold stare, but nothing comes to mind. Not when her son's looking at me like he's planning all the ways he's going to devour me later.

"You and me?" I repeat after him, my voice squeaking when it comes out.

"You and me, baby," he nods, pressing the softest kiss to my lips that makes my knees feel noticeably weaker. "I don't fit into my mother's world, but . . . I'd like to show her mine."

My eyes go wide, my heart stalling in my chest, but before I can speak, he presses a rough kiss to the top of my head, takes my hand, and tugs me toward the backyard.

God, I hope he can't feel how clammy my palm is.

Monica's house is nowhere near as extreme as the Malibu fortress that was the Parker estate, but it's damn near close. The place is huge and straight out of an old Hollywood film.

Parker Estate felt cold. Desecrated and bloodstained. What had once been a grand mansion had been turned into a breeding ground for drugs and rapists.

Now, this new house feels brighter. Less formidable. There's still a stone wall surrounding the house—make no mistake about that, but the sun shines a little brighter here. The air seems breezier coming in off the Pacific. Things just feel . . . calm. Light.

The backyard is full of chatter when Mason pulls me through the gate, his hand tightening as if I'm going to tuck and run as soon as I set foot on the terrace.

"You and me, little doe," he murmurs quietly and he's right.

If I can make it through this, I can make it through anything.

"Mason!" Bailey Carpenter screeches, darting forward and throwing her arms around him for a hug. I attempt to step back and let go of Mason's hand, but he remains steadfast, his fingers only tightening.

So, I stand there awkwardly.

"I've missed you so much," Bailey groans, pulling back.

And then her eyes land on me.

Then they shoot back to Mason with a worried glance.

Then, they fall on me again.

Suddenly, the entire yard is silent. All eyes are on me and I'm certain this is the part where pitchforks and torches come out to play.

And *that's* why I opted for sneakers instead of heels.

"Hi, Bailey," I try my best smile, but I'm sure it comes out as more of a pained grimace.

"Bailey," Mason murmurs darkly. "You remember Hannah."

Bailey falls back another step, teetering on surprise and concern.

Can't say I blame her. I don't know what to do, either.

"She's . . ." she starts and I know she's pointing out the elephant in the room. I'm Melissa Gaines' sister. Her twin.

"Mine," Mason replies without blinking an eye as if anyone would try to challenge him.

"Well," a soft voice that sends a shiver down my spine rings out from behind Bailey. "She certainly is beautiful"

"Mom," Mason greets and she pulls him into a hug while Bailey stares at literally anything but me. "You've met Hannah."

"Oh, I've seen her before, but I don't think I've ever gotten to speak to her. I've always admired her pretty red hair." She turns to me and I'm sure this is the moment all hell breaks loose.

So, imagine my surprise when she pulls me into a hug.

I freeze, unsure what to do. It feels like I'm holding the pin to a grenade and if I let my guard down for even a second, shit's going to hit the fan.

Clumsily, I hug her back and Mason gives my hand a squeeze.

"Monica Parker, dear," she says, pulling back to look at me, her soft voice reminding me of an old film star. "And I'm so happy you came. You know, Mason never tells us about his life."

Worry pools in my stomach. Mason be damned, I can't stay here if I'm not welcome.

"Monica," I start, dropping my voice. "I understand if you'd like me to leave. I know—"

"Stop that," she cuts me off, stepping beside me to wrap an arm around my shoulders. She steers me toward the backyard where everyone is still watching us while pretending not to. "Tell me, has my son been treating you well?"

I debate on making a joke but stop myself. Things are far too tense for that at the moment.

"He has," I admit quietly, while Mila comes over to hug Mason. Finally, he lets go of my hand and butterflies swarm the inside of my stomach at the heaviness in his gaze when he steps away.

"Good. You know, he's a lot like his father," Monica says softly. "Strong and loyal to a fault. He's a good man."

Is this the part where she warns me away from her son?

My stomach falls to my toes in distress.

"You're a good girl, too. Don't let anyone tell you otherwise." I pause for a beat, looking at her. Bright blue eyes like Savannah and Bailey. Soft, gentle smile.

She's nothing like the shell of a woman she was before. I'm happy for her.

"Now, come. Let me introduce you to everyone."

"That's okay," I stammer, even as she pulls me along beside her. I look back at Mason who just snickers and shakes his head, his eyes glinting with something like a promise for later. "I'm not sure they'd care for that."

"Nonsense," she lowers her voice, now that Mason's out of earshot. She stops by the edge of the large in-ground pool and watches the water ripple in the late evening sun. "Let me tell you a story, Hannah."

"Okay," I nod nervously.

"My aunt and mother were twins. Not many know that, but it's true. They were incredibly close growing up, but they went down different paths in life. My aunt was convicted of stabbing her husband and died in a prison cell in upstate New York."

"Oh my God."

"My mother went on to marry one of the richest men in the state."

"Monica . . . why are you telling me this?"

"To tell you, you aren't to blame for what your sister became," she smiles, but instead of the softness she'd displayed earlier, there's a fierce maternal instinct in her gaze. "I think it's time you stopped beating yourself up over it, don't you?"

I stare at her for a moment, tears burning in the backs of my eyes.

"I . . . I don't know how."

I've never said that out loud before.

Monica takes my hand, patting it gently. "It's time to learn. We're all a little fucked-up around here, dear. You're just another one of us."

Across the yard, I can feel Mason's eyes on me and when I glance at him, the carefree smile is gone and replaced with a look of protectiveness.

"My son's in love with you, you know?" Monica says, following my gaze across the yard.

"I don't think we're quite there yet."

"No?" She leans forward, to lower her voice. "Sometimes, it only takes a moment."

Then she straightens as if she said nothing at all and takes my hand.

"Come. I'm sure you're hungry."

If I can say anything about the Carpenters, it's that they *know* how to feed an army.

It's normal food, thankfully—no fish in sight. Cheeseburgers (nowhere near as good as Mason's, but they'll do), steak, potatoes in multiple forms, desserts, and drinks.

Once Monica and I come back to the party, everyone seems to have accepted me. Or at least, they aren't staring me down anymore. As soon as I come back to Mason, he wraps his arm around my waist and pulls me into his side.

"Okay?" His voice is rough and his stubble against my skin sends a shiver down my spine.

"Okay," I nod, thinking back on what Monica had said.

My son's in love with you, you know?

I don't want to get my hopes up, but judging by the look in his eyes when he nods, it's hard not to believe her.

Dinner is an easy affair with everyone sitting down to eat and chatting animatedly. It's nice to see them all so . . . easygoing. Everyone's having a good time. No one's mentioned Marcus Parker or Melissa Gaines and I'm even pulled into the conversation.

For once, I feel normal. Like I belong and not an outsider looking in.

Mason must pick up on this because he squeezes my bare thigh under the table, his thumb running in circles over the goosebumps on my skin.

He smirks at me when a shiver racks through me. Asshole knows what he's doing.

"Who's that?" I ask Mason quietly when an older man comes around the corner of the house. He's probably around Monica's age, gray hair, but it's his eyes that stop me.

He looks kind. Gentle.

"Hope I'm not too late," the man says, holding up a bottle of some wine I can't pronounce.

Monica is the first to jump up.

"Of course not, darling. You're just in time."

Mason stiffens beside me, even as the man's gentle gaze sweeps over all of us.

"Let me introduce you to my kids," Monica says. She names everyone, even me, which surprises me, before wrapping an arm around his shoulders. "Everyone, this is Bob. He's a very good friend of mine."

Judging by the way Bob snickers and blushes, I'd be willing to bet they're a little more than just friends.

"He's her boyfriend," Mila mutters, rolling her eyes. Surprisingly, she's been quiet tonight. Moody. Unusual for her.

Monica actually blushes. "Thank you, Mila. Yes, Bob and I have been seeing each other."

"You didn't tell me that?" Bailey scolds and Savannah nods.

"Well, forgive me for not outing it to the world." Monica looks at Bob, a tender smile pulling on her lips. "It's new. We only just started seeing each other. We met at group counseling."

"Sounds like a match made in heaven," Bailey grumbles, taking a drink of sweet tea while the man beside her, her husband, Charlie, shakes his head and says something quietly in her ear. "Right now?"

He doesn't say anything, but Bailey must understand the glimmer of amusement in his eyes.

"Fine."

Sliding back from the table, she retreats into the house.

"What's that about?" I ask Mason quietly, who just shakes his head, his jaw ticking.

Uh-oh.

"Mom, I have a gift for you."

Bailey returns, placing a small bag in front of Monica at the head of the outdoor table. She looks at it, looks at Bailey, looks at Charlie, then looks back at the bag.

"*I knew it*," she mumbles under her breath, tearing at the tissue paper inside.

Finally, she produces an impossibly small newborn onesie.

Holy shit.

Mason's hand tightens on my thigh, but he doesn't say anything as Monica starts balling her eyes out.

"I knew it," she cries, throwing her arms around Bailey and then, Charlie when he joins them. "When are you due?"

"Six months," Bailey says, cheeks flaming. "And don't get your hopes up. We're waiting until he's born to tell everyone the sex." She pauses for a moment as cheers erupt. "Shit."

"Oh, this is going to be so much fun," Monica beams. "A grandson," she tells Bob, who shakes Charlie's hand.

I place my hand over Mason's squeezing his palm and he interlocks our fingers, his gaze searing into mine. His words from last night float through my mind. They seem like such a lifetime ago, but now, I can't get them out of my head.

The Brethren may be breathing down our neck. The cartel . . . my mother . . . but it's comforting to know that even in these times, something good can come out of the darkness.

"What did I miss?"

Everyone turns as Logan Prince strolls into the backyard, and for the first time since I met him, he's not wearing a suit and tie. He looks handsome in a button-up and jeans, almost normal if it weren't for the devilish smirk on his face.

"We're going to have a baby!" Monica cries as he takes his place by Savannah and brings her in for a kiss.

"Sorry I'm late," he murmurs quietly, stroking a hand over her cheek.

"It's okay. You came."

"You'll be coming later."

Mason clears his throat and Logan just snickers at Savannah's blushing cheeks.

"Where's Christian?" Mason asks, scanning the yard. Is it bad that I find solace in the uncomfortable silence that follows because, for once, it's not because of me? "I haven't seen him."

Monica hushes Mason, placing a hand on his shoulder, and pinning him with her gaze.

"What?" he asks, completely oblivious and Monica sighs.

"He left," Mila murmurs darkly, eyes burning with something repressed I have come to know all too well. She shrugs. "Guess he got all he was after here."

"Mila," Monica admonishes, but Mila just shakes her head, disappearing into the house.

"What happened?" Mason asks, cocking a brow and Monica purses her lips.

"Well, you know your sister. Always wears her heart on her sleeve. He went back to New York. I guess he has family there."

I want to ask who Christian is, but I know—for once—that now's not a good time.

"You should go speak to her," Monica urges, but Mason shakes his head.

"I don't think that's a good idea."

"I'll go," Bailey chimes softly. "She's going to want to hear it from a woman, anyway."

Monica nods and Bailey retreats to the house.

"Don't tell me . . ." Mason grumbles and Monica nods.

"Afraid so."

"Anyone want dessert?" she asks cheerfully, glossing over the elephant in the room. "Or a drink?" she mutters, downing the rest of her champagne.

"Oh, to be young again, my dear," Bob laughs, wrapping his arm around her shoulders.

I give Mason a squeeze of my hand, who still watches the door Mila and Bailey disappeared through as if he could set it on fire with his eyes.

"You can't stop it," I whisper so only he can hear me.

"I can."

"Remember when they tried to stop you from seeing me?"

His eyes find mine and I watch as the anger softens in his gaze.

He pulls me into him, pressing a kiss to my lips.

But he doesn't say another word.

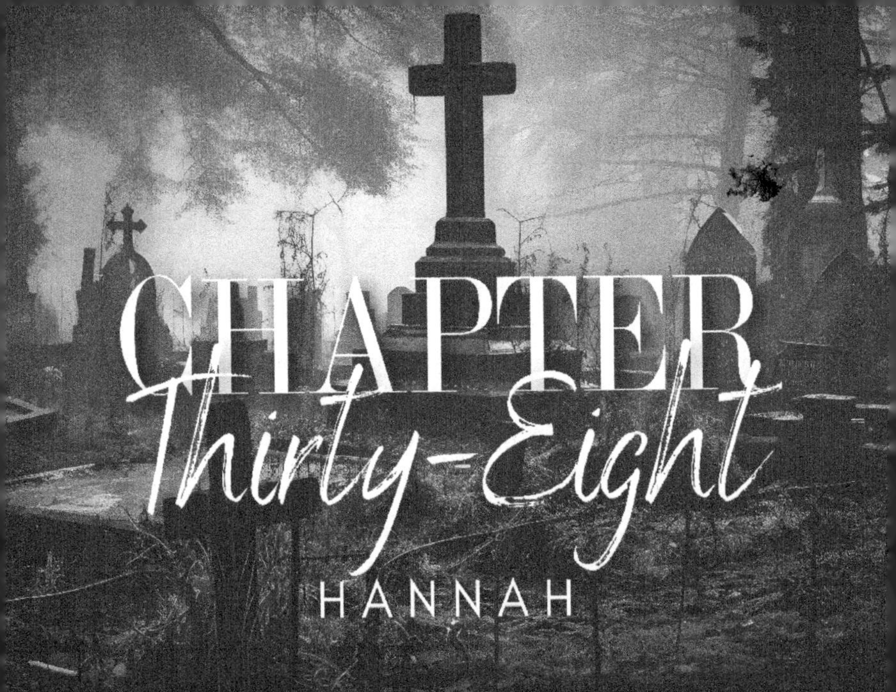

CHAPTER Thirty-Eight

HANNAH

The funny thing about life is even when everything feels like it's starting to fall into place, the universe is actually secretly conspiring against you to fuck that shit up before all the pieces ever land.

I am Hannah Gaines. Daughter of Hank and Laura Gaines. Sister of Melissa Gaines. Guilty as sin, just like the rest of them.

Today, I'm just sad.

Sad for Melissa and what she turned out to be, but . . . she was always a little off, even if I couldn't see it.

Sad that she's dead, now, and there's nothing I could have done to stop it.

Sad that I've roped Mason into this and now, the threat over our head lingers nearly every passing moment.

When does it all end?

Then I look up and spot a person across the street.

Their hood is drawn low over the eyes, so I can't make out their features through the rain, but I can tell it's a woman from the way the soaking wet hoodie clings to her body.

She's watching me.

"Oh, fuck," I whisper, stumbling off of the stool.

Anger rushes through me at the prospect of them thinking they can just show up at Mason's shop and creep on me. I stride toward the front door, prepared to go across the street and give them a piece of my mind.

I'm sick of being tormented by creepy poems and disgusting nightmares. I'm tired of the secrets that we keep uncovering and I'm no longer willing to be controlled.

No one owns me. Not Mom, not Missy.

Not even Mason.

But . . . as I make my way to the front, a truck passes, and when it's gone, so is the person across the street.

I'm so blinded by the confusion swirling around my mind that when the mail truck pulls to a stop, right in front of the shop, I fall to a screeching halt at the door.

"One package today, Miss." The mail driver smiles, completely oblivious to the ominous feeling surrounding the shop.

"Thank you," I murmur, taking it absentmindedly while I stare at the spot across the street where the person was standing.

My heartbeat thuds in my chest, slow and off-pitch.

They were right fucking there.

"Says here I need a signature from a Ms. Hannah Gaines. That you?"

My eyes snap back to the mailman's, nausea bubbling in my stomach. Finally, I glance down at the package. Sure enough, it's got my name on the address label. No return address.

Oh, this *cannot* be anything good.

"Okay," I stammer, voice uneven and I take the pen from him, signing his electronic handheld.

"Great, you have a nice day, now."

I nod and then he's gone, leaving me alone with the creepy box and whatever the hell could be inside.

I look at his back as he retreats. Then the package. Mail guy's back. Package.

Tap tap tap.

Shit, I'm losing my mind.

I suck in a deep breath, a shudder rolling through me. I check across the street again, but whoever was there is long gone, so I make my way back to my desk.

It's just a box. What could possibly be inside that's so deadly?

My first thought is a bomb, but it feels as empty as air.

My second thought is a note.

So what? It's not like I haven't gotten a bunch of those already.

"Come on, Hannah. Not like it can get any worse."

So, carefully, I pull the tape off, opening the box expecting to find a whole lot of nothing, only . . . there's a card, nestled in a velvet wrapping.

Horror washes through me as I read the sprawling cursive, noted elegantly on a bold embroidered card.

DON'T FORGET TO SMILE.

My stomach drops to my toes, but it's when I flip the card over and see the photograph nestled there, that I let out a scream.

And that's when the first shot goes off.

Tap tap tap.

Bullets ricochet around the room and there are shouts, but I can't tell where they're coming from. Seconds later, Mason bursts through the door and jumps at me, his body landing over mine against the wall. He clutches me to his chest, shrinking around me while the sounds of warfare ring out all around us.

The front window shatters and I hear a bullet sing as it barrels past us and into the wall, directly above our heads.

The shop window is blown to pieces next and little shards of glass rain down on us as Mason's grip around me only tightens.

And then . . .

Everything stops, as quickly as it had started.

"*Fuck,*" Mason grits, his hands roaming my body. "Are you okay?"

"I'm . . . okay," I breathe, my voice locked in my throat as my entire body shakes.

Someone just shot up the shop.

Someone tried to kill us.

"Please tell me everyone's alive."

It's Ian, his voice choked and panicked.

Footsteps scramble behind us and then a quiet *shit* sounds out from one of the men as they reach us.

"You're hit," Puke curses, but not to me.

I follow his line of gaze to the dark red blood pouring from Mason's arm.

And then I really start to panic.

"Mason?"

I'm up on shaky knees before I can take another breath. I reach for him, but he stops me, a hand on my cheek and his eyes stern.

"I'm fine, little doe." His voice is rough when it reaches my ears. "It's just a scratch."

His blood seeps through the wound, coating my fingers and I barely register the sounds of police sirens as my eyes lock with his hurricane gaze.

Someone tried to kill him.

Because of me.

"Fuck," he bites again, his hand on my cheek, slipping up to fist in my hair. "Come here."

He tugs me into him and I go, blood and all, and let him hold me, clinging to him just as hard. I feel undeserving of his love, his comfort but I go anyway because it feels like the world is crashing down around us.

I spot the picture, the white back facing the sky and the photograph against the tile floor.

It's a picture that will haunt me for the rest of my life.

"Is anyone hurt?"

It's a new voice, the voice of a cop. Though sweat beads my hairline from the adrenaline coursing through me, a sense of calm sweeps over me. A blackness, tugging me back to unconsciousness.

"Hannah?" Mason's voice barely breaks through, and a sweeping sensation slides over me like a cloak.

"An ambulance is on the way," I hear, as more sirens approach, but my eyes stay locked on the little photograph under the desk.

Tap, tap, tap.

"*Hannah,*" Mason tries again, but it's no use.

I'm already falling into the darkness.

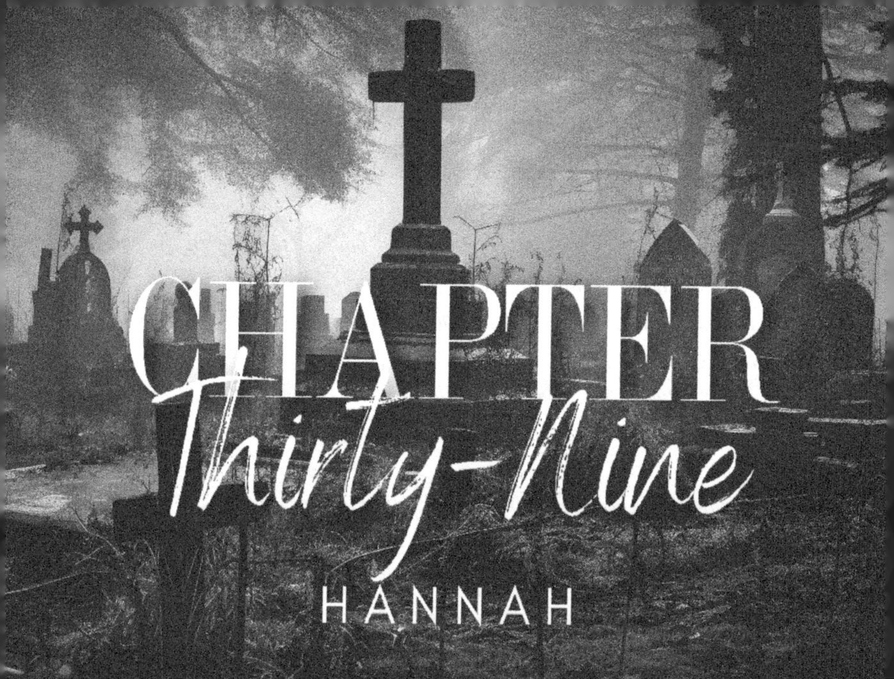

CHAPTER Thirty-Nine

HANNAH

Tap tap tap . . .

"Mama, why does he look like that?"

"Hush, now, Missy dear." My mother silences her, tugging Missy and my hands down the long, narrow passage toward the casket up front. People stare at us as we pass, their gazes trained on us like we're circus performers.

Papa took us to a circus once. There were clowns and I didn't like them. I liked the animals, though. Missy loved *the clowns and declared she would also be a clown when we grow up.*

I just think she said it to scare me.

I don't think we'll be going to a circus again. Mama doesn't like it and now, Papa's not here anymore.

Tap tap tap . . .

What is that annoying tapping? It feels like something hitting my face, but when I reach up, there's no one there.

We were told before we left the house that we must be silent today, or Mama would be angry. I don't like when she's angry, so I've kept my voice locked tight.

"Why is he smiling?" Missy asks as we near and my fingers grow clammy in Mama's grip. I want to tug away from her, but I know if I do, she'll be angry.

Still . . . panic rises in my throat and I feel like it's too close.

I don't want to see him.

That's not *him. That man in the casket holds a slight green tinge to his skin. A sunken decay around his eyes.*

He wasn't green. He was big and powerful. Dark and dangerous. Bad, but willing to be good, just for me.

Gently, I tug on my hand, but Mama won't let go.

She only tightens her grip, pulling me closer and closer to the corpse in the casket.

My breath catches in my throat and I feel like I can smell death. Taste it on my tongue.

"Mama," I choke, but she just pulls harder and I stumble forward when she stops abruptly, right at the edge of the casket. I fall forward, catching myself on the edge and my hand brushes his.

Disgust fills me as bile rises in my throat.

I touched him and Mama told me not to touch him.

Tap tap tap . . .

I scurry back, my head woozy as the blood rushes to my ears, but Mama's face is all I can see, her eyes twinged with disappointment.

Tap tap tap.

Not a single ounce of sorrow rests in that gaze.

Tap.

"See what happens when you don't listen?" Mama nods to the casket, lips pursed.

I follow her gaze, a scream of terror freezing in my throat.

That's not Papa at all.

It's Mason.

His face is twisted in a hellish grimace, mirroring a smile. His eyes wide open, stormy gray, and glassy. But it's the hole in the center of his forehead that fills my veins with ice.

My chest tightens painfully, as the room begins to sway around me, the faces of the crowd distorted and demonic. I suck air into my lungs, but it's not enough and my heart feels like it's going to explode in my chest.

That's not *Mason.*

Tap tap tap tap tap tap.

"Mama?" I think I ask, but before I can focus on her reply, everything goes dark.

Tap.

What the fuck is tapping on my face?

My eyes will barely open, but I can see it's still dark.

Where am I?

Tap tap tap.

"Hannah . . ." Someone whispers from above me.

Mason. I'm in Mason's room. I can feel him beside me, but . . . why can't I feel my legs?

Tap tap tap.

I open my mouth to tell whoever is touching me to stop, but no sound comes out, save for a choking gurgle when the saliva in my mouth pools from the nausea in my stomach.

"Look at me."

That's not Mason's voice.

That's Melissa.

I force my eyes to crack open with everything I have in me.

And my heart stops.

Melissa sits above me, shadowed in the moonlight, a knife raised above her head.

But . . . it's the smile on her face that's the most terrifying thing I've ever seen.

It's *the* smile.

Tap. Tap. Tap.

She pats my cheek, but I can't feel her fingertips. I can't feel anything, save for the heavy weight on my chest like a steel anvil, resting right on top of my ribcage.

"Look at me, look at me, look at me . . ." she whispers, so fast I can barely make out the words. I suck air into my lungs, but none comes.

Panic seizes my chest and tears leak out of the corners of my eyes, but still . . . I can't move.

"Look at me, look at me, look at me."

Why can't I wake Mason?

This must be another nightmare.

I will myself to wake up, fighting with my subconscious for control of my own body. All the while, that wretched smile stays in place.

His smile.

"Hannah."

I scream, all the air rushing back into my body at once and leap from the bed, tangling myself in sheets and blankets before crashing to the floor against the bedroom door.

She's going to kill him.

Mason.

"Hannah," Mason says, jumping from the bed and falling to his knees in front of me. "What the fuck happened?"

He brushes the hair out of my face, too gentle for the nightmares still clinging to the edges of my mind with steel, icy cold grips.

"There's someone in here," I gasp, hand over my chest because I'm still raggedly out of breath. I scan the room around us, even as he takes my face in his hands and attempts to force my gaze to his.

"Baby, there's no one here. It's just us."

He thinks I'm crazy.

"She was," I cry, shoving back from him and falling forward to search under the bed.

Nothing.

Not even a sock.

"Hannah."

I clamber to my feet, searching the closet, the bathroom, the cabinet under the sink, the shower . . . anywhere I can think that someone my size could hide.

"Hannah." Mason's voice is like a whip cracking when I reach for the door handle to check the rest of the house.

Tap tap, fucking tap.

It makes sense now.

The tapping on the other side of my dark prison.

It was Missy. She was the monster in the darkness.

With shaky legs, I sink to the floor at the bottom of the bed and pull my knees to my chest.

Then I cry.

Am I going fucking crazy?

I look away. I can't . . . be *seen* by him right now. Not when the world is falling apart in my mind and that awful night is burned into my brain.

"I'm sorry," I whisper and he growls, tugging me to his chest.

So, I cry harder.

Surprisingly, he lets me, sitting on the rug and tugging me into his lap while I blubber like a baby all over him.

And finally . . . everything makes sense. Everything I've blocked out. Everything I've tried to hide from myself for all those years.

It was me. My fault.

We don't move for a long time. Not even when my back starts to hurt and I'm sure his does, too. When the tears stop, he holds me in silence and I listen to the steady beat of his heart under my ear.

This thing between us has far surpassed anything I ever thought it would. Meeting his family, my promise to stay, his profession of adoration only days ago . . .

I don't deserve any of this.

"I murdered my father."

He doesn't move. He doesn't speak. If I wasn't listening to his heart beating against my ear, I would be sure he'd died.

Finally, when I can't take his silence anymore, I lift my head to meet his gaze.

It's volatile.

"Is that supposed to deter me, little doe?"

My mind struggles to catch up when his fingers tighten on my hips. What is he talking about? I just told him I murdered my own father and he acts like I just told him I have a secret crush on the Pillsbury Dough Boy.

"My mother gave me the poison. I didn't know what it was, but I didn't ask either when she told me to mix it into his dinner." I suck in a shaky breath. "He died because he was planning to leave my mother. He was in love with a woman at his work and he was going to take us away from Mom. He knew what kind of person she was and he always tried to protect us from her. He was a good dad."

Mason looks as unbothered by what I've just confessed to him as he would reading the Sunday paper.

"And now he haunts your nightmares."

"And Melissa. And Mom. Mason . . ." I suck in a heavy breath, tugging my hands away from him.

This is not the response I thought I would get.

"I just told you I murdered my own father and you have nothing to say?"

I move to stand. I need to pace. But . . . he doesn't let me, grabbing my hand and pulling me closer so my front is pressed against his instead. His hand cups my ass while his other the back of my head, like I'm the most precious thing in the world to him.

"I know, Hannah."

My mind threatens to explode.

There's no fucking way.

"How?" I know I sound like I'm accusing him of something, but dammit. My heart feels like it weighs a thousand pounds in my chest.

"Because you're mine," he shrugs, brushing a tear from under my eye. "Because of how he disappeared and the guilt you still carry. Because your mother's never been innocent. And because she's vindictive and cruel when scorned and evil enough to use a child to do her bidding."

Holy shit.

"How long have you known?"

His jaw ticks and he looks away for a split second before those hurricane eyes turn back to mine. "Since Prince's men found his body buried in a shallow grave not too far from your Virginia home."

I want to be angry. I want to fight with him. Ask him how he could keep this from me, but it's my secret, isn't it? I've kept it from him for just as long. I did it. So who's really at fault here?

His arms tighten around me. As if at any moment, someone might snatch me away from him.

Sometimes, it feels like it.

Still . . . even as I soak in the warmth radiating through his skin, I know . . . This has to end.

My mother killed my father. My sister is dead. The cartel is after Mason and I'm bringing all this right to his doorstep with a promise of love.

They had him in their crosshairs. They were prepared to shoot him.

"I need to leave, Mason."

Mason stills beneath me, tension radiating through every tattooed muscle. A beat passes before he drawls, "Want to run that by me again, little doe?"

This is going to hurt.

My mother only wants him because of me. The *cartel* only wants him because of me.

"It's not safe for you to be around me," I murmur quietly, keeping my gaze pinned to the nightlight emanating from the bathroom. I swallow the lump forming in my throat, but my voice still comes out shaky and pathetic. "I need to go."

Carefully, I disentangle myself from him and stand on shaky legs. He doesn't stop me when I step from his bedroom into mine. I don't even know why I came in here, I just needed to walk away from the volatile stare searing a hole into my back.

Unfortunately, it follows me.

"You think that's going to solve all your problems? Sacrificing yourself?" I can *feel* the rage in his voice, seeping into me like toxic waste.

"It's not safe for you, Mason," I snap, whipping around to face him. Big mistake, because if I thought a hurricane was bad, I don't even know what to call this. His eyes have never suited him better. "You have to see that."

"That's not for you to decide."

"You could have been *killed* today, Mason. You were shot!"

He chuckles darkly, the sound sending a shiver through me. He cocks a brow, a dangerous darkness seeping off him in waves.

"This is getting real fucking old, Hannah."

Something in my chest cracks and tears well in my eyes, but I force them back. "I'm not running," I seethe. "I'm trying to protect you."

"You're running alright. Right into fucking death."

"Then that's my choice."

"That's it, then. Your grand plan? Fucking leave and expect me to sit here and lose you?"

"You have to." A tear slips down my cheek and he watches its descent with an icy darkness. "I can't . . . I can't let anything bad happen to you because of me."

"You walk out that door, Hannah, you're doing it with me. I won't allow you to offer yourself up for sacrifice."

I can feel that he means it by the possession in his gaze. The protectiveness in his hands. Call it whatever you want. Toxic. Loyal. I don't care. For once, it feels good to finally meet another person who feels as deeply as I do. Who would be willing to risk their life to save mine, just like I would to save theirs.

I crave to be a part of his life and that's dangerous. He could decide at any moment he doesn't want me here. That the words he says in the darkness of my nightmares are just empty promises. But . . . I accept it. I want to fall into Mason Carpenter, even if it means trusting him completely.

"I'm in love with you," I whisper and the dam breaks. Everything in me crashes around us like an earthquake ripped through the center of the room, as the tears can't be held back anymore.

Mason doesn't say anything, but he stiffens, his spine rigid and his nostrils flaring.

"I'm in love with you," I repeat, "and love means making sacrifices, even if you don't feel the same way."

He stares at me, hate in his gaze that burns every vein in my body.

I guess he doesn't feel the same way.

I shake my head, closing my eyes against the tears. I can't look at him right now. If I do, it'll only make this harder. I move to step around him, toward my bedroom, but before I can, his hand shoots out, grabbing me around the throat and spinning me until my front is against the wall.

"Do you think," he snarls in my ear as shock paralyzes me to my core, "that you can just give me that and rip it away in heartbeat?"

He presses into me, then his hand winds through my hair and he tugs my head back until I'm looking at him straight above me, my gaze filled with only his volatile eyes.

He chuckles darkly when a whimper leaves my throat, his other hand pressing against my stomach to bring my ass back into him. Reaching between us, he rips my shorts down my legs until my ass is exposed, his fingers kneading the flesh roughly.

I clench my teeth, my pride flaring in my chest even as I succumb to him.

"It's for the best." His hand connects with my ass and I gasp at the sting radiating from my skin. Heat envelopes me from the warmth radiating where my core presses into the ridge of his boxers and I resist the urge to move back against him.

"What's your word?" he grits, repeating the motion on the other side until I'm sure there's going to be a welt later.

"Hurricane," I breathe through the tightness in my throat.

"You want me to stop," he murmurs against my ear. "Use it."

I nod, a fever taking over when he smacks my ass again. I arch into his palm, begging for him to touch me, even if his touch is rough.

This is what Mason does. He chases away the demons until he's the only darkness left.

Flipping me around without a word, Mason slips my shirt off, only pulling back long enough to get it over my head before he tugs me back flush with his chest. The cool air hits my skin, but the shudder that moves through me is entirely from the way he nips at my ear, my jaw, and then dipping lower to cup my breast to his mouth.

Expertly, his tongue strokes over the hardened nub and my head falls back against the wall hard enough that I wonder if there will be a dent there tomorrow.

He groans against my skin, his fingers finding my aching pussy before he slips two inside. I gasp from the burn, my fingernails digging into the flesh of his shoulders until I'm on the verge of breaking skin.

"Scratch me, fight me, fuck me," he grits, releasing my nipple with a stroke of his teeth. All the while, his fingers move in and out of me fast enough that I can feel myself opening up for him, begging for more. Just as my orgasm crests and my whimpers turn to deep moans, he stops, tugging out of me. "Your choice."

Abruptly, Mason lifts me into his arms and then drops to his knees. My ass rests on his thighs and I reach between us to work his cock out of his pants before he drops me down to my back on the rug underneath us.

He wastes no time slipping his boxers down his legs and his cock springs free, his thickness straining and angry red from his erection. My mouth waters and I reach for him, but he catches my wrist, pinning it above my head.

"I'm going to enjoy punishing you, little doe."

And then he's filling me. He only manages a few inches before my body pushes him back out, the sting from his size emanating through me and bringing a cry from my lips. The burn as he thrusts back inside, filling me until I can feel him in my stomach drives me to roll my hips into his, my body tightening around him.

He takes my other hand when I try to tug his lips down to mine, denying me a kiss and holding both to the floor above my head. His other comes down to hold my hip in place while he starts a dizzying pace.

"Mason," I groan, perspiration coating every inch of my skin as I work to keep up with him.

This is Mason truly unhinged. Giving me all of him without holding anything back. It's fucking addicting.

"You want my kiss after you just said you were going to leave?"

"Yes," I pant, my back arching off the floor as the pleasure radiating through me draws to a sharp point again.

"No."

Tears collect in my eyes at his denying me, but he doesn't stop the thrust of his hips against mine.

"*Fuck*," he grits, using my hips to slam me down on his impossible length.

My nails dig into his wrist where he's holding me, marking his skin as he has mine. I roll against his groin, my body trembling. It's too much and I can't be quiet as a strangled moan slips free.

"How bad do you want me, Hannah?" he growls, tugging me forward and flipping me over onto my stomach. "How much do you love me?"

"More than anything," I breathe, my nipples straining against the carpet beneath me. Can't wait to see *that* rug burn.

Still, he denies me again, pulling out and leaving my pussy pulsating as the orgasm fades away. He flips me over and I fall forward, my cheek pressing into the carpet beneath me.

"I hate you," I seethe, my head falling back to hit the floor behind me.

"You take my cock so fucking well, Hannah. Even when you're

pissed at me," he rasps, his fingers strumming over my clit until I feel like I'm going to explode. My nipples tighten, my pussy sucking him in greedily, even as my temper flares. "Your love or your hatred; I can't decide which is sweeter."

"I'm not a whore," I whisper, tears streaming down my cheeks from the onslaught of pleasure careening through me.

"No," he bites, his hips against my ass filling the room with rough sounds of sex and flesh on flesh. "But you're my whore. You want me to stop?"

I should say yes. My head tells me to, but my body couldn't disagree more. It wants his hatred as much as it wants his love.

"No," I breathe, moaning when he reaches around and slips his fingers over my clit again.

Leaning down until his front is pressed entirely to my back, he wraps his arms around my chest, his hand at my throat, squeezing.

"You were fucking made for me and only me, little doe," he grits, his thrust pushing me across the carpet with each stroke of his cock against that delicious part of me.

My heart swells and threatens to explode when he presses a gentle kiss—a stark contrast to what he's doing to me—to my ear lobe.

"Even if you ran," he rasps against my ear. "I'd still be there, protecting you from the shadows."

"Sounds like obsession," I pant, my voice strained with the force of his fingers on my windpipe.

"Sounds like you're mine."

"Please don't stop, Mason," I whimper, tears building in the corners of my eyes from the onslaught of pleasure. This orgasm is going to break me, but I'd gladly welcome it if it branded him on my skin for the rest of my short life.

"Come, Hannah."

My body erupts when he strokes over that perfect spot inside me, and blinding, white-hot light shoots behind my eyes. I cry out, euphoria consuming me until I'm lost in the haze, the only beacon back to earth being him as he rears back, takes my hips in his hands, and hikes me to my knees.

He presses my shoulders down into the carpet and holds my legs up because they shake with the orgasm still rippling through me. Then he slides back in.

"Oh, God," I whimper, my sex still pulsing with aftershocks.

"That's it, Hannah," he growls over me, his voice at the back of my neck terrifying as he continues to thrust into me. "Pray for my damned soul. It's always been yours." He presses his thumb to my lips, pushing it inside forcefully. "Suck."

I draw him in at the rough command and lathe him with my tongue. When he withdraws, I let him feel my teeth.

Our safe word isn't just for me.

He hisses out a sharp breath, swatting at my ass before pressing that same thumb to the tight ring of muscles above where his cock is slipping inside me until it gives way, allowing him to enter me.

My body tightens to a breaking point where I think my heart's either going to beat out of my chest or I'm going to come again. His hand on my shoulder slips to fist in my hair. He tugs my head back and with a rough noise, nips the side of my neck.

It's maddening. Deranged. Us.

"You own me, little doe," he grunts, enunciating each word with a thrust of his hips. "No matter where the fuck I am or who I've been with, it's always been you I see."

I whimper, my knees shaking. I can feel my arousal slipping down my thighs and I would be embarrassed, was I not careening toward another orgasm.

His fingers tighten in my hair, bringing my head back at an angle I'm sure will break my spine until I meet his gaze.

"I love you, Hannah. Now come for me."

My body tightens, exploding and tears stream down my face to mix with the sweat on my cheeks. Heat rushes through me, burning me to a crisp when Mason releases my hair and thrusts into me only once more before growling out my name like a prayer to God.

He fills me, coming with a sharp thrust of his hips and a shuddering breath that has him collapsing overtop of me.

When he rests his head on the center of my back, my knees really do give out and he lays down with me, the only sound the racing of our hearts and our heavy breathing.

Still . . . the little voice in the back of my head doesn't shut up.

"Did you mean that?" I pant, chancing a look over my shoulder in his direction to find him watching me.

His steely gaze holds me for a moment, then he rolls me until I'm on my back and he's hovering over me. Somehow, this is more terrifying than anything else I've faced in the last twenty-four hours.

"I'm so fucking in love with you it hurts, Hannah Marie. And I'll fight like hell to keep you."

I swallow past the lump in my throat. No easy feat because it feels like it's the size of a softball.

"And the other. Did you mean that, too?"

He leans down, nipping my bottom lip and soothing the sting with a stroke of his tongue. Finally, he kisses me and it's the kiss of death because it feels like he's sucking my soul out with each stroke of his tongue against mine.

Finally, when he pulls away, his voice is husky.

"Every. Fucking. Word."

"You're bleeding again," I whisper, my fingers running over the red mark in the bandage on his arm.

"And I'll bleed a thousand times more for you, little doe." Reaching up, he wipes the tears from under my eyes with the back of his thumb. "But don't you dare ever ask me to give you up."

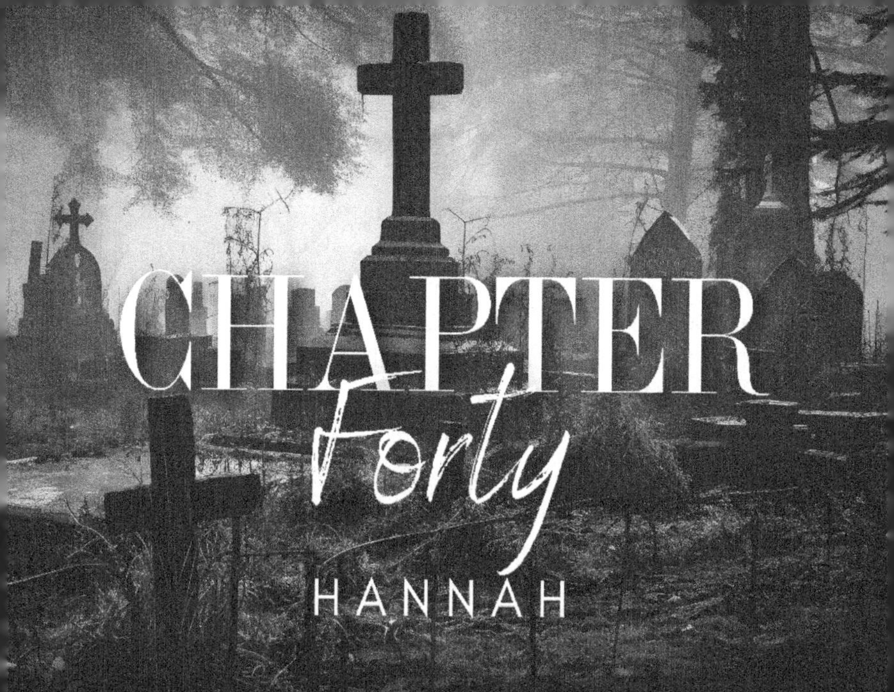

CHAPTER *Forty*

HANNAH

Laura Gaines: It's either you. Or him.

Sometimes, when Mason's asleep, I like to trace the snake on his chest, memorizing it with my fingertips when he's not watching me with those hurricane eyes.

Tonight, he's sleeping peacefully for once, though I know it's because he was exhausted when we got to his mother's house.

We spent the day in the shop, cleaning up and dealing with police and news reporters that wanted to be the first to catch the inside story. It crushed my heart to hear them speaking about his dad's garage—his garage that he's worked so hard to build—as if it were just another passing building.

This is Mason's whole life, and now, it's out of commission until we can make sure it's safe again.

We came to Monica's because someone's out to get us. Logan and Savannah are staying, too, to keep everyone together. It was a strange affair. A quiet, solemn dinner. A quiet, solemn goodnight before we all went our separate ways. I know for them, this is just like old times. When they were all in fear for their life and I hate that I've brought it back to them.

I stared at that picture for a long time today, debating on whether or not I should come clean and tell Mason about it, but in the end, I knew it would only stress him out more.

He'd see it and think this was a threat to me, not him.

What he doesn't see is that this is all my fault.

I dragged him into this mess.

And now I'm going to set him free.

Even if it kills me.

He fell asleep holding me as if I might try to run away in the night. It breaks my heart to know when he wakes up in a few hours, he'll be waking up alone, but I have to do this.

I have to save him.

If he taught me anything in our time together, it's that love isn't just selfish. It's selfless when it needs to be. You give your heart to another person and beg them not to beat it black and blue, but in the end, sometimes you have to do it, just to make sure they're going to be okay.

The fucked-up part about love that no one ever tells you about is how you have to learn to be careless and careful at the same time. You can't worry about every movement, worry that at any time, the person you've given your soul to could up and leave because, let's face it, feelings change. You also can't take them for granted because you never know how much time you have left.

Mason could have died.

Ian and Puke, too.

I can't have their blood on my hands. *His* blood.

Mason said he'd bleed for me a thousand times, but he forgot, I've never bled for him. He's given everything to keep me safe and if love was enough, then I wouldn't be here trying to force myself to slip from the bed. I've been so happy to accept his protection when I have the greatest shield of all time, right within myself.

Turn myself in and he'll be free.

So . . . that's what I'm doing.

I glance at the clock behind his head. Half past midnight. Everyone else in the house has been asleep for hours.

It's time to go.

Carefully, I slip from Mason's arms, the chill of the night settling deep in my bones when I stand from the bed and quietly slip towards my bag on the floor. I can't look at him. If I do, I'll back out of this and I can't do that.

This is not his fight.

I riffle through the bag, trying to pick out something to wear. What is the dress code when you're heading to the gallows?

Leggings? Jeans? Khakis?

I settle on the jeans for warmth because I have no idea where I'm going and the denim scratches my thighs as if it's reminding me this will be the final time I'm ever going to see him.

I hope, after I'm gone, he can find someone who understands him. Who won't take his love for granted, like I did for so long. Who will do everything in her power to show him what real happiness is because, after everything he's been through, he deserves it more than anyone.

Maybe I'm being dramatic. Maybe I'm just in love.

I pull on a T-shirt and some sneakers and tug a hoodie over my head. I don't bother with anything else. What good would it do?

Once I'm dressed, I silently creep back to the bed to lay my note on the pillow beside his. My pillow. He doesn't stir and I take the moment to pause and soak him in, memorizing the strong features of his face until he's burned into my brain.

Fuck, this is going to hurt.

Silently, I slip my gun off the nightstand and into the pocket of my hoodie. It's Mason's hoodie, so it's huge. Luckily, the gun is well concealed.

Leaning down, I place a soft kiss to his cheek and commit his scent to memory. Leather, smoke, forest, him.

"I love you," I whisper, hastily wiping the tear that slides down my chin. Quietly, I slip from the room and shut the door behind me with a soft click, taking one last glance at Mason Carpenter. My life. My soul. My *everything*, before the door shuts.

And then I leave him.

For California in early September, the air is chilly as I walk through the night. The streets are dead. I'm not surprised. It's well past one in the morning, but even the street lights seem dimmer.

Maybe I'm just creeped out.

I've got to hand it to Monica, Santa Monica—funny—seems cozy. If I didn't like home so much, I would definitely consider moving here.

And then it hits me.

Home.

Mason's home, I know, but for a short while, it was my home, too. Maybe it would have even been my permanent home, were I not walking to meet death as we speak.

It's funny. In all my life, I've never really felt like I belonged anywhere. Not until him.

Now that I've found somewhere, *someone* I belong to, it can only be classified as cruel irony that I have to walk away from it now.

I can't tell you how many times I almost turn around and head back. At least a dozen before I reach the end of the street, but . . . then I turn the corner and start down Santa Monica Boulevard.

Tonight I'm giving myself up to my mother and while that might not seem too bad to most, for me, it means this is the end of the line. I'm not naïve enough to believe I'll come back from this.

I texted her from Missy's phone and left mine on the nightstand before I left. I'll have no use for it now, and I refuse to leave it with her.

I'm nearly halfway down the sidewalk when a car rolls to a stop beside me.

"Hannah?"

I'm almost as shocked to see Ian as he is to see me.

"Ian? What are you doing out here?"

He stares at me like I've lost my mind. "What are *you* doing out here? Where's Mason?"

Fuck.

"He's at his mother's." I'm ashamed of how small my voice sounds. And then an idea strikes. "We . . . had a fight."

Ian doesn't look pleased and not that I blame him, but I feel guilty for the disappointment in his face.

"You still shouldn't be wandering the streets by yourself. It's dangerous. Come on. I'll give you a ride."

"No, that's okay. I'd like to walk." I offer him a smile, but I can't say it's very generous. "I need to clear my head."

"Hannah. Come on. Mason will kill me if I just let you roam around at night. Think of the shop."

Dammit.

Conceding that there's no way I'm getting out of this, I begrudgingly trudge forward.

Fine, Ian. Have it your way.

"Can you take me to the Greyhound station up on Wallace?"

He stops and stares at me, his hand on the gearshift of his old Mustang.

"Greyhound? As in the bus?"

I swallow over the lump in my throat. "Yes."

"You're leaving him."

It's not a question.

I suck in a deep breath, a shiver rolling through me, but I don't think it's from the cold.

"It's for the best."

He breathes out a sigh like I've just presented him with the choice of a lifetime. Betray his best friend or betray the woman who just climbed in his car.

"You're going to get me killed," he murmurs, putting the car in drive.

He starts off down the street and I must admit, not being out in the dark quells some of the nausea radiating through me. Just not much.

"You want to talk about it?"

I shake my head. That's the *last* thing I want to do. Just add more lies to my already fucked-up pile. "No. Thank you for doing this."

Ian nods, tapping on the steering wheel to some screamo song that I don't know, quietly playing in the background.

"I must admit, I'm a little surprised, but if this is what you want to do . . ."

"It is."

"Going to hurt him, you know? Just leaving in the dead of night."

I wince. "It has to be done."

Visions of Mason waking up in the morning to an empty bed parade around my mind. Tears flood my eyes thinking about how he'll blame himself, but I hastily shove them back.

I'll think about that later.

Right now, I have to get away from Ian.

"I don't want to hurt him," I admit because it's the truth. My stomach is in knots and it has been since I decided I was doing this. Every time I looked at Mason today, every time his hand brushed my lower back or my hip. Even when he made love to me tonight—a stark contrast to the night before—my chest ached because I knew this was the last of us.

The great Mason Carpenter and Hannah Gaines love affair: A love story with a tragic ending.

I almost roll my eyes. It's a little too much like Romeo and Juliet.

"So why are you?"

"Because it's not safe for me to be around him. He'll see that when I'm gone and things can go back to normal for you guys."

Ian just shakes his head and my stomach drops.

"Listen, I'm sorry, for what it's worth. I didn't know I was going to fall in love with him and I definitely didn't know all *this* was going to happen."

"You're in love with him now?"

I pause.

"I am."

He chuckles under his breath. "Thought you were just using him."

Ouch.

"You know me better than that."

"Do I?" he counters.

"Yes . . ." I grumble, though, right now, I'm not sure what I know anymore. "Are you angry with me?"

"For running?" he asks and after a pause, he lets out a deep breath. "No. Sorry, I've just got a lot on my mind."

"Do you want to talk about it?"

He shakes his head.

"Well, if you do, I'm sure Mason would listen."

"Yeah, I'm sure he would." He runs a thumb over his lip, thinking. "You sure you don't need anything else? Food? When was the last time you ate?"

"I'll eat on the bus."

"You sure? Not always the best."

I offer him a smile. "I'm sure."

He falls silent, staring out the window ahead of him. There's a tension radiating through him that's not normally there, but I chalk it up to helping his best friend's girlfriend leave him.

"The street for the bus station was back that way," I murmur, absentmindedly staring out the window beside me as houses pass. We're heading toward Malibu. The complete opposite direction from where we need to go.

"I know."

I don't move, but the way he says it sends a shot of fear down my spine.

"Got to stop by the store real quick. Can't send you off without something to eat and drink."

"Really, I'm fine."

"Well . . . that's to be determined."

"What?" Icy panic seizes through me, but again, he offers me a calm, gentle smile.

"I mean with all the crazy shit going on. I know you think leaving will stop all of it, but . . . I don't know."

Oh . . .

"He loves you, you know?" Ian says after a moment, his voice quiet.

"I know."

"And you love him?"

I can't help the smile that graces my lips. "I do."

"Yet, you're willing to leave. Listen, Hannah, I've seen him with other women. He just . . . didn't care about making it work. I can see him trying for you, and it's strange to see him that way."

I don't know that I like where this conversation is going, but still, I nod to play along.

"He's my best friend, Hannah. You have to understand that."

"Ian, where are we going?"

"I told you—" he starts, but I cut him off.

"You've passed four gas stations that sell food."

He shakes his head. "We need something better."

"Where are you taking me?" I snap, rearing back in the seat to face him. He holds out his hand to caution me to calm down, but my heart is suddenly racing a mile a minute.

"Hannah," he warns. "You're overreacting."

"I'm overreacting to you driving me out to the middle of

nowhere?"

"We're near the pier. It's not that far."

"We're *supposed* to be back in downtown."

"Let me out," I demand and he doesn't budge. In fact, he slips into the turn lane and heads onto the highway. "*Ian*!"

No response.

I reach for Missy's phone, but he grabs my hand, stopping me.

"I wouldn't if I were you."

"What are you doing?" I jerk out of his grasp, and he just watches me, his jaw feathering as he takes us down the highway toward Malibu.

"I have to do this, Hannah."

"Ian, no you don't. Whatever you're planning, please." I can taste the panic in my voice. *Feel* the guilt pouring off him, but still, he doesn't stop.

Is he kidnapping me?

"You don't understand!" he snaps, voice louder than I've *ever* heard Ian get. Like he's panicking. "They've got my sister. My fucking sister," he whimpers, anger dissolving into tears.

"Ian, who?"

Fear seizes in my throat, my fight or flight reflexes working overtime to come up with a solution. I could duck out of the car, but we're on the freeway and if the fall at this speed didn't kill me, another car would.

"Hannah, the fucking cartel is after us. *You* brought them to us. I'm not stupid! Now they've got Jenna and I'll be damned if I sacrifice her for you."

"He trusted you," I whisper, tears cracking in my voice. "Mason trusted you and you're betraying him?"

"Yeah, and I gave him my all. Helping him with that fucking chop shop shit. Working late. Doing whatever I had to because that's what friends do. And you know what he did? He traded it all in for *you*. The source of all his problems."

In a lot of ways, he's right. I am the source of Mason's problems.

As much as he loves me and as much as I love him, I know it's true. He's put his life on the line for me countless times and yet, it's never enough. There's always someone or something else out to get me and who's there to pick up the pieces? To take a bullet to protect me?

Mason.

"He cares about you, Ian. If you're in trouble, we can help—"

"I don't need your fucking help," he spits, his earlier anguish turning to seething rage. "Haven't you ever noticed you leave a trail of bodies wherever you go, Hannah? It's no coincidence that your sister was exactly the same, only she didn't act innocent when they fell at her feet."

Tears burn in my eyes as the city lights of Los Angeles fade away behind us. As Mason fades away behind us.

"Stop."

"No, face your demons, Hannah. You're the one who created them."

"Do you really think this is what Jenna would want?"

"Don't fucking talk about her," he grits, hand tightening on the steering wheel.

"What do you think she'll say when she finds out you traded another person for her?"

"Shut the fuck up!" He bashes his hand against the steering wheel so hard, I expect the bones of his hand to splinter. "She wouldn't understand. She's just a kid. I have to do this," he says quietly, almost like he's speaking to himself.

"Mason will kill you when he finds out what you've done," I whisper. Tears burn as they slip down my face, but I don't move for fear of pissing him off even more. He's a man on the edge and I don't know if I would survive a crash going the speed we are on the highway.

"I'm doing him a favor. He'll realize once you're gone how toxic you are for him. His little poison apple."

The gun in my pocket digs into my stomach as if it's reminding me it's there. I can't shoot Ian. Ian who was nice to me when I first started at the shop. Who welcomed me. The Ian who's Mason's best friend.

I can't do that.

But . . . I'm also not willing to die for him.

"Pull over." Ian freezes when the cold steel presses to his temple. I can see the vein fluttering in his forehead as the reality of the situation sets in.

"You aren't going to shoot me. We're going seventy on the freeway."

"There's a lot of things I used to think I wouldn't do, Ian. Pull. The fuck. Over."

He shakes his head, pulling off to another highway that will take us outside the city limits. The cars are less here, the streetlights further apart. He doesn't slow down, but I can see his fingers flex on the steering wheel. Like he's going to try something.

"Ian, don't make me shoot you."

He runs his tongue over his teeth.

And then he jerks around and reaches for the gun.

I pull on the trigger and the sound ricochets around the car. Glass shatters and something warm and wet hits my face and slips down as the car skitters along the highway. My ears ring, my head spinning, as I struggle for the wheel, but his foot is on the gas and we aren't slowing down.

Fortunately, or unfortunately, we come to a crash against a dirt bank and the car topples over, crashing onto its roof and lurching me sideways. My head hits something, but I don't feel the pain as the adrenaline courses through me and the car crumples around us.

And finally, we come to a stop.

I can't look at Ian. I know he's dead. My hands are cut from the glass in the car, and the roof is caved in a bit. Everything is upside down and the car is smoking from under the hood. The airbags went off and smoke leaks from them, invading my lungs and cutting off my oxygen supply.

Fuck.

Fuck, fuck, fuck.

I have no idea where Melissa's phone is and there's fluid leaking from under the hood. I don't know how badly I'm injured, but a car is approaching, so I unbuckle myself and nearly fall on my face.

Slipping through the broken window is a painful experience. My limbs ache as the adrenaline wears off and I'm covered in blood and bits of Ian which makes everything worse. I don't even know where the gun is.

I crawl out into the dirt and suck in deep breaths of air, the smoke from the airbag burning my throat as I cough.

"Look what we have here," a sickening voice says above me.

I freeze, sputtering as tears burn in my eyes.

When I look up, it's into the eyes of Cortez.

"I've been waiting for you," he snickers, eyes dark and full of malice.

I suck in a deep breath, through the blood on my face. At this point, I don't even know if it's mine or Ian's.

"Oh, fuck."

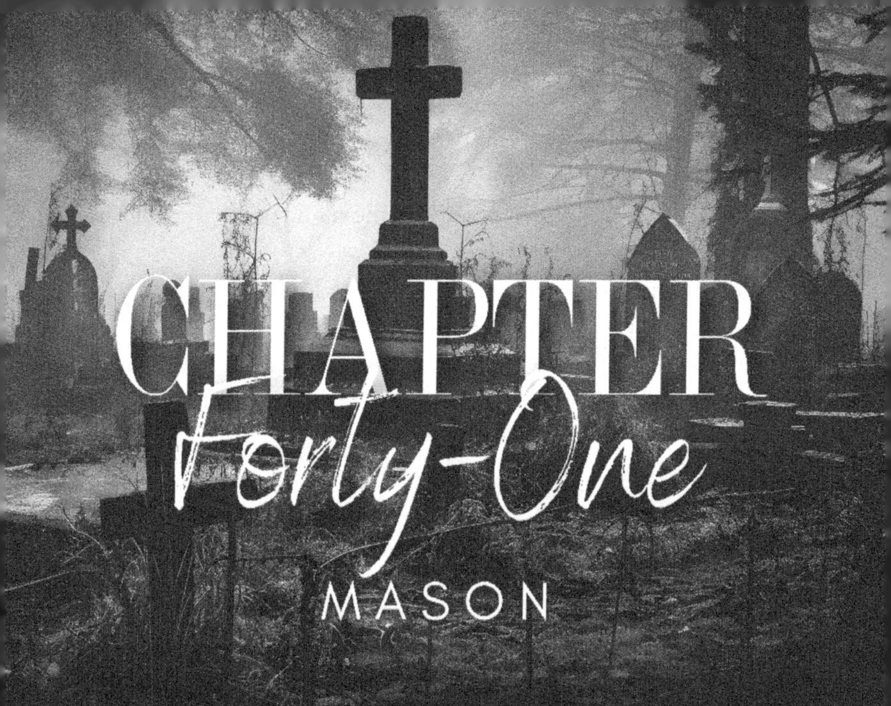

CHAPTER Forty-One

MASON

Something's wrong.

I know it the moment I open my eyes.

My eyes flicker and I gaze around the room, disoriented at first because I forgot we came to Mom's last night. Three in the morning. Reaching out for Hannah, my chest tightens. She's not there.

And then an iciness slips through my veins.

She's not fucking there.

Instantly, I'm wide awake, sitting up to look around the room. Nothing is moved. Her bag's still on the floor where we left it. Fuck, her perfume still lingers in the air, like she was just here.

The bathroom is dark. Empty. I check downstairs, but she's not there. She's not by the pool and she's not in the kitchen.

Something's not fucking right.

I search the house, even going as far as to knock on Mila's door and ask if she's in there, but she's not.

Slowly, a simmering poison seeps into my veins, but I settle it down because I don't know where she could have gone yet.

I pull out my phone. No messages.

Mason: Where are you?

It's when her phone lights up on the nightstand I fucking *know* she's gone.

I check the room again, thinking maybe I missed something, but there's nothing. Just the cold darkness where she should be.

She was right fucking there. I held her in my arms while we went to sleep. She couldn't have slipped out in the night. I would have woken up.

I was exhausted.

"*Fuck.*"

And then I spot it. A piece of paper tucked away in the bedsheets.

My hand shakes when I reach for it and when I see her elegant sprawling handwriting, it takes me a full minute to process what it even says.

This is me bleeding for you. I love you.

She's gone.

She's fucking gone.

"Fuck!"

I sweep the lamp from the bedside table and send it crashing into the wall beside the bed. My reflection in the mirror beside the bed seethes, overcome with violence. My fist shatters it in one hit, the tiny jagged pieces of glass raining down around my feet, but I don't care.

It only takes a second until Logan appears at the door, his eyes glinting black in the night.

"She's gone," I rasp, my chest tightening to the point of pain. "She's fucking gone."

As if on cue, his phone buzzes in his hand and he pauses, his eyes narrowing on the screen.

"It's three in the morning."

He stops to listen to whoever is on the other end of the line and his expression darkens past recognition.

Logan's eyes snap to mine.

"You're sure?"

Dread washes over me. My control barely holding together by a thin thread.

Don't fucking say it.

"Start tracing." He hangs up the phone, his tone reserved. Wary. "The cartel has her."

"Who?" My voice is calm. Quiet. Nothing like the nuclear meltdown bubbling to the surface in my veins.

Logan's eyes go dark and he clears his throat. "Ian."

And that's when my self-control finally snaps.

A deep roar bubbles up my throat, ending on aguish that feels like it might rip me to shreds. Without a second's hesitation, I grab the entire nightstand and throw it across the room until it shatters into pieces at Logan's feet.

This is all my fucking fault.

My vision goes red and hazy, my hands clenching to hit something. To break something. Destroy someone as badly as I am.

"Mason!" Savannah gasps, but Logan wraps an arm around her waist and pulls her back from the room. She stares at me in horror, but I don't stop. I can't.

They fucking took her.

And she let them.

Inky blackness seeps into my veins, caustic and burning full of rage and hate. With a guttural growl, I whip the dresser to the floor and it splinters into pieces. All sense of my humanity slips away until there's just a gaping black void full of wrath.

"Back," Logan orders Mila, who falls back into the hallway, her eyes wide and full of tears.

I grab a vase on the dresser and throw it against the wall so it shatters. And because that does absolutely nothing for me, I grab the chaise lounge in the corner of the room and topple that over, too.

My hearing fades as if I'm underwater, the current battering me down into the dark clutches below the light where nothing but the icy cold black can reach me.

My hands grab for anything in reach and I break it, too. I don't give a fuck what it is, if it's there, I'm shattering it until it lays in the ruins along with my fucking sanity.

She's gone. She's fucking gone and it's because of me.

When I'm done, my body aching and my breathing ragged, I look around at the destruction—my destruction—and fall to my knees.

A throat clears and another vase is thrust in front of me.

"Break this one, too," Mom says, her soft voice absolute. "They're ugly. I always hated them."

When I don't take it, she shrugs and tosses it, watching as the bits of ceramic scatter across her hardwood floor.

We sit there, on our knees, my chest heaving and her silent.

"There's something else."

Mom's gaze snaps to Logan but he and I both understand how this works.

Bad shit happens in threes.

"Ian?" I grit, my teeth clenched to the point of nearly snapping my jaw.

Logan meets my gaze from where he stands, my sister's wide eyes peeking out over his shoulders.

"Dead," he murmurs, expression tinged with something close to pride and acceptance. "She shot him with your gun."

Pride swells in my chest, but it's tainted by something darker.

That motherfucker betrayed me. My best fucking friend betrayed *us.* I trusted him with her life. *My fucking soul* and he desecrated her.

Fuck, I want to bleed the life from his eyes.

"I have it on good authority that they have his little sister, too. Jenna."

Truthfully, I don't give a fuck who else they have. They have *my* girl. My vision blurs at all the possible things they could do to her.

What they could have already done to her.

"They blackmailed him. If that means anything to you," Logan offers, but he knows it doesn't mean shit. I've known Jenna for years. The fact that he wouldn't come to me, tell me what they were trying to do, fills me with an unchecked fury.

I want to rip their throats out with my teeth. Watch them drown in their own blood.

"Shut the fuck up," I grit. I would have never done that shit to him. To anyone. I would have found a way to get Hannah back or died trying.

"This isn't helping," Savannah insists, but I just chuckle darkly and shake my head until the tension radiating through me feels like it's going to break my spine in half.

"Don't you fucking get it?" I snap and she flinches at the tone of my voice. "It's always been her. If she dies, you better find a way to take me the fuck out, too, because I won't stop until every last one of them is dead."

Logan stares at me, black gaze flinting in the darkness.

"I know where she is. I just need a way in."

I shake my head. It's not enough. Every second wasted is another that she could be dead.

I'm going to get her back.

"I don't give a fuck who you have to bribe, who you have to kill, what you have to fucking do. Find a way."

Something devilish gazes back at me from Logan's eyes. "Actually, I have a way . . . it's just illegal. Could get us in a lot of trouble."

"Logan—" Savannah interjects, but surprisingly, Mom cuts her off.

"She's one of us," Mom says, eyes stoney. "Whatever you have to do . . . do it."

And then she leans in and lowers her voice.

"Pull yourself together," she instructs, voice barely audible over the sound of blood rushing through my ears. She places a hand on my shoulder, her eyes firm and her gaze hard. "And fucking find her."

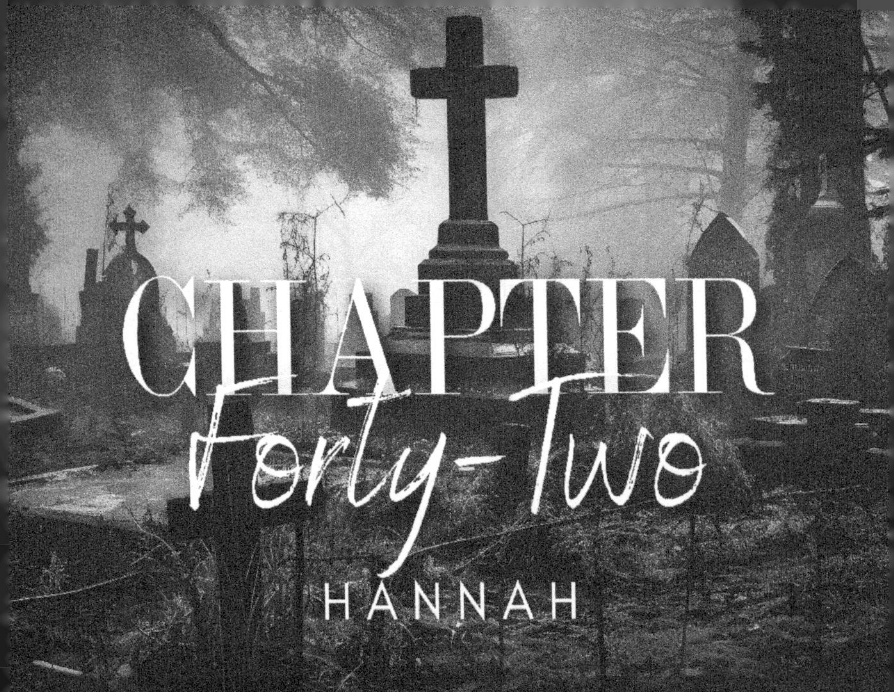

CHAPTER Forty-Two

HANNAH

"What do you think the governor's daughter would fetch?"

I can't open my eyes. I can't move my body. The only thing I can do is listen as I float along. My head is throbbing, pounding with the vibration of whoever is speaking.

"Pretty penny. You think the carpet matches the drapes?"

"Only one way to find out." A sinister chuckle shakes me to my core and I will myself to wake up. Force myself to open my eyes, but nothing happens. I'm trapped in my own body as a slimy hand slides up my stomach under my T-shirt, groping my breast through my bra with a rough hand. Bile climbs in my throat, but I can't push him away.

Wake the fuck up, Hannah!

"What do you think you're doing?" a sharp voice snaps from nearby, followed by the loud crash of a door slamming. "You were explicitly told this one is off limits."

I know that voice.

"We were just looking."

"Well look elsewhere. There are special plans for this one."

Special plans? As in pump me full of whatever drug they choose and post me for sale for all their "buyers" to ogle and rape?

Wonderful.

I focus on my fingers, begging them to move even just a millimeter. Just so I know I'm not paralyzed from the accident.

Fuck. The accident. I forgot.

Visions of the missing part of Ian's head flash through my mind, my stomach turning and saliva pooling in my mouth.

Blood, Jenna, more blood, the sound of glass shattering.

"Jesus Christ," someone groans when I lurch to life, vomiting over the side of whatever operating table I'm on. My vision swims, my head spinning as I wretch the empty contents of my stomach. "Well, she's awake."

"It's about time."

"Lay back," the voice of a woman snaps and someone shoves me down until my head hits the table below. Bright lights sit above me, nearly blinding me, but a face looms over me, blocking it out.

"Hannah, I'm Doctor Pat. I've been treating your wounds."

"Where . . . where am I?" I'm surprised at the croakiness of my own voice.

"You're where you're supposed to be," she answers, pushing the horn-rimmed glasses back up her nose. "You had a nasty accident. Don't you think it would have been better if you would have just complied?"

"Are you going to kill me?"

"Well, *I'm* not. I don't know what their plan is for you, yet, but I do know . . . you're *special*." She says that last part like she can't for the life of her figure out why.

Tears burn in my eyes as she dabs alcohol on a cut on my arm. I don't care. I barely feel it. It's what's inside that's ripping me to shreds.

Mason. He probably knows I'm gone by now. God only knows what happened when I didn't show up. Tears burn in my eyes and a rush of agony courses through me.

"I don't want to die."

"Well, we all die eventually," Nurse Ratched says as matter of fact as she would speak about the weather. "We all have sins to pay for. Just sometimes, we end up paying for the sins of others, too."

"Why are you doing this? My mother?"

"Your mother will pay for her sins, too. As did your sister. My only concern is getting your arm bandaged so I can go home. I'm going to miss my show because of you."

In another world, she could be someone's mother or grandmother. She could be sweet and bake cookies and do other fun shit old people like to do. Not in this universe, though.

"Listen," I whisper because the two assholes that tried to grope me are across the room, chatting about a football team. "They're going to come after you. No one here is safe."

She fixes me with a sardonic look.

"My, you Gaines' are really all the same, aren't you?"

My heart drops.

"You know why I do this, Hannah?"

Somehow, I have the grace to shake my head.

"Because they allow me to do whatever I want. They pay far better than anything you'll be able to scrounge together and this isn't a regulated facility. If you die, well, then you die."

She finishes the bandage on my arm and sits back to admire her handiwork. Ironically, my bandage has princesses on it.

I don't feel like a fucking princess.

"A word of advice," she clucks, cleaning up the mess she left from working on me. "Don't fight them. It'll only make it worse."

And then, as if I'm a piece of trash, she claps her hands.

"She's done. Take her away."

"Wait!" I rush, but they're already coming for me. I try to scramble from the table, but my head spins and I wobble the moment my feet touch the floor, nearly passing out.

Nurse Ratched has the audacity to hand me a pack of crackers and a single bottle of water.

"So you don't die before they're ready for you."

Tweedledee and Tweedledum grab me under the arms and practically drag me through the small surgical room. I struggle against their hold, but I'm too weak and they're much bigger than me. I can't fight them.

"Let's go, princess," one mocks, and the other laughs.

I'm really regretting not shooting Ian sooner now.

They haul me through a narrow corridor straight out of a horror film. Complete with busted wiring and small puddles of standing water, which they have no care to avoid. By the time they reach the end, there's an open door, the blackness beyond looming out at me.

"Please, no," I beg, my heart lurching in my chest when I realize their intentions. "Please don't put me in there. Chain me to the wall out here or something."

"*Explicit* orders," the second guy says cheerfully. "This is where we were told to put you, so this is where you're going."

"Wait!" I screech when I'm thrust forward, stumbling into the darkness and falling to my hands and knees. I wince at the stinging cuts in my palms. The accident wasn't kind to me and I'm sore and bruised. I might have a broken rib or two from the lance of pain in my side.

Still . . . none of that compares to the heart-stopping, all-consuming fear that takes hold of me when they start to shut the door on me.

"Sleep tight, Hannah Banana."

And then it's dark. The only light comes from the small crack at the bottom, but it's not enough.

"Wait!" I screech, pounding my fist on the door, but it does nothing. No one comes to my rescue. No sounds can be heard in the hallway beyond my own personal hell.

I'm alone in the darkness.

You've broken the rules, so you must be punished.

"Go away," I murmur, clenching my eyes shut and wrapping my

arms around myself.

You can come out once you've learned your lesson. Repeat after me. We don't tell strangers about Mommy's work.

I fall to the ground, skittering back against the wall, sucking in shallow, painful breaths as the voices grow louder, echoing around the room.

This is it, I think, clutching a hand over my pounding heart.

There's no one coming to save me. Not my mother. Not Missy.

Not Mason.

I'm well and truly alone.

You're a whore.

No one will ever want you.

—I'm far scarier than anything lurking in the dark.

I slump to the floor, pressing my cheek against the cool, battered concrete. They even took his hoodie from me.

My last piece of him.

Mason's gone now. Home's gone, too. I guess, my consolation prize is that he won't be hounded by the cartel anymore. At least, I hope. Maybe if I'm not in the world he'll be able to live the peaceful life he always dreamed about. He and his family can relax. Be happy, for once.

God, I miss him.

Tears burn in my eyes, and since I'm alone, I let them fall. My brain is foggy, covered in a haze as unconsciousness threatens to pull me under. I welcome it.

All I want to do is fade away.

Would Mason think I was a coward? Would he be disappointed that I wasn't up trying to foolishly pick a lock on a door we both know isn't going to open? Would he be angry with me for falling back asleep?

I hope so. I always secretly loved those hurricane eyes when he was pissed off.

"I love you," I whisper to the darkness because there's no way

I'll ever get to say it to him again. I just hope he realizes, one day, I didn't want to leave him.

Because it's time to face facts.

I'm going to die here.

CHAPTER Forty-Three

MASON

"You sure this shit is going to work?"

Logan tosses his cigarette butt out the window.

"No." He pauses for a moment, his gaze hard as he surveys the parking lot in front of us. "Do we have another choice?"

"No."

He nods, reaching for the handle on his door before stopping. We've been out here for an hour, going over the plan. A plan that could go one of two ways, neither promising a free life after.

"Remember, Mr. Walker," he nods to the nametag on my contraband uniform. "You work for the California Department of Corrections and this inmate is already dying."

"Yeah," I murmur, climbing from the passenger seat of the old prison van, a cold indifference settling in my chest. "Yeah, he fucking is."

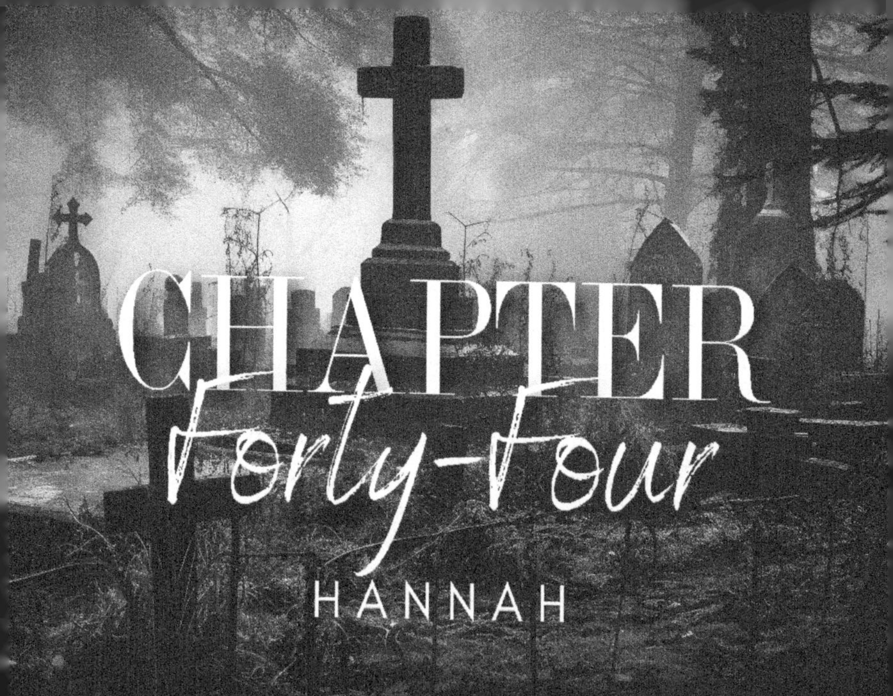

CHAPTER *Forty-Four*

HANNAH

You know those times when everything stops?

Where you have no idea how long you've been out of your mind with no end to the proverbial spinning and the only thing you can do is lay around and wait?

I've made a friend. Well . . . I wouldn't call him a friend, but he hasn't tried to eat me yet.

There's a spider in the corner of my closet the size of my fist. While my fist isn't very big as far as human hands go, the spider is massive. After my eyes adjusted to the near-pitch-black around me, I noticed him climbing down the wall, as if he were coming to check me out.

I don't blame him. My prison is his house and he's being polite by letting me stay here until they decide what to do with me.

It's been hours . . . I think. Or days.

I can't tell which.

By now, everyone will know that I'm gone and Mason is probably already on his way to feeling the weight lifted off his shoulders. He can get his garage back. He can get his life back. His family can be safe while mine lies desecrated in the ruins of what I believe is an old church.

I have no idea where I am. I don't even know *what* I am at this point.

Maybe I'm a spider, too, and I've just never realized it. Twisting little webs of lies and getting people caught in them. Just like Ian said. I leave a trail of bodies wherever I go.

No one comes to check on me during my time in the spider's enclosure. I don't even hear anyone walk by. The only sound comes from the slight *tap, tap, tap* on the outside of the door every now and then.

That's how I know I'm going crazy.

Missy's gone. Melissa. Whatever her name is. Mom's probably out planning her next greatest idea and Michael? Well, who the hell cares, anyway?

It's just me and Mr. Legs—my name for my spider companion.

That is . . . until the drag of feet sounds outside my door.

The first beams of light against my eyes make me nauseous, but it's the face that looms in with features I can just barely make out that really curdles the shitty stale crackers in my stomach.

Fucking. Michael.

"Hannah, sweetheart," he murmurs, his arms coming around me as if I'm a small child.

I open my mouth to tell him to let go of me, but the ringing in my ears stops me.

Fuck. My head hurts.

"I just found out you were here. I'm sorry I didn't come sooner," he murmurs, brushing the hair back from my face before catching a tear under my eye with his thumb.

It's so delicate and tender, I almost forgive him for ever thinking he could force me to marry him.

—Said no woman, ever.

"Let go of me, you freak," I grit between my teeth, feebly

shoving at his arms. He releases me, albeit begrudgingly and I fall back to my ass on the hard concrete floor.

Mr. Legs climbs the wall again and I almost laugh. Good. Michael's not welcome in his home.

"Hannah," Michael growls under his breath. "I'm here to get you out."

"No, you're not," I scoff. "You're working with them."

"I'm going to have you moved somewhere more comfortable."

"Don't," I snap, sliding back against the wall. "I'd rather stay here with the massive spider on the wall. I can actually *trust* him."

"You're acting like a child."

"Maybe."

"I can get you a bed. Something to eat. Get you out of those blood-stained clothes."

I happen to like my clothes, thank you very much. Very apocalypse-chic.

"Why, so you can try to force me to marry you?"

He falls silent, searching my face.

"I wouldn't have forced you."

"That's not what you said that night at the warehouse when you were burning the bodies of the women you raped and murdered. Or did you forget?"

"Whatever you saw—"

"*What I saw*," I correct, "is you working for my mother to traffic people. *Living* people. At least they were alive before you showed up."

"They were members of a cult, Hannah. They couldn't be allowed to hurt anyone else."

I shake my head. "They weren't. Their parents were. You know I met one of the men that you tortured? Dawson? Really sweet, but so scared and unstable after you and Missy got to him. It's no wonder he tried to kill me. Whatever you guys had him hopped up on didn't help either."

"Just . . . black dahlia," Michael rushes. "It kept them calm."

"Oh, because rape when they're unconscious makes it *so* much better."

"I didn't rape anyone."

"No? What about my sister?"

I can see in his eyes the moment he realizes I know too much. No matter what he does, I won't love him and for that, I may as well be dead to him.

Like a black cloak was dropped over his face, the Michael I know is replaced. This Michael, the *real* Michael, is pure evil.

"You know what's ironic?"

I wait.

"I've fucked your mother, your sister, and you. Out of all of you, though, your cunt was the sweetest. Imagine what it'll earn me on the market?" He chuckles to himself. "Almost makes fucking Beatrice for the rest of my life worth it knowing Carpenter will have to live with the knowledge that some rich old bastard is raping his pretty whore every night. Maybe I'll even send him a little video. Really make you scream." He pauses, gauging my reaction. "You think he'd cry? Watching someone else rape that sweet little pussy? Or do you think he'd get hard?"

I don't know why. I've never been a spitter, but I rear back, spitting directly in his eye.

He deserves it.

He pauses, slips a piece of Mason's hoodie out of his pocket—the part that has the Carpenter's Auto logo on it and wipes his face, before tossing it to the floor at my feet.

His eyes flash to the side to Mr. Legs and then, with the palm of his hand, he crushes him, his lifeless body falling to the ground beside me.

"Guess, you really are all alone—"

A bang rings out in the air, so loud, my head spins. My hearing goes and something hot and sick hits my face.

Please tell me that's not more brain . . .

But, when I open my eyes, it's to Michael's corpse on the floor, a hole in the center of his head and his lifeless eyes staring back at me.

I scream, but the sound doesn't reach my ears as Cortez and his men stride toward us and grip Michael by the ankles, tugging him back out into the hallway.

"Never liked that guy," Cortez snickers.

And then the lights go out, again.

Only this time, there's no Mr. Legs to keep me company.

"Time to go."

The heavy metal door creaking open does *nothing* for the pounding ache in my temple. I tried to sleep, but the stench of metallic blood made me sick to my stomach and I couldn't do it.

"Don't make me drag you," the asshole at the door warns, dark eyes flashing venomously.

Dick.

Begrudgingly, I force myself to clamber to my feet. My blood sugar is low because I haven't had anything to eat or drink since my generous rations from Nurse Rachted ran out God only knows how long ago, so my head spins with the weight of my brain.

It's a shame someone so attractive is working in a business like this. My escort is tall, nearly as big as Mason and handsome Mason, and handsome. Like darkness personified, with tattoos and a dangerous scar that spans from his cheek to below the lines of their suit.

Whoever this man is, he's seen some shit.

The big asshole grabs my arm and drags me through the tacky puddle of blood on the floor and into the hallway beyond my prison cell. Michael's corpse lays on the floor beside the door. They didn't even move him. I guess I should be thankful they didn't just shove him inside with me. I can tell it hasn't been that long because he doesn't yet give off a stench, but he will soon.

Somehow, as I pass him, I feel nothing for what used to be my best friend.

Guess he shouldn't have killed Mr. Legs.

My eyes burn in what looks like the later evening sun streaming through the small slits that are supposed to be windows at the top of the walls. The place is old, definitely abandoned, and not unlike the warehouse where they were murdering men and women and burning them in an incinerator.

"Where are you taking me?"

My escort ignores me as if I don't exist.

"I have to pee."

He lets out a sigh and keeps walking.

"Hey," I snap, "I have to use the bathroom. You've kept me locked in that room for hours."

"Fifteen to be exact." He stops by a door and waves me toward it with a cocky smile. "Make it quick."

I swallow past the dryness in my throat and step into the room, wracking my mind to do the simple math of what the hell time it is. Seven? Eight?

I let out a sigh of relief at the sight of a barely functional bathroom. If I make it out of this, let me tell you, I'll never complain about using a public toilet again.

A bucket at the bottom of a landfill would be cleaner.

I start to shut the door, a plan weaving its way through my mind when a boot stops it, nearly jarring me to fall over.

"It stays open."

"I can't pee with an audience."

He cocks a brow, like a father determined to teach his child a lesson. "Then I guess you don't really have to pee, then, do you?"

Asshole.

I force a breath to calm myself, wincing at the pain in my throat as my plan slips further and further away.

Think, Hannah.

"Try anything and I'm authorized to do whatever I see fit," he warns, standing with his hands clasped in front of him like a bouncer at a club. "And I've got nothing left to lose." He shrugs, as if raping me in my disheveled state means nothing to him.

I guess . . . in his line of work, it probably doesn't.

"Are you going to rape me?"

"Fortunately, for you, I prefer blondes."

With a humiliation I'm not accustomed to, I do my business under the careful eye of the creep who watches me like my peeing is most amusing to him.

"See? That wasn't so bad."

"Yes, performance art is definitely my thing," I mock, wiping the smirk off his face.

Taking me by the shoulder, he shoves me down the hall in the opposite direction of my closet hell, this time, staying behind me to watch me like a predator.

"I don't know where I'm going."

"Straight, obviously."

"Well, I'm hungry."

"And a prisoner. Prisoners get food when we feel like it and right now, I don't know that I'm inclined."

I know what he's referring to. A blow job for a scrap of bread.

"I'd rather starve."

"Be my guest."

Silently, I mock him because it makes me feel better amidst the turmoil raging around me.

I miss home. I miss the garage. I miss . . . I miss Mason.

God, I hope he's okay.

I hope he doesn't forget about me. I hope he finds someone to settle down with. Has babies because I know he'd make the cutest ones. I hope they all have his eyes.

A tear falls down my cheek, but I hastily wipe it away because I'll be damned if this asshole sees me cry. I suck in a deep breath, willing my emotions to dissipate and focus on placing one foot in front of the other, even if it means marching toward my own death.

"Through the doors."

Two double metal doors sit at the end of the hall and with a sinking feeling in my gut, I push through them, stepping into what is definitely an exuberant, destructed church. There are holes in the ceiling showcasing the sunlight outside. The walls are peeling from being painted a long time ago and there are piles of dust and dead plants growing through the concrete under our feet.

"Well, well, well . . ."

My spine stiffens at the voice that greets me from the other end of the room.

Cortez.

"There you *are*," he beams, holding out his arms as if I'm the prized pig at the local fair. My escort shoves me to my knees on the hard concrete and I wince, but crumple to the ground under his weight. "Let me tell you, Ms. Gaines, you are one tough cookie to kidnap. You killed my mole."

I shrug. "He deserved it."

Cortez chuckles, shaking his head. "He probably did. I mean, who rats on the man that's like their brother? That's low, even for me."

"Can't imagine many things are lower than you."

He only smiles. "I like you. I can see why Carpenter was so adamant about keeping you."

"What do you want?"

"Well, it's not a matter of what I want, but what the people want." The escort kneels behind me, wrapping an arm around my neck to hold me still while the other bands my arms behind my back. Cortez watches on, cocking his head with that same arrogant smile.

"I'm not heartless. I got you a present." He looks to the back of the room. "Bring out contestant number two!" he yells like a gameshow host.

A scream echoes throughout the room, followed by the movement of footsteps on the concrete.

"Get your hands off me you lousy son of a bitch!"

Oh, great . . .

My mother.

"I always hated presents. Especially when they're wrapped in sinister lies."

"Well, I don't think you'll be getting any more after today, so you better start showing some appreciation now. I know we will."

My mother is shoved to her knees beside me, her expensive Alexander McQueen pantsuit stained with blood splatter and scuffed.

If she was close enough, I'd bite her.

"This wasn't the deal," she spits, completely disregarding me.

"We made a new deal."

"You think I didn't plan for your treason?" Mom's face grows red with rage out of the corner of my eye. Can't really move my head when it's in a headlock. "You don't think the entire country isn't going to come looking for me?"

"Funnily enough," Cortez chimes. "I don't actually give a fuck. If they do manage to find you, it'll be in pieces scattered from here to the equator. Same with your daughter."

"Do it, then," she challenges and I resist the urge to roll my eyes. "Shoot her. Let me go and I'll make you a very wealthy man, Cortez."

Cortez just stares at her in awe, then at me.

"*Wow* . . . and here I thought that slimy little mole was bad. Governor Gaines, willing to sacrifice her daughter to save her own skin."

"Do it. She's no daughter of mine."

Cortez's smile vanishes in the blink of an eye and before anyone can anticipate it, he pulls a gun out of his pocket and aims it in the center of my mother's forehead.

"I would love to. You always did love to bitch."

"Not yet," a soft, cool voice rings out from somewhere behind us. "They're mine."

The click clack of heels sounds on the old concrete floor and as they near, I catch a whiff of perfume.

Chanel No. 5.

My stomach lurches, saliva pooling in my mouth when she steps around where I can see her.

Melissa Gaines.

My sister.

"You look positively perplexed, Hannah Banana."

My words catch in my throat.

"One big family reunion, isn't it?" Melissa chuckles sweetly, looking back and forth between our mother and me like we're pests invading her home.

"Melissa—" Mom starts.

"No!" Melissa screeches face morphing into something sinister. "You covered up my disappearance, *Mom*. What was that about? Were you ashamed of me?"

"Yes," Mom admits, voice shaking in the face of what she created. "I was. I still am."

"Good," Melissa sneers. "Always trying to protect Hannah. Hannah this, Hannah that. I was your daughter, too."

"You were. We just . . ." Mom's voice cracks. "I loved you just the same, you were just so hard to handle sometimes."

"Oh, you hated me from the day I was born. So long as you had your perfect," Melissa stops in front of me, moving a strand of my hair. I flinch against her touch and she snickers. "Beautiful daughter, you didn't care."

"I did care—"

"You did a piss poor job of showing it. Shoving me in that cage? Really?"

Nothing is making sense right now.

"And *you*," Melissa's ire is turned on me. "Always trying to be the good girl with the good grades and the hot boyfriends. There was never any room for me at that house. Not unless it came to abuse and then, you can bet your ass I was first in line."

I resist the urge to roll my eyes.

"We were both abused, Missy—"

"It's Melissa."

"Okay . . . whatever. We were both abused. It wasn't just you that got locked in that closet."

Melissa smiles, her lips cocking up at the side. "No, it wasn't. Except, I also got the board. The rotten food. The slaps out of nowhere. You only had to eat it once. I had it most of my life."

"I was trying to help you—"

"Shut up, you sadistic bitch," Melissa snaps, voice cold. "You were trying to make the perfect little daughters, so we wouldn't tell anyone what you did."

"Missy," Mom warns, but Melissa can't be stopped.

"Haven't you ever wondered how Dad *died*, Hannah? What happened to me when I put one *toe* out of line?"

I freeze, ice filling my veins.

"She's trying to get into your head, Hannah," Mom chimes, voice panicked beneath the cool, calm surface. "You know her, she'll say whatever she has to, to get you to listen to her."

"That's rich coming from you, Mother," Melissa chuckles darkly. "She poisoned him and watched the life bleed from his eyes. When Marcus found out, I confronted her and you can bet I was locked in a cage in one of her warehouses shortly after."

Melissa drops to her knees in front of me.

"Michael saved my life, you know? He was sweet on me, so he'd come in, I'd suck his cock, and he'd let me out. I helped with a couple of his . . . special cases. The ones that were too headstrong for the black dahlia to take it's hold."

"You're too easily manipulated, sweetheart," Mom coos, her

voice changing to that same, sickeningly sweet soft tone that she used to use when she was explaining away her guilt over punishing us. "You listen to her because you love too hard. Don't let her lie to you now."

I look back and forth between the two, my heart thumping heavily in my chest. The man holding my head tightens his grip when Melissa leans in, forcing me to look at her. The same brown eyes that had once brought me comfort now make me want to vomit.

"Hannah. You and I are twins. You know me better than anyone. Would I do those things they're accusing me of?"

I swallow hard over the lump in my throat—a difficult task considering the man holding my head in a vice grip.

I stare into my sister's eyes and finally, everything falls into place.

"You're a monster," I breathe and she stills. The only sound being the shuffling of the cartel watching on idly. "Did you cut off your own finger so everyone would think you were dead?"

Melissa chuckles, holding up a hand dressed in a black diamond-encrusted prosthetic in the place of what used to be her middle finger. The end is sharp, a pointy nail coming out like a knife.

"Oh, that . . . Dear Michael helped. Tell me, did Monica Parker *scream* when she found it?"

"Why maim yourself? So you could stay relevant?"

"Had to get you on the hunt, somehow, sister. *Especially* after you ran off with that mongrel Carpenter." And then she whimpers, just like she did on the phone that night, so long ago. "Hannah, *please* . . . someone's going to *kill me*. Michael and I had fun with that one."

"Mason's more of a man than you will ever have the good fortune of meeting."

She hunkers down, voice dripping in candy-coated venom. "You know, when we decided to go into business together, he would go down on me for hours."

"Shame it took so long," I reply sweetly. "Must be the drugs."

"The black Dahlia . . ." she starts dramatically. "Is an elixir of the gods. Shame you could never handle such a thing."

"Let me guess, you're still drinking it. You know, you might ask if they can insert an IV. Since you can't seem to live without it, and all."

"Oh, I will have *plenty*. There won't be a need. You see, when Parker went to prison, he passed that portion of his business on to me. Haven't you wondered where I've been all this time, Hannah Banana?"

"Actually, it was a nice break from the psychopath I used to call a sister."

Melissa's expression never changes, but even so, I can see the exact moment I no longer mean anything to her.

The moment she decides I'm not her sister, anymore.

"I'm bored . . ." she purrs. "Kill her."

She says it so quick and pungently that for a brief second, no one moves.

Then, the grip on my neck tightens and the cold sensation of a steel barrel digs into my temple.

"I wouldn't do that if I were you."

The voice that rings out behind us may as well be God coming down to rescue me. It certainly feels that way. Though I can't see him, I can *feel* him, and a shiver of grief racks through me.

There's no way we both make it out of this alive.

"Mason, no!" I screech, fighting against the man's hold, but I can't move. I'm only strangling myself.

"It's okay, baby." Mason's voice is both a symbol of hope and a promise of death.

Melissa's gaze snaps to somewhere in the room behind me and then for the first time since she kidnapped me, it falters.

"Marcus . . ." she whispers like she was given the biggest gift in the world.

Marcus? Marcus fucking Parker? You've got to be kidding me.

I jerk in the hold of my jailer, but he only tightens his grip. I need to see him. I need to see Mason. Make sure he's okay.

"Don't . . ." my escort grits under his breath, so quiet, I can barely hear him.

Strange . . .

"You can have him. I want Hannah."

Melissa doesn't look at me as she steps past me, there's a click and suddenly she stops.

"One more step and I'll blow his head off, right here."

"My man can snap her neck before you ever get a shot off."

"Maybe," Mason replies cooly. "But I'll make sure there's nothing left for you to even scrape off the floor if you do."

"My love," Parker's voice sounds strained. Choked, even. "It's been so long."

"It has," Melissa chimes, sounding jaded. "I've missed you."

God, give me a break.

I roll my eyes and the man holding my head chuckles under his breath. At least someone agrees with me.

"I know beautiful, but I'm here now. Just give her over."

Melissa pauses, her lips pursing. I still know her well enough to know what she's thinking. The love of her life or the family that ruined her?

"If you try *anything*," Melissa says after a long moment. "I'll slice her throat and drown you in her blood."

My heart hammers in my chest as the silence drags on.

"Release her."

The man behind me loosens his grip and I fall forward, catching myself on my hands. The cuts on my palms scream out in pain, but it's not enough to drown out the incessant need to get to Mason.

Carefully, I climb to my feet, teetering from low blood sugar, and slowly make my way toward the love of my life who looks at me with a burning adoration behind a mask of sinister indifference.

I pass Parker on the way, who eyes me reproachfully as I go. He looks like shit. His hair has thinned in his time in prison and his skin is pale and sunken. Almost gray.

A walking corpse.

Serves him right.

As soon as I'm close enough, Mason grabs me without a second glance and places me behind him. I soak in his scent, tears pooling in my eyes. Leather, smoke, and spice. I never thought I'd see him again.

This isn't how this is supposed to work. I'm supposed to be saving him. Not the other way around.

But fuck if it isn't great to see him.

"Mason," Mom chimes, still on her knees. "You're not going to leave me here, are you?"

"You know, Laura. Some people just shouldn't be parents."

"You fucking asshole!" she screams and Mason's jaw ticks, but he doesn't say a word. Instead, his hand at his back releases mine and he grabs the pistol there.

And before any of us can blink an eye, he raises it and fires two shots.

One for Melissa. One for Parker.

Mom screams as blood coats the side of her face, the cartel erupts in shouts and gunfire and the FBI swarms the room before any of them can even think about moving.

And there in the middle of all the chaos stands Logan Prince, pointing the barrel of his gun down into Marcus Parker's open, glassy eyes.

And then he shoots him again, just for good measure.

"Governor Gaines," an FBI agent says, stepping up to lift my mother off the ground, who's still shaking and covered in the blood of her daughter. "You are under arrest for your involvement in human trafficking, drug trafficking, as well as first-degree murder."

Mom's eyes go wide.

"I didn't kill anyone!" she shouts. "It was them, I didn't do it!"

Logan snickers, the sound dark and caustic. "Not for the women you had murdered. That's for a different charge. This one . . . is for your husband."

Mom's face goes beat red and she starts screaming profanities as they haul her toward the exit.

"I'm the goddamned governor of this state! You can't arrest me . . ."

Her voice trails off as they haul her to wherever she's going, but I imagine, she'll probably scream at them until her voice goes hoarse.

And finally, Mason turns to look at me.

—and everything in me crumples.

"It's over now."

He nods once. "I know."

I suck in a breath, though it feels like it stops in my windpipe.

"I'm in love with you, you know?"

His gaze burns with an intensity that nearly knocks me on my ass.

"I know."

"Hold me?"

"Get the fuck over here."

He grabs me around the waist and hoists me up into his arms, crushing me against his chest. I wrap my legs around him and he doesn't let go, falling to the ground on his knees.

"*Fuck*," he groans softly, burying his head in my neck and inhaling deeply. I'm sure I stink, but he doesn't seem to care. "I thought I fucking lost you."

For a moment there, I thought he did, too.

"I'm so sorry for leaving you. I'm sorry for Ian and for making you go through that. I'm sorry—"

"Shut the fuck up," he rasps and then he's crushing his lips against mine and now, my head is definitely spinning.

Mason kisses me like it's the first time. The last time. The only time. And he doesn't stop until I'm sure my heart is either going to beat out of my chest or my lungs will collapse.

"I'm so fucking in love with you," he grits against my lips. "But if you ever do something that fucking selfless and stupid again, I'll tie you to our bed until we're old and gray."

I press feverish kisses to his lips in between each word.

"Never again," I promise and this time, I mean it. "You and me?"

"Fucking always. You and me, baby."

And then . . . like most things, all good things must come to an end.

A shot from somewhere up high rings out in the air and Mason's face is suddenly covered in red spots. I panic, the surge of adrenaline rushing through me rendering me speechless as his eyes go wide.

And then everything erupts in blinding pain.

I sputter and Mason screams something, but I can't hear him.

Did I . . . Did I just get shot?

I don't know how it happens, just that I'm on my back on the dirty floor again, staring up at the prism-colored ceiling of broken stained glass before Mason's looming over me.

I take in his face because this really might be the last time I see him. I can't feel the spot where I was shot. Just pain. It engulfs my body in burning lava as if I swallowed the core of the earth.

"Hannah, don't fucking close your eyes!" I hear Mason bellow, but I'm so fucking tired and I really, really need a nap now.

Someone else screams something as my hearing fades in and out, but it's Mason's voice that I cling to.

"I swear to fucking God, Hannah. Don't you fucking die on me."

I don't want to, but . . . I also don't know if I have a choice.

Because again, bad things happen in threes.

CHAPTER Forty-Five

MASON

I don't move. I haven't moved in nearly eight hours. Doctors and nurses have come and gone with shift change, each coming in and saying the same shit. *She's in good hands*. My family has been in and out, all eyeing me warily before helping with whatever menial tasks they think are necessary. Even Puke showed up, flowers in hand that now sit on the table beside Hannah's hospital bed. Little fucker even shed a tear.

Still . . . I haven't moved.

The chair beside Hannah's bed is uncomfortable as fuck, but I refuse to leave her. Not again. I attempted to sleep, but there's too much disturbed energy circulating in my veins.

I lost her. Got her back. Nearly lost her again in the blink of a fucking eye.

Thank fuck Cortez is a bad shot.

He's dead now, but it does nothing to offer any sort of comfort. Not until she's awake and staring at me with those soft green eyes. Not until I fucking know she's real and not just some figment of my imagination.

The shuffling of boots on the hospital floor behind me cause me to snap around, ready to rip someone to shreds. It's been like this since we got here. I keep waiting for something else to happen; some proverbial shoe to drop, but it never does.

This can't be over, can it?

"It's me."

Christian eyes me, a dark expression in his gaze when he steps into the dark room. It's nearly dusk and the hospital is winding down, save for the nurses moving between the rooms.

"She know?"

I shake my head and he nods.

"Thank you . . ." I murmur. "Took a lot to go in there."

"Took a lot to kidnap one of California's most wanted criminals and make it look like an accident."

I shrug. "I had help."

"How's she doing?"

"Alive," I answer, though it feels like a lie. "Nothing major was hit, but she needed surgery to remove the bullet."

Christian's gaze is dark as he watches Hannah in the bed. "And the other?"

I know what he's referring to, but every time I think about it, blinding red-hot rage slips through me.

"They did a rape kit. Nothing, but we'll have to wait until she wakes up to know for sure."

Christian's face is grim and withdrawn. He's always been dark, sticking to the shadows, but now, he looks like a ghost. I understand it.

Helplessness. There was no way that fucking plan should have worked, and yet, it did. Now that every threat has been removed, it's hard to believe things could be normal.

Fuck, what even is normal?

"Any idea why Melissa Gaines did all this?"

"Fabricated this theatrical lie to send everyone on a wild fucking goose chase?" He waits for my answer. "Because she's a narcissist. Probably had untreated bipolar tendencies that only got worse with the drugs." I shake my head. Truthfully, I've been struggling to come up with my own resolutions to solve the mystery that is Melissa Gaines for the last eight hours. "She was so wrapped up in her own life and struggles that she was unreachable."

"And Laura Gaines was more worried about her public image than being a mother."

"Hannah and Melissa were dolls for her to play dress up with. Not people."

"Got to hand it to you, Hannah's a fighter. Even in there, she was ready to cut my dick off because she thought I was one of them. She'll come out of this."

I fucking hate that word. Fighter.

Fight to stay alive. Fight to be free. Fight for your next breath.

It's all the same, isn't it?

Just a euphemism used to bring about false hope.

"You'll be safe tonight."

"Your friend?"

He nods once but doesn't elaborate. I don't bother asking. Whoever Christian Cross's "friend" is took out Cortez before any of us could even see where the shot had come from.

"Mila know you're here?"

He pauses for a moment, before letting out a heavy breath.

"No."

"You want her to know you're here?"

"Haven't decided."

He looks as shitty as I feel. The dark circles under his eyes tell me he hasn't slept in days, much like the rest of us.

Hannah was in that church for a total of eighteen hours. In that time, Christian flew in from God only knows where, Logan and I kidnapped a maximum security prisoner, and I nearly lost my fucking mind before I got her back.

I never imagined shit could hurt this bad until my heart started walking around outside my body in the form of a little redhead with the prettiest fucking smile I've ever seen.

"Because I have to say it," I murmur, leaning back in the chair, holding tight to Hannah's hand on the side of the cot, even if she can't feel me. "I'll fucking kill you if you hurt her."

His jaw feathers and he looks down to Hannah before looking back at me.

"I'm doing this for her."

"We going to see you again?"

He pauses, his shoulders stiff. "Probably not."

And then he leaves.

I don't know how much time passes because my eyes are threatening to close on their own, but when a soft hand startles me awake, I lurch, nearly toppling the chair over in my haste to whirl on whoever got into the room.

But it's just a nurse.

"I'm not leaving her."

She purses her lips together, giving me that stern motherly look as if she wants to scold me.

Then . . . her gaze softens and she places a hand on my shoulder.

"I was just going to let you know we're bringing a cot for you to get some rest. Can't have you sleeping in that, can we?" Her gaze racks over me. "You're pretty big. It might be a little small, but you won't have to leave her."

She gives me a knowing wink before she disappears out the door.

A few moments later, an army cot is wheeled into the room and set up against the wall by the window. I fight sleep for another hour because I don't want to let go of her hand, but when I nod off again, nearly falling out of the damned chair, I concede.

I move it closer to Hannah's bed, just so I can fucking be near her and force myself to lay down. I watch her for awhile. The steady rise and fall of her chest. Like if I close my eyes, she'll be ripped away from me again.

Unfortunately, my body isn't on board.

The nurse was right. The cot's small, but it doesn't take long for me to close my eyes and finally, after more than twenty-four hours, I fall asleep.

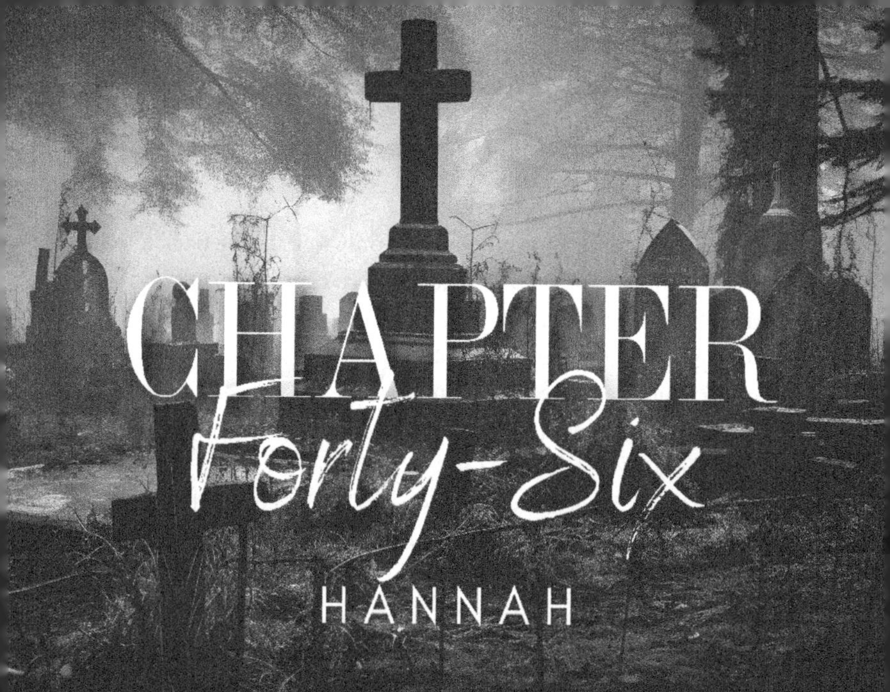

CHAPTER Forty-Six

HANNAH

There is an incessant beeping somewhere around me.

The first of my senses to return is my hearing and that beep settles a migraine in my forehead that feels like a woodpecker is beating the inside of my skull.

The second in my sense of scent.

The hospital.

—Explains the beeping.

The last time I woke up in a "medical facility" it wasn't any fun.

Now, whe n I open my eyes, it's to the dimly lit room of an *actual* hospital, complete with every monitor known to man.

My vision is blurry, but as it returns and I take in the room around me, my heart nearly stops in my chest.

Mason.

He's asleep, his arm draped over his stomach on what looks like the tiniest cot in the world. He's facing me as if he fell asleep watching me. Like I might disappear again. He looks so handsome, though the dark shadows around his eyes tell me he's exhausted and guilt washes through me.

But is he real?

Did I really survive that?

Carefully, I attempt to sit up in bed, only to collapse back to what has to be the most comfortable mattress I've ever slept on.

Maybe I'm just tired.

I try again and this time, pain blooms from a spot on my shoulder and I grunt, but it's nothing compared to the screeching of the alarm that goes off somewhere in the room.

Well, fuck.

"*Hannah . . .*" Mason's voice is gruff and thick with sleep and before I know it, he's by my side, laying me back on the bed.

Those hands definitely feel real.

"You can't get up, baby," he murmurs, voice dark and sleep-riddled. Mason's sleepy voice has always been my favorite thing, though I haven't told him that.

"I'm sorry." I wince at the sound of my own croaky voice. I sound like I swallowed a bucket of sand. Luckily, Mason is there with one of those fancy hospital cups full of water and I drink it down thirstily.

Jesus, how long have I been out?

"Twelve hours," Mason murmurs, eyes glinting almost black in the darkness of the hospital room.

Did I say that out loud?

"I have to pee," I grumble, my cheeks flaming. How the fuck am I supposed to get out of bed if it wails like a banshee every time I do?

"I'll take you."

"That's okay," I start, but he's already slipping his hands under my legs to help me stand.

I'll admit, once I'm on my feet, I'm glad for his help. Funnily enough, I feel like a baby deer, learning to walk for the first time.

I do my business and I have to tell you, peeing in front of Mason is a strange experience. He just doesn't seem to care. It's as if we've done this thousands of times.

By the time I'm done, and making the long journey with Mason and my IV pole back to the bed, a nurse is entering the room.

Doctor Dicky—yeah, that's his name—looks me over, explaining a bunch of things I don't understand. Everything passes by in a blur and I begin to wonder if I'm actually still asleep and this is just a dream.

Maybe I'm in a coma and this is their conversation over my lifeless body.

Maybe I never really made it out of that church.

I have so many questions. No answers, but also . . . no energy to ask, either. By the time the doctor is looking over my shoulder, I'm nodding off.

"Get some sleep," Dr. Dicky says. "I'll be back to check on you in a couple hours."

I nod, though my head feels like it weighs a hundred pounds.

The doctor leaves and then it's just me and Mason. He sits down in the chair beside me and I stare at the x-ray still on the wall across the room.

"Explain."

He lets out a deep breath and leans forward, his shoulders sagging as he leans on his knees.

"You were shot in the shoulder. Nothing major was hit, by some stroke of luck, but you'll be sore for a while."

"Did I have to have surgery?"

"Yes," he murmurs. "The bullet was stuck in your arm. Luckily, it was just a .9mm, or it could have been worse."

"Who did it?"

"Cortez. He's dead."

Something about the way his eyes flash when he says it sends a shiver down my spine.

"And . . . are *you* okay?"

He pauses as if he doesn't know what to say. My chest aches and oddly enough, I don't think it's from the bullet wound in my shoulder.

"I . . . *fuck*."

He gets up walking across the room to look out over the night sky of Los Angeles, his shoulders tense and his jaw hard as he scrubs a hand over his face.

"I'm sorry for leaving you. I didn't want to. It . . . nearly broke me." Tears burn in my eyes and exhaustion waves over me, despite my extra long nap. I just want to hold him. Have him hold me until I can't think about anything else.

"Don't ever fucking do some shit like that again," he says throatily and a tear slips down my cheek.

I deserve that.

Carefully, I maneuver to the side up on the side of the bed, wanting nothing more than to go to him, but I know I can't. Not with all the drugs coursing through my system.

"Okay."

"Fuck," he curses again under his breath and finally, he turns back to me. This time, I can see the despair on his face. "You don't get it, do you?"

"I do—"

"No, you don't. You're the love of my fucking life, Hannah." The room falls silent as he waits for me to protest. "You and me are it. Something happens to you, I'll go to hell to find you and then I'll drag you right the fuck back."

"I love you, too," I whisper, a tremor rolling through me and he bares his teeth. I didn't think I'd ever get to hear him say those things again. I was sure that was the end.

I hold out my hand to him and though it hurts my shoulder, I keep it there.

"I thought I was never going to get to see you again. Please don't be angry with me. You can tomorrow, just . . . right now . . ."

His eyes burn in the night, fury seeping off him. I shiver, but deep down, I know he's not angry with me.

He's angry because, for a moment, he was helpless.

Because Mason Carpenter is the farthest thing from helpless.

Begrudgingly, he takes a step forward and then, surprises the hell out of me and drops to his knees, his head falling to rest in my lap.

"That's the problem," he murmurs, turning his lips into my fingertips. "I can't be angry with you. Even when I want to hate you, I fucking can't."

"I . . . want you to know. It wasn't an easy decision. I made up my mind because I wanted to give you a chance at freedom."

"Baby—" He nips the pad of my finger, eyes darkening when a shallow breath leaves my lips. "—you are my freedom. Anything happens now, we do it together. I refuse to fucking lose you again."

"You won't," I promise, and this time, I mean it. "I'll prove it to you." My stomach clenches as visions of Ian flash through my mind. "I'm sorry about Ian."

"Fuck Ian," he grits, a snarl pulling on the corners of his lips.

"And Jenna . . . Did she make it?"

"Yeah," he murmurs darkly his fingers slipping over a scabbed-over cut on my knee, presumably from the accident. "Though she's in the same state Dawson was."

"I didn't want to kill him. He gave me no choice. I thought I was turning myself in to my mother, but he was taking me to the cartel. I had no idea they were one and the same." My voice catches in my throat. "I had no idea it was all Melissa."

"Tell me . . ." he rasps, "tell me what happened. Everything."

I suck in a deep breath and he leans forward, laying me back against the pillow. When he moves to sit back in the chair, I keep hold of his hand and ignore the dull aching throb from my shoulder.

"Please?"

I can see the hesitation in his eyes while he tries to determine if he should give me what I want or if he should keep his distance.

"Mason," I bite back the tears threatening to break free. "We both almost died."

"*Fuck*," he grits, succumbing. "Let me hold you. I need to feel you're real."

Gently, he slips his arms under me, sliding me over and resting on the edge of the bed beside me. We barely fit, but I don't care. Not when his hand comes up and rests protectively over my stomach and not when I lean my head back against his shoulder.

I start off by telling him about the photograph. The threat against his life the day of the shooting. I tell him about how at war with myself, I was. How I couldn't stomach the thought of leaving him, but I couldn't bear the thought of him not in this world.

I tell him about the closet and Nurse Ratched. I tell him about Tweedledee and Tweedledum, Michael's death and his threat, Mr. Legs, and the escort who he confirmed, was on our side.

"Christian Cross," he murmurs darkly after I tell him about how he watched me pee. "I'll fucking kill him."

"Don't," I breathe and I can't help but smile. "He was only acting the part."

"Yeah," Mason murmurs, though he doesn't sound the least bit forgiving. "And your sister? Did you know she was there?"

I shake my head—a mistake because I'm feeling really, really sleepy and it only adds to the vertigo. "I didn't . . . I thought surely she was gone. She made it look so . . ."

"Believable?" he finishes for me, his thumb tracing circles over the pulse point in my wrist. Almost as if he's solidifying for himself that I'm alive. Tangible. "She had fucking everyone fooled. Don't blame yourself for that."

"For once, I'm not. Melissa was insane. All the best parts of her were snuffed out by our mother a long time ago . . . I was just blind to it."

"The best parts of her were nothing compared to even the darkest parts of you, little doe."

Gently, I reach up, slipping my palm over his face. I want to turn into him, slip inside his skin for a little while, and just breathe him in until I feel like I'll never be without him again.

"How *did* you and Logan manage to sneak Parker out of prison?"

A twinkle of mischief flashes across his eyes and his fingers tighten on my throat. Despite *everything*, my stomach bottoms out with butterflies. "The media is saying two guards helped him escape. If I told you, I'd have to kill you and I plan on keeping you around for a very, very long time."

My heart lurches in my chest. He's so handsome it hurts.

"Easy, little doe," he breathes, running his nose up the column of my throat, eliciting a shiver in response as the goosebumps pebble on my flesh. "You managed to walk away without anything majorly damaged, but you were still shot. You'll be down for eight weeks."

"You mean, no sex for eight weeks?"

He chuckles darkly.

"No sex for eight weeks," he repeats.

"I don't know if my boss will allow that. He can be kind of an ass."

He smirks. "Sounds like a real dick. Imagine what eight long," he pauses to slip his hand lower over my hip to brush over my inner thigh and my breath hitches "—*long* weeks are going to do."

"Imagine how sweet it's going to be when I'm able to return to my duties."

His fingers slip against the goosebumps on my thighs and he growls low under his breath before removing his hand completely.

"Sweet is not the word I'd use to describe the things I'm going to do to you, little doe. Don't think I'm not going to punish you." He presses a kiss to my temple and then another to my cheek and finally, his fingers grip my chin and he gently turns my face to his. I slip my tongue against his, a small whimper climbing up my throat.

He growls against my lips, his fingers tightening on my chin with a small tremor.

He's real? God, how is he real?

He breaks the kiss with a soft groan and leans his forehead against mine.

"Fuck, I love you, Hannah."

"And I love you."

"Get some sleep. You're going to need it. I'm willing to bet my mother will be here as soon as they let her in."

I chuckle, but when he tries to leave, I grip his fingers in mine and wrap them over my stomach.

"Stay."

"Always, little doe."

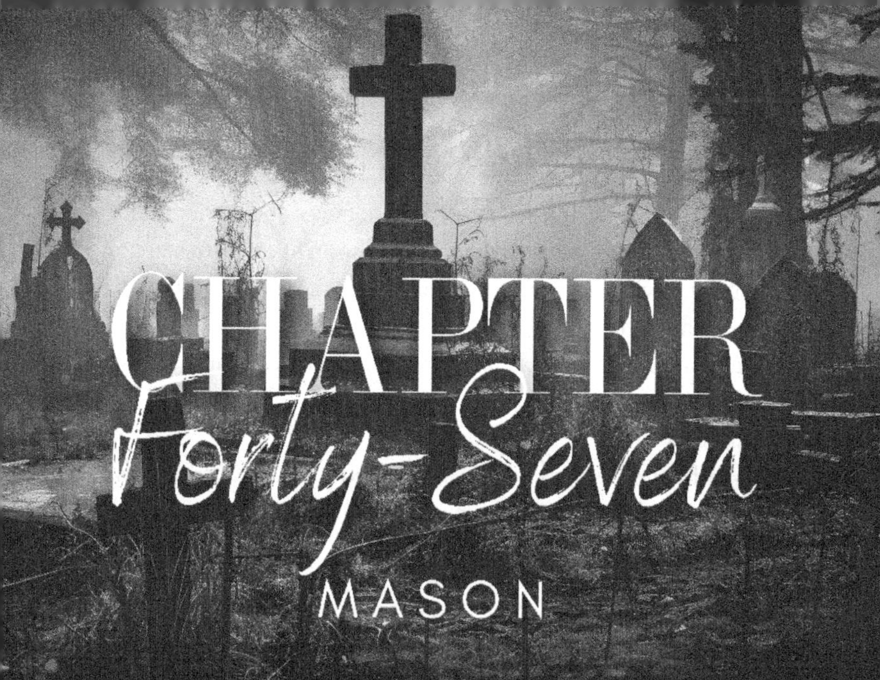

CHAPTER Forty-Seven

MASON

My mother has adopted Hannah like a stray kitten.

"I've already arranged for a nice in-home nurse to come help you take a shower. I *know* you must be wanting a *real* shower."

"Do I stink?"

"Never dear, but it's amazing what a good shower can do for the soul."

Hannah's eyes flit back to me nervously. "It's okay. Mason's been helping me."

"I suppose he could, though, you better keep your hands to yourself, young man. She's off-limits for another six weeks."

Don't fucking remind me.

All I've wanted to do since I got Hannah back is bury myself inside her and not come up for air for days, but . . . with the new wound in her shoulder, I can't. Doctor's fucking orders.

I'm happy to wait. I want her. Not sex.

But fuck if it wouldn't make this shit a little bit easier if I could touch her without worrying I'm going to hurt her.

I've come to a new conclusion. Hannah likes to see me suffer. It's fine. I'll gladly suffer at her hand whenever she wants me to, but when she's licking banana pudding off a spoon like a porn star at noon on a Tuesday when my family is in and out, it's mildly fucking difficult to hide a hard-on.

Judging by the twinkle in her eye when she does it, I know she's doing it on purpose.

Little brat.

"And Bailey sent you this," Mom produces a stack of books from the box beside her, most of which were written by my sister, but there are a few others thrown in there, too.

"Oh, thank God," Hannah groans, taking the first one with a wince. "I was so bored yesterday."

"We're going to have to move out of here," I chime from the wall, but no one pays an ounce of attention to me.

After we left the hospital last week, Mom brought us back to her house and the spare room—with new furniture, of course. I'm not complaining, mostly because as much as I don't want to, I've had to step out to deal with insurance shit at the garage and I refuse to leave Hannah alone right now.

Though she's able to move around and her stitches are healing nicely, I know Hannah and her penchant for doing shit she's not supposed to.

Mom loves it, of course, doting on Hannah, despite her begging to be left to fend for herself. I think my mother is just enjoying having her company, more than anything, but we'll get to that later.

"Oh, and Mila," Mom sighs, producing a box of cookies. "Mason let it slip the other night that you love orange-flavored cookies, so she took the liberty of making these herself. She's a great baker."

Hannah actually looks like she might cry.

"And this is from Bob and me." Mom hands her a small box, popping the lid off so Hannah doesn't have to struggle with one hand.

And then, Hannah really does cry.

"Thank you," she breathes. "You really shouldn't have."

"Well, I know how hard it can be to lose family, even if that family's not worth losing in the first place, so . . . I just wanted you to know you're one of us."

Hannah holds up the little gold locket to show me. It almost completely matches the ones my mother and father had made for my sisters when they were kids.

When I eye Mom, she holds up her hands in defense.

"There's not a tracker in it," Mom says, eyeing me, "but don't think I didn't think about it."

"It's perfect," Hannah smiles and Mom gives her a soft pat on the leg.

God, this is turning into a Hallmark movie.

Honestly, though, she fucking deserves it. We all deserve it. A little peace and quiet after that hell has died down. Melissa Gaines is dead. Governor Gaines is in prison, about to be brought to trial. Marcus fucking Parker is dead. The cartel's gone. Even that rat, Ian.

Life crumbled around us, but now we're standing on top of the rubble. Finally fucking free.

"Now. Let me brush your hair."

"Mom. Can it wait a bit? Hannah's tired."

"I'm fine," Hannah says, completely missing the message.

"She's fine," Mom mimics.

"Mom," I bite, tension radiating through me.

"Fine," she sighs, leaning down to place a kiss on Hannah's cheek.

Fuck, that's something I never thought I'd see.

"I'll come get you in a bit and you can go back to spoiling her."

"Hey!" Hannah chastises from the bed. "I am *not* spoiled."

I cock a brow as Mom tidies up the remnants of the steak dinner she brought for us.

"Only a little," Hannah admits and if I wasn't so tense, I would laugh.

"I'm going to go visit Bob. He should be here by now," Mom smiles, stopping to pat me on the chest. She must feel something there because she pauses, her eyes going wide and her lips parting ever so slightly while I convey to her with my stare to keep the hell quiet.

She clears her throat, righting herself.

"I'll see you at dinner."

"Bye, Monica," Hannah calls as I shut the door behind her.

Fucking finally.

Silence.

"Why are you so quiet?" Hannah asks as soon as the door shuts behind Mom.

I suck in a deep breath. I can't tell you the last time I was fucking nervous for something. Figures she'd be the one.

"I'm not," I murmur, voice gruff when I turn back to her.

She eyes me angrily from the bed, but I know her well enough to know that anger is just hurt.

She thinks I'm upset with her for leaving.

She's right, but . . . this is not that.

"Well, can you just talk to me, please?" The tear slipping down her cheek is like a shot of cement down my spine.

She waits for a moment, but when I can't form the words, her bottom lip wobbles.

"You're being an asshole."

"And you're being a brat," I counter.

You know, for being such a small thing in my pocket, it sure as fuck feels like the weight of the world when you're trying to work up the damned courage to use it.

"If you want to go, we can. We don't have to stay here—"

"Hannah, shut up."

Her eyes go wide, but for once, she actually falls silent.

Thank fuck.

Taking a deep breath, I move back to the side of the bed where she's sitting, sidestepping the chair to get on my knees beside the bed, instead. I'm sure it's not what she envisioned. The hospital and now Mom's, the gunshot wound to the shoulder. The fucking storm that we just came through, but . . . it's us.

"You've been sulking for days."

"I'm not sulking." Far from it, actually. More like shitting myself at the prospect of asking the girl of my fucking dreams to marry me, but you know.

"So what's wrong?"

"Nothing's wrong."

She opens her mouth at the same time my brain just says: fuck it.

Her words catch in her throat, those sexy fucking eyes glinting in the later afternoon sun streaming through the window.

"Mason Carpenter," she croaks, her voice hoarse. "Are you—"

"Proposing?" I stop her, voice rough in my throat. "Yeah, I fucking am."

"You've been quiet because you were . . ."

"Because I was trying to decide if this was the right time, but then I realized, there isn't a perfect time. We aren't candlelit dinners or picnics on the beach at sunset, Hannah. We're darkness and mine has fucking craved yours since the moment I laid eyes on you. I can't promise shit won't be difficult from time to time. We may argue. We may not. But I promise I will *never* stop fucking chasing you, Hannah Marie."

She swallows audibly, slowly reaching up to take the glistening black gold band.

"It's beautiful," she whispers, as if she says it any louder everything around us will slip away.

"The vines are me holding onto you—" I murmur "—with a fucking death grip, might I add. The diamonds are what you gave to me when you gave me your love. And that big stone in the center, with the green bleeding into the clear, is us bleeding for each other because I don't ever want to be without you by my side again."

A tear slips down her cheek and she falls silent, twirling the ring around in her fingers to get a better look at it. "And you said you weren't romantic," she chuckles softly, wiping a tear from under her cheek.

"I don't want to go another second without you being mine, Hannah. I'm so fucking in love with you."

Carefully, she scoots to the edge of the bed, bringing her hand up between us. We both look at the ring and then she holds it out to me.

"Are you asking me because I was shot or because you're in love with me?"

I chuckle because I knew she was going to ask that and produce the receipt from my pocket.

"You bought it . . ." She breathes, eyes going wide.

"Before you left," I confirm. "Does that answer your question?"

"Yes," she breathes and my chest tightens at the word. She looks like a goddess sitting above me, with me at her feet, ready to worship her.

Fuck, I just might.

"A thousand times, yes."

Fuck me.

"I love you."

And then she's surging forward. I catch her in my arms and it's too rough for her with her shoulder, but she kisses me despite the pain. Her lips slip against mine and it's the most alive I've felt since I woke up to her missing from the bed beside me.

"You have to put it on," she says softly against my lips, a tear slipping down her cheek between us. "Please?"

My chest tight, I take it from her, slipping it down her delicate finger and bringing it up to my lips.

"I love you," she reminds me. "And I don't ever want to be without you again."

"You won't be. I don't care when. It could be fifteen years from now, but I'm going to fucking marry you."

She shakes her head, her eyes dancing mischievously.

"You said you don't want to go another second without me as yours, but . . . you forgot I don't want to go another second without you as *mine*, either."

I cock a brow.

"Little doe?"

"Right now," she nods. "I want to marry you, right now."

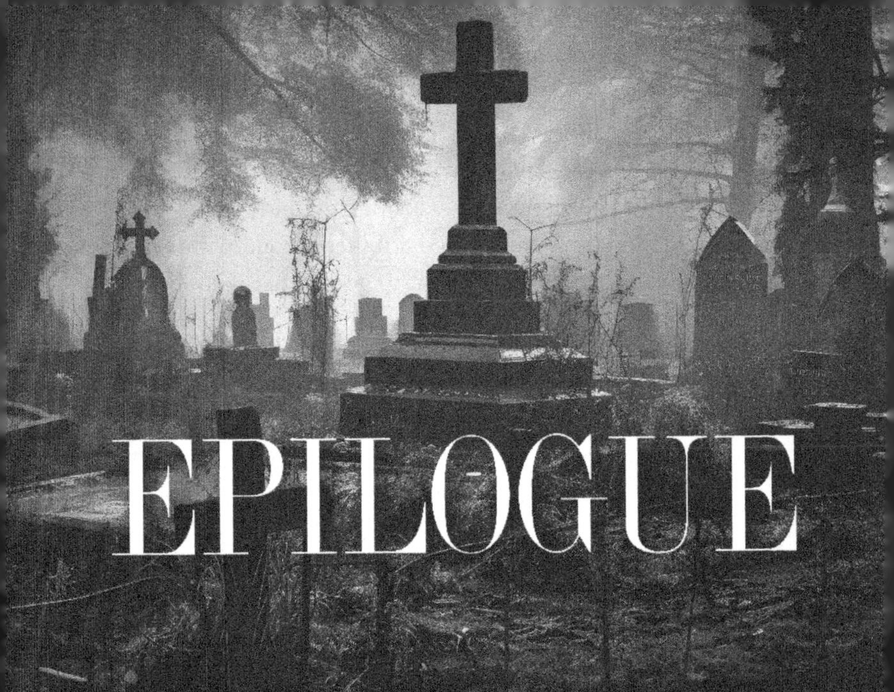

EPILOGUE

Another. Hannah's head falls back against the pillows beneath her, shivers moving through her as she floats back to earth from her last orgasm.

"I've come three times already." She gasps when I release her clit with a draw of my teeth and climb back up her body, aligning myself with her hips and sliding back inside her tight, wet heat.

"And it's been eight weeks since I've been inside this little cunt, baby."

My control slips and I let myself feel her gripping me, my head kicking back on a groan.

Fucking perfection.

I could fuck her for hours.

"I'm too young to die," Hannah pants, still wrapping her legs around my hips.

Leaning forward to give her all my cock and despite her words, she moans, her back arching off the bed. I chuckle darkly, thrusting inside her as if to engrain every cell in her body with me. She can't get enough of me, either.

"Yeah, you fucking are," I bite. I grip her pretty little throat in my hand, squeezing and using my purchase to fuck her deeper. Harder. "So, you better keep up, little *wife*."

"You're going to break me," she whimpers, a war waging inside her. She knows the safe word. She just doesn't want to use it because she gets off on me as much as I get off on her. Her little cries have never sounded sweeter filling this house.

"While I love to break you, little doe, you were fucking made for me," I remind her with a sharp nip to her collarbone. A sexy little moan slips free and her fingernails scour the flesh of my shoulders. We're both trembling, on the precipice of shattering at hour tightly we're fit together, but it's not enough.

It's never fucking enough.

"Now . . . you're going to take my cock like a good girl."

Releasing a deep breath, I wrap my arms under her shoulders and lift her to my chest, caging her against me and driving into her to the hilt. She yelps, but it dissolves on a moan when I circle my hips, my groin brushing against her clit.

It's been eight. Fucking. Weeks. Since I've been inside my wife—*my wife*—and now that she's finally been cleared for physical activity, I don't plan on letting her come up for air for days. Especially with our honeymoon a week away.

She can only blame herself. She made me this way.

"Oh my god," she moans, her voice choked with pleasure at the steady thrust of my hips against hers.

"God's not here right now, baby, but I am." I thrust inside her deeper, emphasizing my point. "You're squeezing me so tight, I can barely fit."

"Please don't stop, Mason," she pants, sweat glistening on her skin.

"Yeah?" I bite back another groan. "You want it deeper?"

"Yes," she breathes, ending on a high-pitched cry when I reach back and tug her legs up over my shoulders, contorting her until the head of my cock is brushing over that sweet spot inside her.

She arches her hips, spreading wider for me and I reach between us to circle her clit with my thumb, drawing out a hushed *fuck* under her breath.

"There's my good little whore."

"Mason . . ." she moans, and heat settles in the base of my spine. I crowd over her, tongue rimming the seam of her lips until she gives me hers. My cock swells, and it's all I can do to keep from spilling inside her.

She tenses, pussy clenching around me while I stroke her clit faster, desperately shoving her toward her climax so we can both fucking come undone.

Like I flipped a switch, her eyes roll to the back of her head and her back bows off the bed. She always comes so hard after the first time and her pussy is like a vice grip, greedily sucking me inside her until there's nothing left of my fucking sanity.

"*Fuck, Hannah*!"

My head falls back and the orgasm that rockets through me is not of this world. My vision blurs, blinding me as the pleasure radiates through me and I fill her with eight weeks of pent-up frustration until it slips down the curve of her ass.

Struggling to catch my breath, a tremor racks through me as I slowly, gently pull out of her.

"Fucking hell," I murmur, my teeth clenched from the electricity zipping through my cock.

I grab a warm rag from the bathroom and come back to clean her and find her still panting in the center of the bed. Right where I fucking left her.

I almost laugh at the look on her face.

"Wear you out, little doe?"

She nods, sucking in deep breaths through her teeth when I pry her thighs open to clean her up.

"I deserve cheeseburgers for that."

I chuckle, tossing the rag in the laundry hamper.

"I'm not sure if that was a reward or a punishment."

"I live to punish you, *wife*, but only if it ends with you coming on my cock."

Even after five weeks of marriage, she still blushes from my mouth.

Our wedding took place at Mom's, in the backyard underneath an old red oak that was probably there before the house was. Hannah looked beautiful, of course, her eyes shining like a thousand fucking stars in the late evening sun.

It was small. Only my family—*our* family—and a few friends. Mom cried—shocker. Puke brought his new girlfriend. Britt from Rummie's came and even, despite my hesitation, Dawson. He's doing better now. Not as skittish and he understands Hannah had nothing to do with what happened to him. I can't believe I'm saying this, but I think he could use a friend and Hannah's the one to do it, if it can be done.

My wife could befriend a caterpillar.

Our wedding was fucking perfect. Now. Finally. After eight goddamn weeks, we're consummating that marriage in every single position I can put her in.

Taking her hips in my hands, I tug her down the bed until she's right in front of me. Then, I sink to my knees, amused at the slight way her legs tremble on either side of me.

I bring her lips to mine and feast on her. My fucking wife—before pressing them to her ear. "Two weeks. You and me on the beach. Not a fucking soul around."

She moans softly, a shiver rolling through her.

"That sounds like heaven."

"Heaven's wherever the fuck we are, little doe."

She smiles but captures my lips again and despite my cock protesting in pain, blood rushes through it.

Fuck. I don't know if I'll ever get enough.

She tries to deepen the kiss, but I catch her hands when her stomach growls audibly between us. I don't know what the caloric burn of two hours of rough, consecutive fucking is, but I know I'm fucking famished.

That and I'd probably hit my knees if my cock got hard right now.

"Cheeseburgers, first. Then . . . we're going to take a bath," I murmur, pulling her to her feet. She wobbles and I resist the urge to make a joke. "Then, I'm going to spend the night showing you exactly what it means to be mine, little doe."

She smiles and my chest feels like it's in a vice grip.

"You forget, you're mine, too."

How could I?

I pull her to a stop at the closet door, tugging her back to me and nipping her bottom lip.

"My soul's always belonged to you. You just weren't ready to claim it."

"Monica is convinced there's going to be a malfunction with the plane," Hannah says from the other side of the kitchen while we make dinner.

Cheeseburgers, of course. I think I created a little monster.

I just chuckle and shake my head. Mom inherited a "bungalow" out in Hawaii in her divorce from Parker. The house is fucking huge and I plan to fuck my little wife on every single piece of furniture. The best part is, it comes with a private beach.

"First name basis with Mom, now?"

She blushes, coming back to the stove.

"Actually . . ." she clears her throat. "She told me *I* could call her Mom, too."

I cock a brow, but otherwise, don't look at her. I know this is big.

"And how do you feel about that?"

"You sound like Kenda."

I can feel her glaring daggers at me. She's told me some about her sessions with Kenda. They seem to be helping, though she's reluctant to go. She's told me about her time in the church. Some of her childhood she's starting to remember. Her father. Her mother murdering him. I want to be the one she shares those dark parts of herself with, but . . . I also understand we have the rest of our lives to worry about it.

For now, I'm content calling her mine . . . and feeding her.

"You don't have to call her that if you don't want to." I place the spatula down and take her face in my hands, pointing those green eyes up at mine. "And even if you do, it won't erase Laura."

I fucking hate saying her name. I fucking hate that Hannah still thinks about her. If I could, I'd take those memories of her time locked away, if it meant she wouldn't have to bear the burden, anymore.

She gives me a soft smile and reaches up, placing her hand over mine, her ring glittering in the kitchen lights. "Is it bad if I said that I would be okay if it did? Erase her?"

"Never, little doe. Family's not family because they're blood. You and I will create our own family. With whoever you want in it."

"That's just your excuse to get me pregnant."

I chuckle darkly because, well, she's not wrong, and lift her ass onto the counter.

"I would love to put a baby in you," I murmur, pressing my lips to hers. "But I'm content with just us for now. We've got the rest of our lives."

She grins, a twinkle in her eye.

"We can practice, though?"

"You fucking bet, we can."

She laughs, but the sound dies down when my phone rings from the counter beside her.

"I think she has a sixth sense for when someone's talking about her," I murmur gruffly, silencing Mom's call.

Listen, I've been working on shit myself. Forgiving Mom. Welcoming her back into my life. Just the other night, she and Bob were over for dinner and it's the first time she's set foot in my house since she and Dad divorced. It was strange at first, but . . . as the night wore on, I found it easier to relax.

Hannah's a big part of that. Bob, too. The fucker's the nicest guy I've ever met. How he convinced my mother, of all people, to go on a date, is beyond me.

"Hi, Monica," Hannah beams when she answers the phone because the little brat knew I was going to ignore it. She hops down from the counter, giggling when I smack her ass, but that laugh falls off, ending in nothing but silence.

"Okay, he's here."

She hands me the phone, her face crestfallen and it feels like someone's stuck a knife in my chest. With an internal groan, I take the call.

"Mom?"

She blubbers something out, her voice unrecognizable from the tears clogging her throat.

"Mom?"

There's shuffling and then the phone is handed over to someone else.

"It's Logan. You need to come to the hospital."

"Now?"

"Right fucking now." My gaze flicks to Hannah and her eyes go wide.

"What the fuck's going on?"

"It's Mila," Logan murmurs gruffly. "She was attacked."

The End

Thank you so much for taking the time to read Never Dig Beneath a Grave. If you enjoyed reading this book, please consider giving it a review on the platform(s) of your choice.

Reviews are like tips for authors, and let us know how we're doing, as well as spread the word of our work. Your opinion matters.

Love,

Jessi

JOIN THE CLUB

If you want to follow along for future updates, secrets, or just want to read the ramblings of a tired, book-crazy writer, click the link below to sign up for my newsletter.

Love Always,

Jessi

jessihart.com

Tiktok: jessihartauthor

Instagram: jessihartauthor

Facebook: jessihartauthor

ALSO BY JESSI HART

NEVER EVER SERIES

Never Kiss and Tell

Never Wake Up in Vegas

Never Deal with the Devil

Never Dig Beneath a Grave

Never Fall for an Angel (Winter, 2025)

The Reaper (Summer, 2025)

STANDALONES

Forget Me Not

ABOUT THE AUTHOR

Hey everybody! I'm Jessi Hart, writer of contemporary and dark romance stories that will probably make you fall in love, cry, laugh, and want to throw the book across the room, all in a few chapters.

I like my hero's grey and my heroine's sassy and full of wit. My characters are human with human flaws that might make you angry, sad, or maybe, relate to them a little more than you thought you would. In the end, though, you can't help, but love them. Because even if they're just on paper, they're real, just like you and I.

-Jessi Hart lives in Ohio with her partner and dogbaby, Rylic. When she's not daydreaming up the perfect scene, you can probably find her gaming, binge-watching a spooky show or pranking her partner, Nick.

Made in the USA
Monee, IL
23 December 2025

40227679R00282